THE RAGE OF A BOY

Grey & White: Book One

Edward Patrick

D1518254

Published by Edward Patrick Writes.

ISBN – 979-8-432-09176-5

Cover art by Johanne Conover (twitter @yirafiel)

edwardpatrickwrites.com

For my Family.
For my Friends.

I ride in fields of endless night,
'neath rays of beautiful moonlight.

Table of Contents

Many stories from our past have been lost to us; we have forgotten much which should have been remembered.

I am determined not to allow that to happen with our story. I have decided to write it down while the events are fresh in my mind, and also while I can easily contact those who can fill in the gaps for the moments which occurred when I was not present.

This is not only my story, but also the story of my bravest friends. It is Tristan's story, and Ella's and Garit's, and countless others. It is the story of the people of Grauberg and Elinton, of Dyta and Felixandria. The war touched three continents and saw great loss to all four nations.

It is a story of great courage and strength, of reconciliation and redemption. It is about fighting to live and about making the ultimate sacrifice.

This is a story of hate and love.

I
Wounds and Memories

Tristan's anger flared to life as he guarded his bruised ribs. His opponent attempted to rain down blows, but he resolved to take no further punishment from the spearman. All around them, the air resounded with the collisions of wood and leather and skin. The impacts echoed off the thick stone walls which closed them in. Soldiers grunted and growled, screamed and roared, but Tristan remained silent.

He focused on his breathing and the movements of the man across from him. Sweat dripped into his eyes, stinging and annoying, but he would worry about that in a moment. Battle surrounded them, but this did not concern him. Only two things mattered now: his opponent's spear, and his own sword.

The man thrust, and Tristan raised his shield to deflect. He lunged with his own attack, but the spearman danced out of range. They reset and measured one another. Tristan lowered his right shoulder, stepped forward, and brought his sword up in a quick stroke. He missed badly, leaving his right flank exposed. His opponent spotted the opening and pushed with his attack.

As the spear came for him, Tristan spun. On the backside of the spin, he extended his left arm and slammed his shield into his opponent. He meant only to knock the man off balance, but the spearman went down face first in the gravel. He rolled to his back, but Tristan moved faster, straddling him and driving his sword down in what would have been a killing strike. The point of his blade hovered above the spearman's exposed chest. "You're dead," said Tristan, and a smirk broke forth on his face.

"Again," said the spearman. "Dammit all, again!" He slapped Tristan's wooden blade aside and lumbered to his feet. "That's what? Five times today? Six?"

"Six," said Tristan. He reached over and patted some of the dust off his friend's back. "You're going to need to bathe twice this month after rolling in the dirt so much." His foe glared at him but chuckled to himself as he continued to brush off. Tristan let his blade rest on his shoulder. "Your problem is that you're too eager, Garit."

Garit met his eyes and raised one brow. "Oh?"

Tristan smiled. "You are. You see an opening, and instead of trying to slip in, you charge forward like a battering ram." He dropped his smile and set his feet in line with one another, then leaned toward Garit. "Push me."

"Oh, now I can score a point," Garit said sarcastically. He raised his voice in a mock shout. "Look, lads. The almighty Tristan is going to let me push him!" Tristan's wooden blade jabbed him hard in the ribs. "Ow! That hurt, you arse!"

"Just push me," Tristan said dryly.

"Nay, I understand what you're saying. I lunged, got off balance, and became easy prey."

Tristan and Garit had been training partners since they were children. Now, they were grown men. Garit belonged to the standing army of Grauberg, and Tristan was part of the auxiliary. They had specialized weapons drills together, and they'd gotten to know each other on both a professional and personal level. "Friends all these years, and I'm still knocking you down because of poor fundamentals," said Tristan.

Garit glowered, which brought the smile back to Tristan's face. "By Rylar, I hate that damned smirk."

"Aye, I know," said Tristan. "You ought to try harder

and not give me cause to do it." His brown hair, lightened nearly to dirty blond by his long hours in sunlight, was bound back in a tail for training. A few loose strands now fell past his cheeks as he tucked the sword into his belt.

The bell sounded, and the training halted. All turned toward the northern wall of the yard, where the chief instructor stood. "That's enough for today. Retire. Rest. If you are hurt, be sure to see the healer." He turned and left, effectively dismissing the soldiers.

Tristan glanced at the men around him. In their younger years, the instruction had been harsher, often coupled with rod and lash. Now, each man stood well-versed in his weapon of choice. Several instructors still observed the sessions and made points as needed, but these were not boys in training so much as men staying sharp.

Garit set the butt of his spear on the ground, letting the shaft rest against his shoulder. "You know," he began, "you are my best friend. I like you—truly, I do—but I absolutely hate the days when I draw you as a partner." Tristan's smirk returned and Garit gripped his weapon. "Don't tempt me, Tristan. I can keep going."

"You want to bathe in the dirt some more?"

Garit growled. "I take it back," he said. "I really don't like you."

The two men clapped each other on the back and headed out of the yard and toward the training barracks. As they walked, Tristan directed their conversation to the evening ahead. "You are coming tonight, right?"

"Well, of course I'm coming!" exclaimed Garit with a cocky smile of his own. "The first autumn dance—where else would I be?"

Tristan nodded and thought about the dancing, the drinking, and the women. While not necessarily the type to sleep with every girl in town, he was known to have a weakness for the ladies from time to time. As he considered the girls and which drink he'd be having first, he and Garit reached the barracks. They found a couple of benches and began peeling out of their training garments.

These barracks had once housed the soldiers of the kingdom of Grauberg, back when it was at war with—and later a part of—the Grey Empire. Now, soldiers lived either in the city or in one of the surrounding villages, with these stations serving as little more than storage and changing quarters after training.

Tristan slipped on a pair of dark trousers and a leather shirt. Garit scoffed. "That's what you're wearing tonight?" he asked. "You? The man of style?"

Tristan hit him with the back of his hand. "No, it's what I'm wearing to go hunting."

Garit slid on a pair of pants. "Hunting? You don't have time to hunt! There's not three hours before sundown!" Tristan began lacing up his own boots, and Garit noted that his mood seemed to have darkened. "Tristan?" No response. "Are you hunting or looking for a chance to spend a wee bit of time alone?" Tristan gave a short nod. "The fight with Ella?"

Tristan grimaced. "Well, aye, I suppose that's part of my issue."

"Another dream?" Garit asked.

"Never a dream," Tristan said, his voice low. "Nightmares. Memories. I think they happen more frequently in the cold months. I never thought about that before, but they are happening more commonly now. Not every night, by any means, but often enough."

Garit moved closer on the bench and patted him on the back. "Want to talk about it?"

"No," Tristan snapped back, his tone sharp. "I talked about it too much when I came here. They made me. I told them what happened—all of them, exactly what happened! They all told me I was either wrong, or lying, or crazy. Then they made me tell it again, so many times that I began to doubt myself. The dreams are so clear, though, I—" He cut himself off, shaking his head. "No!

I've told it enough. No more."

"Tristan, that was fifteen years ago," Garit reasoned. "You were a child. What were you, six? Seven?"

"Seven."

Garit nodded. "What happened to you—to your family—was terrible. I'm sure that anyone in a similar situation would have seen things as well, or—"

"Oh, blow it out your arse, Garit! I didn't 'see things,' dammit!" Tristan came to his feet in a flash, gathering up his padded tunic and breeches and his leather armor. "This is why I didn't want to talk about it. This, right here! Because no one bloody believes me! None of them!" He gave Garit a look which would have pinned him to the wall if possible. "And apparently not even my friends!"

He turned away, shoving the door open as he marched out. Something about the movement woke the pain in his side. Garit had managed to hit him with a solid blow as the training started. He'd felt this discomfort before: bruised ribs, indeed. Now that the heat of battle had settled, it hurt to breathe, which meant everything hurt.

He glanced over to where the healer was always stationed at day's end, and his heart sank as he saw Ella standing there. "Helpers, help me," he muttered under his breath. She hadn't spotted him yet, and he decided that was for the best. After their encounter a week ago, he really didn't want to deal with the fallout.

He decided that bruised ribs weren't too much of a nuisance and dumped his training garments and armor in a bin, pitying the younger recruits who would be cleaning late tonight. He turned and walked in the opposite direction of Ella, opting for the back gate.

Home—if you could call it a home—was just down the street from the training yards. Tristan had been raised as a ward of the kingdom. After reaching what the Grause considered the age of majority, he signed on as a mercenary for a term of five years. For a few more weeks he had room and board. His room served for little more than that. He had a bed, a chamber pot, a small table with a couple of drawers, a chest for his clothes, and a fireplace. Not much else, but it met his needs. Soon, that might be changing.

Leaving through the back gate only added a few turns to his walk, and in a few minutes, he found himself standing inside his small room. He scanned the space, sorting out what he wanted for his little excursion. He saw his journal lying on the table. This was a new hobby, and it had only one entry, but he decided that writing did not strike his fancy.

Instead, he grabbed the small knife he used for carving and the small block of wood which he'd recently started on. He tucked his hunting knife into his belt, hung his quiver on his hip, and reached for his bow. It was unstrung, with a strap attached for transport. He slung it over his shoulder and departed as quickly as he'd come in.

He kept his head down as he ventured out and into the busy streets of the city. Farmers were coming in from the fields for a bit of trading. By the time Tristan returned at sundown, this crowded street would be all but empty. He did his best to not meet anyone's face—a casual conversation was the last thing he wanted.

Some of the men returning were hunters and trappers by profession. They belonged to the city guild, and they'd been busy with their craft all day. For Tristan, this was a hobby. He got lucky sometimes, but the reality was that it gave him time alone more than anything. Today, he wasn't quite sure which he preferred: the thought of no one bothering him, or the desire to kill something. If the chance to take some prey came along, he certainly wasn't going to complain.

Most of the vendor stalls were on his left, and they were packed with people. On his right, standing at the corner of the main street and an alley, a man sputtered nonsense for all to hear. "The day of the dance is coming!

May the pillar stand tall!" The man was positively filthy, with long, tangled hair and half-rotted teeth.

For years, this same beggar had been standing at this spot, spouting his nonsense for any and all who passed by. It had started a few years after Tristan first arrived. He was hardly noticed anymore by those who lived and traded daily in the city, little more than another sound to go along with the carriages and conversations and haggling. The commotion was all one loud discord, and Tristan needed to escape for a few hours.

After what seemed an eternity, he reached the gate. One of the soldiers posted inside raised a hand by way of greeting. "A bit late in the day to be headed out, isn't it?" he asked in a friendly tone.

Tristan had served guard duty with him several times, and the man seemed pleasant enough. "Just going to clear my head a bit. I'll be sure to be back by sundown." By now, he had maybe two hours—two and a half at best—of sunlight left.

"Go on ahead then," the man said. "And good luck!" The other soldier nodded to him and added, "And bring us back something tender. A fat rabbit, or a young doe, perhaps." Tristan gave him half a smile and made his way out.

The central road leading out of the city was made of stone. If a traveler followed it, they'd pass through several villages and farmsteads as it went south before turning sharply east. He glanced that way briefly, though there was nothing to see from here—houses in the distance, and the faint view of the tree line of Camtar Forest at the very edge of the horizon. He turned, leaving the road and moving west.

While Grauberg was nestled against the mountains, a bit of woodland sprung up to the east and west of the fortified city-state. Tristan now ventured into the western woodlands. They were sparsely populated by game, being the easiest of the forests to reach and therefore the most hunted. That made them eerily quiet. Some folk didn't like that, but Tristan treasured the silence.

Beyond the forest, the mountains loomed. The sun still shone above them, but the light wouldn't last. If Tristan were lucky enough to earn a kill, the opportunity would have to come soon so he'd have time to make the trek back to town. For that reason, he only walked about a quarter of an hour or so amongst the trees before he found a large oak, planted himself at the base of it, and strung his bow.

The only sounds now came from the treetops, their branches swaying with the wind. Some of the leaves were beginning to show hints of changing colors. In a matter of weeks, the overhead view would be very different. As a familiar birdsong reached him, he reflected that most of the birds, too, would soon be gone.

There were no owls, though. There had been some that used to live at the edge of the forest behind his family's fields. They called out to each other throughout the night when they were around. They would show up and hunt for a few nights and then disappear for several weeks. Then suddenly, they'd be back.

Tristan set his bow down and pulled out his block of wood and carving knife. He had started on the project the last time he was in the forest. Eventually, he hoped it would be an owl. For now, it looked more like a depressed potato. He remembered why he'd stopped working on the project on his last trip; the knife was duller than Garit, and he'd forgotten to sharpen it. Frustrated, he put away both block and blade and let his head drop back against the trunk of the oak with his bow resting in his lap.

His eyes found the sun above the trees and closed. Orange spots and darkness competed for prominence inside his eyelids. He breathed in deep and winced. His damned ribs were going to hurt tomorrow. Still, this was nice. With his constant training—and especially with stupidity like his conversation with Garit today—he did not often find peaceful moments like this. Slowly, his breathing became deeper, and his chin dipped toward his chest.

"I asked you where your family was, farmer," the stranger said. Tristan didn't open his eyes. In fact, he clenched them tighter. Above him, no one answered the voice. He heard the unmistakable smack of an open-handed slap, followed by a subdued growl from his father. "I'm not the sort of man who asks questions more than once. Believe me when I tell you, this will be much better for you if you answer me."

The voice echoed in Tristan's head—a sound he would never forget. He didn't know what to do, but he had to start with opening his eyes. Willing them open, he looked up. From his hiding spot beneath the floorboards, he could make out the bottom of the stranger's boots, but no more. He dared not risk moving for a better view.

The door opened. His father cursed, and feet scuffled across the floor as several people entered. The man slapped his father again to quiet him, and on the opposite side of the room his sisters whimpered as his mother spoke to them in a soothing tone. He heard a loud smack, followed by the thud of his mother hitting the floor. She lay just over his hiding spot, lying at the feet of the new stranger. "I found the woman and the whelps cowering in the corn," said another man. He sounded younger, but his voice was just as harsh.

"And our men?" asked the first voice.

"They should be finishing up with these peasants and moving toward the city soon."

The older man examined Tristan's mother and sisters. "Those two?"

"Girls," said the younger man. "Twins, I think, but useless."

The stranger overhead turned back to his father. "Consider this a mercy. None of you have to die alone, tonight." The man slid his sword from its scabbard, and

Tristan tensed. Even as a child, he sensed what this meant. Trembling, he quietly made himself as small as possible beneath the floor, just like his father had told him to do. He waited for the sound of the blade cutting through the air, dreading what that would mean. Second after second passed, but the sound didn't come, and then the man put the weapon away. "You need the practice," he said, his voice directed at the younger man in the doorway. "Take your time. Remember how you've been instructed."

Fear and dread welled within Tristan. If he could move a little to his left, there were two boards with a larger gap, and he might be able to see better. "Go! That corner, over there," said the younger voice, and his sisters scurried to obey. Tristan moved as they moved, and now he had an unobstructed view of the younger man. He was hooded in a grey cloak.

"I'll tend to the girls," said the older man, and again the sword came out. His sisters cried while his father cursed and made threats that even Tristan realized were empty. His mother lay prone, breathing heavy, afraid to move. The younger man in the doorway pulled his hood back, revealing pale skin and black hair tied back in a tail. Black paint surrounded his eyes, a thick band which ran from temple to temple.

The man moved over his mother, reached down, and dragged her up by her hair until she was in a kneeling position. She couldn't even scream, she was so frightened. The man stood behind her, and Tristan could see them both—his mother's eyes closed tight, probably in prayer, and the painted man behind her. He whispered something under his breath. Tristan couldn't hear him, but the more the man spoke, the angrier he seemed to become. The invader extended his right hand toward his mother and uttered one phrase loud and clear: "I hate you."

She screamed as an unseen terror went ripping through her body. Tristan knew the stories. His sisters liked to scare him with tales of it at night. In that moment,

Tristan realized the stories were true. This was real power — this was the Grey.

His mother's face contorted as her breath gave out. Still, she silently screamed. His sisters sobbed in the corner, and his father begged and pleaded. The mage raised his left hand, and Tristan's father stopped begging and began roaring out in pain. The stranger had called this 'mercy.' If this was mercy, how did they define torture?

From his spot, Tristan couldn't see his father's face, but his mother's was all too clear. Blood streamed from her nose, and her face began turning from red to purple. Sweat formed on her brow, and a drop of something wet fell between the floorboards and landed on Tristan's hand. He wasn't sure if it was sweat or blood, and he didn't look down to find out.

He wanted to scream or run away, but he knew he could do neither. Then the blood began to trickle out of the corners of his mother's mouth. When, at last, she found her breath again, her shriek rang out like a crack of thunder.

Tristan moved to action. He sprang to his feet, bow in hand and an arrow nocked in a flash — but he was back in the forest. He looked around anxiously, sweat heavy on his brow. The sun touched the peaks of the mountains now. The birds hushed their singing at his abrupt movement, though crickets now chirped all around.

Tristan lowered his eyes and saw a deer standing still, staring straight at him. Any hunting discipline flew away in the face of his sudden rage. With a shout, he raised his bow and drew the shaft back until he felt his finger barely brush his lips. He loosed, and the deer hadn't even turned before the arrow sank in. Everything around him remained silent as the stag hit the dirt, mortally wounded but alive.

He ran forward, shouting his fury. He shouldered his bow and drew out his hunting knife. The young buck made an effort to stand and bolt, but Tristan grabbed an antler with his left hand, plunged his knife into the deer's throat, and ripped the blade through. Blood sprayed forth for a second or two before he let the lifeless body fall to the ground.

He stood, panting heavily, wondering where this rage had been when he was a boy. Useless to consider—foolish even. He was covered in blood, all on his face and arms and clothes. He wondered how he'd managed to make a simple hunt look like an act of war. The thought was so absurd that he almost smiled.

The rage began to ebb as he looked down at his prey. He knelt to perform his field dressing, forcing his mind away from his fury and from his past. He tried to think, instead, of what the night might bring. Tonight, he would go to the Low Hall. He would dance and drink, and possibly he would even find escape from his nightmares in the arms of some local girl.

Tomorrow, he would rise early, determined to work in a training session with the older men. Every day was one step closer to finishing his service to Grauberg—one step closer to his revenge against Felixandria. The field dressing was done, and Tristan slung the deer over his shoulders, unconcerned about the blood and gore which continued to drip on him. He began his trek back towards the gate of the city as the sun dipped behind the mountains. The peace, like the day, had ended.

II
The Brawl in the Hall

Garit has been telling me for years to keep a journal. I don't know what I'm supposed to do with this thing. He's told me to put my feelings on paper, or simply write about what I do on a daily basis. The only time I've ever done this was when I turned fifteen and I was told to write down what I remembered from when my family was killed. Then they told me I'd dreamed most of that. To hell with them.

Still, I'm not sure what else to do, so why not give this a shot? I had an outing with Ella, and it went about as well as I've always thought it would. For years, everyone has been telling me to do it. I'll be happy with her. She's the right kind for me. We have always been friends, so why not?

Well, I don't want or need love. I want a warm body in my bed or her bed, nothing more. For some reason, I thought it would be a good idea to tell Ella as much. Be honest and open right from the start. Well, that turned out about as well as the time Garit and I got caught stealing the lieutenant's mead. I've known her since I fled Elinton, and now —

Why am I even bothering to write this down?

Tristan finished bathing in the guards' steams, then

returned to his room and brushed his hair. When it hung free, as it did now, it fell past his shoulders in soft waves. His beard was by no means full, but he liked it scruffy. Rather, he knew many of the local ladies enjoyed it, and therefore, he did too.

His eyes were a very dull blue, almost grey. It was not common in Grauberg, and while they proved attractive to the women, he also resented them. Grey—anything that was grey—was something he detested, almost as if the color were the same as the magic.

Still, he was glad to have them draw the attention of anyone looking into his face. Otherwise, they'd likely give more notice to the scar which ran from above his right eye and down to his chin, concealed somewhat by his beard. Years had passed since he received the mark, but still the light marking stood out in contrast against his bronze-toned skin.

He slid on a pair of black trousers and black boots and donned an emerald shirt with long sleeves. The fabric pulled tight at his elbows, and he tucked it into his pants to accentuate his slim waist.

A black cloak went over his shoulders, but he'd not need it for long. The hall would be warm with fires, and he never had an issue with the cold once he started dancing. He adjusted his clothes and winced as pain shot through his ribs. He began to second-guess his choice not to see Ella when his eyes fell on his journal, and he thought about the lone entry it contained, written a week ago. A moment later, he forced his mind away and back to the mirror.

He noticed a small dab of blood on his ear as he examined himself one last time before stepping out. He wiped it away and recalled how messy he'd been when he had stripped out of his hunting garb. Never had he made such a mess of himself, not even when skinning and butchering his prey in haste.

The guards at the gate felt certain he'd been attacked

when they first laid eyes on him, and one of them had run forth to check on him. When they realized he was fine and had managed this from a simple hunt, they'd regarded him with anxious expressions.

The man who now emerged from the small room was a much different sight than the bloody beast he could have been mistaken for an hour earlier. The kill had made him feel good. His bath had made him feel even better. This relaxed mood was on him as he made his way out of his home and to the central street.

It was a short walk. Once there, instead of turning right and heading toward the front gate, he turned left. This way lay the lower level's market plaza. The booths and carts would all be deserted now, wares taken home or stored for the night. The focus tonight was on the structure in the center of the area: the Low Hall.

Here, at the far end of the street, Tristan could already hear music and laughter as he made his way toward the building. Light poured from its many windows, the silhouettes of people constantly blocking the rays as they danced inside. The gathering started at sundown, which meant they had been going for an hour or more. Still, the party would last well into the night.

As he neared the building, rapid steps approached him from behind. He spun to see the cause and was shocked to see the crazy street crier standing behind him. "The bones," the man said to him. His words came as a loud hiss, as though he intended to whisper but had never learned how to do so. "The bones will dance." His voice trembled with the night's chill as he spoke.

Tristan stood bewildered. In fifteen years, he could not recall the man ever singling an individual out, and certainly this had never happened to him. The man had always been a voice—just another ruckus in the clamor of the city. Unsure of what else to do, he smiled and reached out to pat the man on the shoulder. The man recoiled, shivering with the cold. "The bones will dance."

"Aye," Tristan said. Perhaps agreeing with the man would comfort him. When the crazed eyes continued staring at him, he motioned toward the Low Hall. "Well, tonight, my bones are going to dance and enjoy a drink or two." He smiled, hoping a genial attitude would go over well.

The man said nothing, only stood there in his tattered rags, rubbing his hands together. Tristan reached up and unfastened his cloak, then extended it toward the poor man. The man flinched. "No," Tristan said. "It's alright. Are you cold? This will keep you warm. See?" He held the garment up, letting the man see the fur lining. The man made as if to reach out for it but pushed it away and stepped back. "You can keep it, if you'd like," Tristan said, offering once more.

"The bones will dance," the man repeated, this time with more insistence in his voice. Tristan debated whether he should turn and walk away when the man covered the few feet between them and whispered into his face. "The Pillar must stand!" The man's foul breath assaulted Tristan's senses, and before he could begin to consider what the cryptic words meant or what to say in response, the man turned and scurried away into the darkness of one of the side streets.

Tristan watched as he faded into the shadows and thought about how chilly the night was. He thought of the coming winter, and how unbearably cold the frosts and snows of these lands could be. He wondered where the man took shelter at night. The answer was, quite obviously, somewhere. After all, the man had been yelling on the streets for all these years, and he hadn't frozen to death yet.

"Making friends?" Tristan jumped, jolted from his contemplations by the voice of a city guard approaching from behind. The man smiled at him. "Tristan? Everything alright, lad?"

"Aye," Tristan said, abashed at how startled he'd

been. This was one of the retired soldiers he'd served with on occasion. "I just — that crazy guy who always yells — "

"I saw," said the guard. "Seems to have a bit more hop than usual in him tonight. Might be the chill. Or, might be he found a drink of something, has him feeling spirited."

Tristan smiled. "Might be," he agreed. "Well, I think it's about time I got a mug of something for myself in the Hall." He bowed his head to the guard, and the guard did the same before he walked on. Tristan watched him as he continued down the street making his rounds. Many times in the past, Tristan had been unable to go to the Hall on nights like tonight because he'd been on duty as well.

Those times would be coming to an end soon. As a mercenary, Tristan had opted to serve Grauberg with his sword arm. The term of that particular contract would be expiring in a few weeks, and when that happened, he would have some choices to make. Formally, at least — in his mind, only one path existed.

He turned his thoughts from the matter and toward the night ahead. As Tristan made his way up the steps that led into the Hall, he felt himself being absorbed into the atmosphere. His eyes swept the room as he walked in, taking in the scene.

The room was far too spacious and busy for one band to entertain everyone, so several smaller groups of musicians performed in various stations. This arrangement meant there was a musical style for essentially every mood. In one corner, a gathering of people danced a frisky jig to a quartet playing fiddles. In another, a man played a tune on his bronze horn, slow and soothing, while the group before him swayed intimately to the melody.

The chamber was lit by torches ensconced all around, and above was an elaborate and huge piece fashioned from antlers which held hundreds of candles and had at least two dozen lanterns hanging from it. Whereas most of the buildings in the city were constructed of stone, the Low Hall was primarily wooden. When compared to many of the finer places in the city-state, one might be forgiven for believing the place to be shoddy, but the style added to the character of the Low Hall, which made the people embrace it even more.

He made his way through the crowd to the center of the cavernous room, to the bar and its numerous tenders serving spirits and the like. As he approached, he observed Garit and a few other soldiers and guardsmen having drinks with several women, some of whom Tristan was quite well-acquainted with. "Good evening," he called out.

"Aye," returned multiple voices at once, Garit's being the loudest of all. From the way he leaned on the bar, Tristan judged he'd already spent a considerable amount of time — and coin — on drinks. "What are you having tonight?" Garit asked.

Tristan grinned at the slight slur in his voice, then managed to catch the eye of one of the more attractive barmaids. "Mead," he called. She nodded and gave him a grin of her own.

"Mead for my friend!" Garit roared at the barmaid, who jumped at the ferocity in his voice. "You can put him on me. Wait, no, I mean you can put his on mine." The woman tried to hide a smile as Tristan and the others began laughing. Garit slapped his own face. "Ah, bloody hell, y'know what I mean — I'm buying his damned drink!"

Tristan came to stand beside his friend and put his arm around him. "And what, my dear friend, has you in such a generous spirit tonight?" he asked. Garit gave no reply but shrugged as he took another mouthful from his mug. Garit did not turn to meet his eyes or even smile. That was when Tristan realized this was either his apology for straining the mood earlier, or his friend was feeling sorry for him and his nightmares.

He didn't have much time to consider it. The barmaid brought his mead over, but any chance of talking to her died as someone else slid up on his right side and bumped him. "Hey, stranger," she said, and he winced, both from the pain in his ribs and at the prospect of the impending conversation.

"Hello, Ella," he said, forcing a smile. "Haven't seen you much lately."

"Well, that happens when you avoid me, you big oaf," she countered. Her words were true, but the lilt in her voice told Tristan she wasn't truly angry. "Truth be told, I've been doing my best to avoid you, as well. So, I guess it's alright." She gave him another light bump, and this time noticed the discomfort on his face. "What's wrong?"

"It's nothing," he said.

Ella put a hand on her hip and raised an eyebrow. "Oh, I'm sure."

Tristan peered over, fully taking her in for the first time that night. Her dark brown hair was loose down her back. Her eyes, normally a dark brown, were amber in the dancing firelight. Many times before, he'd thought about how beautiful they were, but right now they were glaring at him. "What have you hurt?" she asked.

"Nothing."

"Well, what has someone else hurt?"

"It's really nothing." He sighed as he swirled the contents of his mug. "I have bruised ribs."

"Oh," Ella began, "well at least those only hurt when you breathe." He had to smile. Her thoughts had mirrored his own from earlier. They usually did—usually, but not always. "How'd it happen?" she asked.

"Garit got me pretty good today in training," he replied.

"I'm glad to see you're letting the other children have a few shots," she said reproachfully. Before he could give her his complimentary smirk, she slid her hand under his cloak and began prodding with her fingers. She found the spot, and he sucked in his breath. "I believe I discovered the bruise." Tristan glanced over to find her beaming. "You're lucky this counter is here to hold you up, big boy."

He wasn't sure whether to snarl or laugh. She pressed on the injury, and the pain was gone a moment later. No matter how many times he experienced it, he was always astounded by the hands of one of the healers of the Order. "I swear, I'll never be used to this."

"Bruised ribs?"

He shook his head. "The White." Ella gave him a small grin. She let her hand rest on his torso a moment longer before she pulled back and leaned on the bar. Her smile faded and she let out a sigh. Tristan felt sure he didn't want to know, but he made himself ask anyway. "Not having a good night?"

"Frustrated," she said, a slight pout in her voice. "Most of these sods have had too much to be able to dance worth a copper. Worse, there's this one foreign fellow who won't leave me alone." Her face scrunched up the way it did when she was particularly annoyed. "Calls me 'Princess' and keeps trying to put his hands on me."

Tristan tried to hide a bemused smile as he shrugged. "Not your type?" he asked.

She scoffed. "You know me. I don't have a type, but if I did, it would be something that doesn't try to grope me before it knows my name." He gave her a sidelong glance. It was true, she didn't have a type, but that was only because she had a specific target: him.

They'd been friends since they were children, and a week ago they had finally given into the pressure of those around them and gone out one evening together. It didn't take long before he became aware that Ella was not going to be content with a simple tryst. When she tried to pry, he let her know rather bluntly he had no interest in romance, and the night had gone poorly afterward. "Oh Helpers, help me," she said suddenly, but quiet. "He's coming this way."

Tristan was only too happy to have his mind distracted as he glanced about. The Low Hall was packed with people, far too many for him to be familiar with half of them. In the end, he need not have tried to sort it out, for the man in question stepped forward to make it obvious.

"My Princess of Grauberg," he proclaimed with an accent. His arms were spread, and in one hand was a mug, upside down. Tristan wondered if he'd drank it or spilled it. The manner in which the man swayed told Tristan that this had not been his first round. "I feared I had lost you among the swelling sea of common folk. Come back to me now, so I might take you to my tower and make you my queen!"

Tristan snorted as he took in the man's garb. He was attired rather nicely. His coat had long sleeves which opened wide at the wrists and were edged with lace. He wore a high collar, which was trimmed in a similar manner, and long tails hung at his rear. What really captured Tristan's attention was the fact this man had colored his eyelids a shade of red. While the women of Grauberg wore powder and paint—what they called "face"—the men did not. However, men of Dyta, the kingdom to the west across the Far Sea, did. Tristan cleared his throat. "Welcome to Grauberg, my lord."

The Dytan man paid him no mind as he continued speaking to the back of Ella's head. "I say, my lady, are you not hearing me? I have called to you, and I demand a reply!" He bowed his head and extended his empty hand, as if he expected her to turn and walk off with him into the night.

"I doubt you'll have much luck with this one," Tristan said amiably. "I don't think you're quite her type." The man sneered, while beside him Ella suppressed a chuckle. Tristan motioned to the rest of the room. "But the night is lively and we're all friends here. Can I buy you a drink?"

"I did not sail all the way from Dyta to share drink with a peasant!" The Dytan spat the words out, slurred though they were. "I do not desire the company of one such as you."

The other soldiers and guards began to playfully jeer at Tristan. "Such low company," said one, while a couple of others took up the chant of "Peasant! Peasant!" Tristan smiled, but he couldn't deny that the man was beginning to annoy him. "You sure picked a hell of a spot to come to if you didn't want to be around commoners. Come, let me buy you something." He turned to the bar and mumbled under his breath to Ella. "I'm trying to distract the moron. Go!"

"I do not wish for your company, you filthy dog!" the Dytan yelled, and the room began to grow quiet. "I am not here to speak with you! I am here to speak with this woman!" He advanced suddenly, his hand shooting out as if he intended to snatch Ella away. Tristan caught his hand in midair and held firm. The man glared with drunken fury. "How dare you lay your hand on me?!"

"This woman, friend, is spoken for," Tristan said with a hint of ice in his voice. "And I've decided I don't feel like buying you a drink after all. Perhaps you should move on, eh?"

The Dytan had defiance in his glazed eyes, and Tristan recognized the man was going nowhere. It seemed the rest of the chamber was aware as well, for people were backing up and giving them space for the inevitable fight that was about to come. Tristan told himself he didn't want to punch the man—but he'd gladly hit back if the foreign, pompous prick threw the first blow.

The man snatched his hand out of Tristan's grasp. "If I say I have claimed this woman as mine, she is mine," he said.

Tristan tensed. "I'm sorry, but, what was that?"

"I said—"

"I heard what you said, you presumptuous sack of horse filth!" Now the musicians were stopping as well. It wasn't often an argument escalated loud enough to bring the entire hall to a standstill.

Ella leaned over behind Tristan's back to whisper to Garit. "This isn't going to end well," she said. Garit nodded, a simple grin on his face as he took another sip from his mug.

Tristan's anger, meanwhile, was rising. "I don't know how you treat your women in Dyta," he said, "but I can tell you how you will not treat the women in Grauberg." He motioned to Ella with his hand but kept his eyes on the foreigner. "This woman is my friend. And you have the audacity to come into this city—our city—and treat her as a piece of property you can lay claim to?" He began to step away from the bar and toward the man. He fought to suppress the fury, and he forced his words into the harshest of whispers. "Run, little worm. Go back to your ship. Return to Dyta. Go now, or so help me—with Rylar and the Helpers as witnesses—I will beat you out!"

A few other men now came up beside the foreigner. By their garb, Tristan knew they were the man's countrymen. He was anxious at first, believing they were there to attack him, but one of them, a tall blonde man, spoke up. "Our apologies, friend," he said in a placating tone. "We are merchants, visiting your city on business. We mean no offense." Tristan gave the man a nod and a thankful smile and turned back to the bar, believing the matter closed. He was mistaken. "However," this new man went on, "offensive though my friend can be, I do not believe that gives you cause to threaten him so boldly—and in such a fashion as to belittle his honor and reputation."

Tristan had picked up his mug and taken a swallow, but at these words he choked. Mead flew out of his mouth as he laughed and turned back to the others, wiping his drink from his chin. "Honor? Reputation? I daresay he was sullying those on his own!"

"We demand to speak to someone of authority," the man said, not to Tristan, but loud and in a tone noble, confident, and commanding. He gazed around the room as if he expected a magistrate or some such to materialize.

"If you insist," said Tristan, setting down his mug. Around the bar, Garit and the other soldiers and guards set theirs down as well. Tristan saw a brief glimpse of concern and irritation on Ella's face before she stepped out of the way of the inevitable chaos. He turned to address the men. "We, my lord, are soldiers and guardsmen of Grauberg. Defenders of the fortress against outsiders, and guardians of the citizens against wrongs committed within. You'll find none in the Low Hall with more authority than we."

The merchant's eyes flashed with anger. Beside him, his friends were gathering around him and the drunk who'd started this whole affair was cracking his knuckles. Tristan smirked. "Now," he said, lowering his chin to his chest and squaring up his stance, "how would you like to lodge your complaint?"

The first punch was thrown by the man who'd made the initial pass at Ella. Tristan caught it, but this time he didn't settle for holding the man away. His other hand—clenched into a fist—hit the man squarely on the jaw, and the man fell to the ground in a heap of unconsciousness. So it was that the man responsible for the whole ordeal threw exactly one punch, and he received exactly one in turn. However, this did not end the fight altogether.

The other Dytans collided with Garit and the other soldiers. It began as a brawl, but quickly degraded into a remarkably one-sided beating. These merchants were not men trained for combat, and it didn't take more than a few seconds for this fact to become terribly evident. Egos—and much more—were bruised, and a few teeth were knocked out before the fight ended.

Tristan stood over them, wearing his maddening smirk, and Garit and the others smiled and clapped each other on the back. All around them, the rest of the Low Hall cheered them on and shouted insults at the downed foreigners. Tristan was quite pleased with himself—until Ella stepped forward. "Sometimes, Tristan, I think you're an amazing man, but then you prove you're nothing more than a boy sporting for a fight." His smirk faded, and the cheers of those standing nearby died down.

Before he could say anything, Ella turned and knelt beside the men on the floor. She folded her hands in front of her and said a few words under her breath, reached out, and touched one of the men. It was the blonde merchant who had initially defended the drunk. He was bruised, with his right eye swollen shut and his bottom lip split. Ella slid her hand to his cheek, and the man recoiled. A reassuring nod from Ella calmed him, and her hand brushed his face. His left eye opened wide as the people gathered around.

For those in Grauberg who were familiar with the art, this was a fascination. For the Dytans, who seldom had a chance to experience this magic firsthand, it must have been bewitching. After a few moments, the man's split lip closed and the swelling around his eye diminished. The bruises on his face began to fade from dark purple to light, and then to the bronze of his regular tone.

She went to each man, kneeling beside them and healing each in turn. No one spoke as she worked. The last man she came to was the one who had started the whole affair. He still had not regained consciousness as she reached down and touched him. A moment later, he was stirring, and then he was clumsily making his way back to his feet. The White had not been able to do anything for his drunkenness.

"What—" he said, looking around and trying to make sense of what was happening. His eyes settled on Tristan. "Right," he began, "I believe we were about to have words."

Before he had taken more than two steps, Ella grabbed him and spun him around, slapping him hard across the mouth as the crowd let out a collective gasp. The man glared at her in a hilariously affronted manner, and she answered by coming back with a fist that dropped him to his knees. "What do you think you are doing?" the man demanded from the floor while nursing a bloody nose.

"I'm showing you the women in Grauberg can speak up for themselves when they need to," she said, an eerie calm in her voice. "I am not property for you to lay claim to! I don't belong to you, or any man!" Here, she let her eyes glance around the room. They danced over Tristan's face, but she did not meet his eyes. "You were knocked out for your arrogance and childish behavior, and I healed you. Then you repay my kindness by trying to make an arse of yourself again? Out, you imbecile."

She turned her eyes on the men she'd healed. "All of you, out!" The words had scarce escaped her lips before they were stumbling over each other to flee through the door. The crowd cheered again, a boisterous cry louder than their last. A moment passed, the music in the various corners picked up once more, and business carried on as usual.

"It would seem my intervention on your behalf was not needed."

Ella turned and saw Tristan smirking at her. "'Intervention'?" She scowled. "You goaded those men into a fight."

Tristan's brow furrowed. "Actually, I tried to calm the situation down at first."

"'At first'! But then you lost your head! Why? Why do you always end up in a bloody fight?"

Tristan stared at her hard. "I'll not have some idiot from Dyta behave as if you're something he can buy at a stall in the market, Ella!"

"And I'll not have my honor defended by a man who has the discipline of a toddler pitching a tantrum!" She turned and made her way swiftly through the crowd and out the door, not bothering to give him a backward glance as she left.

"Well," said Garit as he slid up beside Tristan, "I'd say that—all things considered—that turned out rather well."

"I suppose," Tristan said. He turned back to his mead, but found the mug overturned. He didn't order another—he decided he really didn't feel like dancing tonight, after all.

Tristan woke to the sound of someone pounding hard at his door. Not only that, but his head was thundering as well. He wondered if he'd taken a punch to the skull at some point and didn't realize it in the frenzy of the brawl. The knocking on his door resumed, louder this time. "Aye, I'm coming!" He sat up and reached for a pair of breeches. "Who is it? This had better be pretty bloody important!"

"Command Walter demands your presence in the High Hall."

Tristan stopped pulling his clothes on and sat stone still. In fifteen years, he'd never once come face to face with one of the commanders. He'd seen them before, at various ceremonies and gatherings, but never up close. To be called before one of them was seldom a good thing. His mind jumped to the fight, and another twinge of pain shot through his skull. "I require a few moments," he called out to the loud voice on the other side of his door. He was shocked to hear the tremble in his own voice.

"I would suggest you be as quick as possible," the voice returned. Tristan abandoned the pair of breeches he was about to put on and went instead to his small collection of clothes. In a moment, he'd retrieved his dress uniform.

He couldn't help but chuckle as he thought about

how many times he'd had to hurry into it for surprise drills and inspections. Never had any of those seemed this important, though. He admired it as he attired himself. A black tunic over black breeches with black leather boots. He wore a shirt of grey mail over his tunic, and silver pauldrons covered his shoulders and his chest. His shins were protected by silver greaves while his forearms were shielded by silver vambraces.

Thankfully, he took care of his equipment and attire; the metal was polished to a shine, as well as the leather boots, and not a single thread was out of place. He was clad quicker than he'd ever known he could be. He pulled his hair back in a tail and emerged from his residence to the appraising eyes of the two guards sent to retrieve him.

"Well," said one, and Tristan recognized it as the voice that had called through the door, "I won't lie—you appear a good deal better than I expected from the tale of the brawl. Still, that shine isn't like to knock the wrath from what you're about to receive."

Any hope Tristan had gained from the initial compliment vanished with the man's last words. "Right, on you get, then." The guards turned him, and they began making their way to the middle level of the city.

The city of Grauberg was tiered into three levels as it rose into the mountains at its back. The lowest was home to commoners and craftsmen, as well as the location of most of the shops in the city. Most commoners lived in the villages outside, but some few lived in the city proper, as well as those the city employed as sellswords. The lower level also featured a vast open area which was used for many events, ranging from tournaments to livestock auctions to celebrations throughout the year.

The middle level was where most of the "higher-ups" worked. These were the military officers and the city planners. The leaders of the city's various guilds met on the lower level for most matters, but some of their more important meetings were held on this level when the hustle and bustle of the lower was not agreeable. The majority of the nobles of Grauberg lived on this level, as well—only a few actually lived on their land holdings.

Though the nation was divided between commoner and noble, it was not unusual to see the higher class venturing down to the lower level to mingle. The distinction between the two classes was not so great as it had been in centuries past, or even in Dyta. Lastly, the highest level of the city held the royal estates and the enormous temple of Rylar.

The High Hall was located on the middle level, and to call it majestic would not do it justice. Whereas everything on the lower level was grey stone, the High Hall was polished marble. Instead of being square and lackluster in appearance, it was rounded and unique in its design. The structure stood tall and lofty, a spectacle to behold, even as the palace and temple looked down on it from above.

It was here that ambassadors met with anyone other than the royal family, as well as where they were housed while they were within the city. It was also the official headquarters for military operations. Though not on the highest level, it was still elevated enough to see out over the walls of Grauberg and into its surrounding area. From here, a general or commander could order troops with flags and horns for signals, while soldiers trained as runners could carry messages back and forth and be dispatched with haste.

In fifteen years, Tristan had never been above the lowest level. His first years had been spent in one of the outlying villages. When the elderly man and woman caring for him and several other misplaced orphans passed away, he was brought into the city as an official ward of the state. Still, he'd never been permitted up these steps. You couldn't stroll up here on a daily walk, and the only way to be summoned here as a soldier—as a general rule—was to do something worthy of either commendation or punishment. Tristan was aware he was not here to be commended.

As Tristan took in the magnificence of the High Hall, he realized that he wasn't afraid at the moment. The building stood in stark contrast to the Low Hall. The "Low Hall" was not, in fact, officially called by that name. There had been, according to stories, a building called the Low Hall centuries ago, but it had been destroyed in the ancient wars, either with Elinton or Felixandria. The High Hall had been built in a more strategic location, and the current "Low Hall" was a moniker foisted upon a much-loved building on a whim.

Tristan's musings about town layout and architecture and history were brought back to the present as he was brought inside the High Hall and the doors closed behind him. The fear which had been oddly absent moments ago now became very real. He found himself being marched down a long hallway, surrounded by four guards. The men were rather tall, with armor as beautiful, polished, and dark as the marble of the walls around him. They stared straight ahead and marched with spears in hand.

Tristan knew, of course, that these guards had been selected for this post to intimidate whoever was brought into these chambers. And yet, they still succeeded in having the desired effect—by the time they reached the large double doors to the commander's office, his heart was racing.

At the doors, the men halted. No one stepped forward to knock. Then, all four hit the butt of their spears on the floor in perfect unison three times, the sound booming and echoing down the hall. This had a dramatic and palpable effect, and Tristan marveled at the difference between the professionalism of these men and those who he had often shared drinks with. As the echoes died, an equally booming voice called out from the other side of the doors. "Enter."

The doors swung open slowly, and Tristan, flanked by the four guards, entered the room. The office was expansive enough to accommodate the commander, two more guards who were stationed inside the office at the door, Tristan, and his escort. It likely could have managed twice the count and still would not have been a tight squeeze. Behind an imposing desk, a man rose. "This is the one?"

"He is, Commander," said one of the guards on Tristan's right.

"Hm. You are dismissed." The four guards saluted, spun on their heels, and marched out while the two guards stationed inside closed the doors behind them. The doors clanged shut, and Tristan winced as he heard the lock bolted into place.

He faced forward and took in the intimidating sight of Commander Walter. He appeared to be somewhere between forty and fifty. He was average in height, but broad with a deep chest. His hair was black and cut short, and his eyes were fixed on Tristan—the commander was evaluating him, as well. "Your name, boy." It was not a question, but a command.

"Tristan, sir."

The commander came out from behind his desk. He began pacing back and forth. "Just 'Tristan,' boy? No more to go with it?"

"No, sir." The commander moved in front of him. Tristan worried if he exhaled too hard, he'd make contact with the man. The commander lifted his eyebrows as if waiting for a more detailed reply. "My family did not carry a surname, sir."

"Ah." Walter stared hard at him. "Lowborn. Perhaps that explains it." Tristan felt some of his fear dissipate. Unfortunately, and to his horror, it was replaced with annoyance. "What's your father's trade?" asked the commander. He turned slowly and walked back to his desk.

"He was a farmer, sir."

"Was?"

Tristan swallowed hard. "He's dead, sir."

The commander nodded. "And your mother?"

"Killed with my father, sir." Tristan shook his head, fighting not just his headache, but now the images which wouldn't stay away.

"And your sisters?"

"They were also—" Tristan stammered to a stop as a massive throb rang through his temples. This was all a game—the commander knew his family history. Tristan gave him an accusatory glare. "They are dead as well, as you are undoubtedly aware, sir."

Walter turned and measured him. "Well, you figured that out quick enough, so I know you aren't a simpleton. Even if you are a lowborn orphan." Tristan tensed. He closed his eyes for a moment and tried to get his feelings under control. "You may want to settle down, Tristan. That temper of yours will get you into trouble one day." Tristan opened his eyes and saw his fists were the object of Commander Walter's gaze. He unclenched them, unaware that he'd even been making them. Walter turned away from him and faced the fire. "Tell me, Tristan, have you been educated?"

Tristan did his best to relax, but it was difficult. "I have, sir."

"Trained in the martial disciplines of Grauberg?"

"Aye, sir."

The commander spun away from the fire, red-faced as he bellowed at Tristan. "Then tell me why an educated, disciplined man in service to Grauberg led an assault against an esteemed delegation from Dyta!" The blood rushed out of Tristan's face. His mouth opened, but words would not form. Commander Walter had no such trouble. "Honored merchants, invited here to renew trade agreements—one of them the son of an ambassador—and you have the audacity to attack them without provocation!"

Tristan now found himself stammering. There were a

dozen things he could say to this, but his desire to speak was now in conflict with his military training. Without the commander giving him permission to speak plainly, Tristan could not defend himself. Walter turned back to the fire, took in a deep breath through his nose, and let it out almost like a growl. "Please, come forward, my lord."

Footsteps sounded from a corner of the room which was shrouded in shadow. Tristan glanced over, and the drunk merchant who'd started everything the night before emerged, a grin plastered on his face. He bore bruises from Ella's strikes, but they did nothing to hide his sheer glee now. "Ah, Commander, you have filled my troubled heart with content. To see him so afraid—to see him learn his proper place—It brings me much joy." He came to a stop only a couple of steps away from Tristan.

"I am glad to be of service," the commander said. "Boy, you will apologize for your behavior last night, and you will pledge to never again be at odds with Lord Turold within the realm of Grauberg."

Tristan's cheeks reddened as the blood rushed back. Still, as bad as his temper was, he also knew better than to let it control him in this situation. "Lord Turold," he began, swallowing hard—both to get his bearings, and to suppress his pride, "allow me to extend my sincerest apology. Had I but realized you were not a peasant yourself, I certainly would not have treated you in such a manner." He bowed his head but had the pleasure of seeing this Lord Turold scowl before he lowered his gaze.

Eyes on the floor, Tristan went on. "Perhaps we can have a drink in friendship, one day. I'm afraid I will have to meet you elsewhere, though. I don't believe it would be prudent if we were to meet again in Grauberg, lest it lead to an awkward situation. In this manner, I believe we can both be certain we will never again be at odds within the city."

The Dytan merchant lord turned these words over in his head, attempting to work out whether Tristan had insulted him or fulfilled the commander's orders. Tristan lifted his head as Turold turned to Walter, who nodded. Turold then turned back to Tristan, his grin renewed, though somewhat diminished. "Apology accepted. Oh, and send my regards to your woman."

Tristan tried not to let his displeasure show at the mention of Ella, but Turold must have sensed it, for his smile grew broad again. "Or perhaps she isn't spoken for after all?" He gave Tristan a sneer that almost dared him to respond. Tristan would not allow himself to be baited here, and after a moment Turold turned back to Walter and bowed. "Commander," he said, and he spun and walked away. Tristan let out a sigh as he heard the guards unbolt the door and open them for his exit.

After Lord Turold was gone, the doors remained open. Walter turned back from the fire and addressed the two guards in the room. "Thank you for your service, gentlemen. You are dismissed. Tristan and I will be fine alone for a time." The guards saluted, walked out, and closed the doors behind them. Tristan noted that he did not hear their footsteps going down the hallway. He looked back at Walter, who appeared much more amiable now. "You may speak free, son," he said. "We are alone now."

Tristan glanced around. "No more Dytan merchants hiding in the shadows, sir?"

Walter smiled and took a seat in the chair behind his desk. He extended his hand toward a chair on the opposite side. "I'm quite certain." Tristan paused for a moment, but then moved and stiffly sat down in the proffered seat. He was unsure what to make of this little scene. "No doubt, you're a bit confused at my sudden change in demeanor," the commander said.

"No doubt," replied Tristan, and he had more acid in his tone than he'd intended.

Walter heard it, too, and his smile lessened. "I know I told you to speak free, but have a care—I am still commander of half of the army of Grauberg."

Tristan closed his eyes and breathed in deep but slow. He tried to suppress the images of his family, as well as his desire to rush out and grab Lord Turold of Dyta and throw him from the High Hall above to the Low Hall below.

He let his breath back out, and when he opened his eyes, he saw a genuine, almost kind expression on the face of the man behind his desk. "I understand, Commander. And it appears I put you in an awkward position last night," he conceded.

Commander Walter let out a booming laugh that would have likely echoed to the lower level of the city if they'd been outdoors. "That's an understatement. Not just me, boy. Your little scuffle last night nearly upended months of trade negotiations with Dyta. And not local contracts, mind you—a contract between the royal family of Grauberg and the royal family of Dyta! Lord Turold's father is a royal bastard of some sort, and the chief Dytan ambassador to Grauberg, no less!"

A small groan escaped from Tristan as his heart dropped into his stomach. He didn't realize how bad he was slouching until the commander laughed again. "Oh, sit up, boy. All is well now! What was damaged has been mended. The entire morning has been spent making reparations, the last of which was a demand from Lord Turold, himself. He wished to be able to witness your humiliation."

Walter leaned forward and grabbed a few grapes from a plate on his desk. Tristan had been so absorbed in everything else, he'd not noticed the untouched food which was set out before him. In all of his dealings, Walter had not had time to eat today, it appeared. "Help yourself," the commander said, motioning to the food.

"I'm fine, sir," Tristan said. In truth, he was starving, but he didn't know if he'd be able to keep anything down just now. He turned his thoughts from food and back to the events which had unfolded. "So, your questions and outbursts were—"

"Playacting, Tristan," said the commander. "Well, at least mostly." Tristan gave him a puzzled expression. "I know well what happened. They came here with their tails between their legs the moment your little healer friend shamed them out of the Low Hall. I spent the entire night sending messengers back and forth, gathering information and questioning witnesses. There wasn't a word you could have said to any question I might have asked this morning that I'd not already have had an answer to." Tristan nodded, impressed by the man before him, but still not feeling at ease. "I do have to say, though, that even if the entitled little arse of a merchant was behaving like a spoiled heap of horse filth, a barroom brawl featuring Grauberg's soldiers is a black eye on us all."

"I have no excuse, sir," Tristan said.

"No, you haven't." Walter stood once more, his gloved hands folded behind his back as he faced the fire again. "But, then again, you aren't actually a soldier of Grauberg, are you? Just a contracted one." He glanced over his shoulder at Tristan. "That contract expires on your twenty-third nameday."

"Yes, sir."

"That would be next month, would it not?"

"It is, sir."

Walter grunted and turned, pacing around toward Tristan's chair. When he was in front of Tristan, he leaned back on the desk and crossed one leg over the other. He let his hands rest on the desktop, tapping a finger on the edge as he did. "Have you given thought to what you'll do when that contract expires? Seek out another profession? Renew the contract for another five-year term? Perhaps choose to join the military on an official basis and become a true citizen of Grauberg?"

Tristan stared straight ahead and told his lie. "I haven't decided, sir."

"You still have time to consider your options, I suppose," said Walter. "In the meantime, I have a special assignment for you."

Tristan smirked. "I've heard it said a special assignment is a fancy way of naming a punishment, sir."

Walter smiled. "Is that right? Well, I wonder how that rumor got started." He reached back on the table and grabbed an unsealed missive. "Seeing as how you almost ruined foreign matters with Dyta, it seems fair you offer your services in helping to mend matters elsewhere."

Tristan nodded, but then stopped and thought about what he'd said. "Elsewhere, sir?"

"Aye," said the commander, his smile now removed. "With Elinton."

Tristan felt as though he'd been kicked in the gut. His heart began thundering in his chest. "With Felixandria, you mean."

"Perhaps," said the commander. "The king of Felixandria still maintains he did not sanction the invasion on Elinton fifteen years ago."

"Sir, it was the crown prince of Felixandria who led the attack!"

"I know," Walter said, holding his hand up. "And Prince Jules still holds the city to this day, ruling as its regent on behalf of the queen." Tristan knew the queen had no power—she was a puppet, kept alive only to have her legitimize Prince Jules' reign. Walter broke through his thoughts. "Regardless of whether he acted on behalf of his father or on his own, the fact is he holds Elinton, and the threat of war hangs over us all while that is the case." He held up the missive. "Or perhaps not."

"Has the queen retaken the city?" Tristan asked, a wild hope bursting forth. The commander shook his head, smothering any hope Tristan held.

Walter gave him a weak smile that Tristan might take as sympathetic, then he cleared his throat and glanced at the missive. "This is a message from Queen Joyce of

Elinton. She is sending her regent, Prince Jules, here to negotiate a long-term peace treaty. We can expect his arrival in about three weeks."

Tristan's hands tightened on the arms of his chair. "Prince Jules? Here?!"

Walter nodded. "To be precise, 'Prince Jules, heir to Felixandria and Regent and Protector of the golden land of Elinton.'" His tone made it plain that he did not approve of these titles.

"The King cannot be seriously considering this!"

The words were barely out of his mouth before Walter gave him an uncompromising glare. "Tristan, I know Elinton was your home. And yes, I'm aware of what happened to your family." His glare softened, but only a little, and he reached out and placed a hand on Tristan's shoulder. "Son, I'm not saying your anger isn't justified. I also had family in Elinton. I lost many of them to Jules. The rest, I can't say for sure how they are faring these days. But here's the reality we face: we've been a nation at peace for, oh, about three centuries now. King Frederic would like for it to stay that way, and I am going to need your help in making that happen."

A bead of sweat began to slide down Tristan's forehead, following the scar on his face — the same scar he'd acquired when his home was taken away. With gritted teeth, he asked, "I don't suppose I can decline this?"

Commander Walter regarded him sternly, but not without compassion. "No, Tristan. You cannot."

III
The Calm Before

The walk back to the lower level of the city was long. A sea of emotions raged inside of Tristan's head, ranging from devastation to heartache to fury. The man responsible for the death of his family—for the fall of the nation he called home—was coming here, and Tristan had to plan the celebration to welcome him and his entourage, as well as the festivities to follow during their stay in Grauberg.

Around him, people seemed to move slowly, as though the world was mired in a fog. He tried not to meet the eyes of those he crossed, but the few times he did, he noted people were giving him confused expressions, and he could not understand why.

Did they know he was going to be welcoming the scum to the city? Surely not—the commander would not have let the news slip. Others within the military would know, though, and the word would soon be out.

At some point in his musing, he realized he had long since passed the street which would take him to his residence. His feet had carried him to another familiar stop: Ella's home. She resided with her parents, and Tristan had always been on good terms with the family dating back to their flight from Elinton.

Before he knocked on the door, it struck him that she may have told her parents about the less-than-happy ending of their recent outing. He prayed she had not. He raised his hand and stopped himself again—why had he come here? He shook his head and tried to clear his mind.

The problem wasn't what he was thinking, but rather that he wasn't thinking.

That had never been an issue with Ella, though. Over the years, they'd often spent hours in total silence over problems which had no answer. He never came to her seeking solutions; he came to her because he found comfort in her company. With that lone thought in mind, he knocked.

"Oh," came a voice as the door cracked, revealing Ella's mother, Braya. "Tristan! Oh my, is—is everything alright, dear?"

"Er, um—I'm sorry?" He was a bit more puzzled now. "I believe so. I was wondering if I might speak to Ella? Is she home?"

"Well, it's just—well—you're in your dress uniform. You're not here on business?" An expression of horror spread over the poor woman's face. "She's not in trouble over last night, is she? She didn't realize the man was the son of some fancy lord. Can't you tell them—explain to them—that she was in the right?"

Tristan now understood the strange looks. "Madam, I'm so sorry. No, Ella's not in trouble. I just came from a meeting with the commander, and I didn't think to change before coming here." He bowed his head, far more sincerely than the one he'd given the Dytan merchant. "I offer you my deepest apologies for startling you. I would never give you or your family undue cause for worry."

When he straightened up, the color had returned to Braya's face as she began fanning herself. "Oh, thank Rylar! But you, you cheeky arse!" She scolded him and gave him a light slap on the shoulder, and her scowl changed to a smile. "Scaring me like that, a woman at my age! Well, I suppose you'd best come in. Ella!" Tristan was smiling as he stepped through the doorway. He'd always been fond of Ella's parents, especially her mother. "Ella, that boy is here for you!" After fifteen years, Tristan was still 'that boy.' "Have a seat, dear. I've a fresh pot of tea.

Would you care for a cup?"

"Yes, please." She disappeared into the kitchen as he moved into the family room. He tried to sit, but the chairs in the home sat very low after the Elinian fashion, and his current attire did not quite allow for easy comfort. So, he stood and waited. He wondered if Ella was still mad at him, and after he had gotten uncomfortable from waiting, he decided she must be.

Braya returned and set the cup on the table in the center of the room. Tristan had to bend quite awkwardly to pick it up. When he caught Braya grinning menacingly at him, he gave her a sarcastic sneer.

He'd just straightened back up when footsteps sounded down the hall. "Tristan." Ella's tone was guarded as she greeted him.

He turned to her and bowed his head and noted the strange glint in her eyes. "Hello, Ella. Do you like the armor? I decided to dress up fancy to impress you." She wasn't smiling. "Well, that—and Commander Walter needed to have a few words with me this morning."

A small grin came to her lips. "Well, at least I wasn't the only one to have had their sleep disturbed, then." He smirked and she rolled her eyes. "Oh, stop."

His smirk broadened to a genuine smile, and he turned to Braya. "Might I walk with your daughter for a bit, madam?"

Braya grinned. "Oh, so formal," she said teasingly. "Go walk, and try to have her back in a better mood than on your last outing." Tristan's face changed to one of struck silence, and Braya cackled at his expression. "Tristan, go, you oaf!" Ella spun Tristan and they headed for the door. "And don't let my daughter get into any more fistfights!"

Ella turned and shot her a glare, but upon seeing her mother's laughing face she instead embraced her and kissed her on the cheek. Tristan held the door open for her as they left the small residence. "So, how bad was it?" she asked as soon as the door had closed behind them.

"Eh, not too bad," he answered. "At least not in response to the fight itself." He glanced down at his boots and chuckled. "Do you mind if we walk over to my place first? I would love to get into something a little more appropriate."

"By all means, yes!" The trek from Ella's to Tristan's was not far. Because his residence was a single room, she waited outside while he discarded his formal wear. He shouted an invitation to her through the closed door— something about needing help getting his trousers off. "Better stuck trousers than a boot stuck in your arse!" she yelled back, and he did not invite her in again. Several minutes later, he emerged wearing leather breeches and a plain white tunic. She breathed a sigh of relief. "Aye, that's much better. So, where to now?"

He smiled at her as he motioned with his head toward the portion of the city behind him, and immediately she knew where he was thinking. "It's been a while, eh?" he asked. He said no more as they moved toward the wall of the city.

As they approached, they followed it along behind what had once been houses for nobles before the upper levels had been built. That meant these structures were several centuries old, and many had fallen into various states of disrepair. The few which were still intact served for storage and such, and what had once been gardens behind the homes were now mostly untended undergrowth.

There were even a few trees here which had to be managed from time to time, though it seemed no one ever came around to clear out the entire mess. This was to their advantage as Tristan and Ella made their way through the growth, looking about to make certain they were not followed.

One of the larger trees had grown up right along the wall. Its branches had not been trimmed back for several years. The area around this tree was the thickest with growth, and this was their target. Tristan stopped for a moment. "How long has it been since we came here?"

"Were we teenagers yet?" They both pondered this for a moment before Ella remembered. "My fifteenth nameday, I think. Just before I began my training with the White."

"That's right," Tristan agreed. "We were able to fit through then. I don't think either of us are much bigger now." Something slapped him on the back of his head. He turned, and Ella was glaring at him, hands on her hips. "Well, I thought it was a compliment—I'm saying you don't seem to have put on much weight since becoming an adult!"

She hit him again. "It would go over better if you'd simply leave the 'much' out altogether, if it please you!" After a few moments, she couldn't help but smile. "Oaf," she said.

They maneuvered to the trunk of the tree and knelt. The roots had worked their way through the wall, and years of rain had left a small opening barely large enough for a man of Tristan's stature to squeeze through. "I can't believe they've never found this," Ella said.

Tristan nodded in agreement. "Well, let's go." As he spoke, he helped Ella to step down into a small hollow at the base of the tree. She laid on her belly and crawled into the small opening in the wall, and Tristan followed. As he did, he inspected the stone overhead, making an examination for the first time as an adult. "I don't believe the roots did all the work," he said. "I think this must have been some sort of drainage ditch, and the roots have only enlarged the area around it."

When they emerged, they were at the base of the mountains at the back of the city. In fact, Tristan doubted he could make his way around to the front gate from here—not without some tremendous exertion and climbing, at least. It was a hidden valley of sorts.

Tristan glanced up at the mountains—the Spears, they were called, for that's how they appeared from afar. They were tall, with points capped in white. Very little grew on them once you were more than a hundred yards or so up their slopes, but the trees here at the base in this small haven had been the home of many of Tristan's and Ella's childhood adventures. This had been their escape when they were both outsiders in a city which wasn't theirs.

"Why here?" asked Ella. They were slowly walking toward a shaded area, where the trees were still thick. The air was cool, and here in the shade it was nearly cold. Still, this was where they stopped.

"I'm not sure," said Tristan. "I'd not thought to come here until you asked where we were going. It's familiar—ours."

His voice had a quality Ella had rarely heard: it was somber. She cleared her throat. "Well, why did you wish to speak to me?" He shrugged, and in place of irritation, she began to feel concerned for him. "Tristan, look at me." He didn't, so she put her hand on his cheek and turned his face to hers. "What's happened? What did the commander say that has you so unsettled?"

He reached up and placed his hand on top of hers and noted how her breath shuddered at the touch. For a brief moment, he longed to kiss her, but he fought the desire down. It would mean more for her than he intended, and perhaps for himself as well. Instead, he slowly slid her hand from his face. Even so, he continued to clasp it. "Before we get into that, I want to apologize, Ella."

Her eyes widened, and Tristan saw her fighting off the smile at the corners of her mouth. "Oh, this is a first," she said. When he didn't give her his usual smile—that damnable smirk—she realized how upset he really was. "You're quite serious, aren't you?"

"I am. I've been avoiding you, and I gave you cause

to avoid me. And I'm sorry." He sensed her discomfort grow. She began to pull her hand back from him, but he held her firmly. "Please, hear me out." She had lowered her eyes and was looking at his chest. He loosened his grip, giving her the option to pull away if she truly wished to, but she nodded her head for him to proceed.

He took a deep breath. "I know what you're looking for, and what I'm willing to give — and what I'm not. I can't tell you why, or even how I feel, but I want you to understand that the reason why I can't give you what you seek has nothing to do with my feelings for you." He fell silent for a moment, struggling to think of a better way to express himself.

He peered down at her and lifted her chin to try and read her face. A curious expression crossed his brow, because instead of the confusion he'd expected, she was snarling. "Ella?" he asked, then suddenly, "OW!" He released her hand and jumped back on one leg, clutching his left shin as she aimed another kick at him. "Bloody hell, Ella — what was that for?!"

"Your feelings have nothing to do with why you won't show your feelings?" she spat at him with as much vitriol as she could imagine. "What kind of nonsense is that? You've said some stupid stuff since I've known you — and that's been nearly all our lives, Tristan — but this may be the most idiotic thing to have ever come out of your mouth!"

He made sure he was out of range of her kicks before he put his foot back down. "Ella, there are things I need to do! Things I can't let go of!" Her anger waned. She was starting to understand. "It still hurts, Ella. I still see them. In my dreams, more nights than I care to count — screaming and bleeding and dying." His hands clenched into fists at his sides as he fought to keep his voice at a reasonable level. "I can't let it go."

Ella crossed her arms. "Tristan, you're not the only one who lost Elinton that day — or family." She had escaped the invasion with her parents. They barely got away before Jules' army took the city, but her grandparents—both on her father's side and her mother's—had been killed. "I know the pain. I will admit I may not sense it as keenly as you, but I understand."

She stared at her hands now, as if she'd find the words to say resting in her palms. "You've got to move on, Tristan." She raised her eyes and glimpsed the outrage on his face. She held up her hands in a placating manner. "I don't say let go, but you have to find a way to move on. You can't let your hate get in the way of your heart." She met his eyes for a moment before he turned away. "And no, I'm not saying this because I love you, or because I wished you loved me."

"Ella, I—"

"Oh, stow it. I won't hide it. You know it's there, and you've known it for a long time. If not me, that's fine. But Tristan—" and here she moved up to him briskly, taking his hand in hers once more, "you have to love somebody. I've seen you when you're happy. You laugh and you dance, and you even sing when you've had too much mead. Tristan, you have it in you to love again."

"No. Not until the scales have been balanced." He fought to keep his voice calm and collected, but he knew Ella sensed the rage which burned beneath the surface. She'd seen him get angry too often, and she recognized when his fury ran cold. He gritted his teeth and turned aside. "And now, when the opportunity is finally presented, I cannot act."

Her eyes narrowed. "What do you mean?"

"Jules is coming here," he said, and a shiver ran through his body. "In three weeks, the bastard is coming here to negotiate a long-term peace, and because I nearly mucked things up last night with Dyta, they're making me plan the bloody welcoming party."

Ella's mouth opened, but she struggled to make words come out. His feelings were so much more understandable now. She closed her eyes, calmed herself, and tried again. "Are they aware of your past?"

"Aye."

"And still, they would have you arrange this?"

He nodded. "Not just the welcome, but the festivities to honor him while he is our king's guest."

Ella turned away and put one hand over her mouth and the other on her stomach. "The very thought makes me sick."

"That makes two of us," he confided, hoping she couldn't hear the fear in his voice. "I don't know how I can do this, Ella."

Her own heart was now racing. She closed her eyes again, breathing in her nose and out through her mouth. After a few moments, she was in control of herself again. "We have our duties we must carry out," she said at length. "You're one of the strongest men I've ever been around, Tristan. And no, I don't mean the size of your arms. You have an inner strength that's kept you going this far. I have no desire to watch you race after vengeance, but neither do I wish to see you in chains for insubordination."

She turned back toward him and motioned to the small vale around them with outstretched arms. "When we first discovered this little place and started coming here as children, we were alone in this city—but not anymore. Grauberg may not be Elinton, but it has welcomed and sheltered us. This has become our new home, and we owe them our best."

Tristan had heard this confident tone in her voice before. His heart began to slow, and he raised an eyebrow at her. "Go on."

She gave him a smile. "Show them how stern and strong the people of Grauberg are. Leave no doubt in their minds that an attack here would lead only to their ruin. Show them we will not be cowed. And if you can, find a way to intimidate them."

"And how do you propose I do that?"

She shrugged. "You're clever—far too clever, sometimes. You'll come up with something." He gave her his little smirk and she groaned, but it gave her the reassurance that he wouldn't do anything stupid—not today at least. Still, it drove her mad. "I hate when you do that."

They sat down on the sloping ground beneath them and lingered in silence for a while. Neither said so, but both were at peace here—a peace which was not likely to last. The sun was rising higher and nearing noon. "We should be going," Ella said after some time had passed. "I have duties with the Order this afternoon, and I'm sure you have something you need to be doing, as well."

"Aye," said Tristan. He stood and held out a hand to help her up. At the wall, they listened to make sure no one was on the other side before they snuck back in. Once inside, he escorted her home. Her father came out as they reached her door. Tristan smiled at him and bowed his head. "Good afternoon, sir."

"Tristan," Ella's father began in a dry tone, "how many times must I tell you to call me by my name? You're a grown man now."

"My apologies, Brice," Tristan replied, the sensation still weird every time he was forced to say it. "Old habits."

Brice smiled. "I know." He turned his gaze to Ella. "And how's my little champion of the barroom doing today?" She hit him in the shoulder, grinned, and wrapped her arms tightly around him. Brice gave Tristan a grin. "The benefit of having a daughter in the Order of the White is if I taunt her into hurting me, she loves me enough to make it better." All three laughed. Brice hugged her back, but then shrugged her away. "Believe me, I would love to stay and talk, but I've left my stall with my apprentice, and the boy still struggles with counting coins. Helpers, help me." Ella kissed him on the cheek, and he turned and disappeared around the corner.

"I had best be off as well," Tristan said after Ella's father was out of sight. He turned to her and gave her a genuine smile. "Thank you for seeing me."

She rolled her eyes and grunted. "Stop being so formal. I swear, one minute you want me to come into your room to see you in your smallclothes, and now —"

"Actually, I wasn't wearing anything when I invited you in."

She hit him and continued without missing a beat. "And now you're all 'thank you, and fare thee well my lady.'" She made a mock bow to him. When she straightened, he playfully tapped her on the cheek, and she wrapped her arms around him. "Don't be stupid," she said, and she squeezed him a bit tighter. "But do be careful."

"I will," he said. He backed away and gave her a mock bow of his own. "Fare thee well, my lady." He raised his eyes in time for the door to close in his face.

"They want you to do what?!" Garit could not believe what Tristan had said. He was at a loss, not just at what they wanted Tristan to do, but also that his friend wasn't raging. "I'm not sure what I'm more confused by... the fact they want you, of all people, to throw your arms open to the people who ki—" He cleared his throat, "...the people who sacked Elinton, or the fact that you haven't killed six men and a goat in a rage."

"Excellent recovery," Tristan said in a flat tone. "But aye, I wanted to kill six men — and maybe a goat — but I spoke with Ella, and she talked me around to seeing things differently."

"Oh?" Garit asked, genuinely intrigued. "How's that?"

Tristan finished lacing up his leather greaves and took up his wooden sword and shield. "She told me to show them our fortitude. Our grit." He pointed at Garit with his practice blade. "And, if possible, she said I should intimidate them."

Garit laughed. "Perhaps you should take them to the Low Hall for drinks and let Ella slap them around a bit. She's been the talk of the town all day." Tristan smiled. Men were less likely to harass her if she had the reputation of punching out a visiting dignitary for being too friendly. Garit amended his statement. "Well, she was the talk this morning. This afternoon, it's been the rumors about this visit. I didn't believe it, though, until you told me all this."

Tristan nodded. He had figured word would start getting out soon, but he hadn't expected it this quick. Still, the whole story wasn't out yet. His role had not reached Garit's ears, and if anyone in town was inclined to hear gossip, it was Garit. His friend didn't say much about others, but he loved hearing the latest news and rumors before they became common knowledge. "So, got anything in mind for how to scare them?" Garit asked.

"Not yet," Tristan admitted. "I have some time to think on it. They aren't expected for three weeks. Still, I need to be quick about coming to a decision. I have a feeling that events of this magnitude don't get thrown together at the last minute."

"Yeah, it's not quite the same as a night at the Hall."

The two men made their way to the training yard. Today's session called for the men to change partners every quarter-hour, drilling defensive and offensive poses. For three hours, they worked. The yard typically hummed with small talk here and there, but today was eerily quiet.

None here had any love for Jules. The refugees from Elinton had left a clear impression on the people of Grauberg, and the Grause had no desire to see this foreign army up close. The men in the yard battered one another until all muscles were bruised or aching or both.

As they progressed, the mood changed from solemn to determined to angry. It seemed the blows which followed each parry hit harder than the last. It was a mercy when the chief instructor called a halt to their day.

Tristan had not paired with Garit that afternoon, but he promptly found him in the barracks after. Garit's black hair was slick with sweat, and his body covered with bruises. Tristan smacked him on his bare back with his flat palm, and the loud clap made the nearby soldiers wince. "Ooh, that smarts," said Garit, sitting up and arching his back. "And what, pray tell, has you in such a fine, bloody mood?" He made as if to reach for the stinging spot on his back, but his aching shoulders would not let him.

"I know what we're going to do," Tristan said.

"Oh? About Jules, you mean?" Tristan nodded, and some of the men who were standing nearby turned to listen. Garit gave Tristan a cautious glance. "What do you have in mind?" Tristan smirked, and Garit knew the answer would be interesting.

> *Games. As far as ideas from Tristan goes, it could be worse I suppose, but that's what he is proposing to me, and what he plans to propose to Commander Walter tomorrow morning. Bloody games. Not the sort where you lose coin betting on dice, but a tournament. He hasn't worked out the details in his head yet, but now that the notion is there, I have no doubt he will.*
>
> *I can't deny it might be a great idea. Our men are clearly on edge, judging by the way training went today. Mayhap this sort of news will lift their moods and they won't be so angry. Rylar knows, I don't want to go through another day of training like that. I feel like I'd been tied to a rack and tortured.*
>
> *Still, I can't imagine what must be going through Tristan's mind. We've been friends for far too long for me to believe he's taking this as well as he is. Ella may have calmed the beast today, but these people killed his family. Not only that, but the way he says it*

happened... I know it can't be true, but he's so sure when he tells it that I almost believe it. Tristan is a lot of things, but a liar isn't one of them.

I have a bad feeling about these talks. Jules wanting peace is the biggest jest I've heard all year, but Tristan may be on to something here. Perhaps this will give Jules a glance at our own force. If we fight in a tournament in any manner at all resembling today's training, I know I'd be nervous in his place.

Well, that's all for tonight. The White serves well for healing bruises, but it does nothing for fatigue, and I'm beat. May Rylar and the Helpers help us in the days to come.

IV
The Gathering Grey Clouds

Today is the day Jules arrives. We had a rider in the night who informed us he'd spotted the party yesterday evening, and we expect their arrival some time this morning. There is a mood over the city I can't explain. It certainly isn't excitement. Anxious, perhaps? Just this feeling of something looming, even if no one can say for sure what that something is.

Commander Walter has kept me busy. I've been in charge of preparing a welcoming banquet for tonight, and the tournament is set to begin tomorrow. I believe the people are excited for that, but it's masked under the uneasiness surrounding the arrival. What if this sense of dread lingers and no one comes to the tourney? Surely, they'll come.

The commander had an idea yesterday for the welcoming party. I had anticipated that the general and the commanders would wish to meet with Jules at the gates, but he suggested I do so with a group of men from Elinton. This is supposed to be about peace, but I'm more than certain our guest will take this as a slap to the face.

I don't know. Perhaps it's about a show of strength. Something to make it clear to Jules we aren't going to hide behind false smiles. I can see that going either way with the *negotiations, but I am glad to see that they don't believe in Jules' goodwill.*

I sent out messages last night, stating any men of Elinian birth can meet at the High Hall in dress uniform this morning if they wish. I won't force any of them into this: this is as hard for them as it is me.

Tristan walked to the residential district on the middle level. He'd received a message from Garit's father asking him to be here at sunrise, an hour or so before he was to report to the High Hall. Tristan had never been to the residence, though he and Garit had been friends since childhood.

Everyone with a home on this level was a noble, and because Tristan had been raised as a ward of the state, his place had always been at the bottom. Still, he had met Garit's parents several times over the years, and he'd always been welcomed in their company. Nobles, true, but they had never belittled him. Sadly, Garit's mother had passed away two summers ago. It had been a terrible sickness, and Garit did not speak of it easy.

Tristan was in his dress uniform again, and he was meeting the day with a combination of dread, apprehension, and expectation. He worked hard to minimize the prospects in his head—the best way to be disappointed was to set an expectation too high and see it fail. He tried not to imagine what may go wrong over the course of the coming days.

He had no issue in being allowed to the second level. He'd been this way several times in the past three weeks for planning, and each of the guards was familiar with his face by now. At present, he walked in the opposite direction of the High Hall, and there was no mistaking the moment he entered the housing zone.

The homes of the nobles were immense, made of fine, polished stone and dark oak. Huge, arching windows looked down on the streets below, and most of the doors were adorned with a family crest. Tristan had received exact instructions, so when he recognized the golden spear on one of the doors, he knew he was at the right place.

He inspected his uniform once more and knocked. Seconds later, the door opened, and he was met by a serving man. "Welcome, Tristan," said the older man in dark velvets. "Master Garit shall be along presently. May I direct you to the sitting room?"

"I would appreciate that, thank you," said Tristan, bowing his head in gratitude. The man smiled at him and led him down a corridor lined with richly colored tapestries. This opened into a room which was easily three times the size of the one-room home in which Tristan resided.

Exquisitely carved furniture and many thick cushions indicated that the family was used to entertaining guests. Tables and plants and looking glasses surrounded the perimeter of the room. Tristan's eyes scanned the space in a few seconds, and quickly settled on the fireplace at the far end of the chamber. Corridors ran off to either side, but the fireplace itself—and the spear which hung over it—commanded much attention.

"It has been in the family for centuries." Tristan turned as Garit came into the room. He'd been so focused on the spear, he'd not noticed his friend come in, nor the servant leave. "Over three hundred years, to be exact," he continued. "Since Grauberg rebelled against Felixandria and broke free of the Grey Empire." They stood side by side now. It was a basic weapon, Tristan observed. The head had no etchings or ornamentation, and the shaft was simple oak, banded with thin iron. "It may not seem like much," said Garit, "but this is our greatest heirloom."

A bell rang, and the same manservant who'd admitted Tristan came past them, going down the hallway to the right of the fireplace. Tristan had seen the man with Garit's parents over the years at different events, but he couldn't recall ever actually speaking to him. He turned his head to Garit and saw him smiling after the man was out of sight. "His name is Hardi," Garit said. "He helped raise my father, and he's been a dear friend to me all my life." Tristan glanced back down the hall as the servant knocked on a door and disappeared inside. "My father summoning him," said Garit. "Strange of him to call us here like this."

"You don't know his reasons?" asked Tristan.

Garit shook his head. "Not a clue, but I suppose we will find out soon enough."

Hardi returned a minute or so later. Garit had begun to show Tristan around the room, telling him of how his parents had once been involved in the social scene in the city and often entertaining lavish parties, but no such gatherings had been held here since his mother had died.

Hardi stepped out of the corridor and proclaimed, as though he were addressing an audience, "Lord Gerald of House Tyon, Honorary Captain of the Guard, and Defender of the Keep." The title 'honorary captain' was given to all soldiers of Grauberg when they passed into retirement unless they'd achieved a higher rank in their career. "Defender of the Keep," however, was only earned by those who had seen true battle.

Tristan wondered at the formality of the moment, and he stood in awe as Lord Gerald appeared in his dress uniform. He was clad in silver mail, a cape fastened about his right shoulder and bearing the golden spear of his family crest, and he carried his helm in the crook of his left arm.

When he came before Tristan and Garit, both men stood at attention—giving him the deference and respect owed to a senior officer—and they saluted. Lord Gerald, likewise, laid his right fist over his heart and bowed his head to them. "At ease, my son. You as well, Tristan."

The pride in Lord Gerald's face as his eyes met his son's was evident. His short hair, once black like Garit's, was streaked heavily with grey, and his years showed on his face. You could see at a glance that he was still strong, and though Tristan had never thought of him as frail, it now occurred to him he'd have no desire to take him on in sparring practice.

Lord Gerald cleared his throat and resumed a more stoic expression. "No doubt, this is a bit more than you were expecting," he said, his words chiefly directed to his son.

"It is a pleasant surprise, Father," Garit replied, and Tristan could tell without looking at him that he was smiling.

Gerald could not help but smile back. He placed his right hand on his son's shoulder and fought with his own emotions, but only for a moment. He turned to the fireplace and spoke with a clear voice. "This spear, Garit, has been passed down through the years of our family. It has belonged to the eldest son of the eldest son, and it is past time it was handed down to you."

He took his hand from Garit's shoulder and reached up, clutching the spear and taking it down. He stood with his back to them for a moment, staring down at the weapon in his hand. "Years ago, the Grey Emperor attempted to force the people of Grauberg to kneel in worship to Emjar, the Cursed Helper. His oppression of our people was met with steel and iron, and this spear was amongst those which rose in defiance. This was a tool for fighting against tyranny."

He turned and faced both Garit and Tristan, determination burning in his eyes. "I'm not a young man, and I'm not as sharp as I once was," he began, "but it looks to my old eyes as if tyranny is reaching out for Grauberg again. It has reclaimed Elinton," he said, turning his dark eyes to Tristan. "Now, it reaches for Grauberg. I'm not sure what our current commanders, or the general, or even the king will say when these ambassadors arrive, but I have learned our history, and I can tell you why this spear is the symbol of my family. If peace truly is their intent, so be it, but if not..." He extended his arm, offering the weapon to Garit. Tristan took a step back to witness the moment. Lord Gerald lifted his chin, and Tristan heard the pride in his voice as he spoke. "With this, I pass on this command, my son: if the shadow of tyranny again threatens us, fight it."

"I will do this, Father," Garit said, his voice breaking on the last word. He took the spear in his hands and clutched it firmly, and his father relinquished his own grip on it. Garit stared at it in wonder for a moment, as if he'd never seen it before. He placed the butt of it on the floor and stood at attention, saluting his father once more. Lord Gerald did likewise, and they embraced for a long moment.

A few minutes later, Tristan and Garit were leaving the residence. Garit now wore the spear on his back. It seemed out of place with his dress uniform, but this did not concern Garit. He had an air of solemnity about him which Tristan was not used to, and yet he understood it. As they made their way back in the direction of the High Hall, it was Tristan who spoke first. "It seems to me your father does not look approvingly on the situation with Prince Jules."

Garit shook his head. "He can't openly proclaim as much—it could stir others to disdain our visitors and unsettle everything. The talks are upon us, and we need peace." He adjusted the strap which held his spear. "Have I ever told you how he earned the title 'Defender of the Keep'?" Tristan shook his head. He'd wondered, because Grauberg had not been in a war since the fall of the empire. "It was when we were children. Grauberg, of course, sent out patrols after Jules took Elinton. Sometimes, there would be skirmishes in the forest, and my father got caught up in a couple of them. The attackers never wore any sigil, and the few of them who were taken prisoner never broke in interrogation. Jules never claimed responsibility, sending messages stating that it must be the small villages of the forest rebelling. A pathetic lie — there can be no doubt they were his own scouts and small squadrons. Likely testing our defenses. It would seem the men of Grauberg passed his test: he never tried to invade, and the skirmishes ceased. Still, that was nearly fifteen years ago."

"I see," said Tristan. He wanted to talk more, but he looked up at the sky and realized they were pressed for time. "Come, my friend." They picked up their pace, moving as quick as they could without jogging.

The streets were not lively at this hour on the second level. Below, people would already be hard at work, either setting up their shops for daily trade, or on their way out to tend the fields and hunt. People from the villages would be making their way in to barter, and breakfast was being placed on the tables of a thousand households in the city and its surrounding lands.

Still, as they moved on and came nearer to the High Hall, the busier the streets became. Most of these were soldiers, milling about or adjusting their uniforms or polishing armor. One man was sharpening his sword, and Tristan wondered what thoughts were going through his mind. Was he a worried Grause soldier? Perhaps he was one of the former Elinian refugees here to volunteer for the welcoming party and thinking of home.

Commander Walter and his private guards were outside when they arrived at the High Hall, as well as several soldiers, attendants, and pages. Walter raised his hand in greeting as they approached, and he motioned them over. "Sir," they said in unison, saluting as they came before him.

"Tristan, Master Garit," said Walter, returning their salute. Garit had taken an active role in helping Tristan over the last three weeks, and the commander was well acquainted with both men now. Walter wore silver-plated armor, and Tristan marveled at the size of the breastplate and wondered how much it weighed. A broadsword hung on the commander's back. "The preparations have been made, yes?"

"They have, sir," said Tristan. At that moment, the doors to the High Hall opened, and the other commander of Grauberg, Harman, emerged with his personal guard. Behind him came a man in armor which put Walter and Harman to shame, and Tristan recognized immediately that this was General Arnold, despite having never seen the man before in his life.

Tristan had gotten tense without realizing it. He started as Walter laid a hand on his shoulder. The commander laughed. "Settle down, son. They're not here to inspect you." Tristan took a deep breath. His nerves were on edge, but he could handle it.

Walter gave him a pat before moving his hand away. "This hasn't been easy, Tristan, and yet, you have carried out your duties well—or should I say, your 'special assignment'?" A smile passed between the two. "Harman," Walter called out, turning aside. "This is the young sellsword who has undertaken much of the planning on our behalf."

Commander Harman was taller than Walter, though not as broad. Tristan and Garit saluted him. The man inspected them from head to foot. After a moment, he gave Tristan what seemed to be a reluctant salute in return. "You are well met, Tristan," he said, but the tone in his voice said otherwise. "Are you pleased with your promotion?"

Tristan's brow creased. "Promotion, sir?"

"Blast it, Harman, you've spoiled the surprise," said Walter. He scowled at his counterpart before turning his eyes back to Tristan, his scowl replaced briefly with a broad smile. He quickly suppressed it. "Tristan, there are some men here who you need to see."

He turned and called the soldiers who were standing about to attention. They formed up, and as Tristan looked upon them, he was able to pick out a few faces. The man in the center of the front row had been the son of a farmer in Elinton, the same as him. A taller man in the second row had been the son of a nobleman in Elinton. He'd come to Grauberg as an orphan and served as a ward with Tristan. When he turned eighteen, he'd not chosen to be a mercenary, but rather he had enlisted into the Grause army and been made a citizen.

More faces stood out, and Tristan realized these were his volunteers. "These men all have something in common," Walter said, speaking Tristan's thoughts aloud. "They were all boys in Elinton fifteen years ago. Some come of common birth, some of noble. Yet, they are all now men in service to this nation. Some are still training, and others are sellswords, the same as you. Others have become citizens of Grauberg, making the choice which yet lies upon you." Tristan's time to make that choice was near—his nameday was but days away.

Walter swept his arm across the assembly. "Every one of them, though, are here today to represent the Elinian men of our forces—those who were driven here because of a foreign invader. While it is true that we would rather avoid war with Prince Jules, we will not turn a blind eye to what he has done to your home."

Tristan examined the faces of the men. Their eyes reflected the same resolve which he had cultivated within himself all these years. These men desired blood, but mixed with this was a desire for peace. Tristan was shocked at the number of men before him. Dozens had turned out, and he knew there were more who were engaged elsewhere. Still, he had never stopped to consider how many others there were. Orphans—or at the very least, soldiers in a nation which was not their own. Yet here they stood. "My brothers," he whispered under his breath.

"Indeed," said Walter. "In honor of your service for this momentous occasion, Tristan, you are hereby named

Honorary Captain of the Elinian Guard." The men before Tristan, already in formation, now saluted him. Though the title was only an honorific — and therefore temporary — Tristan was still overwhelmed by the moment. Tears stung his eyes as he looked on at the columns of men. "Well go ahead, son," said Walter. "Your men are saluting you."

Tristan returned their salute and held it for several seconds. He returned to attention and spun to face the two commanders. "The Elinian Guard is prepared to receive your orders, sirs."

Harman scoffed, and under his breath Tristan heard something which may have been "riffraff." Walter paid it no mind. "Captain Tristan," he began, "you will ride for the front gate. You and your men will be the first to welcome Jules when he arrives. You will escort him through the lower levels and rendezvous with us here at the High Hall.

"From here, General Arnold, Commander Harman, and I will escort them to the palace. At that time, you are to begin making your preparations for the night's feast. See to it you also are prepared for the events which are set to begin tomorrow. Master Garit, you may go with them to the lower levels, where you will rejoin your own unit."

It was almost midday before the horn sounded. Jules and his party were now visible from the towers. The signal was meant as a call to arms against foreign invaders — under normal circumstances. Tristan wondered if it might not be now, as well.

He was sitting on a mare, chestnut in color. At his back were the men of the Elinian Guard. They were spread to cover the breadth of the entrance of the front gate. Every man was horsed. Even with the sun high in the sky, breath could still be seen coming from man and beast — winter would be upon them soon.

There was a silence over the countryside before them, as well as in the city at their back. The central street was lined with Grause soldiers, and townsfolk were packed behind them. However, this was not an atmosphere of celebration.

Tristan felt in his gut that peace talks should be welcomed with shouts of joy and a festive mood, but the tension was almost unbearable in Grauberg. The very knowledge that men of Felixandria were arriving—even if they came under the banner of the queen of Elinton—had set everyone in the city on edge.

Faintly, Tristan became aware of the sound of hooves in the distance. They grew noticeably louder with each passing second. He watched the bend in the road, which was partially blocked from here by some of the houses in the village nearest to the keep.

Then they appeared—a dozen men on grey horses led the way, filed in two columns. Behind them sat a man on a large black horse, which was bedecked with grey livery. This man had long, straight black hair, though he was balding on top. As they drew closer, Tristan could tell he had a thin, sharply sculpted black beard. The man was thin as well, and he was dressed surprisingly plain.

As Tristan stared at the approaching men, he realized the entire party were simply garbed. They did not wear ornate robes or gilded armor, but were clothed primarily in leather, and what little plate and mail was worn was basic, without decoration or embellishment of any kind.

Behind the man on the large horse came two carriages, each pulled by a team of oxen. Behind those came a group of less organized travelers, which Tristan assumed to be freeriders—people who were neither guards nor a part of the royal court, but who had chosen to come along anyway. Of these, he guessed there to be about thirty or forty.

As the group approached the gate, Tristan called for his men to dismount. Despite the fact they'd never drilled together as a unit, every man here had the Grause training deep in their bones by now, and as one they were off their mounts, holding the reins while standing at attention. Tristan led his horse forward a few steps.

When the foreign party was about a dozen yards or so away, they halted. The two columns of horses veered to either side, opening a lane for the man on the tall black horse. He rode forward, past the two columns of his own men and right up to Tristan. Tristan's own horse whinnied and began to shy away, but he held her firm and quietly shushed her.

When the man on horseback stopped, he was so near that Tristan could have kissed the horse's nose without needing to lean forward. He had to step back to bow. "Welcome to Grauberg, Prince Jules of Felixandria, Regent of Elinton." He'd considered the words a thousand times in his head, but never spoken them aloud. He hated them as they scraped past his lips.

A long moment passed in silence. Tristan stood with his head bowed for a while, until it became clear the prince did not wish to acknowledge him. Finally, he stood back upright.

He did not like the fact that Jules did not dismount. He'd remained on horseback to look down on Tristan. It was an intimidation tactic, and Tristan knew it. He was not daunted by it.

Instead, he turned to his men and shouted. "Elinian Guard, remount." He and his men swung themselves back into their saddles fluidly. When Tristan looked again, Jules had an expression of amusement on his face.

"Elinian guard," came the voice of the man, distinct and sharp. "How charming." At the sound of the voice, Tristan's pulse quickened, and he felt lightheaded. Jules spoke louder. "I am Jules Cornelius of Felixandria, heir to the throne, and Regent and Protector of Elinton by order of Her Grace, Queen Joyce." He narrowed his eyes in Tristan's direction and gave him a crooked smile. "You nearly had it right. You'll learn it properly in time. Perhaps by then, I'll have some new titles, as well."

A cold sweat ran down Tristan's brow. "My apologies, Your Highness," he said, but he did not bow his head in deference.

"And who might you be?" As he asked, Jules stared straight into his eyes. Tristan could almost feel his gaze.

"If it please you, my lord, I am Tristan, Captain of the Elinian Guard." There was a slight tremble in his voice, and Tristan himself was not sure if it was prompted more by anger or fear.

"And what, Captain Tristan, is the 'Elinian Guard'?" He wore an expression which made it clear he was fully aware of what the answer would be.

Tristan sat up straighter and took a deep breath to compose himself. "We are soldiers of Grauberg, Your Highness." He waited a moment before adding, "But before that, we were of Elinton. Dire circumstances forced us here."

Jules did not pretend to smile. "Delightful greeting."

Tristan found his nerve and managed to force some semblance of his usual smirk. "If you will allow me, Your Highness, I will escort you to General Arnold." As they sat looking at one another, the light dimmed around them. Tristan glanced up and saw a lone, grey cloud covering the sun. In the distance, more were gathering. Tristan did not believe in omens, but the scene was unsettling.

Jules did not respond, and Tristan was done waiting on him. He turned his horse toward the city. His riders did likewise and formed up into two columns of their own. They entered first, followed by Tristan and Jules, and behind came the rest of the foreign guard. The sentries who regularly handled the gate held the wagons and freeriders outside, speaking with them and finding how best to accommodate them, but also making a headcount.

Inside, the riders made their way slowly up the thoroughfare. The streets and alleys were packed, but no cheers were raised. There was only the sound of hooves on pavement and some uncomfortable murmurs. Prince Jules did not speak, and Tristan had no desire to hear the man's voice again.

As he rode on, Tristan spotted both Garit and Ella. Garit was standing at attention with his unit, but still he shifted his eyes to meet Tristan's. Ella wore a concerned look, and Tristan did not doubt she could see his anxiety — but could she feel how truly uncomfortable he was? He hoped not.

They reached the second level of the city at last, and Tristan led them directly to the High Hall. General Arnold sat his own horse, with Commanders Walter and Harman behind him on either side. As soon as he approached them, Tristan dismounted and saluted them. He then turned to Jules. "If it pleases, Your Highness, I present to you General Arnold, Commander Walter, and Commander Harman."

He begged leave to prepare the welcoming feast. Walter noted his haste with a raised eyebrow but nodded to dismiss him as Harman scoffed. The general was speaking his own greeting to Jules, but Tristan had already turned, remounted, and was trotting away. The rest of the Elinian Guard remained, now under the command of Walter.

As he left them behind, Tristan struggled for breath. He thought back to a time when he saw his mother's face, trying to scream but unable — and he thought about the voice which ordered her death — the voice which commanded the death of his entire family.

The voice of Jules Cornelius of Felixandria, heir to the throne, and Regent and Protector of Elinton.

V
Feasting & Fighting

The day of Jules' arrival seemed uncommonly long. Business was slow and people were quiet, almost as if they were sneaking about, worried about who or what they may come across. Tristan had returned to the city gates and sorted out the carriages and the travelers who formed the rest of Jules' party.

He was never able to get a clear picture on who these people were—whether they were members of the noble court of Elinton, or if they were his supporters from Felixandria, or simply people who had wanted to come along and to witness what would unfold on this momentous and unprecedented meeting. In the end, Tristan concluded that they were likely a combination of all three.

Most of his energy should have been spent toward preparations for the feast that night, but Tristan focused on trying to suppress the sound of the voice in his head. He was certain this was the voice he had heard in his home all those years ago.

He tried to shake the thoughts from his mind, but they persisted. Even if his suspicions were true, what could he do about it? There would be time for that soon, after his nameday had passed.

The sun set, and the kitchens in the High Hall were bustling as last-minute arrangements were made. Tristan went into the dining hall to ensure the attendants were presentable. Plates and silverware were arranged in the custom of fine dining of Grauberg for most of the seats.

The places reserved for Jules and his party were set in the Elinian fashion. Tristan had been unsure if he should plan the settings this way, or after the Felixandrian manner, but he settled on the Elinian in the end. Even in matters such as this, he would not recognize them as Felixandrian in any official capacity if he was able to avoid doing so. Still, the settings were a bit much for him—the most complex setup he'd ever used was a single fork and knife.

"Captain Tristan?" He turned to find a runner with a solemn look on his face. "The general wishes to know if everything is set."

Tristan nodded. "You may inform him all is ready for the entrances to begin." The boy turned and left, and moments later Grauberg's nobles began to come in. These were people who, under normal circumstances, would likely have been announced as they entered, but that was not the case on this night. Tonight, they were the visitors, not the attraction.

Tristan had expected Elinian nobles to come in as well but had been informed none would be in attendance. The only people Jules was keeping nearby were his personal guard. As the Grause nobles took their seats at the table, the immense double doors of the hall opened. A trumpeter entered, accompanied by a crier. As the fanfare sounded, those seated at the tables rose, and the crier called out the names of those entering.

The first in were the commanders, Walter and Harman. They stood behind their chairs on the far left of the high table, which was on a raised dais above the others. Next came General Arnold. The next name was new to Tristan's ears. "Vincent, Chief Lieutenant of the thirteenth legion of Felixandria and Commander of the forces of Elinton." The man who entered was older than Tristan, maybe in his early thirties. Tristan assumed this had been one of the riders in the columns accompanying Jules. Vincent went to the far right of the table and stood behind his seat.

"His Royal Highness, Prince Jules Cornelius of Felixandria, heir to the throne, and Regent and Protector of Elinton by order of Her Grace, Queen Joyce." The room was filled with murmuring. No matter how quiet they tried to be, the sound of every noble in the room whispering at once was noticeable. Jules, if he was aware of it—and he had to be—paid no mind.

He entered garbed in the same manner as when he'd rode into the city: plain leathers overlaid with simple armor. His face was stern as he surveyed the room, and Tristan gave a visible flinch as the man's eyes scanned over him. He was happy their eyes did not meet—seeing Jules again made his blood boil. Jules moved to the side of Vincent, and Tristan was struck by the similarities between the two. He wondered if they were kin.

The trumpeter blew a second fanfare, this one longer than the first. "Her Royal Highness, Adelena of the House Hendry, Princess of Grauberg and heiress to the throne. She is being escorted by her father." Here, all in attendance raised their glasses. "His Royal Majesty, Frederic of the House Hendry, King of Grauberg, Defender of the Keep and Lord Protector of the City. All hail the king!"

"Hail, King Frederic!" The Grause nobles lifted their glasses higher, then drank. The king and his daughter entered, both garbed in deep blue. The princess had a necklace of blue gems, while the king's crown, an elaborate circlet, featured one immense sapphire at its center. When the king and princess took their seats at the center of the table, all others took theirs as well. Attendants who had been standing in the background stepped up and refilled the glasses of the noble lords and ladies. This was followed by servers emerging from the kitchens to bring out the first course. The room filled with polite conversation, and for the first time that day the mood seemed a little lighter.

Tristan was not feasting. He was circling the room, standing well back from the tables, observing and ensuring everything went smoothly. After a time, he glanced up and noted all at the high table were enjoying their meal—all except Commander Walter. His plate was empty, and he had not bothered to remove his gloves. Tristan motioned one of the attendants over to him. "Can you explain why Commander Walter has not been served?" he asked.

The attendant was an older man who appeared unfazed by Tristan's anger. "Begging your pardon, sir, but the commander does not eat in public. Everyone in the High Hall knows that." Tristan said nothing, but his face was one of curiosity. The man glanced around, making sure no one else was within earshot. "His digestion has been unsettled since, well—since his captivity all those years ago."

"Captivity?"

The attendant raised his eyebrows. "You don't know? And you, a soldier and all that? Well, I suppose you would have been just a lad. You see, the commander was captured during the skirmishes. You know, the ones with Jules's scouts, if the rumors are true. It was three years before he escaped. No stories have ever come from his lips about it save to his superiors, but we all suppose it must have been rough on him. Those present when he entered the city said he was all skin and bones. He doesn't eat in public now, and the word is he holds the Felixandrians with an abiding hatred."

Tristan was stunned. He raised his eyes, and Commander Walter was staring straight at him. He wondered if the commander guessed at the topic of their conversation. For the first time he realized Walter was not solemn—he was angry. He couldn't believe he had not recognized this before. "He hates them as much as I do," he said.

"I would imagine he hates them more than just about

anyone, sir," said the attendant, thinking the comment aimed at him. "I should be about my duties, sir. Is there anything else?"

"No," said Tristan, shaking his head. "That is all. Thank you." The man bowed his head and walked away. Tristan thought back to what Garit's father had told them about skirmishes in the years after Jules arrived, but he'd not known anything about prisoners—much less that Commander Walter had been one of them. As the rest of the courses were served, Tristan considered how his superior felt about these talks. Had he come to terms with what had been done to him, or did he crave vengeance as well?

Towards the end of the meal, General Arnold rose to his feet. The room fell silent, and all eyes focused on him. "On behalf of my king and my princess, our soldiers, and our noble citizens, I would like to say welcome to Prince Jules. May the coming days prove prosperous for both of our realms." He raised his glass and drained it, and all those in attendance—from the nobles to the king himself—did likewise. The glasses were filled once more, and the general continued. "To commemorate your visit—and to mark this historic occasion—it has been decided a tournament is to be held in your honor, Prince Jules. Your Royal Majesty, Your Highness, lords and ladies—I present to you our valiant warriors."

Doors on either side of the hall opened, and a line of men entered from both the left and right of the room, opposite the high table. The men were richly garbed, though not in armor. As they came in, they stood at the back of the hall. Tristan waited by the door on the right and fell in behind the last man to come in. The general's voice called out once more. "I present the warriors who will honor you on the morrow, Your Highness." The lords and ladies clapped, and a few even cheered.

Then, Jules stood and gave the men standing at the far end of the hall an appraising look. His eyes traced each, and when he reached Tristan, their eyes locked. An anger suddenly surged within Tristan's chest, and his heartbeat quickened. The scar which ran along the right side of his face became numb, a sensation which happened only when his fury was ready to boil over. Still, he managed to keep his composure—but only just.

"I thank you for your welcome, General Arnold," said Jules after several uneasy moments of silence had passed. "I hope, as all here surely do, these meetings shall prove most prosperous. I look forward to seeing what develops over the coming days, as well as observing these—what did you call them? Oh yes. 'Warriors.' Let us all be witnesses to how well they perform in the *games*." He said this last word with an obvious disdain, and an air of uneasiness descended on the dinner. Beside him, his lieutenant smiled. "To unity!" called Jules, raising his glass.

"To unity!" answered those in attendance. Again, and for the last time that night, everyone drained their glasses together, but no one could be sure what was to come next.

> I hardly slept. I just keep hearing his voice. I've heard it for years in my head, but to hear it come out of his mouth—I realize my mind is probably playing tricks on me. Perhaps a similar voice in the same dialect. My brain keeps repeating it.
>
> I have to focus. Today is the day of the tournament. Of everything that has been planned, this is the most important. I worked with Commander Walter and several of our highest officers to narrow the list down to fifteen men—and me.
>
> This is an opportunity to make Jules recognize the spirit of the men he'd be fighting if he were to come against us in battle. This is also my chance to show him just how angry he's made me.

Putting those words down on paper, I realize how childish this sounds. Ella would scold me for thinking this way, but I can't help it. This is how I feel and I won't fight it. I've been told too many times that I think with my heart and not my brain. I can't say those people are wrong, but it's gotten me this far. I'll see how much farther it takes me.

As much as I have dreaded this visit, I admit I'm looking forward to the tournament. This won't be like the tournaments most of the lords and ladies are used to, where men ride horses and joust. These will be duels. The swords will be dulled and the heavy weapons padded, but these will be real fights. Whoever the Order of the White assigns to heal the wounded will likely be busy, and I won't be winning any favors with them for choosing this format.

Sixteen men in eight matches. And after, the victors in a winner-take-all grand melee. I hope no one gets hurt, but I won't be holding back. Not now.

The sun dawned behind grey clouds the next day, but the city was already stirring and loud. The mood was much different than what had met the arrival of Jules' and his people the day before. Today was the day of the tournament, and the excitement rushed through the veins of every citizen, from the oldest men and women to toddling children.

Tournaments were rare in Grauberg, but not unheard of. Tristan had seen a few over the years to commemorate major promotions—such as when Arnold had been named General—or when Princess Adelena had come of age. Never, though, had he participated in one.

As a rule, the only combatants allowed to enter were either lords—men who held their own titles and property—or masters—heirs who had not yet come into their inheritance. For his help in arranging these festivities, and also because the contest was his idea, Tristan had been permitted to enter. This would not be conducted in the manner of the usual tournaments. Tristan had chosen a unique format, one which would thrill those in attendance and send a message to Jules and his people.

The tournament would be on the lower level. Behind the Low Hall was an enormous open area. Typically, it was filled with merchants and their stalls. On days like today, though, the vendors had needed to bid for spaces. Those who won lined the perimeter, so tightly packed they were practically prisoners behind their own booths, carts, and goods. Business would be outstanding, as essentially everyone in the realm of Grauberg—both the city proper and its surrounding villages—would be there.

The arena consisted of a fenced-in field, surrounded by various tiers of raised seats. On the north side was a covered platform. From here, the king and princess of Grauberg would attend the contest with Jules.

As people poured into the city and gathered at the trading stalls, those participating in the event began to make their way toward the combat area. Each man gave the others plenty of room. This was not for any animosity—indeed, most of the men were at least familiar with one another—but men need space before a tournament.

All except for Tristan. He may be part of the auxiliary, but he was not considered a true soldier. He'd never been alienated by those in the army whom he trained with, but he'd also never been accepted completely in. He was simply there.

Of the men in the tournament, one other was originally from Elinton. Unlike Tristan, he had not been orphaned. He'd made the journey to Grauberg with his family, the same as Ella. He had enlisted into the Grause army years ago, and he was now a citizen of the nation.

His parents had been nobles in Elinton, and their titles were recognized in Grauberg, even if they'd lost their lands. This fact enabled him to claim entry to the tournament.

Still, there was one he called a friend. "Good morning, Garit," Tristan said. "A fine, gloomy day for fights, wouldn't you say?"

Garit turned and gave Tristan a smile. "A grand day, indeed," he said, extending his hand and clasping Tristan's. "Today, we shall give our people sport to cheer and our enemies cause for fear."

"Did you mean to make that rhyme?"

"Shut your hole," Garit said, giving Tristan a playful rap on the chin. "Perhaps I'm considering a future as a minstrel." He scanned the perimeter at their prospective opponents. "I wonder who I'll draw for my first bout." He finished looking about and turned his eyes back to Tristan. "How do you feel about your chances?"

Tristan shrugged. "I'm not so worried about the opening fights. I think I can handle myself against any man one-on-one." He turned his eyes from left to right, sizing up the men he may be matched up with. "It's the melee which concerns me." He glanced back and caught Garit grinning. "What?"

"I'm amused you entered yourself into a format which concerns you," he said with a chuckle. "Especially considering you were the one who organized this!"

"Aye, well," Tristan began with his usual smirk, "I'm a fighter, not a scholar. I'm not known for my wits or clever thinking."

Garit's smile faded slightly. "You jest, but one day, that might get you into more trouble than you can handle."

"Perhaps," Tristan agreed. "Not today, though. Today, my fighting is all I need."

The time crawled for Tristan. It was one thing to be a spectator, enjoying a day of festivities and bargains. It was quite another to be one of the combatants, waiting around, wondering if being festive would be wise, or if passing on the opportunity for a bit of levity was the true mistake. The others found ways to pass the time, but Tristan was still battling the sound of that monster's voice—trying to hear the words from fifteen years ago, and yet resisting at the same time.

"How're you feeling?" came a voice from right behind him.

He jumped and spun to find a shocked look on Ella's face. "You scared the hell out of me!" he said, trying to catch his breath but smiling.

"Well, likewise, you big oaf!" said Ella, her look of fear transforming into a smile, and then a laugh. "Oh, the thought of you being frightened by little ol' me so soon before you're to face off against another of these big lads!" They both chuckled, but as the laughter faded away, she stepped closer to him and took hold of his arm. "Really, though—how are you feeling?"

He shook his head. "Rattled," he admitted.

She nodded. "I can imagine. This is your first tourney, after all, and—"

"No," he cut in, "it's not the tournament. It's..." His voice trailed off, and he wondered if he should say anything to her.

"Don't do that," she said quietly. "For all I know, your jaw may get broken and you won't have a chance to say anything later. What's got you rattled?"

He met her eyes. "Prince Jules."

"Oh," she said. "His presence? Or has something happened? I could tell that you were on edge while riding through the city with him at your side yesterday."

"His voice," said Tristan. "I've heard it before, Ella. I'm sure of it. Fifteen years ago."

Her eyes went wide. "Tristan, it's been so long." His lips made a straight line, and she shook her head. "I'm not saying you're wrong or lying. Please, understand that. I'm not saying that at all, but—are you sure?"

"I think so," he said. "I mean, aye, it sounds crazy. The chances do seem unlikely, but the moment he spoke to me yesterday for the first time, Ella, it just hit me. All of it. If this was the sort of thing I could bet on, I'd wager my life on it."

She shook her head fervently. "Tristan, no! I don't know if you're planning something drastic, but please, no!"

He reached out, pulled her to him, and wrapped his arms around her. "Don't worry. I'll not do anything rash. Not today."

Even with her face buried in his shoulder, he heard her scoff. "You have as much control over your rashness as I have over the rain, Tristan." He let her go, and she relinquished her hold on his arm. "Speaking of which," she said, lifting her eyes to the clouds overhead, "I do hope it doesn't storm during the contest."

"Aye, so do I," said Tristan. "I need sure footing."

She smiled uneasily. "So, this is to be a first for both of us." He gave her an inquiring look. "The tournament. Your first to compete in, and my first to heal." Tristan now gave her a look-over from head to toe. He'd been so preoccupied when she came up, he hadn't even realized she was wearing her healer's robes. She looked down and brushed a bit of dust off the pure white garment. "They tell me this isn't going to be like the tournaments which have been held in the city before. Not that I've ever seen one, anyway."

"Really?" Tristan asked. "Never? In all our years here?"

She shook her head. "I'm trained to help people, Tristan. To heal them. It pains me to think about them hurting one another for sport."

He smiled. "Well, I shall do my best not to come away with too many injuries for your sake."

"Or to deal out too many, I should hope." He nodded

to that, but he made no promise. After a few seconds of silence, she pushed him lightly on the shoulder. "So, how is it done?"

"Well, in the beginning there will be a drawing. The first two names drawn will fight one another. The same with the third and fourth, and so on. There's sixteen of us, so that makes for eight matches."

"Oh," said Ella with a shrug. "That doesn't sound so bad. I'd imagined all manner of mass carnage."

He smiled. "Well, that would be the second part. After the winners have had a bit of rest, they'll all fight one another in a melee. Every man for himself. When you yield or fall, too battered to rise, you're done. Last man standing wins."

Ella went pale. At length, she swallowed and managed to speak. "Oh." She closed her eyes, and Tristan figured she was imagining a thousand ways for everything to go bad. For the first time, he regretted that the tournament was his idea. "Um, and what does the 'last man standing' win, exactly?"

That brought the smile back to Tristan's face. "Glory." He looked at the raised platform and the place where Jules would be seated. "Glory, and the chance to see the look on Jules' face when he sees our fighting spirit."

At noon, the sixteen combatants stood in the center of the arena. The stands were filled to bursting, and people who had not been able to find a seat had found ladders and boxes and other designs—both brilliantly creative and idiotically haphazard—to watch the events. Some were even seated on the roof of the Low Hall, or on the roofs of other surrounding buildings.

King Frederic and Princess Adelena sat on one side of the platform—the left, from the perspective of the fighters—while Jules and his lieutenant, Vincent, sat on the right. Two men stood between them in the center of the platform, drawing the names of the men out of a sack. Garit's name had been selected for the third match, but

Tristan's name had not yet been called.

He glanced to the side and saw Ella, shining in her bright white robes, with her hands clasped and her eyes closed. He wondered if she were shutting out the scene or if she was sending a prayer to Rylar or the Helpers. Perhaps he should offer up a prayer himself.

"Tristan, Captain of the Elinian Guard," yelled one of the men on the platform. Ella's eyes snapped open just as he turned his eyes away from her and back to the men drawing names. He held his chin up high as he faced the criers, but he let his eyes drift over to where Jules sat, watching him intently. "Master Randall of House Terric. This shall be the fifth match."

Tristan and Randall both stepped forward two paces, bowed to those on the platform, and turned to salute one another. Randall was larger than Tristan, but he was clumsy. They'd sparred before on several occasions, and Tristan thought his chances were better than good. After a few more minutes had passed, all the matches had been called, and the men left to sit in designated spots outside the combat field.

The first two contests could not have been any more different from one another. In the first, a young lord named Ingram defeated his opponent in under half a minute. Armed with a lance, Ingram came out fast and swept the other man's legs from underneath him. Then a second swing connected, the flat side of the head hitting the enemy's jawbone, just beneath where the man's half-helm ended. The man was unconscious and in a heap, and Tristan's thoughts went to what Ella had said about a broken jaw earlier.

Ella came rushing in with concern plain on her face. She knelt beside the downed man and uttered a few words no one else could hear. After a few minutes, the man stood and walked out with nothing hurting except his pride. Before she left, she shot a glare his way. Tristan figured she, too, was thinking of her earlier musings, and possibly regretting them.

The fans were in a frenzy over the quick finish, but Tristan was not pleased. Ingram had been impressive, sure, but what impact had the match had on Jules? Tristan stared at the man. He wore an expression which betrayed no feelings.

The second contest, on the other hand, was one of true skill. The men were brothers, and it was clear from the outset they were familiar with one another in sparring. Their names were Rolfe and Raif, sons of House Winter, and both fought valiantly, Rolfe with sword and shield— the same as Tristan—and Raif with a two-handed Warhammer.

After a quarter of an hour had passed, both men were exhausted, and the editor of the games stood and called them to a halt. It was now up to Prince Jules, because the tournament was in his honor, to select a winner. "I cannot choose between these two men," he said without standing. Tristan was not happy he remained seated, but he was contented that the brothers had impressed him. Jules spoke again. "It seems to me that if either of these men were worthy of being in this grand tournament, he would have the ability to win a single fight. Neither of these men can do even that. I say continue until one of them lies in the dirt. If they are not able to do this, they should tuck their tails and go home."

Tristan was stunned. Those in attendance were as well, and after a few moments of silence, jeers filled the air. Tristan believed it to be the people of the city directing them at Jules, but as he looked about, it was the freeriders garbed in grey scattered throughout the crowd, and they were jeering the brothers. These men had given this contest their all, and Jules and his cronies had seen fit to insult them.

Tristan resolved to show him the true fury of a soldier when his turn came. As for the men in the arena, they exchanged weary and exhausted looks. Then they nodded to one another and raised their weapons. The crowd came to life with cheers which drowned out the booing foreigners.

This second part of their fight was not quite as exciting, though it was much briefer. They were slow now, and their blows had no true force behind them. After a time, Raif swung, missed badly, and fell to his knees in exhaustion. Rolfe moved over him, but Raif extended his hand and waved his brother away, a signal the bout was over. The crowd cheered as Rolfe collapsed beside him.

Though they were greatly wearied, Ella found she had little mending to do. However, while her power could heal them, it could not give the brothers back their energy. Tristan wondered how well Rolfe would be able to perform in the melee to come.

Garit was up next, armed with his spear, though not the one his father had entrusted to him the day before. He faced an older nobleman named Hugo, who was equipped with a mace and shield. Tristan was at the edge of his seat, cheering hard for his friend.

The two men began their contest slow, feeling each other out. After a few feints and half-lunges, they committed to full battle. Garit was keeping Hugo at a distance with his spear, but the man was lightning-fast with his shield and footwork, able to deflect or dance around any jabs or swings Garit made. Tristan hoped to move as fast as this man when he was older.

After a few minutes, Hugo made a wild swing with his mace and missed, exposing his flank. Garit stepped in for a lunge and Tristan winced. Hugo was using the same trick Tristan had used recently to best Garit in training. He looked on in horror as Hugo turned and swung his shield around to take advantage of his friend's mistake.

Garit ducked under the shield, pivoted, and put his shoulder into Hugo's side. The man sprawled in the dirt, and Garit spun and stood over him, the dulled point of his competition spear at Hugo's neck. The crowd cheered,

Tristan roared, and Hugo dropped his mace and waved his hand in surrender. Garit, it seemed, had learned a new trick.

Tristan skipped the next match. He now busied himself with making sure he was properly outfitted. He checked the lacings and bindings on his armor no less than half a dozen times. He was getting jittery, not from nerves, but anticipation.

Unable to stand still, he turned back to the ongoing bout in time to see it end. The larger of the two men, Norman Hodge, almost took his opponent's head off with a swing of his greatsword. The weapon was dulled for the event, but the ferocity of it in the hands of a man this strong could still kill anyone.

As it was, the man was able to duck just enough for the blade hit him in the helmet. It still knocked him out, and Ella had to work on him for several minutes before he regained consciousness. When the man had been helped out, Tristan made his way to a gate at the southern end of the arena. It was time.

"Master Randall of House Terric!" yelled the crier, and Tristan turned to a second gate several yards away as his opponent entered with two swords. He was wearing iron armor on his shins, forearms, and torso, and the breastplate was a work of art. It bore an image of the city-state of Grauberg, nestled into the protection of the Spears. From where he stood, he thought the hilts of Randall's swords were golden. At least he looked good entering— Tristan hoped the same would not be said of the man as he left at the end of the bout.

"Tristan, Captain of the Elinian Guard!" He took a deep breath and stepped forward. The crowd cheered, though not as loudly as it had for Randall. It was to be expected; Randall was, after all, a citizen of Grauberg.

For his armor, Tristan was wearing greaves of thin steel to protect his lower legs and a helm of similar make, but he'd chosen leather elsewhere to allow him to move about faster and easier. His tunic was crimson, but naught else had color to it.

Tristan was not here to look pretty. His only desire was to appear fierce once he started moving. Let the people cheer who they wanted—the only audience which concerned him was Jules.

Tristan and Randall came to the center of the arena and clasped hands for a moment. "Try not to bleed too much," said Randall. The man motioned to where Ella stood. "I'll try to keep you pretty for your little friend."

Tristan didn't rise to the bait. This was a fight, and he knew Randall was trying to get into his head. "No worries there," he said after a moment. "Tell me, Randall—when was the last time you bested me?" It had always been easy to get under Randall's skin, and that had not changed. The man scowled, shoved Tristan's hand away, and spit on the ground at his feet. Tristan smirked and stepped back a few paces.

Both men turned to the royal platform and bowed, first to the King, and then to Jules. The Prince appeared to barely notice them, and Tristan was annoyed to see how little interest the man seemed to be taking in the tournament. Tristan and Randall turned toward each other. Tristan raised his sword and shield, and Randall raised his blades. "Begin!" called the crier, and both men advanced.

Tristan held his shield up to protect his chin, but it did not obstruct his view of Randall's movements in any way. He focused on his opponent's shoulders but glanced down here and there to see the man's footwork as well. It had been several months since they'd been paired together, and he wondered if Randall had learned any new tricks. He wanted to beat the man down, but he also wanted the bout to impress his true target on the platform.

"Aaah!" Randall shouted and rushed forward, swinging wildly with his right sword, then his left, one after the other. Evidently, he still yelled like a novice before striking. Tristan didn't even deflect the blows, choosing instead to step back out of range. He ducked under another right and turned a left away with his own blade.

Both men reset. Though focused on the line of Randall's shoulders, he could tell the man was snarling at him. It was the sort of thing which had never made sense to Tristan. Why snarl when your enemy knows by your blade that you intend him harm?

Randall advanced half a step. His right shoulder began to drive forward, and Tristan raised his shield. He deflected the thrust and watched Randall's feet. The man stepped forward, throwing several quick jabs with his blades in succession. His opponent stepped back, and Tristan momentarily dropped his shield and shrugged at him. "Is this all you've got?"

Randall snorted and spat, and Tristan flashed a mocking grin. Randall charged with another shout, both swords raised above his head. The audience fell silent in anticipation of some great strike, but Tristan stepped to his right and extended his leg. Randall rushed straight into it and went down like an oak, his face slapping hard against the earth before he rolled over and climbed back to his feet. Tristan noted Randall was already breathing heavy.

"Randall, my dear friend, I beg of you—mind your step."

Randall's mouth was filled with blood. He spit it, not to the side, but toward Tristan. "Why don't you quit backing up and fight like a soldier?"

"If you insist." Tristan tapped his shield with his sword. Before Randall could get his own blades up, Tristan had darted forth and forced him back with a knock from his shield. They were near the edge of the arena, and Randall's back was against the fence. Tristan wasn't sure if it would be able to support Randall's weight, but he wanted to find out.

He ducked under a slash from Randall and came up

with a shield blow which landed hard under Randall's chin. The big man did not go through the fence, but rather flipped over it. Fans cheered, Tristan smirked, and Randall yelled in anger.

He came back to his feet, his heavy armor weighing him down, and lumbered back over the perimeter. Tristan jogged back to the center of the arena, and Randall unwisely ran after him. Gasping for breath now, it was a labor for him to raise his swords.

Tristan could toy with him at this point, but he had no desire to gloat. He stepped forward and deflected two slow strikes from Randall and began battering him with attacks of his own. He scored a slice across the man's breastplate and ducked down and slashed across his shins. He was purposely hitting every piece of armor his opponent was wearing, and now he was firmly in favor with the crowd.

Randall managed to raise his left sword in time to deflect a strike, but Tristan hit it so hard, the blade went flying several feet and to the ground.

Randall swung with his right, and Tristan raised his shield to block it. Randall brought his arm back for another blow, and this time Tristan brought his shield back with such force the second sword was knocked from Randall's tired grasp as well.

Exhausted, the man went down to his knees. Tristan stood over him. "Wish to yield?" Randall glared at him and spat blood again, a bright red which landed on the steel greaves covering Tristan's shins. "Well," said Tristan, "I suppose that's a 'no.'"

Randall appeared ready to speak a word of defiance, but Tristan did not care to hear it. He backhanded Randall hard with his shield, the flat wooden surface smashing violently into his opponent's face. Where before there had been only a trickle of blood coming from his nose and busted lip, he now wore a crimson mask. He lingered on his knees for but a moment, teetered back, and fell to the dirt and grass to the roar of the impressed crowd.

Tristan turned to stare at Jules. Their eyes met, and Tristan shrugged and wore an expression of disinterest. He bowed stiffly, and when he glanced back up, Jules was giving him a faint smile. Tristan turned to leave but stopped at the glare on Ella's face. "You just had to try and take his bloody head off, didn't you?" she asked as she hastened past him to Randall. She was out of earshot before he could offer a reply. This was likely for the best; he wasn't sure what he could have said that wouldn't have made it worse.

He missed the sixth and seventh matches getting cleaned up and finding water to sooth his parched throat. He returned for the eighth, which went much like the first. Here, the other Elinian soldier named Malcolm, bearing the largest ax Tristan had ever seen, came out and swung for the legs of his enemy. The man stepped over the swipe but was hit next by Malcolm's shoulder in the chest.

The man went down as Malcolm raised his blade. It was blunted in hopes of preventing a fatal blow, but Tristan wasn't sure that would make any difference in the hands of this massive contestant. This would be a wound Ella could not heal.

When Malcom brought the ax down, he drove it into the earth beside his opponent's head. Padded or not, the blade still sent chunks of dirt flying. By this point, the man on his back was crying for mercy and waving his hands frantically.

Malcolm left the head of the ax buried there as he raised his arms in triumph. His opponent got up and fled from the arena. Tristan's discerning eye noted a patch of wet fabric on the front of the man's breeches, indicating just how scared he was. He hoped, for the man's sake, no one else had been able to tell.

"We will now break until the mid-afternoon bell tolls!" the crier called out. While some few people remained in their seats, most broke away and moved to check the wares of the stalls or to relieve themselves or stretch their legs. Tristan walked around the arena to see if Ella was at her post. He found her there, slumped forward with her face buried in her hands.

She raised her eyes as he approached and held a hand up to stop him. He halted as she grabbed a bucket and gripped it close to her face. A few violent heaving moments later, she lowered it as he stepped toward her. "This was your idea, remember?" he said jesting. She peered at him, lost for a moment. "You told me to try to intimidate them."

She glared but nodded as if to acknowledge his point. "The fights have upset your stomach," he said, and not in a teasing manner. "I do apologize for making it worse than it needed to be on my part." He wasn't sure he meant this, but he didn't like to see Ella in this state.

She shrugged. "You are an arse, but no, that's not what has me retching." She sat still a moment, and Tristan thought she would vomit again. After a few moments, Ella managed to compose herself. "It's the White," she said at length, wiping sweat away from her brow. "I've never expended this much energy. When the soldiers are done training and we treat wounds, I am usually accompanied by others—and all we have to tend there are bumps and bruises, mostly, but this..." She said no more, and Tristan nodded as if he understood. He didn't. He'd never realized using the magic could take a physical toll on a user. "I'm having trouble finding it," Ella said after a few more moments had passed.

"What do you mean?"

"It's difficult to explain," she said. "The power to use the White is something we can feel in the air. Sometimes it's so rich, you can almost smell it—but it's always there. Lately, though, we've had trouble sensing it."

He tilted his head. "Not just you?"

"No," she said. "All of us. And now, in this very moment, it's barely present—and the worst of the fighting is yet to come."

Tristan thought back to the stories he'd heard as a child. Long ago, his sisters had told them to him. "Perhaps the magics are out of balance?"

Ella gave him a measured look. "What?"

"You know, the old tales. The Grey and the White. When one ebbs, the other flows. The Balance."

She smiled faintly. "Those are just legends, Tristan," she said. "The Grey hasn't been used in centuries. It was stamped out when the Grey Empire was thrown down. If the stories were true, we'd have ceased to be able to use the White long ago."

Tristan pursed his lips. He'd seen it when he was a child. He'd told them all when he came to Grauberg, but they didn't believe him. He'd told Ella as well. She had never called him a liar or told him he was wrong—until now. "You know what I saw the day Elinton fell."

She sighed. "I know what you think you saw, Tristan." She met his eyes, and he knew his face told her his feelings. "I'm weary, Tristan. I don't have the energy to argue with you just now. We can discuss this another time."

"I don't have anything more to say," he said. Without another word, he turned and walked away. He thought she might have called after him, but it was weak if she had.

He did not turn back. He had no desire for further words. They'd never done any good on this topic, and he had no reason to expect additional conversation to change anything. He had planned on seeking out Garit, but now decided against it. He was already in a foul mood, and he needed to be clear-headed. Garit was his friend, but he was about to be one of his opponents. One of seven.

When the fourth bell after noon sounded, people came hurrying back to the stands. There were a few fights which had to be broken up by guards because of people claiming seats which had not been theirs during the opening round, but after a time the crowd settled. The king and princess returned to their places, as did Jules and his lieutenant.

"And now," began the crier, "we present our grand melee. We welcome back to the arena those eight warriors who fought their way here. In this contest, the last man standing will be declared our champion." The gates opened, and Tristan and the others took the field. He tried not to, but he couldn't resist the urge to find Garit on the perimeter. He found his friend already looking back at him, and they smiled and nodded to one another. The crier introduced them all once more, and Tristan evaluated them. His greatest challengers would be Garit and Ingram with their spears, Norman Hodge with his greatsword, and Malcolm of Elinton with his ax.

"And now, your Royal Majesty, King Frederic; Your Royal Highness, Princess Adelena; Your Royal Highness, Prince Jules, and Lieutenant Vincent—"

"Hold!" yelled Jules. The crier stopped short, shocked by the interruption. All fell silent as Jules rose to his feet. "I have no doubt the men standing before me have attempted to do me great honor." His eyes traced the perimeter of the arena at the eight who were set to do battle. "Yet, they seem to be little more than boys playing at war."

From the corner of his eye, Tristan watched Princess Adelena go from a healthy copper tone to pale. He'd never seen such a stark change in an individual. Beside her, King Frederic flushed with anger, and his fists clenched and unclenched.

Jules spoke on. "Was this façade orchestrated to try to impress me? I will admit, it likely would work as planned with many who now reside in my homeland of Felixandria. But know this: I hold to the old ways, and I desire more than a game. Show me your true rage, mighty warriors. If you would honor me, let me see your fury!" He took his seat again, and no one quite knew how to respond. The field remained silent.

The crier looked at the king as if seeking guidance. The king's jaw was set firm as he gritted his teeth, but he nodded towards the arena and said not a word. The crier bowed, turned, and raised his hands. "Warriors, begin!"

The moment the call went out, the crowd came back to life. Tristan and most of the others began to measure one another, but Rolfe, the fatigued winner of the second bout, charged. He ran full speed toward Malcolm of Elinton. Tristan supposed Rolfe thought to take out the strongest man in the contest first by catching him by surprise. That, or he understood he had no chance of winning and wished to go out in style.

His fatigue from the opening round showed clear in how he ran, and whatever his plan had been, disaster was the result. He leapt high, only for Malcolm's ax to smash him hard in the chest and send him crashing to the ground. He did not rise again. Mere seconds into the melee, and already one man was eliminated.

Tristan had assumed the match would not be overly long. There would be chaos, or at least what appeared to be chaos to the crowd, and at all times every man was in danger.

He now thought of an element which had not been a factor in the singles bouts: alliances could be formed. He wondered if the same thought was crossing Garit's mind. If so, they could aid one another in the bout against the others. He realized what a fool he'd been to not even mention this to his friend earlier.

To his right was Ingram. To his left, Norman Hodge. The three of them stayed on the outskirts of the fight, watching as the others did battle. Garit wisely teamed up with Malcolm, and together they made quick work of the winners of the two bouts Tristan had missed.

When they turned their attention to the three who had refrained from combat, Garit mouthed something to Malcolm. The man with the ax nodded, and Garit waved

Tristan over. Tristan took the message and joined them. It was now three on two: Tristan, Garit, and Malcolm against Norman and Ingram.

Tristan longed to rush forward because the numbers were on their side. He advanced, anticipating Malcolm and Garit to come with him, but they hesitated. He stepped back and regarded them both, and he could see the apprehension in their eyes. They were being cautious—overly cautious. Norman and Ingram, likewise, did not seem too keen on engaging in battle.

"I called for fury, and I get timid mice!" The five men turned to find Jules standing, his face red and contorted with anger. "It is no small wonder your kingdom almost tripped over itself to make these peace talks a reality—it is clear your people have no stomach for war."

This time, the crowd booed. Not Jules' camp followers, but the people of Grauberg. Tristan only hoped they were booing Jules and not the fighters. This was not going according to plan. The tournament was meant to be a display of prowess, but Jules was twisting it into a platform to exercise his own form of mental intimidation.

Around him, Garit, Malcolm, Norman, and Ingram continued to measure each other. Inside, though, something snapped. His rage burst like a dam. He spat and rushed forward.

His eyes narrowed on Norman Hodge. The man stared, shocked by the sudden charge. He began to lift his two-handed sword, but Tristan jumped high, his knee hitting Hodge's chin. He practically felt the crunch of it as his foe fell back. Hodge did not move again during the contest.

He turned to find Ingram had taken his spot beside Malcom and Garit. He looked to his friend and recognized fear in Garit's eyes—fear of him. Tristan had been singled out as the biggest threat, and he welcomed their advance.

As they closed in on him, his blood quickened. They couldn't decide how best to handle him, and he used their tentativeness against them. He ran forward, between Malcolm and Ingram.

Ingram gave a thrust with his spear while Malcolm made a wide swing with his ax. Tristan dropped and slid along the ground between the two. Ingram hit nothing, but Malcolm's ax came across and pummeled the spearman in the chest.

Malcolm looked on, stunned, and Garit seized the opportunity. He drove the point of his spear into the spot where the plates were separated between the shoulder and breastplate of Malcolm's armor. The head sank in, dulled though it was, and the force of his thrust drove the mountain of a man to the ground.

Malcolm dropped his ax as Garit stood over him. He ripped his spear free and threatened to drive it down again, but Malcolm was waving him off and scooting to the perimeter. He was eliminated. Garit turned as Tristan was throwing the injured Ingram out of the fenced area. Ingram lay at the foot of the spectators in the stands, making no effort to rise. It was now down to the two friends.

Garit was slow to come forward, his weapon gripped tight, but Tristan charged ahead. He moved within range of Garit's spear. It came at him and he ducked, deflecting it up with his shield as he stabbed with his sword. Garit narrowly avoided the attack and circled away, and both men faced off again.

Garit gave his head a shake. He was tired and sore, but still he came forward. He thrust at Tristan's feet. Tristan stepped back and the point of the spear hit the ground. Tristan drove his shield down on the shaft, snapping it in half. Garit cursed as Tristan kicked the broken head aside.

Tristan knew his opponent now had little more than a stick. His mind raced. Jules was still watching. Tristan wanted to show him what violence he was capable of. He faced his enemy, not even considering his name or who he was. This was a foe, nothing more. The man's eyes flickered between defeat and resolve, and the confusion left him exposed.

Tristan charged forth and gave voice to his fury, breaking his own rule about shouting in combat. His opponent gave way, falling back a step as Tristan came on him in his wrath. The man raised the bit of weapon he had to deflect a blow, but Tristan's sword snapped it in half and came down on the enemy's shoulder. Though dulled, it hit with enough power to break skin and a great surge of blood erupted from the wound.

His foe let out a cry of pain as he sank to his knees. Blood poured from the gash, the man waved his hand in submission, and collapsed. Tristan stood over him, poised to deliver a killing blow, when Jules interrupted him.

"Excellent!" he yelled. Tristan suddenly snapped free from the grasp of his anger. He realized what he was about to do, and let his eyes fall on his foe. He had a name—this was Garit. Had he been so blinded? Is this what he was prepared to do? He took a step back, horrified, as Jules' voice continued behind him. "I might almost believe you were a true warrior if not for the evidence to the contrary."

Tristan turned, not daring to consider he now spoke to a prince. "What's that?" he yelled back.

Jules appeared taken aback for a moment, but he smiled, nonetheless. "If you had not proven yourself a coward in the past, I might almost believe you were a man of courage."

Fury now mixed with confusion within Tristan. "And when did I prove myself a coward?" The crowd was silent. All in Grauberg, from the lowest peasant to the king himself, would bear witness to this confrontation.

"Well, you are a man of Elinton, are you not? The mere fact you are here in Grauberg tells me that, at some point in your life, you fled."

Tristan shook with anger. The man who had taken his

unarmed family from him was now insulting him before his adopted home. "I was seven, you bloody sack of—"

"Captain!" The voice was that of the king, and Tristan's stomach churned and his mind snapped back to where he was, who he was, and who he addressed. "Enough of your insolence." The king was standing, and he now turned to Jules. "Let us retire. Your tournament is over, Your Highness."

That was the ignoble end to it. The crier never even proclaimed Tristan as the winner. He'd won no glory. He stood in the arena, watching as Ella strove to heal those who had been injured, and he stared as his best friend bled from the wound which Tristan had dealt him with all the animosity he could muster.

All warmth left his body. A moment later, a hard rain began to pelt him. He remained there, cold inside and out as the people fled the stands to find cover. There were no cheers.

VI
Decision

What have I done?

Tristan sat quietly by Garit's bed. He had been required to perform many duties over the last two days following the tournament, but every moment of his free time was spent here. His friend had stirred several times and managed to ask for water on a few occasions, but no more.

Half a day had passed since even that had happened, though Tristan and Hardi took turns forcing his mouth open to pour small sips for him. Ella had told them he would need the fluid to help regain the blood he'd lost— and he'd lost a lot. She had healed the wound, but now Garit's body had to do the rest. Tristan worried whether he would wake again.

"I'm sorry," Tristan said for what must have been the thousandth time.

Hardi was sitting across from him on Garit's other side. "He was aware of the risk, sir. I doubt he would think the apology necessary."

Tristan shrugged. "All the same, I'm still sorry." Hardi gave his shoulder a light squeeze, then reached up and touched Garit's forehead with the back of his hand. A door opened somewhere in the home, and footsteps sounded down the hall. Tristan glanced over to see Lord Gerald enter the room. "Sir," he said.

Gerald did not speak, though he nodded in response. "Any change in his condition?"

"No, my lord," said Hardi. Garit coughed, and his eyes fluttered open. Tristan, Hardi, and Gerald all crowded over him. "Master Garit?" asked Hardi, reaching down and taking one of Garit's hands.

"Your hands are freezing, Hardi," Garit said with a shiver. A smile came on his wearied face, and Tristan breathed a sigh of relief. Garit's eyes found him. "Ah, the champion. How's this morning find you?" Tristan smiled but before he could respond, Garit spasmed as if he were alarmed. "I didn't piss myself, did I?"

They all laughed. "No," said Tristan. "You passed out before you were able to disgrace yourself."

"The hell with that," Gerald said, "he would have disgraced me!" Garit shifted his gaze to his father, whose eyes brimmed with unshed tears. "I'm glad you're awake, my son."

"Aye," said Garit, "You'll not have to worry about losing an heir today." A rumble sounded in the room and Garit grabbed his belly. "Then again, you might be without one if I don't get some food."

Hardi stood, but before he was out of the room, a loud knock echoed down the corridor. "Someone at the door. Let me tend to this, and I'll bring you a bite, Master Garit." He was gone for only a minute before he returned. "Apologies, Captain Tristan, but a guest has come seeking you."

Tristan's heart sank. He'd feared a summons would come at any moment for the past two days. No matter how sorely provoked he'd been, he was still only a soldier—and not even a true soldier, but a mercenary—and he'd had the gall to address Jules in such a manner in so public a place.

"Is the message from the commander? Or the general?" He winced as he thought of the next and worst possible person. "The king?"

Hardi shook his head. "No, sir. He is garbed as one of the party from Elinton. He says Prince Jules has requested an audience with the champion of the tournament."

Tristan's blood went cold. He began to rise when a hand gripped his wrist. His eyes dropped to Garit. "Be prudent, my friend," he said. Tristan gave him a blank stare. He was certain Garit could not tell what he was feeling, which made sense—he wasn't sure himself.

"I'll do my best." Tristan said the words without emotion. His head was light as he made his way to the front door and met with the man who'd come to call on him. They were at the foot of a flight of stairs which led to the third level before Tristan realized the man walking beside him was Vincent, Jules' chief lieutenant. Standing this close, he had to look twice; at first, he thought the man had been Jules, himself.

"Something the matter?" Vincent asked, disdain evident in his voice.

Tristan found his nerve and cleared his throat. "Aye, Lieutenant."

Vincent faced him as they made their way up the stairs. "Then give voice to your thoughts."

"I shall," replied Tristan. "Very soon."

Vincent scoffed and turned forward again. "Insolent boy."

Tristan smirked and continued doing so until Vincent caught sight of it. The glare Vincent returned made it clear that he'd gotten under the lieutenant's skin, and with very little effort. He kept the expression plastered on his face, and he did not say another word. Instead, he began to take in the sights of the upper level of Grauberg.

Only two structures stood on this level. They were massive, and they would have filled half of the middle level and a quarter of the lowest. They were the royal palace and the temple of Rylar. Tristan had always seen them from a distance, but from below he'd never been sure which spires belonged to which building.

They passed first by the temple, which consisted of four imposing towers. The greatest stood behind the other three and was far larger on its own than the others combined. This tower was meant to symbolize Rylar, the god who reigned over all.

The three lesser towers were immense in their own right, but they paled against the tower of Rylar. These symbolized the three still-living beings who helped govern Rylar's affairs here below. They were the Helpers: Peyth, Hufa, and Luka.

According to the teachings of the priests and scriptures, two other Helpers had existed at one time. One was Gui, who was the chief of all the Helpers and gave birth to the White. The other was Emjar, who gave birth to the Grey.

As they passed by the towers, Vincent spat and said, "Emjar be praised!"

Tristan gave him no response. He recalled that, at least in days of old, the Felixandrians had given their worship to Emjar. They had also tried to force Grauberg and Elinton, then provinces of the Grey Empire, to pay homage to him.

While other factors existed as well, this was the chief issue which brought about the rebellion of Grauberg and Elinton. The Grey Empire was destroyed, and the Felixandrians were driven back to their home on the harsh, mountainous continent of Ruxtuma. None in Grauberg would ever praise Emjar. Tristan wondered if they were forced to do so in Elinton.

The temple was imposing, but the palace was massive, easily dwarfing the High Hall and Low Hall combined twice over. This was the residence of the king and his daughter, as well as their servants. Many nobles were often guests in the castle, and some were on such good terms with the royal family that they were reputed to spend more nights here than in their own homes.

As they approached the massive doors which led to the greatest portion of the palace, several guards snapped to attention. Tristan stopped, not sure how best to proceed at this point. Then he remembered hearing Garit speak of coming here with his father in the past. Tristan bowed his head. "Hail, King Frederic," he said. "Long may he reign," was their response. Two of the guards opened the doors, and the others bowed and remained that way until Tristan and Vincent had passed them.

Inside, Tristan marveled at the height of the ceiling in the grand corridor in which he found himself. He walked on a carpet of rich scarlet, and enormous pillars stood to his left and right. Beautiful windows lined the wall, and they were nearly as tall as the hall itself. Their glass was stained in every color imaginable, and the various stained pieces were assembled in such a way as to tell stories, each window depicting a different event in Grauberg's past.

He was ashamed that he was not familiar enough with history to identify what many of them illustrated. One image which stood out to him showcased figures in grey garb, and they were retreating from the city. Tristan noted that Vincent picked up his pace as they passed this particular piece.

They turned right, into a small corridor. Before long, they had moved through several smaller passages, up a flight of stairs here and another there, and soon Tristan had no concept of where he was in the labyrinth which was the royal palace.

He did not let his bewilderment show, but one thing did bother him. This man, Vincent, who belonged to the force which raided his birthplace, was this familiar with the palace after being in the city for but a few days, but Tristan had never been allowed to this level a single time. He did his best to shake the thought from his head and focus more on the matter at hand.

They came to a corridor which was well-lit. The guards on duty here were not Grause, but rather belonged to Jules. Tristan wasn't sure of what to call them—were they Elinian or Felixandrian? A drop of cold sweat ran down his spine as he considered they may be a combination of the two. Four of them stood outside a doorway.

As Tristan and Vincent approached, the guards came to attention. "Emjar be praised," said Vincent. "His enemies, cursed," they responded. Tristan did his best to give no indication that he was appalled. He didn't consider himself to be a religious man, but this exchange was still shocking to behold. One of the men opened the door, and Vincent led Tristan in.

Tristan had expected the room to be richly colored and ornate. What he found was plain stone walls, a fire burnt low, and an open window letting the cold air of autumn flow in. The room was furnished with a simple desk, a wash basin, and a table surrounded by chairs. Aside from these simple items, the only decoration was a grey banner without emblem which hung over the fireplace behind the desk. Under this banner, in a high-backed chair, was Prince Jules. "That will be all for now, Lieutenant," he said, dismissing Vincent with the wave of his hand.

"Your Highness," Vincent said as he bowed. He glowered at Tristan and walked out, pulling the doors closed behind him. Tristan glanced around to ensure he and Jules were truly the only two present.

"Relax," said Jules, reaching out for a glass of wine which was resting on the desk before him. "We are alone. Please, help yourself to some of my vintage and take a seat." A second glass was set for Tristan, but he did not fill it as he took his place across from Jules. The prince drank his wine and reached for the bottle. "Very well, then," he said as he poured more for himself.

"You have no cup bearer," said Tristan. Though he'd never sat with the king or princess or any sort of royalty a single day in his life, he'd heard tale of how little they were reputed to do for themselves.

Jules drained his second glass. "I have no need of one. I can pour my own wine. We are not so lofty or pathetic that we need people to do everything for us, though I understand the stories told in Grauberg say Felixandria was crushed centuries ago, and my nation is now populated by old men and eunuchs who have no lust for blood."

"Well, I can't say much about the state of Felixandria today," Tristan said, "but it *was* crushed centuries ago. You may have climbed back, but you were — quite undeniably — crushed."

Jules mused on this for a moment. "A fair point, I concede, but we are not helpless dotards."

"There are some who believe otherwise," Tristan admitted.

"But not you?" Jules kept his fingers wrapped around the empty glass as he stared into Tristan's eyes.

Tristan shook his head. "No, not me," he said, but offered no more.

"Go on, then," Jules said. "Tell me, what does the mighty champion of the tournament think of Prince Jules of Felixandria?"

Tristan was not sure if this was a trap or not, but the urge to speak freely was upon him. He did his best to consider the last bit of advice Garit had given him. "Perhaps it would be prudent if we changed the —"

"It would be prudent if you answer me when I ask you, Tristan, Captain of the *Elinian* Guard, what you think of me!" Tristan realized he'd offended the man simply by having the honorary title placed on him.

"Do I have permission to speak my mind?"

Jules smiled. "Of course. I hold to the old ways, Tristan. When two adults speak, they should do so with clear intent and understanding. I don't need simpering subjects looking to say what I wish to hear."

Tristan leaned forward and grabbed his glass. "May I?" Jules offered him the bottle. By its weight, Tristan gathered that Jules had already enjoyed a bit prior to his arrival. He poured, sat back, and drank it in seconds. The wine warmed him in the chill of the room. "The 'old ways,' you say? I'm not familiar with them. I wonder, Prince Jules—do the old ways include attacking sleeping farmsteads and slaughtering people with no defiance given?"

Jules stared at him with a blank expression which betrayed none of his thoughts. For a while, they sat in silence, studying one another. "Is this what the people of Grauberg tell you? They say we attacked without cause?"

"No," said Tristan, leaning and pouring another cup. "The people of Grauberg tell me that what I remember is wrong. They don't believe me when I tell them what happened the day my family was taken from me. They say my eyes deceived me. Some have called me a liar."

Jules raised his eyebrows and folded his hands together on the desk before him. "And what, Tristan, did your young eyes see?"

Tristan drained his second glass and poured the last of the wine. "My father, on his knees. He was a farmer, and he was held at the point of a sword as if he were a criminal. My mother and sisters were dragged in. I watched as my family was tortured. Not by blades, though. By something else, Prince Jules—something unseen."

Jules regarded him carefully. He pushed his chair back and stood. Tristan rose to his feet to meet him as he approached, drained what was in his glass, and remained perfectly still as Jules stared hard at his face. He watched his enemy examine the scar which ran down over his eye and cheek, and he noted the way Jules' eyes narrowed for a brief instant. "I wonder, Tristan—how did you earn this mutilation?"

Tristan fought down his desire to drive his forehead into Jules' nose. Instead, he took a deep breath and found the boldness to smile. "Oh, I think you have a good idea as to the answer to that, Prince Jules, Regent of *Elinton*." He put the same inflection on the title as Jules had on his.

Jules observed him for a few moments more and did the last thing Tristan expected: he smiled. He returned to his side of the table but did not sit. Neither man did. "I will be departing Grauberg as the sun rises tomorrow. These talks of peace have bored me, and I long to return to my own land."

"Felixandria?"

"No," said Jules, his words sharp. "I said my own land. Felixandria belongs to my father and will not be mine until his death. My land is Elinton. It belongs to me, Tristan, because I took it."

"You did," said Tristan. "Cherish it while you can, Your Highness." He did not finish the thought. He didn't need to. Jules had caught the implication.

"I understand that with your coming nameday, you will have a choice to make," said Jules, undaunted by the threat. He'd clearly found out all he could about the champion of his tournament. "You can choose to pledge your sword to Grauberg in perpetuity, thereby becoming a citizen, or you can choose to forge another path for yourself. I wonder, have you yet made your decision?"

While he'd not let it be known, Tristan had made the choice—the only one which had ever existed. He was curious where the prince was guiding the conversation. "I have not, Your Highness."

Jules smiled. "Well, I'll be blunt. I've seen your fury. More than that, I've seen that you have the nerve to stand with the man who took your home from you and speak your mind, both here in this room and in the arena. Some would call that foolish, but I call it daring."

"My friends tell me I talk too much."

The prince laughed. "To be sure, you do. Your friends don't lie. You speak boldly with your accusations, though I confess I'm not sure how well you would be able to back your threats up." He let a silence hang for several uncomfortable seconds. Tristan's face reddened. "But," continued Jules, "I would still make an offer to you."

"An offer?"

"Yes. If you should refuse the Grause and choose, instead, to find another path, one is available for you in Elinton."

Tristan's eyes widened. "I beg your pardon, Your Highness, but I'm not sure—"

"I could make much use of a man like you in my own army. You would be home, after all, and—"

Tristan flung his glass at the table and sent the empty wine bottle crashing to the stone floor, where it shattered into a thousand pieces. The doors flew open, and the guards rushed in, spears pointed at Tristan. "A simple accident," Jules said, his tone flat. The men raised their weapons but remained in the room. "I do, however, think my time with my guest is done. Please escort him back to his friend's side. I do hope that Master Garit has not suffered too much from the wound you dealt him in the tournament. So much anger, to drive a man to do such a thing to a companion he's held close since childhood."

Tristan suppressed a growl and bowed stiffly. "Your Highness," he muttered. He was hastily ushered out of the palace. He did not dawdle or take time to admire the scenery as he made his way back to the front.

Once he was out, he did not go back to Garit's, but instead went to the lower level and the training yards. He'd been excused from his exercises these past several days because of his duties regarding the prince's stay. Today, he needed to feel his sword in hand. He glanced up and scowled. The sky was still grey, and when night came, no stars shone.

Tristan was in his dress uniform again the next morning. With him were the men who had served under his command during the past days as the Elinian Guard. They sat in front of the High Hall, and after a time, Prince Jules and his party descended from the upper level, and the two parties came together.

As they made their way toward the lower level, Jules' soldiers rode in front. Behind them came Tristan and Jules side-by-side, and the Elinian Guard behind. They found the streets to be desolate. The crowd which had been there to witness Jules' arrival was nowhere to be seen.

Word had trickled down and spread that the peace talks had failed. Every person in town knew this man would likely be their enemy soon, and they were not too keen to lay eyes on him. Tristan wondered if they stayed indoors out of prudence, or anger, or fear.

The two of them spoke no words as they left through the front gate. As the last of the Elinian guard came out, they formed up in a line across the gateway. Tristan sat his horse before them as Jules and his soldiers rode on. The carriages and freeriders were assembled, waiting on them.

After they had ridden fifty yards or so, the foreigners stopped and turned. One of the riders came up beside Jules, and Tristan recognized him as Vincent a moment later. The prince's lieutenant drew his sword and aimed the point toward the city. Behind him, the other soldiers did the same.

Tristan and the men at his back unsheathed theirs in response. Rather than pointing them, they laid their blades across their knees, bare steel exposed to the men who had just been their guests. The two sides stood like this for a time, until Jules and Vincent and the rest of their party turned and rode away. This was an old custom — the drawing of weapons to signify a challenge, and the promise of steel in kind. Tristan and his men did not sheathe theirs until Jules' entire train was out of sight.

Tristan shuddered as a cold wind snapped around him. He turned his horse and faced his men, scanning their faces and meeting their eyes. In some he saw fear, and in others hatred. The peace hoped for was not to be, and war loomed on the horizon.

He closed his eyes, took in a deep breath, and spoke loud for all those present. "It has been an honor to serve with you, brothers," he said with tears in his eyes. He had not thought to speak to the men like this, and the sudden sentiment which rose in him caught him off-guard. "And to be clear, I do not mean 'brothers in arms.' No, you are my brothers from home."

"'Home,'" one of the men repeated. Tristan could not tell which soldier had spoken, but as his eyes roamed from man to man, more than a few mouthed the word.

"Aye, home. A home which was taken from us. Now, war appears to be the path we must take. Some of you probably feel conflicted about raising a sword against your home. Mark well these words, my brothers: we do not go to war with Elinton. We go to war with Prince Jules of Felixandria, the man who styles himself the regent of our home."

He thought to fight down his emotions but decided not to. He fought to master them, but not to shield them. He may not have given voice to his feelings, but they were evident in his tone. "It has been my honor to serve as your captain. Now that this occasion has concluded, I must lay down this title. You will each rejoin your units. In time, probably in the near future, we will likely be on a field of battle. On that day, I will be proud to know the men of the Elinian Guard, whether side-by-side or scattered across the field, will be fighting to liberate the home which was stolen from us.

"For some of you, Grauberg is now your home. You have become citizens of this city, and there is no wrong in that. Yet you can help ensure Elinton is free for all who are to come after." He placed his right fist over his heart in salute. "Brothers, may the peace of Rylar and His Helpers be upon you." They returned his salute, and, one by one, they turned and rode back into the city.

Tristan brought his borrowed horse back to its stable on the middle level and walked back down to his home. He had a meeting scheduled at noon with Commander Walter, and he intended to sit and think for a while before he had to leave.

When he walked into the room, something was lying on his bed. It was a garment of some kind, but the room was too dark to see well. He opened his door to let in as much light as possible, but the cloth remained colorless. It was a cloak—a grey cloak, like the ones worn by the soldiers who rode with Jules even now.

As the fifth bell of the day—the last before the noon bell—rang out, Tristan left his small home, bound for the High Hall. He'd barely closed his door before Ella appeared before him with a smile on her face. "Looks like I caught you just in time!" she said. "Where are you off to?"

He motioned his head upward, toward the middle level. "I have to meet with the commander in an hour," he said.

"Ah. Well then, I won't take up too much of your time." He realized she was holding her hands behind her back. Before he could ask what she had, she brought them around in front of her. "I hope you like it!"

In her hands was a rich emerald cloak, with an inner layer lined with dark brown fur. It unfolded as he took hold, and his breath caught. Stitched into the center with golden thread was an owl. "Ella—" he began, but the words were choked.

"I know your family had no crest," she said, "but I remember you telling me often of how you would sit outside at night and listen to the owls call to each other across the fields."

"I—I don't know what to say, Ella. This must have cost you—" He knew the cost was beyond her means, but he didn't want to ruin the moment by bringing up the value. A gift was a precious thing, in both Grauberg and Elinton—something to be cherished. That said, they were rarely given without reason. "What's the occasion?" Tristan asked after a few moments.

She gave him an amused expression. "Well, it's not every day that you celebrate falling out of your mother's underparts."

"My nameday," he said. He closed his eyes and counted up the days. They'd been a blur since the tournament, one flowing into the other. Then his eyes shot open. "It's today!"

She laughed at him. "I suppose you haven't exactly been tracking the days lately. Unless it was counting them down for when that arse of a prince would be out of the city." Ella beamed at her gift in Tristan's hands before she noted the cloak he was already holding. "What's that?"

His smile dimmed, but he fought to keep some semblance of it for the sake of his friend. "A parting gift from that 'arse of a prince,' it would seem." He unfolded the cloak and showed it to her. While her response was not as evident as his had been, the disdain was plain on her face. "I don't know if I'm the only soldier who received one. I plan to show it to the commander."

"I see," she said softly. "Well, I know you can't wear the new one while you're in uniform, but I had best see you in that cloak soon." She walked up and put her arms around him and pressed her cheek to his chest as he rested his chin on the top of her head. "Happy nameday, you big oaf."

"Thank you, Ella," he whispered. For the briefest of moments, he recalled the last words they'd shared alone, when he learned she didn't believe him about the Grey after all. In that brief moment, he felt his anger begin to surge, but she squeezed him tighter, and he knew they'd sort it out somehow. This was Ella, and he couldn't stay angry with her.

She released him and turned to walk away. After a few steps, she turned back to him and pointed up. "The sun has come back out. Let's hope it's a sign for a good day."

He smirked. "Let's hope." She smiled, turned, and

disappeared around a corner. Tristan came back into his room and placed his gift on the bed. It looked warm and comfortable, and he knew it was a far greater gift than Ella could afford without great difficulty. Though he'd never worn it, it was already one of his greatest treasures. He left the room again and lifted his eyes to see the dark clouds had indeed parted. The sun shone brightly, but he felt only chill.

He was early when he arrived at the High Hall but was still called directly into the commander's office. Walter was not there, and so Tristan paced as he waited. He walked to the corners of the room and made sure no Dytan merchants or other surprises lurked there.

After about a quarter of an hour, footsteps sounded in the corridor outside. "Is he here?" he heard the deep voice ask, and a muffled "Aye" from one of the guards. The doors opened and the commander came in with a red face. Tristan could not tell if it was from the cold wind or his temperament.

"Sir," said Tristan, coming to attention and saluting. Walter returned it and moved behind his desk. Tristan helped himself to a seat across from him. He considered how comfortable he'd become in the office in the last three weeks, despite his first encounter here.

"I wonder, Tristan, how much longer you will be saluting me." As he said this, Commander Walter laid his gloved hands flat on the table before him, occasionally tapping with his forefinger. "I understand today is your twenty-third nameday."

"It seems everyone remembered this except for me, Commander," said Tristan with half a smile. "I only realized it when a friend stopped me on the way here."

Walter grunted. "I can understand how the days have gotten away from you here. Still, the decision you make today will have heavy implications for your future. I trust you have given it some thought."

Tristan was not prepared for this. "I'm not sure I'm

ready to give an answer yet. I—I wasn't even aware it was due today until I came here."

Walter's eyes met his levelly. "Surely another five minutes or five days or five weeks won't change what you've considered. You may have others convinced that you're more interested in drinking and dancing than aught else, but I see what drives you. I know you've given this a considerable deal of thought, yes?"

Tristan gave him a solemn nod. "I have, sir." He said no more.

Walter gave him an understanding smile. "So, you've decided to go your own way." Tristan lowered his eyes and nodded. "I thought you might," Walter said with a grunt. "I'd like to be the first to wish you the best of luck with whatever you decide to do."

Tristan stared at him, bewildered. "You're not going to try to talk me out of it?"

Walter rose from his desk. Tristan began to stand as well, but Walter motioned for him to stay where he was. "No, I have no desire to convince a man to do anything against his will. It is one thing in military matters. A soldier must obey, and sometimes I have to make him do so, but today, your contract is up. You're a man with the freedom to make your own decisions. It would be an injustice on my part toward you to try and take your choice away."

Tristan smiled. "Thank you, sir."

Walter returned the smile. Then his face tightened, and he grew serious. "Still, there are a couple of things I would like to discuss with you." He walked around his desk and to the doors. He pushed them open but did not walk out. Two men stood sentry, one on either side of the doorway. After a few moments, one of them turned his head. Seeing the commander right there, he faced forward once more. "You lads have been on duty for some time, yes? Why don't you make your way to the kitchens and find yourselves something to eat?"

Now they both turned to him, their uncertainty at the request clear on their faces. "Oh, and take your time," Walter continued. "There's no need for you to hurry back." The guards gave what Tristan could only describe as an uneasy salute and strode away. Walter closed the doors firmly, locking them from within, and turned back to Tristan. "Now, let's discuss Jules."

Tristan was very unsure of what kind of territory he'd wandered into now. "Sir?"

The commander walked back and peered down at Tristan. He leaned over a bit, their eyes locked. Tristan noted that Walter's eyes were greatly faded and dull—almost grey. Like his own. He wondered if they'd once been vibrant. Had the color faded with time, or possibly with his torment as a prisoner of Jules all those years ago.

Thinking of this gave him an inkling of the direction this conversation might be headed. After several moments had passed, Walter straightened and returned to his chair behind the desk. "There are no ears to hear us. Let us speak plainly." Tristan nodded, and he saw Walter had focused on the grey cloak in his lap. "What have you got there?"

"I believe it is a recruitment attempt from Jules, sir. He told me yesterday that he would value a man like me in his army." Walter scoffed, but Tristan continued. "My initial thought was to burn it, but I realized I should show it to you. I'm not sure if he made the offer to any others. Thought you'd like to know he was trying to turn some of your own men."

"Oh, I doubt he seriously believes there is a shred of a chance you'd join him. He has ways of getting under your skin, Tristan. He enjoys it."

"What, behaving like a bully?" Tristan asked with a hint of a sarcastic chuckle.

"No," Walter said with ice in his tone. "Torture. He enjoys the torture of the mind, lad. This may be just a cloak, but I know it doesn't sit well with you that he left it, now does it? He's inside your head, son. He may be riding to a city on the other side of this bloody island, but he has made sure he stays right here in your head. It's nothing but pure hatred, Tristan. The only thing he loves is hatred."

Tristan sat in silence for a while, but Walter offered no more. The moment stretched on, and Tristan began to feel uncomfortable. He wanted to know for sure where this was going. "What can you tell me about him, Commander?"

Walter inhaled deeply. "He's dangerous. Years ago, he sent out his scouts to test us. We answered them with iron and steel. We honestly thought we were teaching him a thing or two until some of our men went missing. At first, we thought they'd fallen in the skirmishes, and we'd simply not been able to reclaim them from the battlefield, but it became common. For every small battle, there would be one or two men we couldn't find, nor could anyone recall seeing them fall to the sword. They were being captured.

"We couldn't declare war on Elinton because Jules had not claimed responsibility for the attacks. Still, it had to be him. There's nobody else on this bloody continent. I often wondered why we had to follow such a strict decorum on this matter. Later, I'd learn the truth— Grauberg wasn't built for war anymore, no matter how hard we wished to believe otherwise. Still, the fights persisted, and we continued to lose a man here and a man there. One day, I was the man who was lost.

"For three years, they held me. They didn't ask me about our defenses or our techniques. They didn't ask me anything. They just tortured me. Every day, for three years. Sometimes only for a minute or two. Sometimes for hours. Sometimes, Jules came to me personally, and at other times it was his bastard." Tristan raised an eyebrow to that. Walter went on. "Vincent. I'm sure you saw the similarities. He's Jules' bastard. Well, one of them anyway.

He's his father's favorite, even more than his own trueborn son. They both tortured me. Sometimes, I'd see them daily. Then they'd be gone for weeks, and it would be other men."

Tristan shook his head. "I can't believe I never heard of this."

Walter shrugged. "When I finally escaped and made my way back, it became common gossip around the city for a while. This would have been about twelve years ago now, mind you. I was given a promotion for my supposed valor and called to serve in the High Hall. I was never fool enough to believe that. They just wanted to keep me close, but I wasn't complaining. I didn't exactly want to be out and about. Over the years, I made as few public appearances as I could as I quietly made my way through the ranks as men above me either passed away or retired. In the years since, I have made sure we brought our forces up to full strength.

"Back to what I was saying, though—after a time, people got used to not seeing me, and the stories about my capture and escape faded as yesterday's news. But it happened. The people in town may no longer speak of it, and many have forgotten or never heard about it, but it happened. I think of it every day. I still feel the blasted pain."

Tristan nodded. "I think it says a lot about you—your strength and your will to live—that you can even stand, sir. I've heard tales of men crippled for life from but a few days of torture, and you were there for three—"

"It was not a torture of my body, Tristan. Well, I suppose it was. I felt it in my body, of course, but that's not where the pain comes from. I thought it was—at first—but the more I felt it, the more I became aware of the true source."

Tristan narrowed his eyes. "What do you mean?"

Walter leaned forward and spoke slowly. "They tortured my soul. That's what the magic attacks. It wasn't with a sword or a whip that I was struck. I wasn't stretched or flayed or half-drowned. They tortured me with their hatred. That's what fuels the magic."

Tristan swallowed. "Sir, do you mean—"

"I do," Walter said with a grunt. "I know what you reported when you came to the city. You weren't the only one, but it was quickly hushed up. Men in charge fifteen years ago said it wouldn't do for everyone to know what Jules and his men were capable of. I'm not so certain in their wisdom, but what's done is done. But you were right, Tristan. You were always right. It's the Grey."

Tristan's breath wouldn't come. He stood abruptly and turned away, the affirmation bringing all the memories to the fore of his consciousness. A gasp escaped, and he was breathing heavily. After all these years, he finally had acknowledgement that he wasn't crazy or a liar, and yet, there was no joy to be found in the revelation of it.

Instead, all he could see were the faces of his parents as they were held under the power of the evil magic. All he could hear were the screams of his sisters in the final moments before their lives were taken from them. "I don't know what—I can't—I—"

"Breathe, son," Walter said, standing behind him and putting his hands on Tristan's shoulders. "Breathe, nice and slow."

Tristan nodded and did his best to do as Walter suggested. Soon, he was master of himself again, and he came back to his seat. "Apologies," he offered, taking one last deep breath.

"None required," Walter said. He patted Tristan on the back and leaned on the edge of his desk. "So," he said, crossing his arms across his broad chest, "let's talk about your plans."

"My plans, sir?" Tristan rubbed his eyes with the palms of his hands and faced Walter.

The commander smiled. "Well, you are planning on

going after him, are you not?"

Tristan's eyes widened. "How did—"

"Oh, give me more credit than that. I knew that look in your eyes the first time we met in this office. It's the same one I see when I look in the mirror." Tristan gave him no response, but instead reflected on his earlier musings of the similarity of their eyes. "I'm not going to hinder you. If I wanted to do that, I'd have foiled you already. I sent my men away for this reason, son: so we might talk openly about this." He moved to his fireplace, added another log, and poked up the flames. "Might be here for a bit," he said as he returned to his chair. He rested his gloved hands on the desk before him. "So, Tristan—let's talk."

VII
Leaving Grauberg

Well, at least I'm healed enough to be able to write. I feel so weak, but I'm told I will mend soon enough with food and drink. I plan on having an ale or two tonight, if nothing else. Maybe Ella won't find out.

A quick note to myself, though: never fight on the side AGAINST Tristan. Bastard doesn't yell so much as release the screams of hell when he's pissed. I felt sick in my stomach when he let his war cry out and came at us. I won't be on that side again.

Well, I'm being told to come eat something else, but I really don't want to. Hardi will skin me if I don't listen, though. More later.

The walk back to his residence gave Tristan plenty of time to consider everything. In the span of a few hours, the direction of his life had changed. This had happened once before, when he was seven. It was completely out of his hands that time. On this occasion, it was a change he freely chose.

Not only had he desired this, but he went with the blessing of Commander Walter, albeit unofficially. The city could not condone the actions of an assassin for obvious reasons. War may be looming, but there was still time to draw up battle plans, make provisions, and attend to other concerns. Grauberg would not provoke Jules prematurely. As far as anyone was concerned, Tristan's actions would be his own if he were discovered.

In any case, his service to Grauberg was done. When he had departed to meet with the commander, he had not considered that this would be a possibility. He'd understood the time was coming, but not today.

Mere hours ago, Tristan had stood at the gates of the city with his Elinian brethren and told them that soon enough he would be fighting by their sides. Now, his sword no longer belonged to Grauberg. He still intended to ensure none of his brothers ever needed to step on a field of war. If he failed, he would end up at their side anyway — that is, if he wasn't dead.

He tried not to think of that. As he walked, he began to feel an overwhelming exhaustion. This was not physical, though his body had certainly been drained by all his activities over the last several days. This was more of a mental and emotional fatigue. The confirmation that his family had been killed the way he'd always said had left him weary.

He longed to fall to his bed, and as he reached his room, he did just that. He'd not paid attention when he fell face-first to the mattress, but he became aware of his new cloak bundled up beneath him.

Without standing, he kicked off his boots, wrestled out of his dress uniform, and considered how much easier this all would have been had he simply stood. He draped the cloak over himself as if it were a blanket. Ella had truly outdone herself with this gift. Her face swam up before him as warmth spread through his body.

A moment later, he was staring at his mother's face. She screamed, and blood trickled from her nose and mouth. Beside her, his father roared his pain and fury, but Tristan was not able to see him from his hiding place under the floor. He watched his mother closely, praying for a miracle which wouldn't come. Her eyes were clenched tight in prayer as well. She had always been a follower of Rylar and his Helpers, and Tristan wondered why they weren't helping her now.

In the far corner of the room, Tristan's sisters screamed. Suddenly, the screaming ceased, and he understood what that meant. He had little time to consider this, for that was the moment his mother's eyes opened.

To his horror, he saw recognition in them; she'd spotted him through the crack between the floorboards. Her cries stopped as she gasped in terror. Her eyes, which had been filled with tears, now turned red as blood began to run down her cheeks. She mouthed his name, but no sound came out. He dared to raise his face to the boards above him, hoping that by being closer to her, she might be comforted.

Two things happened in the next moment. One was that his mother's face seemed to spread open, and her blood poured through the crack in the floor. The second was a pain which writhed through Tristan's own face.

For a moment, he recognized the blade of a sword. It had ended his mother's physical suffering and made Tristan's begin. His own blood ran out and mingled with his mother's on his face, and he recoiled in agony. He couldn't help himself—he screamed. Was it fueled by pain or rage? Likely both.

The boards overhead were being ripped up, and fingers wrapped into his hair and hauled him out of his hiding spot. He frantically wiped blood from his eyes and tried to take in the scene. The man holding him was young—perhaps not yet twenty—but the other stranger was a bit older. They had their swords drawn, and both were slick with blood.

Tristan was suspended, held tightly by his hair. Beneath him were the bodies of his parents. In the corner, his sisters lay on the floor. He couldn't tell if they had been killed with blade or magic, but they were dead, and beside them lay their dolls.

"A boy," said the man holding him by his hair. Before

anything else was said or done, Tristan began to jerk in the man's grip. A moment later, he dropped to the floor. As soon as he was on the ground, he ran for the open door. He was not pursued, and he fled fast and far into the forest which bordered his family's fields.

After a time, his pains intensified, as though his face had been sliced in half. His head ached, and he reached up and realized how much of his hair had ripped free from his scalp when he escaped the man's clutches. The pain became secondary to his exhaustion, and soon everything turned black.

The sun had set by the time he came to, and someone was holding him. He began to struggle, but a voice spoke to him in the darkness. "It's alright," someone said. "I've got you." This was a woman's voice, but not his mother's. He couldn't open his right eye, but he was able to find the woman in the night as his left adjusted. She was about the same age as his mother, he thought.

Someone was crying, and he turned his head to find a man and a little girl a few feet away. Tristan thought she was a little younger than he was. The woman cradling him lightly touched his chin and turned his face back to hers. "Let's get this clean, and I will see what I can do for bandaging," she said. They were in the forest, and a stream was flowing nearby.

"They killed them," he said with a trembling voice. He hadn't realized he was crying until he heard himself.

"What's that?" asked the woman as she dabbed at his injury with a wet cloth.

"Mother and father, and Vanora and Miriel. They're dead. They're all dead." He sobbed and curled into a ball in the stranger's arms.

When he opened his eyes again, the cloak Ella had given him was pulled up beneath his chin. The room was black, and he realized he'd slept through the entire afternoon. His pillow was wet with tears.

Wearily and shakily, he rose from his bed and

stumbled about as he reached for his lantern. Once lit, he dressed hastily in clothes fitting of a night in the Low Hall, and he threw his new cloak about his shoulders and fastened it in place. He needed distraction, and the Hall would be busy tonight now that Jules' party was gone.

"Well, look who chose to grace us with his presence!" The voice greeted Tristan nearly as soon as he entered, and with great surprise he beheld Garit at the bar. The Hall was not as crowded as he'd expected, but his friend who'd been gravely injured less than two days ago was not going to miss out.

"Aye," said one of the soldiers standing with Garit, "look who it is." His tone held more disdain than greeting, and Tristan assumed the word had spread that he was no longer under the employ of Grauberg.

Tristan approached the bar, and the soldiers—save for Garit—stepped aside a few paces. "Guess they aren't too fond of me at the moment," Tristan said as he put his hand on Garit's shoulder. "And what are you doing here? Shouldn't you be in a bed mending?"

Garit gave him a dismissive wave of his hand. "The wound is mended, thanks to Ella and the White. I've been told to drink plenty to help my body replace what blood I lost." He raised his drink to his lips, but a hand shot out and snatched the cup away. "Who in the bloody hell—"

"Me, that's who!" said Ella, seeming to materialize out of nowhere. "And yes, you were told to drink, but water! Not this poison! You'd think Tristan had given you a head wound I couldn't heal!" She slammed the cup down on the bar in front of her. Garit made as if to reach for it, so she lifted it again and drained the contents herself.

She eyed Garit for one more moment before she shifted her gaze over to Tristan. She held him with the same glare before her eyes were drawn to the cloak he wore. Her expression flashed from anger to confusion and back again. She made a noise which may have been a growl, turned, and walked out.

Garit and Tristan exchanged glances. "What was that about?" Garit asked. "The look she gave you, I mean."

Tristan gave a slight shake of his head. "I'm not quite sure, but I think I should go talk to her."

"I'll come with you," said Garit. "No man should die alone."

Tristan winced at the words. They were too close to what had been said to his father when his mother and sisters were brought in by their captors. He bit his tongue and said nothing. "Aye, come on then," he said, and they made their way to the exit.

They found Ella standing at the foot of the steps. As they approached, Tristan knew she was crying by the rising and falling of her shoulders. "Ella?" he asked softly.

"Why didn't you tell me?" she asked. She turned to him, the hurt evident in her eyes. "You're leaving, aren't you?"

He sighed as he pulled her into his arms. "I had thought the decision was yet a few days away," he said. "It was thrust upon me to make today. I'm sorry."

Behind him, Garit cleared his throat. "I don't mean to sound ignorant, but—leaving? And where, pray tell, might you be going?"

Ella's hands gripped the cloak she had gifted him, as if holding him tight would make him stay. She knew where he was going, and deep down, Garit had to know as well. Tristan met his eyes. "I'm going home, Garit."

"Oh, well, that's not so bad. It's not too terribly far," Garit said, walking up and pointing. "You see that street? You walk down about a block, make a right, and quick-like you turn left again. That's where your home is. Here, in Grauberg. I have this funny feeling you think you're talking about some place out east. So, to clear up any confusion you may have—that place in the east is not your home. This is home!"

Tristan shook his head slowly. "No, my friend. My home was taken from me. I've a chance to take it back, and that's what I mean to do."

Ella released him and stepped back, wiping tears from her eyes as Garit began again. "That is one of the most ridiculous things you've ever said, Tristan. Take your home back? What, alone?" He grabbed Tristan by the shoulder and spun him, staring his friend squarely in the face. "Tristan, we are about to be at war with the bastards! We will all aid in liberating Elinton. Why do you think this is something you would have to do alone, or even something that you *can* do alone?"

Tristan debated what to tell them. If he gave them no reason, they would hate him for leaving, and the last thing he wanted was for the two people who meant the most to him in the world to despise him. That said, they had never believed him when he spoke of his past. Would now be any different?

He resolved not to leave them in this manner. He looked around, and several others were standing about. "Come with me," he said. "Let us speak in my room."

Garit and Ella exchanged unsettled glances, but both nodded their assent. "Lead the way," Ella said, her voice shaky. The tears had stopped, and Tristan believed it more from the cold than emotion.

He led them away from the Low Hall. He turned and looked back and thought about the soldiers inside and realized he was bothered by how they'd regarded him. He pushed the thought from his mind, and soon the three friends were in his room.

Tristan relit his lantern, and Ella walked over to his small fireplace and got to work. She had much better luck than he usually did, and a blaze was going within a few short minutes. "Alright," she said as she knelt by the fire. "Let's have it. What madness makes you think you have to go out there alone?" The shake was still in her voice, and Tristan now recognized this was not caused by sorrow or cold. She was angry.

He sat down on the edge of his bed, and Garit took a place beside Ella on the floor before the flames. "I know you've never believed me," he began, "but this enemy will be fighting with more than swords and spears. They have a dark and terrible magic on their side, and—"

"Tristan," Ella cut in, attempting to keep her voice soft and reassuring, "we've been through this before. The Grey—"

"—is real, Ella," Tristan countered, his voice not quite as soft as she had attempted to make hers. "I'm not the only one who's seen it, either. There are others."

Silence filled the room. His two friends were dark silhouettes between him and the fire, and he could not make out the expressions on their faces, but they appeared uncomfortable by the way they shifted. Garit cleared his throat. "Who else has seen it, Tristan?"

Tristan took a deep breath. Walter had not sworn him to secrecy or silence, but he understood this was knowledge which was not meant to become common. "I was told this in the confidence that it would not get out to the entire city. I know I can trust the two of you, so I will not ask for vows of silence. Just understand that this cannot leave this room." Ella and Garit both nodded.

Tristan leaned in closer, as if to ensure the very walls could not listen in. "Commander Walter was a prisoner in Elinton for three years. He saw it. Hell, he experienced it. They tortured him with it." Ella and Garit turned to one another and exchanged what must have been shocked glances. "He also told me that others reported as much when we first fled here as refugees fifteen years ago. It appears only a handful of us witnessed it firsthand, and we were all shamed or bribed privately to keep it from becoming widespread. The Palace, Temple, and High Hall all agreed the information could—and likely, would—cause a panic."

"It would," said Ella. Her voice was a bit higher than

Edward Patrick

usual. "It scares me to consider it. I know how powerful the White can be when it comes to healing a broken body. If the Grey is as strong in breaking someone—"

"I won't let it come to that," said Tristan. "The army doesn't realize what it faces. They will either go forth ignorant and unprepared, or they will be terrified before they get there if the officers are allowed to tell them about it. They've not had years to consider this. If the knowledge is thrust upon them without warning, fear will conquer them." He shook his head. "Keeping this a secret was a mistake. A grave one, and one whose damage cannot be undone at this late hour."

Garit rose to his feet and began pacing. With his arms folded across his chest, he turned to Tristan. "What's your plan?"

Tristan cleared his throat. "I will travel to Elinton. Alone, I have a chance of sneaking in. I will find a way to kill Jules. Even if I have to wait days or weeks for the opportunity to arise, I will kill him. Without their leader, they may lose heart and run back to Felixandria."

Garit scoffed. "Such an elaborate plan. You're wasted in the auxiliary. We should make you our chief strategist." The sarcasm was thick, and Garit saw by the slump of Tristan's shoulders that his barbs were hitting home. "That's a mighty high hope. What if they don't 'lose heart'? What if you actually succeed and this act of yours forces the war? Or even if you fail, the mere attempt would be enough preamble!"

"If I succeed, they will still be without Jules, and that will be a blow to them. War is coming, Garit—there is no doubting that. It doesn't matter if I go or stay, and it does not matter if I succeed or fail. The war is coming. At worst, nothing changes. At best, I can rob them of their leader."

"You say the inevitable war is the worst which would happen," said Ella. "But you're wrong!" She stood quickly and advanced on Tristan. "What if they kill you?"

He shook his head. "If they kill me, only one man has

124

been lost. My death will be insignificant when compared to the harm Jules' assassination would mean for them. This is well worth the risk."

"And if they don't kill you?" Ella asked with a hint of desperation in her voice. "What if they capture you? Walter was taken and held for three years. I can't bear to think of you being tortured!"

Again, he shook his head. "They'll not capture me—I'll not allow that. I will end my own life before they take me."

She let out a laugh of absurd astonishment. "You hold your life in so little regard? They will either kill you, or you will kill yourself, is that it?"

"Or I will kill Jules. It will be one of those three." The silence swept in once more. Ella had no words, and Garit was considering all Tristan had told them. Tristan let out a deep breath. "I don't ask you to forgive me for leaving. I don't expect you to understand. Not now, at least. I do hope, with time, you will come to accept that this was the only path I could take."

Both of his friends turned to him, and the angle of the firelight revealed enough of their faces for him to see the solemn expressions they wore. Ella's brown eyes and Garit's blue were barely visible to him. "This has been the only path I was ever going to take. Staying here permanently was never an option. Jules took that option away from me fifteen years ago—took everything away. My family. My home." He looked at Ella. "Our home."

Her eyes began to fill with tears, but she turned before any could fall. Even Garit looked as though he was on the verge of crying. "When do you plan to leave?" Garit asked at length.

Tristan bowed his head and stared at his hands resting on his knees. "I'll be making my final preparations tomorrow morning. I'll depart as soon as I am able."

Ella turned and bolted. Tristan rose to give chase, but she was out and down the street, her vanishing form swallowed up in the darkness. He called her name, but it was no use. He was about to follow when Garit stepped out and put a hand on his chest, gently pushing him back. "I'll talk to her, Tristan. You've already got enough on your mind." Tristan balked at this. He could not stand the thought of leaving her in this manner, but he didn't have a choice. If she didn't wish to talk, he'd not be able to force her. "I'm sorry, Tristan."

"Sorry?"

Garit sighed. "That I never believed you. That this is what it took for the truth to finally be made plain." He lowered his hand and held it in place before him. Tristan clasped it, and Garit pulled him into an embrace. "Will I see you tomorrow before you go?"

Tristan shook his head. "Please, no. I don't think I can do this again."

Garit shrugged. "I don't want you to go, my friend, but I won't dare try to stop you."

"Thank you." Tristan had not planned on goodbye, and tears came unbidden to his eyes. He wiped them away, only to find more had taken their place.

Garit pushed away from him. "Travel well, and stay safe, Tristan. May the Helpers watch over you." His voice cracked on these last words as he released Tristan's hand and he, like Ella, disappeared into the night.

Tristan stood a moment in the cold before stepping back into his room to get what little sleep he could. Tomorrow was going to be a long day.

VIII
Companions

Sleep was not easy to come by that night, nor was it restful. Still, Tristan rose before the sun and began to put his room in proper order. Ella's fire from the previous night had burned out, and he had not bothered to rise and keep it going. He stared at the remains and considered starting another but decided against it. The flames would be one more thing to tend, and he was preoccupied enough already.

As he scanned the room, he was struck by how little he owned. Most of the clothing was uniforms. He had some clothes for personal use — some of which were rather nice — but most would not be making the journey.

He decided he would sell what he wasn't taking with him. He'd need provisions and a horse, but he was painfully short on coin. His armor and weapons belonged to Grauberg, so he'd be leaving those behind as well. He was alright with this, but he'd need to buy a new blade.

He sank down to his knees and retrieved a carrying sack from beneath his bed. Into this he sorted his garments, judging what would be suitable for the trip and what should be sold, and he was shocked at how little would be practical for his purposes.

"I never realized how much I took advantage of Grauberg and how well I've been provided for." He spoke the thought aloud and felt a twinge of something in his gut. Was it guilt, or perhaps a sickness at the thought of everything — and everyone — he was leaving behind? He shook his head and began to tuck some of the garments into the sack.

He placed the block of wood on top of the clothing, and he paused a moment to sit and sharpen the dull knife before he did anything else. The chore took little time, and he tucked the blade and its small sheathe into his pack beside the wood. He grabbed his journal but hesitated. He pulled up his small chair and sat down at the table, and he reached for a quill and the ink bottle.

> *This is the last entry I will be making from inside the walls of Grauberg for the foreseeable future, and I'm at a loss for what to say. I did not expect this to happen so suddenly, but perhaps it is for the best. If I'd had the time to think on the matter, would I have doubted my course? No, I think not. My mind has been made up for years, and yet this hurts more than I'd have ever suspected.*
>
> *It isn't the thought of leaving the city so much as the people. Ella. Garit. The soldiers, those I know well, and those who were able to wound me with their gazes last night. I didn't expect that, and I don't know that I can simply shrug it off. It matters little in the end — I leave today.*
>
> *I'm not sure how I'm going to do this, but I must try. For Ella and Garit, and for those soldiers. May Rylar watch and guide me, and may the Helpers help me on my way. I shall certainly need all they can give.*

He let the ink soak into the page and tucked the journal into his pack. He capped the inkwell and stowed it and his quills, as well. Perhaps he'd have opportunity to write on the road. He felt sure his evenings would afford him plenty of spare time.

Last, he retrieved the grey cloak which Jules had left for him. Walter had told him to keep it. "Burn it if you wish," he'd said, "but do with it what you will. Don't leave that damned rag with me, though." Tristan now packed it with the rest of his belongings. This would be the first thing he'd see every time he reached into his pack, a reminder of his hatred for the man he now went to hunt.

As he pulled on his boots, he noted the leather at the toes was beginning to pull loose. He had other pairs, but none suited for the long rides and marches. This would be another expense, and he realized leaving would be more costly than he'd hoped.

He made his bed and arranged his dress uniform and sword on the blanket, and he made sure the rest of his uniforms were in presentable condition. He restacked the small bit of firewood and swept the loose ash back into the fireplace, then he shouldered his pack and tucked his other garments under his arm. He gave the room one last glance and walked out, pulling the door firmly shut behind him.

He made the trek to the main street. Many of the vendors were already setting up their stalls for the day, and the actual shopkeepers were busy inside their own stores. He walked up to one of the shops that he was most familiar with and reached out. The door was still locked. He peeked through the window, but no one could be seen. He moved down a few doors to another shop he had frequented for clothes. The door was open, and he made his way in. "Buy, sale, or trade?" came a voice as soon as he was over the threshold.

About half an hour later, he emerged with a better pair of boots than he'd expected but also less coin than he'd have liked. Still, he'd made a decent amount for the clothes, and that—added to what he was owed for his last month of service—should be enough. This being the case, he walked down the road and to the training grounds for the soldiers.

Some boys were in the yard, drilling in the fundamentals which would build them into the future soldiers of the city. Tristan watched and recalled well his days in their position before turning his attention to the small shack beside the grounds. Inside, he found two men deep in conversation as they sat behind their desks. One of them peered at Tristan and snorted. "Heard you'd tucked tail." The contempt was evident in his tone.

"Is that what you heard?" Tristan asked with a raised eyebrow. "That's news to me."

"Oh?" asked the second man. "Not here for your final pay, then?"

Tristan shrugged. "No, that's why I'm here. Oh, and if you would, send someone to my residence to collect my armor and weapons."

The second man grunted as he got up and walked into a back room. The first man held Tristan's gaze. "Moving out of the city? And what trade will you be taking up? Did Jules scare you enough that you don't care to stand with the likes of us any longer?"

"I'll always stand for the people of Grauberg, my good man. Even the ones who don't know what they're talking about."

The man came to his feet, but at that moment the other clerk emerged with a coin purse. "There's to be none of that in this shack," he said, eyeing his colleague behind the desk as he approached Tristan with the payment. "Your wages for the last month of your service, Tristan. Can't say I understand why you're leaving, but it is what it is. No matter what you do, good luck, lad." He gave Tristan a genuine smile, despite the hint of bitterness in his tone.

"My thanks," said Tristan, taking the coins from the purse and slipping them into his own pouch. "And I'm not bloody running from anything." Neither of the clerks said anything, and Tristan tossed the empty purse on one of the tables. "Good day." He turned and walked away, wondering if all his former comrades had the same thought. He shook his head, wishing it could be otherwise but choosing not to focus on it.

He ventured back to the market and glanced to his left and right, debating whose wares to peruse regarding a new sword. He'd barely begun examining his surroundings when someone called his name. "Tristan! Here, son!" He turned to see Ella's father, Brice, smiling as he waved Tristan over. "You seem like a man in need this morning," he said as Tristan stepped up to his stall. "Might I be of service in any way?"

Tristan smiled. "I appreciate the gesture, sir, but—"

"'Brice.' Must I keep telling you to call me by name?" He smiled as he spoke, and Tristan couldn't help but smile back. "My daughter seemed quite upset when she came home last night." His smile remained, though Tristan could tell it was slightly forced. "She mentioned you, though she'd not go into detail. Anything I should be aware of?"

Tristan considered what to say. He didn't want to leave on bad terms with Ella's parents. They'd had a close relationship since the departure from Elinton, and that was something he treasured. "I'm leaving, Brice," he said bluntly. "I'm going back to Elinton."

Brice's eyebrows rose nearly to his hairline. "Back to Elinton?" Tristan nodded, but he gave no more details. He could see Brice's eyes darting about as he considered this. The man's gaze traced over Tristan. "Well, I can only think of one reason you'd go back, and it sure isn't to join the bastards." He pointed to Tristan's hip. "Where's your sword?"

"No longer mine," Tristan said. "My weapons were property of the state. That's actually what I'm in the market for."

"Walk with me," Brice said, stepping out from behind his stall. "Boy, mind the goods!" A boy of twelve or so stepped up and swallowed hard, but he nodded his head. Tristan gave a puzzled look, but Brice took hold of his elbow and turned him.

"Where are we going?"

"To my home." Tristan tried to slow his step, but Brice pushed him along. "Don't worry, lad. Ella won't be there to attack you. She was up and out before dawn to tend to Order business." Tristan wasn't sure which was worse: the thought of running into her again, or not seeing her at all. He didn't want the previous night to be their final parting. Regardless, he followed along.

There was a numbness growing inside him as he walked down these streets, and he couldn't help but wonder if this would be the last time he'd pass this way. His musings were short lived, as the residence was not a long walk. Brice opened the door and Tristan walked in with him. "Braya? I'm home for a moment with a guest."

Ella's mother entered the room with a perplexed expression on her face. It changed to one of annoyance when she saw who the visitor was. She marched right up to Tristan and put her hands on her hips. "I don't know what you did to upset my daughter last night, young man, but I expect you are here to apologize!" Tristan didn't have a chance to say anything before she went on. "Well, she's not here. Left early this morning. I've seen that girl cry many times—more than I care to try counting—but never like this. Not when we left Elinton, and not even when she's cried over you in the past. Never anything like this!"

"She's cried over me before?"

Braya's eyebrows rose. "Oh, you big oaf, you're not blind or stupid! You know how she feels. Of course, she's cried!" She breathed in deep and let it out slow, her eyes closed as she muttered a prayer to the Helpers under her breath. "So, what did you do this time? She wouldn't say a word—not a single, solitary word!"

"He's leaving, Braya," Brice said.

"Oh, no he's not. Not until he tells me—"

"No," Brice cut in, "I mean he's leaving the city."

Braya turned her head from Brice to Tristan, trying to

make sense of what her husband had just said. Then she narrowed her eyes on Tristan. "Where are you going?" she asked hurriedly, her voice shriller than Tristan had ever heard it.

"Home."

Braya's arms fell to her side and she visibly slumped. Brice hurried over for fear she would faint and helped her into a chair. "Elinton," she said after she'd been sitting for a moment. "And what's waiting for you in Elinton?"

Tristan knelt beside her. He glanced up to meet Brice's eyes and looked back to Braya. "I don't expect anything is waiting for me. I only know Jules is there."

Brice squatted down, and all three were on the same level now. "Tristan, do you understand how crazy this sounds?"

"Aye, I do," he said in response. "And I understand that if I can succeed, it might save thousands of lives." He took in a deep breath, wondering how much he should say. "I'll tell you everything," he said after a moment's reflection. "This may be my last chance, and I want you two to understand why I'm doing this, and—" He swallowed hard and realized tears were building up in his eyes. "And I want you to explain this to Ella when you can, because I did a poor job last night."

He told them about Jules and Vincent and about his revelation that they were the ones who had personally killed his family. They listened as he laid out his logic behind going alone rather than going in with the army. His tone was calm and collected as he spoke, but he wondered if he sounded like a complete lunatic. Brice and Braya hung on his every word and never once stared at him as if he were crazy.

When he was done, he rocked back on his heels and waited for a response. Brice's forehead was wrinkled as he sat in thought. Braya had gone pale, but she was the first to speak. "Tristan, I love you," she said, her voice shaking. She reached out her hand, and Tristan took it. "I don't want you to do this. You make perfect sense, and I'm sorry for what you've learned, but you have to realize this is a one-way journey. You see that, don't you?"

Tristan tried to force a smile, but it was poorly done. "Probably, but I can't help but feel that this is what I have to do."

Brice cleared his throat. "We've known you since you were a small boy, Tristan, but now you're a man — and as a man, I feel like I would do you a disservice by trying to talk you out of doing what you've made up your own mind about."

Tristan's smile became genuine at these words. "Commander Walter said the same."

Brice grunted, stood, and walked out of the room and down the hallway toward his bedchamber. Tristan turned his eyes back to Ella's mother, but the two said nothing while Brice was out of the room. She continued to hold his hand as her tears flowed down her cheeks, and he smiled for her as he sat quietly.

A short time later, Brice returned. He carried a thin, narrow bundle in his hands. He slowly unwrapped it and revealed an old scabbard with a shortsword. He unsheathed it, and Tristan noted a bit of rust about halfway up the blade. "Forgive its state," Brice said, a slight hint of shame in his voice. "I'm not too familiar with weapons or how to maintain them. This was my father's. He gave it to me, but I've never used it. He didn't have me learn how, and several years have passed since it has seen the light of day."

He slid the blade back into its sheathe. "It has no true value that I'm aware of, and it's never seen battle or anything of the sort, and it's done nothing in my care except begin to rust. So, I want you to take it."

He proffered the weapon to Tristan, who reached out and received it with shaky hands. "I have no words, sir."

"'Brice.'"

Tristan smiled. "Thank you, Brice." He looked at each

of them and didn't try to stop the tears which began to flow freely. "Thank you both for everything. I owe the two of you so much — more than I can say."

Braya and Brice approached him and wrapped their arms around him. Braya and Tristan cried openly, and Brice stood with one arm around his wife and one around the young man they'd met all those years ago. After a few moments, Tristan pulled back from them. "I hate this — but I'd best be on my way."

Braya met his eyes, her cheeks wet with tears. "Will you not wait for Ella, at least? She will be back for lunch."

"I can't," Tristan said hastily, though reluctantly. "I made things bad enough last night. I can't — " He struggled for a moment and took a deep, shuddering breath. "I can't go through that again. I can't keep saying goodbye to the people I love, much less having to do so a second time to the one I hold dearest." His voice broke, and Braya dipped her head to hide the new flow of tears. She turned away and buried her face in her husband's shoulder. Brice wrapped both arms around her and regarded Tristan with a gentle expression. "Go then, lad. May the Helpers help you. And — " He swallowed hard as tears threatened at the corners of his eyes. "And know you take our love with you."

Tristan departed, and he was staggered at how emotional the parting had been. He'd not anticipated speaking to Ella's parents, nor had he stopped to consider the depths of his affection for them or theirs for him. He straightened and took a deep breath. Now it was time to clear his mind and press on.

He made his way back to the market and procured a chunk of cheese, a couple of loaves of bread, some salted pork, and a bit of dried beef. He planned on hunting for most of his food along the way, but he'd need the extra supplies. He also purchased several water skins to fill as he went. With this, his pack, and the sword on his hip, he headed towards the stables near the front gate.

The old man running the stable was one Tristan had dealt with for years. He was a retired soldier, and he'd held this post since shortly after Tristan had begun his training. "Morning, sir," Tristan said as he approached.

"Aye, good morning." The man turned and saw who was speaking to him and sniffed. "Heard you left the service."

Tristan stopped a few steps away and braced for the man's contempt. "Aye, I did."

The stablemaster gave him a sidelong glance, but his expression remained blank. "What can I do for you, lad?"

"I find myself in need of a horse," Tristan said as he patted his coin pouch. "Are these all boarded, or do you have any for sale?"

"I do," said the man. "Two, in fact. One is carrying, though. Owner passed away last week, and she was entrusted to me. The second is one of our service mounts. Well, leastways he was. He's getting on in his years, but he should serve you well enough, I suppose."

Tristan scratched his chin as he considered this. "May I see him?"

"Aye, this way." The stablemaster led Tristan to the stalls, and they stopped in front of a horse who appeared to be in great shape, especially considering what the man had just said about his age. "He's set to go up for auction at the end of the month. I'm not supposed to sell him." Tristan tensed, expecting the man to try and wring every coin out of his pouch. "Where are you bound?"

Tristan had not expected the question, and he stammered for a moment. "Camtar Forest," he said after he found his tongue. This wasn't quite a lie, for the forest did stand between Grauberg and Elinton.

"I see. Well, I'm not one to tell someone his business, but I will say that if you're headed in that direction, you need a mount what can care for you. This here fellow can do that."

Tristan reached out and patted the horse's flank. The

animal turned and let his black eyes meet Tristan's stare. "How much?"

"Twelve." Tristan choked. It was only about a third of what the horse was worth. He began to say something, but the stablemaster cut him off. "I won't be haggled with, lad. You've always been good to me, and I like you, but ten is absolutely as low as I'll go, you hear?"

Tristan smiled. "You drive a hard bargain," he said, and the old man winked at him. "What's his name?"

"Traveler," said the stablemaster. "Funny name, seeing as how he was never used anywhere except right here around the city. I suppose he'll finally have a chance to live up to his name at long last now, eh?"

"Aye, I suppose so," Tristan said with a nod. He pulled his pouch open and retrieved a few coins. "I could also use a saddle and a few other things."

"Aye, let's go and get you settled."

The man was not too keen on conversation, but Tristan came to realize over the next few minutes just how fondly he was viewed by the stablemaster. By the time his dealings were done, he'd practically stolen a saddle and blanket, two large saddlebags, and the horse as well. He tried to offer more, but the man wouldn't take it. Still, Tristan left a few coins behind on the man's desk. He didn't suspect he'd have much need for them once he was beyond Grauberg's gates. Grause coins in Elinton would only arouse suspicion.

The morning was drawing near to noon as Tristan packed the last of his belongings into the new saddlebags. He took the reins of Traveler and stroked his new steed's nose. "Well, old fellow, it's you and me now. I'll do my best to take care of you—I only ask that you do the same." The horse nuzzled into his hand, and Tristan smiled. "I'll take that to mean we have a deal, then." He mounted at the gate. The guards on duty did not smile as he approached, but they nodded as he rode through. At last, he was on his way.

He traveled south toward the first small village outside of the city. He would have to pass through a few of these small settlements before he reached the forest. He eased Traveler into a canter, and they made their way along at a decent pace. The horse's movements were familiar to Tristan, and the beast responded perfectly to both rein and touch. It wasn't long before they'd ridden through a second group of homes.

They now passed by fields of green grass on either side of the road. In the distance lay the last few houses, and beyond stood the forest. As he slipped past the small, simple homes, Tristan wondered what the rest of the journey would hold. Multiple routes ran through the forest, some of which wound through and went to small villages.

He had no intention of following these, nor of seeing anyone else until he reached Elinton. He'd be taking the most direct route through the forest: the Treaty Road, which led directly from Grauberg to Elinton. At least, this was what he planned.

As he neared the forest, he became aware of horses approaching from behind. He glanced over his shoulder to find two riders advancing at a trot. He pulled his horse to the side of the lane to let them pass and shielded his eyes against the sun as they drew nearer.

It was almost noon now with no clouds in the sky, and as the riders approached, Tristan made out the figures. His heart began to thunder in his chest as his friends slowed their mounts. "Ella?! Garit?!" His words caught in his throat. Garit grinned at him while Ella remained unreadable. "Why are you here?"

Garit laughed. "Oh, just enjoying a pleasant ride. Nothing more."

"I'm sure," said Tristan. His eyes moved to Ella, whose lips formed a flat line as she stared intently at him. Tristan dismounted and walked toward her. He held out his hand to help her down from her saddle. She hesitated but a moment before she allowed him to take her hand.

As her feet touched the ground, he pulled her into a deep embrace. She was tense as he held her and placed his lips to her ear. "I'm sorry for how we parted," he whispered, and in an instant her tension faded as she wrapped her arms around him. "I'm so sorry."

A silence hung between them for a moment, but she held him tight and buried her face in his shoulder. "I know you are," she said at last. "I know you meant nothing against me by it." She gave him a squeeze before pulling out of his embrace. Tears threatened at the corners of her eyes, but none had yet fallen. "Besides, we're here now."

Tristan gave her a puzzled expression and he shifted his eyes to their horses. Both were laden with travel bags and supplies, as if they were stocked for a long journey. His eyes went wide. "You intend to come with me?!"

Garit hit his forehead with his palm. "Well, you didn't truly believe me when I said we were out for a pleasure ride, now did you? Of course, we're coming with you. Why else would we be out here at the edge of the bloody forest?"

"But—you're deserting?!" Tristan was terrified by the thought. "Garit, if they find you—"

"I obtained permission to come after you, Tristan," Garit said, cutting in before his friend became too anxious. "I met with Commander Walter this morning. We worked it all out, and I was given a leave of absence. He said he'd tell them that he'd become acquainted quite well with me over the last few weeks, and he trusts me as a courier. He's putting the word around that I'm carrying a message to Elinton on Grauberg's behalf. Something about 'hopes to renew talks.' Nonsense, of course, but enough reason to get me out of the city without raising suspicions."

Tristan turned to Ella. "And you? What of your obligations to the Order of the White?"

She motioned to Garit. "He talked Walter into

speaking to the head of the Order. He's requested I go along to make the trip appear more diplomatic, less aggressive."

"Again," said Garit, "mere pretext to get us out. We brought extra provisions too. Looks like you hardly brought anything. We have enough for the journey to Elinton, and some feed for the horses as well, though they'll have to be happy with grass more often than not. I've got some coin so we can stay the night in some decent beds along the way. Surely you weren't planning on spending every night under the trees!"

Tristan threw his head back and laughed. "Actually, I was. I'd fully planned on bypassing all the villages in the forest."

"The nights are cold, Tristan!" Ella said. "Winter is just around the corner, and you can't build fires at the best of times. You'd have been dead in two nights!

"Then I'm glad to have my saviors come to the rescue." He smiled as he said this, even if he was a bit annoyed at the prospect of the trip taking longer now. More worrisome than that, though, was the knowledge that his friends would now have to face the same danger he would. "I suppose we should talk about a few things," he said, his expression becoming more serious.

"Well, let's ride while we talk," said Garit as he gave his horse a pat on the neck.

"Aye," said Tristan. He assisted Ella back on her horse and returned to his own. They turned and made their way toward the forest, and Tristan considered where best to begin. "Did Walter tell you any more of what we discussed?"

Garit shook his head. "No. He recognized my urgency. Told me to ask you about it after we caught you."

Tristan thought back to his conversation with the commander the day before. "The whole thing was a ruse," he said. Both his friends gave him curious glances. "The peace talks, I mean. King Frederic never considered making a treaty with Jules. Commander Walter said the king is wise enough to realize he couldn't trust the man. Assigning the Elinian Guard as the welcoming committee always seemed odd, but I'd figured it to be more of a show of strength rather than a slight against Jules. Turns out, a slight is precisely how it was intended. Also, the feast was deliberately held in the High Hall and not the palace. Meeting the leader of another nation—even a self-proclaimed leader—should have been a matter handled entirely in the palace. Instead, the king met Jules there for only a few minutes before sending him back down a level."

"I'm liking our king more every moment," said Garit.

Ella was more wary. "But why provoke Jules?"

"I don't think they ever believed for a single second that Jules was coming for peace. It isn't in his nature. The king consulted General Arnold and Commanders Walter and Harman, and all agreed this was no more than a pretext for Jules to assess an enemy. So, they opted for a show of strength."

Ella shrugged. "I suppose that does make sense."

"It does," said Garit. "To have offered only hospitality would have encouraged Jules to believe we were desperate for peace, and possibly would have led him to strike all the faster. Seeing Grauberg unafraid may have bought us some time to prepare." They rode on for a few minutes in silence, but after a time, Garit spoke again. "I'd imagine Jules brought some spies with him."

"Commander Walter believed so," said Tristan. "During the tournament, the commanders stationed men around the city. Most of them reported turning back several men of the Elinian contingent who were 'taking in the sights.' Likely they were looking to take advantage of the festivities to search for any weaknesses."

"Sounds like Walter really thought this through," Ella said.

"Aye," replied Tristan. "They all did. I don't believe

anyone thought Jules could be here out of any goodwill, and there can be no doubt he didn't leave with any." They were into the forest now, and the ground was rising and falling as they went. They'd be passing through hilly terrain along the way. If they had followed the road which went straight to Elinton, they'd have had a slightly smoother time of things. "I don't mean to sound ungrateful—I am glad the two of you chased after me, but—"

"You're upset with us for changing your plans on your behalf?" Ella offered. "Tristan, this is just as much our trip now. In fact, we've likely been planning for it longer than you have."

"What do you mean?"

"Well, for one thing, you're not as hard to read as you seem to think," said Garit. "We've known for years that you'd be leaving when you could. Of course, we didn't expect it to be so sudden—and we did not anticipate Jules coming, nor everything which surrounded his presence in the city—but we knew you were going back to Elinton one day, and we knew if we couldn't talk you out of it, we'd have to find a way to come with you."

Tristan said nothing, and they rode forward for a while longer. Their chosen path wound through the trees and around the hills as they went. "I didn't mean for it to be obvious, but I can't say I ever tried to hide it. Still, I didn't think you two would be plotting together to thwart me." He grinned as he spoke.

"We're not here to thwart you, silly," said Ella. She had a strange look on her face. "At least we don't mean to. There's a part of me—a large part of me—that doesn't want you to go. I'm aware of what's there, and it's more than Jules." She met Tristan's eyes. "Your past. Your memories. *Our* memories." His face told her he understood the hurt she felt. She cleared her throat and turned her gaze back to the east. "I also know your heart, and I would never wish to talk you out of pursuing what you feel you must. So, I'm with you." She smiled at him once more. "Besides, if we weren't here, you'd be sleeping on the side of the road, either frozen to death or starved before you arrive anywhere."

They all laughed at this. Tristan shrugged and gave up any hope of talking them into his original plan. "So, what's our destination?"

"There are several small villages in the forest who trade with Grauberg. King Frederic claims them as a part of his realm, but they govern themselves in all but the most severe of matters. Still, they host people from the city from time to time. Mostly hunters, but occasionally other traders, and they also have visitors from the other villages. We'll come across an inn in some of them, or at the least someone willing to take us in for the night."

They rode on for a while after that, discussing provisions and weather. The trip would not be terrible on horses, but the days were still growing colder. After several hours had passed by, they approached one of the small villages Garit had spoken of. For being a 'small' village, it was larger than Tristan would have suspected, with many simple wooden homes and a small trading square. It was set in the middle of a clearing, with a few thin streams of water coursing to the north and south of it.

The few people who were out and about eyed them cautiously as they approached, but they settled down once they realized the travelers were from Grauberg. Tristan soon gathered that the villagers were aware of Jules' traveling party, though they'd not passed this way. The three learned that inns would not, in fact, be found in the forest, despite what Garit may have naively believed. However, more than a few people in the market were willing to board the travelers for the night.

They accepted the hospitality of an elderly couple, and as they were stabling their horses and grabbing some items from their packs, Tristan suddenly had a thought. "What about your parents?" he asked.

"Whose parents?" Garit asked.

"Well, both of you, I suppose."

"What about them?"

"Why, the fact you left the city with no bloody notice, of course!"

"Oh, right. Well, my father is for it," Garit said. "For obvious reasons, I didn't tell him what we were doing, but he's clever enough to realize we're not off to deliver a message. 'That's a load of dung,' he said when I told him. I couldn't just lie to him after that, but neither did I tell him the whole truth. I think he figures we are off as scouts to assess their strength." Tristan was about to turn the question to Ella, but Garit pulled one last item from a long sheath which hung along his horse's flank. "I brought this, as well." He held his family's ancestral spear in his hands. "Thought it would be fitting for the trip."

Tristan nodded his head. "Seems right. After all, it was used in this very forest during the old wars, right?"

Garit's eyes went wide as the realization dawned on him. "You're right! I'd not even thought about that. Why, we must not be more than a few dozen leagues from the old capital, eh?"

Again, Tristan nodded. "Emjaria."

"Don't name it!" Ella's voice was low but sharp. She'd been headed inside the home they were staying at for the night, but she now turned and pinned them both with her eyes. "That is a place of evil. We will do well to stay on this road and go nowhere near it!"

"We'd have to go well out of our way to see it," said Garit. "Besides, nothing lies there but a ruined foundation and a few crumbling structures, I'd imagine—if any still stand at all."

"All the same," began Ella in a measured tone, "we should avoid it—even talking about it."

"Very well," said Tristan. "We need not speak of it again." An uneasy silence followed, and Tristan saw the discomfort in Ella's expression as though the mere mention of the capital of the Grey Empire had upset her deeply. Before he could say anything more, she turned and made her way into the home of their hosts.

Garit had offered them enough for the night that they'd be able to enjoy a nice meal and pleasant company. Still, the three were ready to retire early in the evening, and they found themselves set up in a room with three floor pallets. They laid their bedrolls atop them, and Tristan was thankful that Garit and Ella had insisted on this course. "This beats the thought of sleeping outdoors."

"Aye, just a wee bit," said Garit with a lighthearted chuckle.

Tristan glanced over at Ella, who seemed to be absorbed in thought. "Ella?"

She started at the sound of her name, but quickly regained her composure. "I'm sorry," she said with a faint smile. "Just lost in my head."

"I understand," said Tristan, but then he thought back to earlier. "You never answered me."

"Hm?"

"What did your parents think of your sudden departure?"

She gave no response. Garit began to make some comment about his spear, and Tristan realized that his friend was trying to turn his attention away from Ella's reply. He raised his hand to halt Garit and gave Ella a piercing glare. She met his eyes, but only for a moment. "I couldn't tell them," she said as she turned her face away from him.

"You couldn't tell them?!" Tristan exclaimed, leaping to his feet. "Ella, your mother is going to die of fright! If your father finds out where you are, he's likely to come riding for you himself!"

"Keep your voice down," Ella said, her voice steady. "And don't speak to me as if I'm not a grown woman, able to make my own choices!" She was on her feet now as well, standing before Tristan and looking up into his face with a determination which had not been present a moment before. "I know how much they'll worry and how hard they would have fought to stop me. There's nothing I could have said that would've convinced them that I need to do this!"

"No, Ella, *I* need to do this. This journey is my choice, not something you—"

"Yes, Tristan, it is something I need to do! I can't just sit in Grauberg while you're gone, not knowing if you'll come back. I couldn't even consider that. I understand this is your journey, and that's why it has to be mine, as well!"

Tristan shook his head, confused. "What is that supposed to mean?"

Her face turned a deep shade of red which was noticeable even in the darkened room. "I know I call you an oaf, but if you don't understand what I'm saying to you, then you really are a bloody idiot, Tristan." A few moments passed, and his face changed to one of possible understanding. He held his tongue as he and Ella continued looking into each other's eyes, their expressions unreadable.

"Well," said Garit suddenly, "the hour is late, and we all want to make an early start. I say we all bed down and catch some sleep, eh?"

Tristan and Ella continued to stare, neither knowing what the other was thinking. For Tristan, he wasn't even sure of his own thoughts. After a few moments, he nodded. "Garit's right. We should sleep."

Ella scoffed before she turned and went back to her bedroll. She lay down with her back to them. Tristan and Garit exchanged glances, and then they lay down as well. It had been a good start for the first day, but Tristan wasn't quite sure what to make of the end. He closed his eyes and fell asleep, considering the days ahead and hoping their journey would be a simple one.

IX
Mishandled
Misunderstanding

My friends are with me, and I should be happy about that. Yet I find myself in a foul mood this morning, and I don't know if it's because I'm angry or disappointed or confused or what — I hate it.

Why do I have to feel this way? Why can't I just focus on what I have to do? Why do I struggle so much every time she's around? I know what I am supposed to say and do until she's near, and then I say and do all the wrong things. Helpers, why don't you bloody well help me?

The next morning dawned far sooner than it should have in the eyes of the three companions. They found themselves sore from the previous day's journey. While they were all accustomed to riding, they couldn't say they were used to going for such a long time.

As he considered how much his muscles ached, Tristan wondered if every day would be like this until they reached Elinton. Perhaps his body would adapt quickly. Then again, it might be a nightmare going forth.

He'd gotten up just before the others to write a bit in his journal, but this had been a short entry. He stood with a groan, as did Garit and Ella. He'd slept the full night but was not rested, and he busied himself with tidying up his belongings.

They all began making their preparations to leave, and it became obvious that Ella was doing her best to avoid him. Garit said nothing, not wishing to make the silence any more unpleasant. Ella headed outside with her pack, and a few minutes later, Tristan followed suit. He found her in the stable, talking to her mare. He approached her from behind and tapped her on the shoulder. "Good morning."

"Morning," she muttered, facing away from him. A moment later, she breathed in deep and let out a sigh. "Good morning, Tristan." She turned and gave him a gentle smile, and with that, she'd let the awkward moment pass. He smiled back and nodded. "So, we're fine?" she asked.

"Aye. We're always fine," he said. "At least, I am." She rolled her eyes and punched him in the chest. He laughed as he gave her a small nudge on the shoulder. "So, what's the plan for the day?"

She shrugged. "Well, I think breakfast should come first." He nodded to that, and they walked back to their hosts' home together.

Garit studied them as they came in, and he discerned by the expressions they wore that they had patched things up. "Oh, praise Rylar," he said with an exaggerated sigh. "I thought the day was going to be positively miserable—perhaps the whole damned trip. I'm making a rule now that we all have to get along for the rest of the journey. No matter what." Tristan smiled and Ella shook her head.

The three of them made their way to the common room and were greeted with a warm breakfast by the couple who'd housed them for the night. They enjoyed a vegetable soup and fresh bread, and when they'd said their goodbyes, Garit paid their hosts handsomely. "Thank you," he said as he bowed. "Your hospitality has been most appreciated." The couple bowed back, and Garit made his way to the stables with his own supplies. Once there, they all saddled their mounts and prepared to get underway once more.

"Seeing as how the two of you have taken control of my plans," Tristan began, "what is the plan for the day?"

Garit led them to the path, and they began making their way deeper into the forest. "Well," he began, "I believe we'll head east. At some point, we will need to eat again. Sleep tonight. I'll have to take a leak eventually, and possibly the other one, which—ow!" Ella had thrown the core of an apple at him, and Tristan was laughing. "Don't hurl food at me, my lady! He's the one asking stupid questions!"

Tristan shrugged. "I supposed the path and plan is straightforward enough." The leaves overhead were a brilliant red, with some of the smaller trees taking on a shade of yellow instead. Many had lost a decent amount of their foliage, and the last traces of pink and purple had faded from the dawn sky.

They'd be watching the sun as it rose, and Tristan hoped for a pleasant and leisurely day of riding. "On horses, this should take, what, another three days?"

"Three or four," said Garit, who was now riding on Tristan's left. "If we ride hard, we can certainly get there in three. Should the weather be poor, it may take four or five, but I wouldn't expect the journey to take longer than six or seven in the worst of circumstances. Even on foot, we'd make the trip within a fortnight in the most horrid conditions. The only thing which would take up too much time would be leaving without proper provisions and thinking of sleeping miserably on the cold ground every night." Tristan gave him a sidelong glance, but Garit just shrugged. "Don't look at me like that. You're the one who set out on your epic quest with half a loaf of bread and bad cheese."

"That's not true," said Tristan, his tone light. "The cheese isn't bad."

"Oh, trust us," began Ella as she rode on Tristan's

right, "it was bad. We had to smell you while you slept, and it was not pleasant."

"Then, for your sakes, I'm glad I'd only had a couple of bites yesterday."

"Praise Rylar," Ella said dryly. "Otherwise, we'd be dead already."

The morning passed quickly. The roads here ran from village to village, and it appeared that those who dwelled in the forest maintained them rather well. The three traveled at a decent pace, alternating between brisk trots and walking their horses. There was little reason to push their mounts too hard. "Elinton will be there, no matter how fast or slow we go. Best to let the horses get there comfortably," Ella counseled when Garit asked if they should launch into a full gallop.

"A stablemaster now, are you?" Garit asked playfully.

"No, but I've spent plenty of time helping with her," she responded as she gave her mare a pat on the neck. "Her name is Rose, and I've cared for her since I came to Grauberg. I'll not mistreat her."

Tristan had ridden out with Ella often over the years. He seemed to always end up on a different horse from the soldiers' stables, but Ella had always been with Rose, her beautiful mare. He understood how much the horse meant to her, and he'd supported her view when Garit pressed again a short time later for a gallop. He figured Garit just wanted the thrill of a race more than anything.

The day was pleasantly warm as the sun rose higher in the sky. They came into an open field, and though autumn was edging closer to winter, the grass was healthy and green. Ella suggested they let the horses graze a bit while they prepared a small meal of their own.

They decided against cooking and settled on dried beef, bread, and cheese, and each enjoyed an apple. Ella took an extra one from her pack to share with Rose, and so Tristan did the same with Traveler. Garit was too invested in his own food, and his horse was likewise very focused on the grass.

"I still can't believe the two of you came after me," Tristan said. "And I don't have any idea how to express my gratitude."

"I'm quite certain you've said as much at least a dozen times," said Ella.

"All the same, I'm glad," said Tristan as he lay back in the grass. He gazed up at the clear blue sky and closed his eyes, enjoying the warmth of the sun on his face. "It is far more than I deserve, and I'm ashamed to think you were both so much more prepared for my departure than I was. You planned all along to come with me, but I never expected it of either of you, and it shames me that I had so little faith."

"In us?" asked Ella.

"No," said Tristan. "That I was worthy of having friends who cared so much." He turned to face them. "Thank you for having more faith in me than I had in myself, and for always being there—for being *here*." They smiled at him, and he returned their looks with his characteristic smirk.

"Oh, don't give me that damned look," said Garit with a groan. "I'd have stayed in Grauberg if I'd thought for a moment about having to put up with that smug grin. We're here on serious business, lad. Be stern and somber— like me!"

Ella sighed loudly, and Tristan felt sure that if the day had been any quieter, he'd have been able to hear her rolling her eyes. Then a new sound came to him, and he pressed his ear to the ground. "Riders are coming," he said, sitting up and looking back in the direction they'd traveled from.

"What's that?" asked Garit, drawing still with a half-chewed bite of bread in his mouth.

Tristan stood and faced west. "I heard horses."

Ella turned her head and cupped one ear. "I can't

151

hear anything. Are you certain you—"

Tristan shushed her, and after but a few moments of silence, all three discerned the distinct sound of hooves. "Other travelers?"

Garit shrugged, appearing relatively unconcerned save for a slight narrowing of his eyes. "May be villagers from nearby. I doubt it is of any concern to us."

"Should we make for the trees?" asked Ella, looking around the clearing.

"No time," said Garit. "We've not the time to remount and make for them. If anything, it'd look suspicious. Probably will be best to stay put and see who it is. Besides, they're coming from the west, and we have no enemies in that direction. They're close. We'll see them in a few moments."

His words proved true as the riders appeared a few seconds later. Their garb was dark, and as they neared, Tristan was able to identify the deep blue banner which they flew: these were men of Grauberg. There were four of them, and they wore the colors and attire of the personal guards to the commanders.

"Never seen them so much as leave the High Hall. Where do you think they're going?" Tristan asked as they came down the lane. Before either of his friends had a chance to respond, the men turned and came directly for them, their horses slowing as they left the path and approached. Each rider carried a long spear, as well as a sword on their hips. They came to a stop a few yards away from the group as Tristan and his companions rose to greet them.

"Good day," Tristan said, moving forward. "May we help you?" The riders sat still, offering no reply. Tristan glanced to Ella and Garit, but they shrugged. He searched for words. "We have some food if you need something—"

"What are your names?" the lead rider asked. He sat tall and imposing in the saddle. As he cut off his words, the other three guards began to move around them. They were being surrounded, and Tristan realized it with startling clarity. Something was wrong here.

"I'm Tristan, and these are my comrades, Ella of the Order of the White, and Garit of House Tyon." As he spoke, his eyes scanned from left to right and back again. Ella and Garit moved in closer as the riders encircled them. Tristan understood they'd not done so purposefully, but it played into whatever was happening. They were trapped now. His heart pounded in his chest, and he fought to control his breathing.

"I thought as much," said the guard. "You are free to go, Tristan. My business is not with you." He turned his eyes to the others. "Master Garit, Lady Ella, I'm afraid you two are under arrest. Men, bind them."

"Under arrest!?" The words exploded from Ella. "For what crime?"

The guard's eyes narrowed. "You will learn more when you reach Grauberg," he said, his tone harsh.

Tristan glared at the man. "She has a right to know what crime she's been charged with!"

"No," said the guard. "Only citizens have that right. She is a refugee, as are you. In fact, *you* have no ties to Grauberg at all anymore. I am given to understand that you recently abandoned your brethren, did you not?" Tristan tensed, but the guard continued. "I'll not waste breath on you, coward. The fact is, neither of you may demand anything of me."

"Then what crime am *I* charged with?" shouted Garit, his hands moving to his belt where he had a knife sheathed.

"Keep your hands away from that, lad!" shouted the leader. The other three guards dismounted, and one of them hit Garit in the back of his knee with the butt of his spear. Garit went down to a kneeling position and felt the point in his back. "Garit of House Tyon, you are charged with desertion."

Garit's eyes grew wide. "Desertion?! I'm here on

153

orders from Commander Walter. You know this! You're wearing the livery of his guard!"

"I do not serve Walter," the guard said coolly, his voice full of disdain as he said the name. "I serve Commander Harman."

"All the same," said Tristan, "he has come by leave of Commander Walter. Your orders are in error."

The three guards around them glanced at one another. None said anything, and Tristan could see the leader considering the matter. "What are these orders?"

Garit tried to stand, but the tip of the spear dug into his back a bit harder. He grunted. "The commander dispatched me as a courier to Elinton. He gave me permission to take a horse and a message, and he also gave leave for Ella to accompany me."

The lead guard nodded his head. "So, you have a missive with you?"

Garit inclined his head to one side. "A what?"

The guard peered closely. "A letter—a message of some sort. If you're a courier, you have something to deliver, yes?"

Tristan and Ella both turned to Garit. The word of being sent out as a courier was a ruse by Walter that was meant to quell suspicions, allowing Garit and Ella to easily leave the city. Why had Harman not been told of this? With a sinking suspicion, Tristan recalled the way Harman had always regarded him and the other Elinians—the man did not hide his contempt toward them. Was this truly a matter of his pettiness?

Garit stuttered, struggling to come up with a response. "It was a verbal message for Prince Jules of Elinton," he managed, but even as he said this, his eyes clinched tight. It was a poor story, and everyone standing there knew it. Behind the guards, Ella's mare and the other horses knickered as if they sensed the tension.

"Seize them!" the lead guard commanded, lowering his spear and pointing into their midst. Tristan found himself shoved aside. The guards seemed to think that because he was not under arrest, he was worthy of no further consideration. Tristan realized that though they were elite guards, this type of work was clearly not common for them. If they believed his presence here was of no consequence, they were quite mistaken, but he couldn't face them alone.

"Hold a moment!" Garit said as one of them attempted to force his hands behind his back. "How many deserters do you know who would sit here while you approached and offer you food?" The shaft of a spear hit his back, and he struggled against the guard who tried to wrestle his wrists firmly behind him.

Ella slipped out of the circle and backed away from the lone guard who tried to approach her. He lunged, and she stepped to the side. "I'm not about to stand still and let you take me back without telling me why!" she yelled at the man.

"You will come as commanded!" the man growled at her, frustrated by her defiance. Ella stopped moving and slapped the guard. The sound made every head turn to her. She stood firm with her hands on her hips, almost as if she expected him to respond like a chastised child, just as the Dytan merchants had. The guard tackled her forcefully, smashing his shoulder into her and driving the air from her.

"That's enough," said the leader. "Take them now!" Garit found himself on the ground, his face forced into the dirt as the butt of a spear held the back of his head down. He expected a guard to bind his wrists, but instead he received a kick to the ribs and a stomp to the small of his back. The leader turned to go assist the one guard with Ella while the other two handled Garit. "Hold that wench down!" he shouted as he approached.

Garit struggled to push up against the spear and the foot which was still planted in his back when he heard a loud smack, followed swiftly by another. Both spear and boot were gone, and Garit pushed up to find Tristan wielding a spear—*his* spear. The two guards lay on the ground, one with a split nose and the other pulling a bloody hand from the back of his head.

Tristan tossed Garit's spear to him and unsheathed his sword. He put the point of his blade to the throat of the man with the bloodied face. The leader, halfway to Ella, now turned back to face them. Tristan directed his words toward him. "I say we take the time to talk this out," he began. "You're a reasonable man. I know this seems rather bad, but please, listen to us." He hoped the threat of killing one of his men, coupled with his calm tone, would buy them time to figure a way out of this mess. He was wrong.

"Kill the bastards!" came the reply from the leader. Tristan cursed. His bluff had been called—he had no desire to kill any of these men. He'd served beside them for fifteen years, and he didn't want their blood on his hands over a misunderstanding. He looked down the edge of his sword to the man at his feet and decided to spare him. The man seized the moment and attempted to rise, but Tristan delivered a quick kick to his face. Garit, now armed with his spear, parried attacks from the other guard Tristan had attacked.

Ella still lay on the ground, but she'd gotten her breath back. She held tight to the guard on top of her, preventing him from joining the fight against her friends. The man's spear was pinned beneath her, the shaft digging into her back. Still, she refused to roll off it, lest the man bring it to bear against her or the others.

Suddenly, pain ripped through her neck and shoulder. She shrieked as she turned her head and found the man biting her. Blood trickled from the corners of his mouth as his teeth sank into her flesh. Her cry intensified, and a few moments later her ears were filled with what seemed to be thunder coming from the ground.

"What the hell—" the guard began, releasing her

flesh and glancing up to find Rose bearing down on him. She reared, and her hoof took him in the face. The man fell back, Ella relinquishing her hold on him as her mare moved to protect her.

As the horse came back down on all four legs, she missed Ella by only a few handspans. The beast neighed and the white of her eyes was visible. She ducked her head and bit at the guard who'd been attacking Ella, then reared again and brought her hooves down on his torso. Rose began trampling him, a brutal dance which soon turned from sudden shock to violent horror.

The leader of the guards came at the mare, convinced that she was the most dangerous enemy on the field. The horse paid him no mind at first, but as he came in range, Rose stopped her assault on the downed guard and aimed a kick with her hind legs at her new foe. She bucked, and though she presented a large target, the man could not seem to strike her with his spear. Every time he found solid footing to aim an attack, she reared or bucked or charged or darted away.

Behind them, Garit and Tristan continued to battle the lone soldier who stood against them. Tristan's first foe still lay unconscious on the ground. The standing man backed away, trying to keep Tristan and Garit at bay with his spear. Tristan circled him, and both he and Garit used their footwork to keep him between them.

They took turns lunging, making their foe wear himself out with missed counterattacks. Finally, Garit struck him hard in the ribs with the butt of his spear. The man doubled over and dropped his weapon, and Tristan ran in and drove his forehead into the man's jaw. The guard went down, out cold but still alive.

They turned their attention to Ella, who scooted away from the carnage as her horse and the leader stood against one another. Tristan and Garit began to jog over, but as they closed the distance, the leader's spear hit his target. Rose made a sound that could only be described as a scream.

Tristan could not tell where the spear had pierced her. As the man pulled the weapon back, blood gushed out and Rose turned and bolted. Ella screamed after her, watching Rose gallop into the distance. Behind her, the leader came with his spear raised for a strike. "Ella!" Tristan shouted, realizing he'd never reach her.

The wind whistled above Tristan's head, and he looked up and saw Garit's spear flying through the air. Tristan stumbled, and as he went down, the missile pierced the guard's back. In front of the guard, blood drenched Ella. The man dropped to his face and made as if to reach under his body for the spearhead, but his hands never reached their mark. A mere moment after he'd fallen, he was dead.

Tristan turned and saw Garit's face, pale and stricken. As Tristan surveyed the rest of the scene, the two guards he and Garit had fought were both stirring, though they were not yet up. The horses belonging to the guardsmen had clumped up near the road, and Garit's and Tristan's were out in the field. He searched for Rose, but she was lost to sight. She'd charged into the forest, and her hooves could no longer be heard.

Tristan stood and ran to Ella, who was kneeling and staring at the body of the man in front of her. To his side, the trampled guardsman lay in a puddle of his own blood, his face mangled and his chest caved in. Tristan found himself hoping the man had not suffered long.

"Garit!" Tristan called, seeing the other two men rising. Garit turned, but it made no difference. The guards were not running to them, but rather they moved toward their own horses. Before Tristan even reached Garit, the men mounted and took the reins of the beasts belonging to the two dead guards. They raced back to the road and turned west toward Grauberg. "They'll return," said Garit as Tristan reached him. His voice had a tremble in it. "If others were dispatched behind them, we'll not make it far — not with only two horses for the three of us."

"Let us see to Ella," Tristan said, "and then we can figure out our next move."

Ella stood behind them, her eyes scanning this way and that. They approached her, and she gave them a quick glance. Her gaze was hollow, lacking focus. "What just happened?" she asked, but her words were directed more to the wind than to them. "How did this happen?"

Tristan didn't know what to say. He wrapped his arms around her. "I don't know," he said.

"Traitors," came the voice of Garit beside them. Tristan and Ella turned and found him looking at the guard with the spear lodged in his back — Garit's spear. "They called me a deserter. And now..." He walked over and pulled his weapon free and stared down as blood dripped off the head. "Now I'm a traitor."

He walked away in the same direction that Rose had galloped. Ella tore herself free of Tristan's grasp, rushing off in that direction. In seconds, she passed by Garit, and soon she disappeared into the forest. Tristan watched after them both. Garit stopped, grasped the spear in both hands, and snapped the wooden shaft across his knee. He let both pieces fall to the ground.

Tristan ran up to him, but Garit held up a hand and turned away. "Let me be, please," he said. Tristan sighed, but acquiesced. He trotted toward the forest, hoping to find Ella. Sadly, it was not difficult.

The trail from Rose was a bright red, and after a short time he found Ella squatted beside a puddle of blood and gore. The underbrush was thick here, and he knew they could not pursue the horse through it. Not that it mattered — the size of this puddle made it clear what had happened to the mare. There was no way she could have survived this.

As Tristan approached, Ella turned to him, her face soaked with tears. Their eyes met, and she spun from him and collapsed in a heap, her body spasming with each sob.

The sun was still high above them, but this was a darkness which Tristan had not known since the day his family had been taken from him.

X
Pursued

Camtar Forest should have been easy to navigate. There were many trails, as well as full roads which wound through the trees and led from village to village, but Tristan and his friends had decided to keep off them. They soon found the forest was thick and untamed in many places, with an unforgiving underbrush which made traversing with their remaining horses very difficult. Garit was lagging behind—again.

When they'd prepared to set out, Tristan had essentially been forced to drag him out of the clearing they'd been in. He'd been on the verge of leaving him there when Garit at last rose and came with him. Tristan had left Ella at the edge of the forest. She was still struggling to breathe, but at least she'd regained control of her emotions.

Tristan had walked to the spot where Garit had broken his spear—his family's most precious heirloom—and knelt beside it, still within sight of the Grause soldier his friend had killed. Tristan understood that Garit was no traitor—yet the blood on the spear testified otherwise. This knowledge did little to alleviate the sense of agitation he felt toward Garit. The sun was getting low, they were struggling to find any conceivable path forward, and Garit was doing nothing to help their plight.

Ella was emotionally exhausted and physically drained, yet she took it on herself to take the reins of Garit's horse when it became clear he wasn't fit to guide the animal. When they'd started into the forest once more, the horse had pulled free from Garit's grasp, and Tristan only noticed after they'd walked a fair distance. He'd turned back, only to see Garit falling behind, his mount nowhere in sight.

Had the reins of the beast not become entangled on a branch, it would have quite possibly gone astray. The trio had already lost the provisions in Rose's saddlebags — not to mention the horse itself — and they could scarce afford the catastrophe of forfeiting more of their goods.

"Hold a moment," Tristan said, and Ella acknowledged him with what sounded like a growl. He passed Traveler's reins to her and turned back for Garit. As he neared him, Garit hardly took note. "Garit, we need you to keep pace. We can't move this slow. If we aren't being pursued yet, you know we will be soon." Garit mumbled something under his breath, but Tristan didn't understand him. "What was that?"

"I'm a traitor," his friend repeated a bit louder, but there was no energy in his delivery. He peered up, his gaze hollow and his voice monotone. "I'm a traitor."

Tristan clenched his fists, unsure which urge was strongest: to slap Garit and bring him back to his senses, or punch him on the jaw and sling him over a horse so he'd keep pace better. "Riders on the road," came Ella's voice behind them, her tone urgent but controlled. Tristan grabbed Garit by his collar and drug him forward.

When they were with Ella and the horses once more, he shoved Garit to the ground and took Traveler back in hand. The road was out of sight but well within range of hearing, and the unseen riders passed by at a gallop. "More from Grauberg?" Ella asked.

"Probably," replied Tristan, patting and stroking his horse's neck and hoping he'd not make a sound or sudden movement. Soon, the riders were out of earshot. "We were wise to move away from the road," he said.

"How many do you think pursue us?" Ella asked, an edge of apprehension in her voice.

Tristan shrugged and shook his head. "I've no idea, Ella. I've never seen this sort of problem dealt with before." He surveyed their surroundings. The hours had passed slowly as they'd plodded what he considered to be far too short a distance. Night was falling, and he couldn't see what lay ahead. "We should find somewhere to bed down for the night."

"I think we should keep moving," Ella said.

"We're like to kill ourselves in this thick brush. What if one of the horses goes down on a root and breaks a leg? At best, we lose the horse. At worst, the cries would call those riders down on us. We must move when we can see." He looked down at Garit, who'd not shifted an inch since Tristan had forced him into a sitting position. "Besides, we can't do much with this dead weight." He made no attempt to hide the frustration in his tone, and Garit didn't heed him.

Ella glanced first to Garit, then back to Tristan, her eyes revealing the same aggravation. "Has he said anything?"

Tristan shook his head. "Nothing of note," he muttered. He gripped the reins in his hand and began to turn his horse. "We should move a little deeper while we still have a bit of light. Watch your step, and no fires tonight. We'll simply have to make do."

"No worries," said Ella. "My flint was in Rose's saddlebag." The words were laced with bitterness. "Come," she said, nudging Garit in the ribs with her boot as she turned the horse in her care forward. When they made camp a bit later, she used Garit's sleeping roll. If he was aware, he didn't object.

Tristan woke to the sound of hooves in the distance. He was groggy and not able to get his bearings about him, and he couldn't tell if they came from west or east. By the time he was on his feet and shaking the weariness from his head, they were gone.

The sky overhead was beginning to turn the faint grey of morning, though he couldn't see much for the dense forest. Many of the leaves had fallen, but the branches of the surrounding trees were thick and interwoven, and very little light penetrated here.

As his eyes adjusted, he saw the horses with their heads down. Ella was still sleeping in Garit's bedroll, her blanket gripped tight about her. He took the cloak she'd gifted him and laid it across her for extra warmth. He supposed Garit would also likely need something, but he was still annoyed and in no hurry to help in that regard. Still, he turned to see how his friend was faring, only to find Garit was nowhere to be seen. He'd been left at the trunk of a tree between Tristan and Ella, but the spot was now vacant.

"Garit," Tristan called in as loud a whisper as he was willing to risk. The only response he received were the chirps of a handful of birds overhead, beginning their calls for the day. About a stone's throw away he spotted what may have been a silhouette. He crept forward, and as he approached, he saw that it was indeed Garit, facing the direction from which they'd come. "Garit!" he hissed in a whisper.

Garit turned, the blank stare gone, replaced by an expression of anguish. Tristan knew at once that he'd been crying. "Tristan," he said, lowering his eyes as he turned and walked toward him. Tristan stood still, unsure of what to say or do. "There were four more riders headed east a few minutes ago," Garit said. "There were others in the night, but I'm not entirely certain which way they went. They're looking, though, and they'll start combing through the forest soon." He met Tristan's eyes and opened his mouth to say more but stopped himself and let his gaze fall once more.

"Garit," Tristan began, but he quieted himself, and a long silence passed between them. "Garit," he tried again, "about your spear—"

"No," Garit said quickly. "I don't wish to speak of what happened back there."

"That's not on you, Garit," Tristan said. "You had no choice."

"I could have gone with them. Straightened this mess out when we got to Grauberg and then turned and came back. Sure, we'd have lost some days, but—but no one would have had to lose their life. I wouldn't have had to take one."

Tristan took in a deep breath through his nose and exhaled slowly. "That's easy to say now, when you've had time to think through everything—but they didn't give you that time. Things happened the way they did, and there's nothing to be done now but move forward. You saved Ella, Garit. That's all that matters. If you'd not thrown your spear—"

"That's enough, Tristan," Garit said. "Perhaps I'll come to see it that way, but not now." He took a deep breath of his own. "Now I'm a traitor—an enemy of Grauberg. I've dishonored my house and my father." A sob erupted from him, and he collapsed into Tristan's arms. Tristan lowered him to the ground and sat with him, cradling him as he wept.

After a few minutes, Garit's shaking body became still and his sobbing ceased. Another minute passed, and a gentle snore reached Tristan's ears. Garit had likely not slept at all in the night. Pursuers would soon start searching, and yet he couldn't bring himself to stir his friend back to wakefulness.

It was in this state that Ella found them. "Is he alright?" she asked gently as she gazed down on them.

Tristan shook his head. "No, but he will be, given time."

Ella scoffed. "Time. If only we had that. We might as well go ahead and turn ourselves in if he's not going to be able to march soon. We can't move at his pace."

Tristan nodded. "I think he's moved past that point,

at least. I was frustrated with him, too, but we have to stop and consider what he's going through. He killed a man, Ella—a man who should not have been an enemy. Your Order values life above all else, doesn't it? Surely, you can try to understand what he's going through."

"Oh, you're being a voice of reason?" she said, her tone making it plain that she believed it to be anything but possible.

"You know, Ella, you may not want to admit it, but you have a temper and a stubborn streak that would rival my own." She tensed her jaw, and he could see her grinding her teeth. "I'm not saying it happens near as often with you as it does with me, but you're prone to become lost in your anger and frustrations sometimes. We all do, but we can also lose ourselves in grief or sadness." He let his hand rest on Garit's forehead.

She closed her eyes, took a few moments, and nodded. "You're right." She gave Tristan a weak smile. "I suppose that if I can be as stubborn as you sometimes, then you can occasionally be right." He smirked back at her. She rolled her eyes and made her way back to camp.

Tristan stayed with Garit, listening for the sound of more riders, but no more passed. After a while, he caught the distinct scent of a fire. He wondered how Ella had started one, and he knew he should go and tell her to put it out, but then he distinctly noted the scent of salted pork.

The morning was cool but not cold, and history told him warmer air was on the way. If so, storms may lie ahead. The thought was pushed aside as Garit began to stir in his sleep. "You've not slept long," Tristan said softly.

"No, but that smells too damned good, and I'm too damned hungry," Garit said in a tone which was almost lighthearted, and Tristan knew for certain his friend would be alright. "Think she made any for me?"

"I'm sure she did," Tristan said, though in truth he wasn't sure if she'd made any for either of them.

When they reached camp, Ella was sitting on the ground with a helping of pork and a chunk of bread. The fire was between them, but on their side were two small wooden trenchers, each with bread and meat as well. Tristan and Garit sat and began to eat. There were a few awkward moments at first, but as they sat there, each met the others' eyes. All smiled, Tristan and Garit nodded to Ella in gratitude, and she nodded back. No words were spoken, but Tristan hoped this meant things would be better.

They moved as briskly as they dared for the rest of the day. Knowing the soldiers would be patrolling the roads, the three had elected to move deeper into the forest. Passage was harder, but safety was paramount. They led their horses now, rather than forcing each to carry too heavy a burden in this unknown terrain.

The land rose and fell with rolling hills, and the roots of these trees were thicker. They were spread out, though, and the companions were not impeded as much by undergrowth the further they went. The ground was covered with fallen leaves which would serve well to aid in concealing their tracks.

"We should eat soon," Tristan said after they'd been moving for several hours. A moment later, they crossed over a small footpath, and he frowned as he turned back and realized how it had been marked by the horses' hooves.

"I wouldn't worry too much about that," said Garit. "This isn't one of the true forest roads, and even if the guards do come across them, these paths are well-travelled by the people of Camtar. It's likely a trail that leads to a village." He stopped to consider the thought. "Should we follow it?"

"No," said Tristan. "We can't risk any more villages. We'll camp in the forest tonight. No fire."

"Then you're right, we should probably begin

looking for a suitable place," said Ella. "Not only to eat, but to make camp. We'll lose the light faster than we think. We'll bed down and start as soon as the sun is up."

Tristan and Garit nodded in agreement and continued deeper into the forest. After a time, they found a clump of trees which would serve to keep most of the wind off them during the night. Bright green winter grass was already growing in the area, and the horses were unsaddled and allowed to graze as the three made ready for the evening. Ella watched Tristan as he laid his sword belt aside. "I have a question, but I don't want to sound like an idiot," she said.

"You're in company with Tristan," said Garit. "You'll never sound as ignorant as him. What's your question?"

Ella smiled. "I'd never really thought about it until recently, but—" She bit her bottom lip, considering how best to ask. "Every soldier seems to have a different weapon in Grauberg," she said at length. "In Elinton, they all trained with the same equipment. Even the Felixandrian soldiers who traveled with Jules were outfitted identically."

"An excellent observation," said Garit, taking the mock tone of a scholar. "Why do you feel ignorant asking about it?"

Ella shrugged. "Because I've lived in Grauberg all these years, and never asked—or even noticed—until now."

"Well, I shall be more than glad to educate you," Garit continued. Ella and Tristan both shook their heads and smiled.

"By all means, Philosopher Tyon, proceed," said Tristan, leaning back against the trunk of a tree and enjoying a chunk of bread.

Garit cleared his throat. "Training for the Grause soldier consists of two portions: training to be part of a unit and training as an individual. When we train as a unit, we are armed with spear and shield. We work in unison to form a shield wall, with each man protecting himself and those beside him. The spear is best for this type of warfare as it allows for maximum range and thrust.

"Each soldier, though, is also trained to handle himself in the event he becomes separated from his allies or is assigned a duty in which he doesn't have his unit with him. For this, each soldier is allowed to train with the weapon of his own choosing. The idea is that he should not be forced to defend himself with a spear if he can do it better with a sword or an axe or a hammer."

Ella nodded and turned her eyes to Tristan. "Why have I never seen you with a spear?"

"I've been schooled in its use," Tristan said with his mouth half-full. "But not as extensively as Garit, since I'm not a soldier in the Grause army." He drank some water and noted Ella's eyes were still on him. "I was trained as a harrier, you see."

"What's that mean?" she asked.

"Well, as you know, I was only a mercenary in the employ of the military. I wasn't a part of the main force."

"No, I mean, what's a harrier?"

"Oh. Well, harriers are typically small units—only a handful of soldiers or so. We're trained to stay on the edge of battle if possible. Our job is to dash in and upset the enemy formations. We're not meant to engage them directly, but rather find ways to harass them. This frustrates them, breaks their focus. It—" He was cut off by Ella laughing. He and Garit shot her a look, and she tried to cover her mouth to suppress it, but she succeeded only in laughing harder. "What's so funny?" Tristan asked when she at last stopped to take a breath.

"That's the most perfect thing I've ever heard," she said, struggling with each word.

"What?" asked Garit.

"Tristan's role. He's the most annoying oaf I've ever met, and the military actually trained him to use that in battle. It suits him perfectly!" Garit chuckled, and Tristan found himself laughing as well. Ella wiped tears from her cheeks. "I needed that," she said as she at last gained control of her breathing. She got up and looked to the horses. "I'm going to bring them over and brush them down."

Tristan was glad to see her smile. She was keeping herself busy, and that was also a good sign. He felt there were few things as distracting as caring for something else, and he hoped her tending to the other horses would keep her mind from her own mare. So far, it had been the perfect diversion for her wounded heart.

The shadows of the trees grew longer as the sun neared the western horizon. A couple of birds called out nearby, but most were gone for the year. Not too far in the distance, they heard the flow of running water, as if from a spring or a creek. "I hate to be the voice of reason," Garit said, reluctantly breaking the peace. "We can't do this for much longer. If we walk the entire way, we're going to run out of food quick. We'll need to hunt, which means we'll need fires. We're not using the roads, so the way is going to be more difficult, to say nothing of having to be careful to avoid leaving signs of our passage and hoping we don't come across any of the Grause patrols."

Ella and Tristan both grunted an agreement but said nothing. Garit fell into silence once more, and the three lay there, not sleeping but enjoying the rest. The warmth of the afternoon was now replaced by the cool air of the autumn evening, and Ella sat up and faced the others. "So, what are we to do moving forward?"

Tristan propped himself up on his elbows. "I say we water the horses before we lose the light altogether. After that, we should scout out the area. We need an idea of where we're going, and we need to see if anyone is on our trail."

Ella looked about. "We're surrounded by these small hills. It's going to be difficult to—" She cut herself off and lifted her eyes to the trees. "Have I ever mentioned that I'm an excellent climber?"

Most of the trees had trunks which were too large to climb easily, but Ella was able to make her way up one of the smaller ones. Tristan gasped as she leapt from the upper branches of the tree she was in to the lower limbs of a larger one. "She climbs like a squirrel," Garit said. Before long, she'd reached the top.

Tristan and Garit stood at the base of the trunk and looked up. They were about to call out but were able to make out Ella's hand waving them to silence. The light was quickly fading, and it wasn't long before she was lost to sight. "Should we go ahead and tend to the horses?" Garit asked.

"I suppose," said Tristan. "Might as well clean ourselves up while we're at it." They took some clothes from their packs and went with the horses in the direction of the running water in the distance, which turned out to be a wide creek flowing from north to south. "Must be an offshoot of the Nuum River," Tristan said.

The water was brisk and cold, but the horses drank their fill, and Tristan and Garit took it in turns to watch the mounts and bathe. Tristan also made sure to refill their water skins. The air chilled them as they made their way back in damp clothes to the camp. As they arrived, Ella's dim form was descending the last of the branches.

"Well, I don't believe anyone is on our trail. There was no significant movement I could make out, and we're well off the roads best I can tell. Two villages in the distance—several fires in the windows, smoke from chimneys, but nothing else of note." She turned and pointed north. "Except for that way. Half a league at the most, there's a single fire. It seemed very out of place. Perhaps a hunter?"

"Perhaps," said Garit. "But perhaps not. Soldiers?"

Tristan nodded. "It's worth looking into. Let's go check it out?"

"To what end?" asked Ella. "We're trying to get away from them, not closer. We've done well so far."

"Aye, we have," said Tristan, "but we might be able to do better. I'm not suggesting we stroll in and surrender ourselves. Just a bit of reconnaissance."

Ella was still unsure, but she relented. "I'll stay here with the horses. Follow the base of those hills that are due north and you'll come upon it. I believe they were camped out on one of the forest trails." She bit her bottom lip. "Are you certain this is safe?"

"No," Tristan said truthfully, "but the soldiers aren't woodsmen. They aren't like to be blundering about in the forest at night. We'll have a better chance of discovering them than they do of finding us."

Ella let out a shuddering sigh, and Tristan wasn't sure if it was the night's chill or her nerves. "Be careful," she said. "Nothing reckless."

"Nothing reckless," Garit and Tristan said together.

"Leave me a bow," Ella said after a moment of hesitation.

Garit regarded her curiously. "I didn't know you could shoot."

"I'm decent with it," she muttered.

Tristan laughed. "Don't let her fool you. She's an excellent archer." Even in the dark, Tristan could tell Ella was blushing. She rarely praised her own skill, but he knew how much she liked it when he complimented her. He walked over to Traveler's packs and removed his carefully stowed bow and quiver. "Stay alert," he said as he handed them off to Ella.

She nodded and then sniffed the air. "You took the time to bathe," she said.

"Aye," said Garit. He moved his head in closer and breathed in deep. "You should do the same." She stuck her tongue out at him and lightly punched him in the shoulder. Garit laughed, and he and Tristan made their way north.

The way was uneven, but not too difficult. All about them, the land rose in gentle hills, and the stars were visible overhead. Tristan was not skilled enough to navigate using them, but he'd made a note of where the constellations were in the sky and the direction they needed to go. Ella hadn't been wrong; the path was not quite straight, but it led more or less to the north.

"Do you think they'd rather kill us or capture us?" Garit asked after they'd been walking for several minutes. Tristan shrugged as if he weren't sure, though he had a pretty good idea of the soldiers' intentions. Garit gave voice to the thought running through Tristan's head. "I would imagine they set out with the idea to capture us. Now, I'd wager a spear through my chest would suit them just as well." Tristan grunted an agreement. "I hate this," Garit added. "I wonder how far they'll pursue us."

"Well, they know we won't be trying to return to Grauberg—there's nothing for us there any longer." Garit gave no response, and a moment later Tristan realized the horrible truth of what he'd said. He glanced over to find a wide-eyed expression on Garit's face and immediately regretted his own words. "Garit, I—"

"Nothing to return to," Garit echoed. "My father..." Tristan reached out a hand and placed it on his friend's shoulder. "Tristan, what are we to do after we finish this?" There was desperation in Garit's voice. Tristan struggled to come up with an answer, but the sound of hooves on hard earth interrupted them. He and Garit stopped moving and dropped to their bellies.

Two riders passed over the hill to their left, both bearing torches. Tristan shook his head to himself, knowing the lights were likely hindering the men more than anything by blinding them to the forest around them. The two were garbed as soldiers of Grauberg, and they were moving in the direction of the suspected camp.

They spoke to one another, but Tristan was unable to pick out more than a few snatches of conversation. What little he did gather was that the men were hungry and on their way to a meal. After a few moments, they were out of earshot, and their torches disappeared over the crest of the next hill. Tristan rose to his feet. "Come," he said, "and we'll figure the rest out later." Garit gave him a pensive look but nodded and stood.

The distance had been shorter than Ella had believed. Half an hour after they'd left her, Tristan and Garit smelled meat over a fire. A few minutes later, they could overhear bits of talk. At last, they saw the flames, mostly concealed in a small circle of trees. This wasn't a small camp with two or three guards as Tristan had assumed it would be, but rather the base for the entire party which had been sent out against them.

Once they had the camp in sight, Tristan and Garit paused long enough to calm their nerves and their breathing. They both took a drink of water and waited to let their hearts slow. After several minutes, they went down on their bellies and crawled as close as they dared, concealing themselves in the darkness beyond the reach of the fire's light.

The soldiers were not being as careful as they should have been, talking loudly and laughing. It was not shocking that the bulk of their conversation revolved around the pursuit, but the unmitigated hatred these men had toward the three for the death of the comrades was unnerving.

"I'm telling you, they're lost. Rylar alone knows when they'll emerge—if they ever emerge at all." This from a soldier who stood off to the side of the fire, his mouth half-full of food. His tone was harsh, and Tristan couldn't tell if he was pleased that he believed his quarry was lost in the forest or upset that he might not find them.

"We weren't ordered to chase them into the forest and leave them be," said another, a soldier with a deeper voice. He was sitting by the fire, his face illuminated by the flames. "We were ordered to find them, and we'll not be returning until we've done that." The man reached down and picked up a cup and took a long drink. "Besides, the filthy bastards killed two of our brothers. I won't hear any more talk of leaving them to the forest. Am I understood?" The first man appeared annoyed, but he bowed his head in deference, and Tristan and Garit realized the man sitting by the fire was the commanding officer.

"We don't have the provisions to search much longer," said another soldier.

"If need be, we can always send two or three back," the officer said. "Or we can get what we need from the villages. We have ten men out here. We can spare a couple." He stood and tossed the last bit of his drink into the fire, which blazed up momentarily. "We'll hound these traitors all the way to Elinton if we must, but I'll not be satisfied with that. Dead or alive, I fully intend to bring them back to the commander!"

The other soldiers grunted in approval of this, including the man who'd initially wanted to leave their quarry behind. Tristan counted six of them and wondered where the other four might be. He didn't have to wait long. Horses approached from the east, and the six men who were gathered around the fire stood and drew their blades. As the riders neared, they revealed themselves to be the other four. They were riding hard and fast, and Tristan wondered what had them in such a hurry on the dark paths.

"We can go no farther east," said one of them as he pulled up hard. "Trouble ahead!"

"Our traitors?" asked the officer.

The men on horseback all shook their heads. "Prince Jules," said the one who'd first spoken. At the mention of that name, the rest of the men appeared to catch their breath and stand a bit straighter. In the grass, Tristan crawled closer. "We spotted some of their party in the distance. They were moving in the direction of the old capital." The man said these words with a dread which Tristan didn't quite understand, but the other soldiers—and even Garit—seemed uncomfortable at the mention of the place. "It would seem he's not moving straight for Elinton. We went no farther, lest we risk an encounter with them." The men around the fire cursed, and the riders could not hide how unsettled they were. "Sir, what should we do?"

One of the other riders moved forward, and as he neared the light, Tristan recognized this was no soldier, but a healer of the Order of the White. His name was Bartram, and he'd often helped with injuries following training. His hood was thrown back, revealing a thin, clean-shaven face, and his voice was stern as he spoke. "If I may, sir?" The officer nodded to him. "There is a power which lies in those ruins. What it is exactly, I cannot say. It's spoken of in the greatest of secrecy in my order, and I am unsure of its nature. Only a few vague prophecies exist in the teachings of Rylar, but whatever it is, we are always warned to stay clear of the ruins in the sternest of ways. I pray I'm not breaking my vows to the Order in saying this much, but I feel compelled to say that—ghost stories though they may be—I would strongly urge we go no closer to that cursed place." The conviction in his voice was nearly enough to mask his fear, but Tristan noted the tremble in Bartram's voice. How could one be afraid of something so shrouded in mystery?

The officer nodded to these words and looked down as his men stared hard at him. "Not only that, but we can't risk a skirmish. It's the sort of thing that could start a war, and I can't imagine the commanders or the general would be too pleased if that were to happen before they're ready." He took a few steps away from the fire and began pacing. The mood of the camp was uneasy, and Tristan could practically feel the tension.

Finally, the officer stopped and turned back to his men. He looked each in the eyes, and then settled his gaze on the man who'd proposed leaving Tristan and the others to fend for themselves in the forest. "Bloody hell," he began, then he spat in the fire and growled as if he were disgusted with himself. "They were pursued into the forest, and we were unable to find their trail. Then, we encountered Prince Jules' retinue and were forced back." He looked up, and the camp remained silent as he laid it out for them. "We're not waiting for the morning—it wouldn't do for Jules' scouts to backtrack and find us here. How far to the road for Emjaria?"

"Perhaps a league," said the man on horseback.

"Shite! That's too bloody close!" He glanced around at the camp and nodded to himself. "Right. Break camp and mount up. Back to Grauberg!"

The words were barely out of his mouth before every soldier was busy. Tristan and Garit were impressed with how efficient they were, especially considering these were not men who were used to work in the field. In a matter of minutes, everything was stowed away, the fire was snuffed out, and nine Grause soldiers in the livery of the commander's personal troops and one white mage were riding for home.

After they were out of view, Tristan and Garit rose and walked to the site. They found a few discarded items here and there, and one pack with some loaves of bread. Garit picked it up and prepared to move back into the forest when he spotted Tristan staring down the trail, facing the east. "Come on," Garit called. "It's past time we got back to Ella."

"Jules isn't in Elinton," Tristan said, not turning his eyes away from the road. "This is our chance—we can take him unaware here, in the forest!"

Garit stared in the same direction and shuddered as he considered where they might have to go. "That may be, but we must return for Ella first."

"Aye, you're right," Tristan agreed. He turned and began making his way back to their own camp with Garit.

"Let's get some rest, my friend. Tomorrow is going to be a busy day."

XI
The Old Capital

The Helpers smile on us! We need not travel all the way to Elinton to accomplish our goal. Jules has travelled to Emjaria, and we shall follow.

I'd be lying if I said the very name of that ancient city doesn't fill me with dread, though it seems to affect Garit and others even more. There's a reason why it's been forsaken: it's named for the Cursed Helper, after all, but there is no reason for this to be a curse on us. My hope is that Jules will be the only one to carry a curse away from the ruins, and I pray I'm the one who delivers it.

After we have concluded our business with Jules, I plan on returning to Elinton. If Rylar is willing, we will enter triumphant, our foe already vanquished. Tomorrow, we make our plans.

"Absolutely not." Ella had not wanted to hear another word of Tristan's thoughts once Emjaria was mentioned. "There is nothing you can say that will convince me to go toward those ruins."

"What's the threat?" Tristan asked, and Garit waited for her response as well. Ella pursed her lips, but she gave no reply. Tristan persisted. "You wouldn't speak of it last night, and you'll not speak now. If I'm walking into danger, I would like to know what it is."

"I told you, I'm not going," Ella repeated, her voice sterner.

Tristan nodded. "I know, and I'm not asking you to. Still, I'm going, and I'd like to understand what I'm facing."

Ella's eyes opened wide. "You'd leave me behind?"

Tristan shook his head. "Not by choice, but I can't force you to go." She gave him a wounded look, as if to say he was betraying her, and he struggled to suppress a growl. "Ella, now you're being silly. You're acting like I'm stabbing you in the back. Need I remind you that I left Grauberg to kill Jules, not to have a pleasure stroll with you? I'm sorry if you're not comfortable with it—I'm not either, truth be told—but I'm not here for comfort. I'm here to put a blade between his ribs."

Ella closed her eyes and took in a deep breath to center herself as a silence stretched out between them. Garit shifted his gaze from one to the other and turned back to the last of his breakfast. Tristan stood in front of Ella, unsure of what to say or not say.

After several tense moments, Ella let out a slow sigh and met Tristan's eyes. Her expression was calmer, though still uneasy. "I can't say for certain what they're up to, but I was always ardently instructed to stay as far away from that place as possible. There are secrets, buried deep." Tristan began to interrupt, but she held up her hand to cut him off. Garit listened intently once more. "Let me finish. No, I will not speak of what these secrets are. I made vows to the Order, and I'll not easily break them. But something evil lurks there, even without Jules being present. It may be nothing more than a superstition, but I don't want to go, Tristan. The mere thought scares me."

Tristan nodded and reached out, placing his hand on her shoulder. "I won't ask you to go, Ella. But I feel like I have to. I'll not ask you to break your promises, if you can only tell me this: if I go, am I in danger? Aside from Jules and his party, that is."

Ella's eyes exposed her fear, but she turned his question over in her head. "I don't believe so. If the stories are true, they hold no direct threat to you or Garit—so far as I can tell."

Garit stood once more. "Does that mean the danger is for you? Is it because of the White?"

Ella said nothing, and Tristan knew Garit had hit close to the mark. "We'll ask no more for now." He turned and peered at Garit as he said this, who nodded in agreement, and moved his eyes back to Ella. "We'll keep camp here. This is near enough to Emjaria for us to move in, and far enough away that scouts shouldn't venture here."

"That struck me as odd," Garit said. Tristan and Ella turned to him as he came back beside them. "Last night, the Grause soldiers sounded as though they'd ridden right up on them. Jules should have had lookouts posted. How did the commander's men reach them undetected? I know he has no reason to suspect attack, but still—I'd expect him to have men posted. He strikes me as the kind who'd sleep with one eye open."

"He was most likely trusting that they wouldn't come near Emjaria for fear of the ruins," Ella offered.

"That's absurd!" Tristan said.

"You think so?" she asked. She moved her eyes from Garit to Tristan, and back again. "It worked, did it not? The men realized where Jules was, and they fled. Don't think it was all because of fear of Jules. It was as much because of *where* he is as *who* he is, I can assure you."

Tristan turned this over in his head as he surveyed their belongings in the camp. "Garit, you're coming with me?" His friend nodded without hesitation. "We'll have to decide what to take with us, then." He swung his eyes back to Ella. "You're comfortable staying behind and watching over the horses?"

"No," Ella said. "I'll be coming with you. The horses will be fine on their own for a while."

"But," Tristan began, more confused than ever, "you're against the idea! You're scared of the damned place!"

"Aye, but I didn't come along just to stay behind when you need me, Tristan."

He fought back a smile. "You're maddening, you know?"

"You've no room to talk," Ella and Garit said in unison. They both laughed, but Tristan did not. "Come on, Tristan," Garit began. "We can use her help. Weren't you the one talking about how good she is with a bow? It'll be nice to have her present to watch our backs."

Ella's eyes widened, and Tristan knew the possibility of killing someone had never entered her mind. She shook her head and opened her mouth, but it took her a few moments to find the words to say. "I don't think I could do that—take a life."

Tristan regarded her with pity, but Garit laughed and scoffed. "You don't think you can kill, and yet you've come along on a journey where our sole purpose is assassination?"

"Aye, because my friend needed me," she said. Her voice was defiant, but her eyes were downcast. "That's all that mattered. He needed me, and so I came to him."

Tristan studied her, but she'd not so much as glance his way. He was thinking of what he could possibly say in response when Garit continued. "You're telling me you wouldn't take a shot at the man who put your home to the sword?"

She gave a tiny shrug. "Garit, my life has been devoted to the training of how to save lives and heal hurts. If the Grey does indeed exist, then it is born of hatred, but the White is born of love. I realize I'm snappy and I lose my temper, but I don't think I have the ability to truly hate anyone."

"Not even the man who took your grandparents away from you?"

Ella dipped her chin even more, and Tristan couldn't tell if she was weary of the questions or ashamed of her answers. "That's enough," he said. "If Ella does not wish to kill—or even to hate—then we should hold that as precious. This is who she is, and it's a quality to be protected if possible." At this, Ella lifted her eyes and gave him an expression of gratitude. Tristan went on. "I hate Jules with all my being. I hate him so much that I don't have it in me to give love to anyone. As much as I want him dead with my blade through his heart, I'd rather have peace and not harbor this hatred."

Garit grunted, and then he reached over to what had been Tristan's trencher and took a leftover bite of cheese. "Well, we'd all love peace, but that's not what's looming over us, now is it?"

Tristan's expression darkened, and Ella felt pity for him as she sensed him yielding to his darkness. "No," he said. "And so, I will continue to hate."

A moment passed which threatened to become an awkward silence. "Well, I regret breaking up the cheerful conversation," Garit began, "but since we are all in agreement that the only way forward is through Emjaria, we should figure out what we need to do."

The tension was broken, and Tristan and Ella relaxed a bit as they rejoined Garit. "Aye," they said in unison. After that, the remainder of the day was surprisingly relaxing. All agreed that no true plan could be made without gathering information, and scouting would be best done after the sun had set, and so the time passed in relative peace. Tristan and Garit went hunting, only to return to camp empty-handed. Ella, in the meantime, managed to bring down a small buck while in the middle of sorting their meager supplies. "Great! You'll be able to feed us as we go along," Garit said with a mouthful of the bounty.

Ella laughed. "I'm glad to know I'll be able to care for myself." Though she said this with a smile, Tristan nodded in heartfelt agreement. It reassured him to discover how capable Ella was. He and Garit had received plenty of survival training, but this was all new for Ella. She adapted well, and she was smart, and that would take her far in a lot of potentially rough situations. He squirmed at the thought, hoping they'd encounter nothing worse than what they'd already seen.

"Sun will be down soon," Garit said, breaking Tristan out of his thoughts. "I think we should start making our way while we have the light. By the time we arrive, it should be dark enough to cover most of our movements." The mood became solemn once more, but they were not robbed of their resolve.

Tristan finished his meal as Ella moved away to the horses. "I'm going to tie them, but loosely. There's plenty of grass about, and if something happens and we don't come back, they'll free themselves easy enough. Perhaps the suggestion of being tied up will keep them from wandering."

"Hopefully," said Tristan. They really had no other choice. He walked over to one of his packs, and the first thing he saw was the grey cloak which had been left in his room by Jules. He scratched his chin as he inspected it. "This might actually be useful now," he said. Garit and Ella watched as he took the garment out and held it up for them to see. "Should I take it?"

"I don't see what it would hurt," said Garit as his eyes narrowed on the garment. "Why do you have that?" Tristan realized he'd not told Garit about the cloak, and he did so now. When he finished, Garit stared in disbelief. "For him to think you'd actually consider it..."

"Commander Walter believes he did so to get under my skin," Tristan confided. "Said it was likely his way of torturing my mind from afar. He says the prince is full of hate."

"Seems more like pettiness to me," Ella said. She'd shouldered the bow Tristan had given her and hung a quiver of arrows from her hip. Garit gave her a raised eyebrow, and she placed her hands on her hips and returned his stare. "I said I don't think I can kill anyone, but that doesn't mean I'm going into danger empty-handed. I'm kind-hearted, not an idiot."

Garit smiled. "Can't argue with that. So, shall we?" At that moment, a faint roll of thunder sounded in the distance. All three glanced up and noted the darkening clouds. "Well, that just makes things far more cheerful, now doesn't it?"

"The rain will aid our approach," Tristan said flatly. He rolled the grey cloak and tucked it under his arm. "Let's be about it, then." Ella and Garit nodded, and all began moving toward the east.

Half an hour passed before the rain began to fall. The three pulled their hoods up as they pressed forward. The way was mostly flat, and the trees they were now passing had grown large. They navigated through a bit of undergrowth, and the rainfall became heavier.

"We'll be soaked to our bones before long," Garit grumbled. Ella grunted in agreement, but Tristan kept his eyes on the path. For him, the rain was nothing more than an inconvenience. The only thing which mattered now was the task. He raised his eyes and peered ahead. "There," he said, pointing to a stone structure in the distance. "What is it?"

"The beginning of the ruins of Emjaria," said Ella. Her voice trembled, and Tristan wondered if it was the fear of the place or the cold of the rain. "We should be on our guard." She let her bow slide from her shoulder and noted the water running down the string. "Should I—"

"Leave it strung," Garit whispered. He squatted down as he spoke, and Tristan and Ella did likewise. "A torch, just beyond the ruin. And there, a soldier." Tristan spotted them at the same time. A man with a long spear marched along a perimeter which Tristan and his friends could not see, and behind him came a second man bearing the flame. Garit leaned in close to Ella. "Leave your bow strung," he repeated, "and have an arrow at the ready. Stay vigilant."

"Aye," she said. A shiver ran down her spine, and Tristan turned to her. "I'm alright," she said.

"I know," he said. "And you're nervous, too. So am I, and so is Garit. Breathe—that's the key. Don't focus on the soldiers, but on yourself. You can handle this." They stayed where they were for several more moments. After a time, the two guards turned and began to walk in the opposite direction. "With me," said Tristan, and they quietly advanced toward the crumbling building. It appeared to have once been a small one-room structure. The roof had collapsed, but they moved in and against one of the walls. This provided some small amount of relief from the rain, which now angled in as the wind began to pick up. "We may have quite the storm to contend with," Tristan said as they settled down.

"Yes, but so do they," Garit added. He pressed against the opposite wall, enduring the rain and looking out of what had once been a window. "The storm is getting worse. What's our next move?"

"Divide and gather information," Tristan answered. Worry was clear in Ella's eyes and he reached out a hand to reassure her. "Don't fret, Ella. I'll not be sending you into the city alone." He rubbed her shoulder as he spoke, and she gave him a faint smile in return. "I think the two of you should observe from a distance. Ella, you stay near to Garit. As you move in, watch for anything and everything. Sentry numbers, their movements. Structures, the people—what are they doing, why they're doing it—anything at all, make a note of it. Remain alert, and don't get too close."

"And what are you going to do?" Garit asked, looking over his shoulder as the rain dripped from the hood over his face.

Tristan smirked. "I'll move in among them."

Ella nearly choked, but Garit shook his head. "Tristan," Ella began, "are you certain that's wise?"

"Not at all," Tristan said, "but we need information, and I have this cloak. With this, I can move in close."

Ella glanced to Garit, who shrugged. "He's right, Ella. Our options are limited."

Tristan placed his finger under Ella's chin and nudged her to meet his eyes. "Don't worry. I'll not do anything rash."

She laughed and covered her mouth to silence herself. "The least reassuring thing you could have done is try to reassure me." She shook her head and reached up, putting her hands on top of Tristan's. "Please be careful."

"And remember why we're here," Garit added. "We are here to gather information tonight, not to act. We're not sure what's going on here, and until we are, we learn. Then we plan. Aye?"

"Aye," Tristan replied. He still smiled, but his tone sobered. "No matter how good the opportunity appears, I'll not act. That goes for the two of you as well, though. No one gets careless tonight, eh?" Ella and Garit both nodded. She let her hands slide off Tristan's, and he stood. "What do you see, Garit?"

"A few torches here and there, but I can't make out what lies ahead." He wiped the water from his face and turned to the others. "I think I keep catching something bright in the distance, but it's hard to tell in this downpour."

Tristan placed his hands on his hips as he considered what to do. "I'll move in. Alone, I should be able to stick to the shadows and avoid the patrols. I want the two of you to go in shortly after, but be careful."

"And you stay safe," Garit said in return. Tristan unrolled the cloak and slid into it. He turned back to Ella, and they nodded to one another. Then he moved out of the structure and soon faded from Garit's sight. "Helpers, help us — the crazy lad's gone in alone."

"Helpers, help him," Ella said.

Tristan passed in the rain, unseen and unheard. Trees and rubble aided him in his approach. The forest became less imposing as he moved forward, giving way to more ruins of what had once been the chief city on the continent of Camtar.

Some of the buildings had fallen into disrepair with time, while others had been destroyed in battle. Many had been completely razed to the ground. In places where a structure had clearly existed, not a single stone remained. Tristan thought about this as he passed from shadow to shadow, and he wondered what they had housed that necessitated such hatred. It had not been enough to bring them down; they'd been obliterated from history.

Now and again, he saw the strange rays of light in the distance which Garit had spoken of, but they'd vanish again moments later. It was as if a great lamp were being exposed and hidden. People milled about, but their numbers were too few to be the whole of Jules' party. Where was everyone else? Had some of them gone on to Elinton and only a portion was here in Emjaria's ruins? If that were the case, then which group was Jules with? Tristan wasn't sure, and so he moved closer to find out.

Another patrol passed, and he spied nearby members of the party who appeared not to be guards. Their cloaks were the same as the one he now wore, and they moved about as though they were simply on a stroll in the rain.

He stayed to the shadows as he continued forward and witnessed more people as he went. Most lingered near the ruined buildings, and they were not all guards. Beyond them, the bright light appeared once more, and now he realized it seemed to come from within the very earth. A sound of grinding stone marked its appearance and disappearance. A couple of the people turned their heads to the light, but none seemed surprised or confused about its presence.

Tristan decided the time had come for a risk. He wasn't going to gather any information from here, and so he moved from the shadows. As he revealed himself, no one seemed to take notice. A guard passed by and gave him a cursory nod but never once stopped in his movements.

As he made his way toward where the light had appeared, a blast from a horn filled the air. He stood as still as stone, hoping he'd not been caught. All around, those who were sitting or milling about in the rain began to walk in the same direction as him. He breathed a sigh of relief as he realized they were moving *with* him, not *toward* him. He fell in with the group, wondering where they were destined and what he would find.

A number of guards stood as a barrier. As the group approached, the guards moved to the left and the right, and between them stood two small stone posts. The people filed in, as if they planned to walk between the posts. Confused, Tristan continued on his way. A moment later, his ears were filled once more with the sound of grinding stone.

The stones between the posts gave way, revealing a stairway which led into a pit of light. The glow of a thousand torches nearly blinded Tristan as he reached the stairs and moved down with everyone else. His jaw would have dropped if he'd not been so focused on keeping his response to himself.

The city above may have been reduced to rubble, but here was a chamber of gold, untouched by time or destruction. This was no simple cavern, but an inverted pyramid. Tristan estimated that from the ceiling to the bottom was no less than a hundred and fifty meters. Every surface was golden, from the sconces in the walls to the stairs on which he walked. The light of the torches reflected brilliantly, allowing the few flames to blaze as bright as the sun.

There were no structures to be seen on the way down, but an immense building was erected at the bottom. It was built in the fashion of a great catacomb, and Tristan tried to think back on his history lessons as to who might be buried here. No one came to mind, and he turned his thoughts away to other concerns.

The group moved down, wet grey cloaks dripping as they went, and Tristan noted that many others were already inside. Seeing the assembled group, Tristan now believed this was indeed the entire party that had traveled with Jules from Elinton, renewing his hopes that his target would be present.

The walls of the pyramid were not smooth, but stepped, cut in deep layers as if they were steps for a race of giants, and a narrow stairway was cut into the middle of this side which descended to the bottom. The people moved away from the stairway to the left and right, using the shape of the structure like a theater.

They sat, facing forward and waiting for something. Tristan, likewise, moved to his right. He sat near a few others—close enough to not appear isolated, but far enough away as to not draw their attention. As everyone settled, some of the assembly began to talk. Tristan turned his head to hear all he could.

"How many more nights of this are we going to be forced to endure?" asked a young woman. This drew gasps from the two who sat with her. "Oh, don't give me that! You're just as bored as I am!"

"Hush now!" came the voice of another woman. She sounded older. "This isn't so bad. Look at this place! Have you ever seen the like?"

"It's a golden hole, Mother," said the young woman once more. "Gold or dirt, a hole is a hole."

"Guard your tongue," said the other figure, a man with a deep and commanding voice. "This is no mere hole, but sacred ground for the Felixandrians, and you know it. You're more familiar with their ways than our own. I'm almost jealous of that, truth be told. Now, if you've nothing constructive to say, keep your lips sealed and your eyes and ears open. See what you can learn when the regent speaks."

The young woman sighed. "I'm sorry, Father. I don't mean to be disrespectful. You're right, I know what this place is. But—" and here she gave him a pleading expression to make him understand she wasn't merely complaining, "I don't know why we are staying here is all. They're dead. They were never even alive. They're not gods or helpers worthy of worship. I just don't understand what the regent hopes to accomplish here."

The father shrugged. "Then wait and have patience, my girl. We will learn soon enough, I'm sure."

Tristan pulled his hood down lower, hoping to conceal the expression he knew must be visible on his face. This family was not Felixandrian, but Elinian. These were *his* people! How could this father and mother encourage their daughter to sit and learn about the culture of their conquerors?

He felt disgusted and confused. The terrifying thought entered his head that this might not be rare—how many of his people in Elinton felt this way? He clasped his hands in front of him, fighting hard against the anger that rose inside.

Footsteps descended from the entrance above, and Tristan glanced over his shoulder. Jules approached, with Vincent and several guards at his side. Slowly, so as to draw no attention, he turned his face back forward.

Just in time, he realized everyone else had risen to their feet and bowed their heads. He did likewise, a bit delayed but not enough to draw scrutiny, or so he hoped. The footsteps drew nearer, and his heart pounded faster and faster in his chest. Then the men passed him by, and he let out his breath. He'd not been caught, and now he was closer than he'd ever dreamed he'd be.

He had sworn to Ella and Garit not to act, but this

opportunity was too good to pass up—or was it? He took a moment to consider. He stood surrounded by enemies in an underground temple with only one exit. He stayed his hand and remained in place. Jules moved in a deliberate manner, but he reached a point about halfway down the stairs and stopped as he turned to face his followers. With a wave of his hand, he acknowledged the gathering. Everyone took their seat, Tristan among them.

"My people," began Jules, "we now sit in the very midst of what should have been the supreme act of the true chief of the Helpers. It was here that Emjar was to give his greatest gift to the world: life. A race of people made for his own delight. The other Helpers had been given this chance to create life, and yet when he made so bold as to do so, he was cast out." His tone was as harsh as ever, and Tristan wondered what he'd found himself mixed up in.

Jules motioned to the bottom of the structure with an outstretched hand. "Emjar was attacked, and his gift lies there, entombed—the Children of Emjar. His only lasting legacy is the one which we carry: the Grey. Those devoted to Emjar have spent years trying to solve the riddle of how to grant life to those he created. 'Only an offering of Death and Life will wake them,' it is said. And for years, we have been looking at it wrong. I believe, at last, we have the answer to the riddle!"

Murmurs sounded all about, and a few people began to applaud, but the act seemed out of place in this setting. After a few moments, all quieted and Jules raised his left hand, palm facing outward. With his right hand he revealed a knife. He drew the blade across his palm, and bright red blood ran down his hand and arm, dripping onto the golden stairs on which he stood. "For years, we believed the offering to be blood. The essence of blood is that it holds the key to life and death, both. And so, we have made sacrifice after sacrifice.

"Our forefathers slaughtered cattle. Later, we turned

to the sacrificing of people. At first, they were volunteers, those loyal to the teachings of the Grey. Later, we spilled the blood of prisoners. None of this mattered. Nothing yielded results. So much death and misery to our own people."

He clenched his left hand into a bloody fist as he brought it back to his side. He lifted his head and smiled, tucking the knife back beneath his robe. "No more. I firmly believe we have discovered the missing piece of the puzzle. Death and Life: the Grey and the White exist in a delicate balance. They are harmony, not discord. And so, we must offer a balance of death and life. And fate has delivered an offering of the White into our hands this very evening."

Tristan tensed. There was only one White mage in the area, and he'd brought her with him. They'd captured Ella, and now they were going to sacrifice her. Multiple people were descending the steps now, and he turned, his hand going beneath his cloak.

He stopped short as he perceived that they did not have Ella, but rather Bartram, the mage who'd been accompanying the guards from Grauberg. He walked in chains, his white robes covered in mud. Crusted blood covered his right cheek, and both of his eyes were swollen nearly shut. Two guards walked before him and another two followed behind. As they passed by Tristan's seat, the two following behind halted. The others led the prisoner down to Jules, who waited with a smile.

"You did well," said one of the men to Tristan's side. He recognized the voice as Vincent's, and turned his head slightly to listen in. "It is no coincidence you were the one to find him. This is the hand of fate."

"I am glad to serve, Lieutenant," said the other voice. Tristan could not see the man, but he sounded young. "If your people had not come, I would have been doomed to a life without meaning. Prince Jules and the Grey have given me purpose. I am honored with the task that lies before me."

"We are honored to have you among us," Vincent replied. Tristan pondered these words, but his thoughts were interrupted. "My father speaks," Vincent said, pride heavy in his voice.

Bartram now stood beside Jules, his head hung low, all resistance seemingly beaten out of him. Jules raised his voice for all to hear. "This is a most welcome turn of events. We will adjourn for the night, for there are preparations to be made. Tomorrow night, brothers and sisters, we will make an offering to Emjar. An offering of Death and Life—of Grey and White!"

Jules began to march up the stairs, the prisoner and his guards trailing behind. After they'd passed, the rest of the assembly began to break up. The young woman and her parents walked past Tristan before he stood. "What do you think he means, an 'offering of death and life'?" the girl asked.

"I—I'm not sure," her father replied, a tremble evident in his voice. He stared at his wife, and they shared the same expression—one of concern.

"How exciting!" their daughter said, and she walked out as they followed, both lacking in her enthusiasm.

Tristan rose and trailed after them. He discovered the storm had worsened as he exited the underground chamber. All around him, the people scattered to find shelter. He scanned the area but found no sign of Garit or Ella.

His eyes fell on Jules, Vincent, their prisoner, and his guards. He stalked after them, taking care to keep his distance. The cloud cover meant no light shone above from moon or star, and Tristan discerned them only by the torch one of the men carried.

The torch disappeared around the corner of an old structure, long fallen into decay. Moments later, he reached the same corner. He flattened himself against the lone standing wall of it and peered around the edge.

The guards led their prisoner several paces away, and the wall they approached had iron rings in it. One guard bound the mage's hands together, then tied the rope to one of the rings. Jules and Vincent walked on, disappearing into the night. With Bartram secured, the guards moved away.

They were soon lost to sight, but Tristan knew they'd not be far. He considered Bartram as he surveyed their surroundings. The forest lay only a short distance away. He could free this man, and both would be in the safety of the dark woodland in seconds. He'd told Ella and Garit he'd not act, no matter what, but this was different.

He stepped around the corner and began to move toward the prisoner. Something crunched behind him, a boot on loose rocks. He didn't even turn before he felt the strike to the back of his head. "Thought I smelled a rat," he heard from Vincent as he toppled over.

XII
First Blood

We warned the bloody fool, and he said he'd not act. We even joked about how easily he could muck it up, and then he went and absolutely mucked the whole thing up. Now, instead of having all three of us here to plan an attack on Jules or an escape for that damned mage, we only have two. And HE'S the one we need to save. Helpers, bloody help me, because if we come out of this alive, I'm going to shove my boot up his arse.

He was still hiding under the floorboards, his hand clutching his face. The sword had slashed from above his eye and down to his chin. The flesh parted, and he wondered if he had an eye any longer. The boards were being ripped up over head, and he was snatched up by his hair the moment he was revealed.

As he struggled to look around the room, the bodies of both of his parents were sprawled on the floor beneath him. In the corner lay his sisters, their dead hands still clutching their dolls. Twin girls with twin dolls, wearing little blue dresses.

His hair ripped free of his scalp, and he fled, escaping into the woods. He passed out and later woke to the woman bathing his wound. He cried for the family he lost, but the woman soothed him with soft words and sweet songs as she continued to clean his face.

A small hand touched his cheek, and as he opened his

left eye, he found that the little girl had approached them. She was crying too, and yet here she was, reaching out to offer him a comforting touch. Tristan reached up with his own hand and took hold of hers. Through her tears, the girl tried to smile for him.

Tristan opened his eyes, and his vision was blurry. A woman patted his forehead with a damp cloth. "Ella," he said, but as his eyes focused, he realized this was a stranger. Not only that, but she was clothed in a grey cloak. His mind raced as the events of the previous night came flooding back.

He raised his hands and found them bound with tight cords. The sun had not yet risen, though the eastern sky showed the faintest hints of light. The storm had passed, and only a few clouds were in the sky. He moved his eyes to his left and discovered the mage, Bartram, sleeping soundly. Tristan let his chin drop as he let out a groan. "Helpers, help me," he intoned.

"Empty prayers," said the woman tending to him. "Spiteful beings, your Helpers. Only Emjar is worthy of devotion." Tristan said nothing in response. He'd not uttered the words as a true prayer so much as a habit, and a theological debate was the last thing he cared for at the moment.

His head pounded from the blow he'd taken the previous night. Whatever Vincent had hit him with had done its job—he was struggling to focus, both mentally and physically. He closed his eyes and tried to stop thinking.

"You're lucky they only bound you," the woman said after he offered her no argument. "Trespassing on our sacred ground—I don't care if it brings the Children back or not, they should spill every ounce of your blood just to find out." She dropped the cloth in a bucket, and her footsteps retreated in the distance.

At some point he must have dozed off. The next time he opened his eyes, the sun had risen, though it was still early after dawn. His head throbbed, but not as much. He may have slept, but he was not rested in the least.

His hands were purple from the tight bonds. He struggled against them for only a moment before concluding it was useless. He scanned about and noted three guards watching him. As he let his hands fall and his shoulders slump, one of them smiled, glad to find how readily he accepted his defeat. Tristan resisted the urge to smile back. Letting the men assume he had no fight in him would work more to his favor than showing defiance.

Tristan wished to nudge Bartram awake, but he figured he'd be punished if he attempted to speak to the man. Instead, he focused on one of the other guards, ignoring the one who'd smiled at him. "What's to be done with me?" he asked, hoping he sounded defeated but not quite feeble.

"Keep your damned mouth shut, filth!" said the guard that he'd purposefully not addressed. "You'll have plenty of time to talk when the lieutenant says you can."

"Vincent, eh?" Tristan said, his voice low. He sat still and pondered his situation. Escape was not an option, and he had no idea what his captors had planned for him. His fate was completely out of his hands. He clenched his teeth and let his head fall back against the wall behind him. That was a mistake, and intense pain once more thundered through his skull. "What the hell did that bastard hit me with?"

"A rock," answered Vincent as he appeared around the corner of a nearby structure.

Tristan rubbed the back of his head. "Hit me pretty damned hard."

Vincent shrugged. "Not hard enough, it would seem. I wanted you dead." Tristan glanced up and found no jest in Vincent's face. "My father is glad to hear you yet live. He has questions for you. Bring him." These last words were delivered to the guards around him. Vincent turned to lead the way but spun back to face the other prisoner.

"Make sure the mage eats."

"We've tried, sir," said one of the guards. "Won't touch anything."

"Try harder," the lieutenant said. "Force him if you must." He walked over to the sleeping prisoner and put his hand on the man's shoulder. "I know you're awake. Eat. I tell you, old man, there are far worse things for you to endure than your hunger."

Bartram sat up quickly and shook his head. "Please, not—"

"Oh, yes," said Vincent before the man said any more. "You've heard about it your whole life, haven't you? Your people have spoken of it as a myth. Perhaps as a tale, one your children use to tease each other with, eh? Why have a monster in the dark when the Grey sounds so much more terrifying?

"But you know better, don't you? You're an elder of the Order of the White. Even your acolytes aren't told the truth of it, are they? But you've been told. You know it's real, and it scares you." He moved his hand away from Bartram's shoulder and reached up to cup his trembling chin. "Have no fear, old man—do as you're told, and you need not learn about it firsthand."

Vincent did not smile as he said this, and Tristan didn't sense that he enjoyed making the threat. It was simply a thing he had to do, and that made it all the more chilling. Vincent turned back to Tristan and the men who were untying him from the wall. "Now, follow."

Tristan's hands remained bound as the guards took the other end of his rope. One pulled him as the other prodded him from behind, and Vincent led the way. They moved through the camp among the ruins, and Tristan did his best to observe his surroundings. He soon realized there wasn't much to discover beyond the looks of contempt from nearly every face he passed. Word of his capture had spread, and hatred stared back at him in the eyes of those who returned his gaze.

However, he noted some avoiding his eyes, and a fair portion of those wore troubled expressions. Were they uneasy about him, or was this something else? He thought back to the previous night and the way the parents of the young woman had reacted to the capture of the White mage. Maybe they were not the only people uncomfortable with the events which had unfolded — or perhaps they were more afraid of the potential events yet to come.

He had little time to muse. The camp was small, and soon Tristan was led inside one of the few buildings which was still largely intact. A grey shroud covered the entrance, and two men stood sentry outside. They came to attention as Vincent passed between them, pulling the shroud aside for the guards to bring Tristan forth.

Once inside, Tristan could see nothing. No candles were lit, and the room was in near total darkness. The only light came from the mostly obscured doorway, and Tristan's eyes took several moments to adjust.

When they did, he observed a figure seated in the middle of the room on a stone. He was clad only in his breeches, his feet and torso were bare, and even in the poor light Tristan knew this was a man who was starved. Nearly every rib the man had was visible, and yet he held himself in a state of composure. Tristan didn't know who this prisoner was, but for the first time he feared what his captors had in store for him.

"I have brought him, Father," Vincent said, snapping Tristan out of his worrisome thoughts. He peered about for Jules but found no one else in the room. The skeletal figure lifted its head, and Tristan recognized the face of the prince. He couldn't help but gasp, which earned him a prod in the back from the point of a spear. "Hold your tongue," Vincent growled.

"He knows not our ways," Jules said. He slowly gathered his legs beneath him and stood. "We do not all fast in this fashion, and few who do are as avid about the practice as I am." He walked to one corner of the room and retrieved a shirt. "Light some candles," he said, and the guard who'd led the way passed the rope off and did as he'd been ordered.

Soon, the room filled with light. It was a simple arrangement, much like Jules' chambers in Grauberg had been. The prince moved to a cushion in one of the corners and let his head drop back against the wall. He looked faint. "You believe me to be weak prey at the moment, no?" The thought had barely entered Tristan's mind before Jules spoke it aloud.

Vincent put his hand on the hilt of his sword. "If you so much as twitch, I will show you a pain you've never even heard rumors about." Tristan made no moves aside from tensing, forcing himself to be as still as possible. He did not doubt that Vincent meant what he said, and he was in no place to challenge him.

"He'll be making no attempts, Lieutenant," Jules said. He motioned for Tristan to sit on a stone in the center of the room, the one which he had been sitting on to meditate. Before he was given a chance to move of his own accord, the guards forcibly moved him to the stone and set him down. "Not too uncomfortable, I trust?"

"I typically sit a bit more gently," Tristan said, and Jules laughed.

"Still as impudent as ever, I see. No matter. Guards, you may leave us. Vincent, I would have you remain." The other men saluted and departed, and Vincent came to take his place at his father's side. "Tell me, son, what do you make of our guest?"

"I call him a poor spy, Father." He inclined his head to one side and gave Tristan a piercing glare. "Or perhaps an even poorer assassin."

Jules scratched his chin. "I wonder," he said. He motioned to a small table in the other back corner of the room. "Water," he said, and Vincent moved to obey. Jules never took his eyes off Tristan. "I like your attire."

Tristan looked down instinctively. The grey cloak was still wet from the night's storm. "Where did you get that?" Vincent demanded as he abandoned his task of getting the water. "Did you kill one of our people?"

Tristan rolled his eyes. "Has any alarm been made about someone missing?"

Vincent began to stalk over to him, but Jules raised his voice. "Settle down, Vincent. The cloak is his own."

Vincent's head snapped around. "What?"

Jules nodded. "It was my parting gift for him. A token to let him know he had a place here, should he wish to accept."

Tristan's mind raced. He'd not thought to take this route, but Jules had opened the door for him. Vincent knelt nearby. "And yet he used your gift to sneak in like a thief, intent on freeing our prisoner."

"I wasn't after your prisoner," Tristan said, thinking fast. "I was following your father." He looked past Vincent and directly at Jules. "I was following you."

"You admit you were here to make attempt on the Prince of Felixandria?" Vincent asked vehemently.

Tristan made a show of rolling his eyes. "No, but I figured he's the only one who'd know I wasn't here as an enemy. Anyone else would challenge me and likely strike me down with a sword, or a big rock at the very least." Vincent glared, informing Tristan that he didn't believe a word of what he said.

Tristan chose to focus all his attention on Jules. "You left the cloak for me. If I could approach you, you'd recognize me. No one else would."

Jules said nothing, but he allowed for a hint of a smile to grace his face. Vincent's eyes moved from Tristan to his father, his fists clenched. The silence lasted for several moments before Jules chuckled. "Tristan, I have no doubt you are a fine soldier. You are not, however, a clever liar. Get him on his feet, Lieutenant." Vincent was only too happy to oblige as he roughly hauled Tristan up. "Take him back. Put a guard on him." He paused a moment and seemed to be considering something. "Ask Nigel to keep him company for a while. Perhaps Tristan will enjoy that."

Vincent nodded, and Tristan wondered what sort of brute this Nigel would be, and how much of a beating he was in for. Was this to be a slow execution by the Grey? His mind raced in a thousand directions as Jules dismissed him.

They returned him to the wall of the previous night, and Vincent motioned for two guards to come over. "You, bind him once more. And you, go and fetch Nigel. The Regent wishes for him to meet our guest." The second soldier moved to obey with hurried steps.

After Tristan was securely bound to the iron ring, Vincent moved forward, close enough to speak but still out of reach. "Don't fret, boy. You're not about to die. I think my father wants you to witness what he has in store for tonight." He spat at Tristan's feet. "But don't get any ideas in your head of escape, nor of attack. I'm watching you, and if you so much as twitch around my father, I'll gut you." He turned and disappeared around the corner of a building.

Several minutes passed, and Tristan slid down the wall. Bartram was now awake and watching him. Three guards stood around, but none too close. Tristan decided to risk speaking to the man. "Are you hurt?"

Bartram tensed, but when the guards did not turn to chastise them, he shook his head. "Not bad. They roughed me up a bit, but I've had worse." His eyes went distant. "They killed the men I was with, or most of them, at least. I'm not quite sure. Everything happened so fast."

"But you were riding away from them," Tristan offered. The man regarded him curiously, and Tristan smiled. "I was outside your camp. You returned, told them of Jules' party, and then you all made for Grauberg."

The mage chuckled bitterly. "I wish the captain could have heard this. He'd piss himself with fury." He threw his head back and laughed harder, and one of the guards turned and scowled. Bartram quieted down but kept his smile. "Aye, lad, we rode away, but we were pursued. We made camp after we'd travelled a few leagues. Thought we were out of harm's way. Jules was headed east—why would any of his people move back west?

"I don't know why they came for us, but they did. Maybe they had spies who'd seen us, same as you. In any case, it appears they wanted a White mage—and they found one." His smile faded, and he went still after these words. A few quiet moments passed, and he glanced at the guards and back to Tristan. "I don't know if anyone is out there, but I'd feel better if I knew someone was looking for us."

Tristan recognized the hope in his eyes and nodded his head. "I'm sure someone is out there. Somewhere." Bartram gave a look which could only be described as relief and fear mingled together, and Tristan shared the same expression. The mage slumped, visibly exhausted. "Did you eat?" Tristan asked. Bartram nodded. "Get some rest, then. I know your sleep last night was fitful, and I'm sure it won't be pleasant now, but try."

The mage tried to lie down, but his rope was short enough that he couldn't quite lie flat. He sat back against the wall and let his head loll to one side. His neck would be hurting in a matter of minutes, but he had no other option.

Tristan pitied him before he realized he was in the same position. He tried to get comfortable, but the sound of someone drawing near made him sit upright. His fears of impending torture returned, and then he saw the approaching person. He was no brute, but a young man who seemed to be about Tristan's own age. The man came closer, and Tristan recognized him as the one who'd been commended on the previous night by Vincent for catching the mage. "Might you be Nigel?"

The young soldier came before him, appraising him.

After a few seconds he nodded. "I am. And you are Tristan, the man who won the tournament in Grauberg, are you not?" Tristan couldn't help but smirk, which made Nigel smile in turn. "Aye, I witnessed that expression more than once during the combat. 'Cocky, but not overconfident,' I remember thinking." He turned and walked a short distance away. He entered one of the disheveled structures and emerged moments later with the remains of an old chair. Tristan marveled that it did not fall apart as Nigel sat across from him. "Do you mind if I join you?"

"I don't really think I have much of a choice, now do I?"

Nigel laughed. "No, I don't suppose you do." He leaned forward in his seat, and for several quiet moments the two men stared at one another, both full of curiosity. There were questions to be asked, and Tristan wasn't sure where to begin. Nigel, however, was. "They introduced you as the captain of the Elinian guard?" Tristan gave a nod. "So, you're truly from Elinton, then?"

"Aye," Tristan said in a low voice. "I escaped the night Jules invaded. The men who served under my command for the days of your visit were the same — we were all refugees."

"Your entire family fled?"

"No," Tristan said. He stared hard at Nigel under a furrowed brow. "No, they were killed. By Jules and Vincent."

"By the Regent and the Lieutenant," Nigel corrected. Tristan glared at him, but the man shrugged. "I can imagine you hate them, but you've got to understand where you are now — a prisoner under their care. Those are their titles."

Tristan shook his head. "Not my regent. Not my prince. I don't care how he styles himself, he's a murderer to me. He destroyed my family and my home."

"He may have destroyed your family — I'll give you

that—but he did not destroy Elinton. The city is much stronger now than before. Things haven't gotten worse, but improved."

"That's what I'd expect a Felixandrian to say."

"But I'm not a Felixandrian. I'm Elinian, like you."

Tristan's eyes widened, and he thought about the words of the family the night before. "How can you accept the rule of a man who conquered your own people? Why are you following him?!"

Nigel shrugged. "My life's gotten better since he came, and conditions have improved for nearly everyone. You don't know the whole story, Tristan. He didn't come here and invade because he's evil. He came because he had to. He—"

"He didn't have to come and kill my family!" Tristan snapped back. "That's horse filth! The man is a monster who destroyed everything I love. I lost my home because of him! And so did you, even if you're too blind to see it!"

"My home..." Nigel's voice trailed off as he nudged a small pebble with the toe of his boot. "Do you want to know about my home, Tristan? Because it appears we have two very different notions of what Elinton was. To me, Elinton was a den of vermin. My pa was lame in his right leg. He'd hurt it one night when he was patrolling. He'd been a city guard, and when his leg got hurt, they turned him out. He had no other trade, and he was struggling. Got caught stealing a loaf of bread and was tossed in the city jail to await the Queen's justice.

"Problem was, the jailer was the baker's brother. My pa had stolen bread, so the jailer decided he shouldn't have anything to eat while he waited. He never made it to the queen because he died in that bloody jail. They said it served him right, seeing as how he was a thief and all. But a man's got to eat, and so does his wife, especially if she's pregnant."

Tristan had the grace to drop his eyes. "I'm sorry for your loss. But that doesn't justify—"

"Oh, I'm not done!" Nigel rose to his feet, his tone deeper and sterner. "My mum was a pregnant widow. Not many men want to take on that burden, and her family wouldn't take her back because she was the wife of a thief. Not much she could do except join the whores. She cleaned for 'em and emptied their chamber pots until she'd given birth, and then she went to work with 'em. Fine life to raise a lad in.

"I remember the night the chap followed her home. Knocked in the door and told her she'd cheated him, and he wanted his next round for free. When she fought back, she got a knife between the ribs. I ran out screaming and two guards found me. They were both quite upset: one of 'em because my mum happened to be his favorite girl, and the other because now they'd have a new street orphan running around under foot. Only took me a few seconds to realize he meant me. They didn't bother coming back to our place.

"I was five when I drug my mum out of town to bury her alone, and the good people of Elinton stepped aside and watched. That's the city you're so upset about!" Nigel roared out the end of his story, and Tristan had no words for him. "When the Regent came, he took us off the streets. There's work and wages, and a place for everyone. And there are no bloody children dragging their dead parents out to bury them!"

Tristan let his head drop and thought about the anger he had about his own family. Here was a man of his own kingdom, a man who had just as much hatred inside of him—and he respected the man who Tristan hated. He opened his mouth to speak, but he only stammered. Pity and sympathy mixed with rage and fury.

"Got nothing to say?" Nigel asked. Tristan tried for a few more seconds before he clenched his jaw tight. "Didn't think so. Maybe your cause isn't as righteous as you thought. And you still don't know the whole story—only mine." He turned and walked away. He was out of sight, and Tristan pounded the ground until his knuckles were bloody. He roared his fury to Rylar and the Helpers, but he received no reply.

The day was long and boring. Tristan attempted further conversation with Bartram, but the guards decided to no longer be tolerant. After the sun set, people began moving toward the underground chamber once more, torches in the distance marking their passage.

After a time, Vincent and a group of guards came to him and the mage. "Bring them," he said. Tristan glanced around, hoping to discover some sign of Garit and Ella in the distance, but found nothing. He turned to Bartram and saw the resignation in the man's eyes. He'd already accepted death, but Tristan had not.

When the guards grabbed him, he struggled. He found himself on the ground, being kicked and stomped and spat upon. The wind was knocked out of him, preventing him from screaming his pain or anger. Vincent halted them before they did any lasting damage, and Tristan offered no further resistance. Like cattle being led to slaughter, he and the mage let the men lead them to the golden pit.

Once inside, the room was much darker than it had been the night before. Only a couple of torches were burning at the entrance, and two more were lit halfway down the stairway, giving the scene an otherworldly glow.

The rest of the people were already assembled, and Tristan made out a few forms near the lower torches. One was Jules, he was sure. Beyond them, shrouded in the dark, lay the tomb of what Jules claimed to be the Children of Emjar. Even now, Tristan scoffed at the notion.

Down he was led, the mage going before him. As they neared Jules, Tristan noted two large, flat stones. The White mage was directed behind one of them. Tristan was forced to sit, quite near but off to the side. "You will watch from here," Vincent said to him, "and you will behold our greatest moment of glory."

Another figure descended and took his place behind the second stone. It was Nigel, and he briefly met Tristan's eyes in the torchlight. The assembly, who'd been standing as everyone assumed their place, now took their seats as Jules stepped forward.

"An offering of Death and Life! This is the prophecy which has been passed down by our people. This is the prophecy which has been stricken from the common teachings of Grauberg and Elinton, and this is the prophecy we shall see fulfilled tonight!" He reached beneath his cloak and revealed a dagger. The blade appeared to be cut of stone, with notched and jagged edges. Nigel tensed, but only slightly, while Bartram struggled against the two guards who held him.

"My people, I present to you Nigel of Elinton. In the years which he has served, he has been ever loyal. It was an honor when he presented himself to me several years ago, confessing he believed himself to be a vessel of the Grey. He was tested and trained, and he now stands among the most devoted of our Grey mages. An offering is required, and he has presented himself to be this offering. I give to you, our offering of Death!" No one applauded, but the chamber was filled with murmurs. The faces of the onlookers were a collection and conflict of emotions, from pride to fear to dread—and even elation.

"And here, my people, is a White mage of Grauberg. His people were found in the forest nearby, and they were discovered by none other than Nigel. Emjar truly blesses us, for when we arrived here to perform observance of his glory and his children, we were fated to chance upon an offering which should have eluded us. An offering is required, and this man shall be presented as such. I give to you, our offering of Life!" At this, Tristan witnessed the range of emotions once more. Some stared at the mage with hatred in their eyes, while others were disturbed by what they knew was about to happen.

"So, human sacrifice and murder, is that it?" Tristan spoke aloud, and a boot crashed against his jaw.

"You will keep quiet," Vincent hissed into his ear, "or else we'll make an additional offering." Tristan was about to speak more when someone shoved a cloth into his mouth, and he found himself gagged.

"Prepare them," Jules said. Nigel removed his grey cloak. Beneath, he had a short sword. He unbuckled his belt and handed the weapon over, as well as his shirt. His clothes were placed in front of the stone before him.

Beside him, the guards wrestled the white mage out of his robes. He was stripped down to his smallclothes, his bundled garments likewise discarded before his stone. Nigel sank down to a kneeling position, and Bartram was forced down to his knees.

Jules raised the flint blade above his head. "Emjar, your Children were denied the life they deserved. Tonight, we shall finish the task!"

Tristan shook his head at the madness. Jules turned his attention to Bartram and stepped toward him. "Be at peace, mage. What we do, we do for the divine."

Tristan lunged for Nigel's discarded blade. He stumbled up to his feet, but guards were on him before he was able to raise the weapon in his bound hands. All around them, the chamber filled with the uproar of the gathering. Vincent came forward, his lips moving fast as he uttered something under his breath, and then Tristan understood—quite clearly—"I hate you."

The pain which ripped through his body was beyond words. The blood in his veins turned to ice, and a cold agony coursed through his entire being. He couldn't think, only stare forward and cry wordlessly.

Even had the gag not been present, no sound would have escaped him. He managed to meet Vincent's eyes, and he found the same expression he'd seen eighteen years before, when this same evil had been done to his mother, and by this same man.

The torches at the top of the stairs went out. Something flew past him in the dark, and then a second. Vincent took his focus off Tristan, and the pain subsided. Tristan scanned about for what had flown by: arrows. Two guards were down, dead or wounded.

Two more arrows sped past. Vincent ducked aside in time to avoid the first, but the other struck Jules in the shoulder. The guards and Vincent surrounded him as Tristan kept hold of his blade and turned. He knocked over the other torches, and the entire chamber was pitched into near total darkness.

Slowly, he crawled up the stairs. People constantly bumped into him, but he continued crawling forth. After a time, he was near the top. Moonlight and starlight streamed in, and hands suddenly grasped him. "I have him," came a voice. It was Garit's. "Move!"

Tristan slipped on one of the steps, but one of the hands gripped hard on his cloak and kept him upright. "Come on, you bloody oaf!" This was Ella, and even in the chaos around him, Tristan found relief in knowing that they were both alive.

He stumbled up and found himself outside the chamber. Two guards lay on the ground, either dead or unconscious. From the pit, it sounded as if a thousand men were preparing to burst forth in pursuit. Garit took Nigel's blade from Tristan and cut the cords from his hands and returned the weapon to him. "Which way?" Tristan asked.

"Away," said Garit.

"What about Bartram?" Ella asked.

Garit growled. "I'm sorry, Ella. We can't get in there." He turned, and no one argued with him as he began to run. Their only hope was to outrun the pursuit and lose them in the darkness. Tristan hated retreating. He wanted to turn and fight, though he knew in both head and heart this would be foolish. He tucked the blade into his belt as he and Ella ran after Garit, and soon they caught up with him.

Almost as though she sensed his reckless yearning, Ella gripped his hand as she ran forward. If he stopped now, he'd have to make her stop too. Something about her grip assured him that she'd not release him. "Keep going," she said, glancing back over her shoulder. Some of their foes surfaced, and as she looked back, they spotted her and began their chase. She faced forward once more. "Keep going!"

Vincent was running with his men, and above the shouts of the other soldiers, they heard his curses. He was calling Tristan by name, declaring a multitude of reasons for abhorring him. To his dismay, the pain began to seep into him once more. It was not so great as it had been — probably because of the distance which now stood between him and Vincent — and yet it was there.

He stumbled, and Ella stumbled with him, but they kept their feet under them. She did not let him go, but he found his strength leaving him as the pain grew. He moved slower by the second, allowing Vincent to gain ground. As the enemy drew closer, the Grey intensified.

Finally, Tristan dropped to one knee. "He's hurting me," he gasped out, clutching his chest, though he could not exactly say where the pain was. "It's the Grey." Ella knelt beside him, and he regarded her with a pained expression, his eyes white and haunted. "Ella, run!"

"Tristan! Ella!" Garit yelled, looking back and seeing them on the ground with the soldiers closing in. A few pursuers blazed ahead of the others. Garit ran back, grasping his sword and cursing himself for breaking his spear.

"Run with Garit!" Tristan urged Ella.

"No," she said, meeting his eyes with iron resolve. She rose to her feet and pulled her bow from her shoulder. Her quiver hung at her hip, and she quickly nocked an arrow. The advancing men slowed as they realized what her dark form was doing, and she let the missile fly. She couldn't tell where it struck the first man, but one of the soldiers went down, clutching somewhere on his torso and screaming. This gave the other pursuers pause, and the pain gripping Tristan lessened.

"Come!" said Garit, pulling Tristan to his feet and urging Ella back with a gentle push. Again, all three were up and moving. Their pursuers hesitated, possibly out of fear of more arrows, and after a few moments, the hunters fell out of sight.

Ella ran first, with Garit still supporting Tristan. Something whistled in the air behind them, followed by a thud and a sharp intake of breath by Garit. Tristan tripped and fell, sprawling on the ground as Garit went down beside him, his bow dropping in the dirt. When Tristan lifted his head, he discovered the shaft of an arrow protruding from between Garit's shoulders.

"No, no, no," Tristan said, crawling over to his friend. An arrow flew overhead, but he gave it little heed. A second arrow flew, and he realized they came from Ella. "Garit!" Tristan said, gently shaking his friend's shoulders. As he tried to roll Garit onto his side, a cry escaped from him. "Help me get him up!" Tristan said to Ella, who loosed a third arrow.

"Helpers, help us," she said. Somewhere in the distance, Vincent was shouting, but the words were indistinguishable. Had the chasers split up? Ella looked down. "We can't move him with that, Tristan. The shaft is like to catch on something."

She was pointing to the arrow. Tristan stood and grasped it, bracing with one hand and snapping it with the other. As quick as the motion had been, the arrowhead still moved, and Garit let out a cry of untold pain. Tristan squatted, unfastened the quiver of arrows from his friend's belt, and lifted Garit in his arms.

"I think they split into different parties when we lost sight of them," Ella said, confirming Tristan's thoughts.

"That cry will bring every one of them this direction. How many do you see?" She did not answer him. "Ella! How many?"

"None," she said. Tristan turned back and discerned the forms of two men on the ground with arrows protruding from them. He assumed a third lay somewhere, but he couldn't find him in the dark. His heart sank as he recognized the torment on her face. Her eyes turned and met his. "I had no choice," she said.

"You had no choice," he agreed. Garit twisted in his arms, trying to take a deep breath. "We must move," Tristan said. "This way."

As they fled through the forest, the effects of Vincent's attack wore off, but as fast as it departed, it was replaced with the exhaustion of running through the unknown while carrying the weight of a full-grown man. "I can't go much farther," he said.

"What's that sound?" asked Ella.

Tristan stopped for a moment and listened. There was a tremendous noise ahead, though he was just barely able to hear it over his heavy breathing and the thumping of his own heart in his ears. "I'm not sure," he said.

"Is it water?" Ella asked. "Which direction are we running?"

Tristan tried to think of which way they'd gone when they fled the camp, but after falling and rising again—and after hefting Garit—he had no way of being sure. He glanced up, only to find clouds were now covering the stars. "I don't know," he said.

Ella looked back as the sound of soldiers' voices grew louder. "Come," she said, and she leapt forward into the dark, with Tristan doing his best to keep up with her. "How bad is his bleeding?"

Tristan dropped his eyes, and though he saw little blood coming from the wound in Garit's chest, he felt it coating his arms and tunic and breeches. Garit still breathed, but he appeared to have lost consciousness. "It's bad," said Tristan. "We have to find a way to staunch the bleeding soon."

Ella cursed. "All my bandaging is in my pack with the bloody horses."

"What about the White?"

"It takes time," she said. "I feel it—but there isn't much to draw from."

As they ran, the sound they had noted before continued to grow louder, and soon there could be no doubt what it was. "It's the Nuum River," Tristan said. "It has to be."

"Do we turn back?" Ella asked, never slowing her pace.

Shouts behind them sent Tristan forward just a bit faster. "We can't," he said.

They continued running, and the voices grew closer and louder. When Tristan distinguished Vincent's voice again, dread crept up his spine. He'd experienced the Grey twice already, and he realized that he was afraid to feel it again. Fear was something he did not often feel—not on the training grounds, and not when he got into fights. He'd not felt it in the tournament, and even in his worst dreams—his worst memories—it was not fear. Or if it was, it wasn't like this.

Suddenly, they stood on the edge of a cliff. Ella stopped just in time to keep from falling over, and Tristan almost ran into her from behind. Unable to stop himself, he let his legs give out to avoid hitting her. He tumbled hard to the ground, and Garit tumbled harder.

Ella knelt beside them, but in the dark, she couldn't make out much. The stars and moon were veiled behind clouds, but she saw enough to know the arrowhead was coming through the point where Garit's left shoulder met his torso. "I think it missed his lungs," she said. Tristan took this as a good sign. "He's lost a lot of blood," she continued. She searched for a pulse and lowered her face to his nose. "I can't feel his heart, but he breathes. It's weak, but he breathes."

"We have to move," Tristan said, pulling himself to his knees. As he tried to stand, exhaustion pulled him back down.

"We can go no farther," Ella said. She peered over the cliff. "I don't think we can survive from this height." She turned back to Garit and shook her head. "He can't. The shock of the cold water would likely kill him."

"If we stay here, Vincent will kill him." That's when Tristan's fear became real again. From the approaching noises, Vincent's voice rose above the others. Tristan looked down, and Garit's body began to seize and shake. "Into the river!" Tristan shouted.

Ella started to protest, but Tristan surged to his feet and grabbed her, pulling her up. She moved to the edge and hesitated. "I can't do this, Tristan," she said, her voice shaking. "I can't—"

Tristan knew if she didn't die from the fall, she'd kill him when she got her hands on him. This was the only choice. He put his hands to her back and shoved, forcing her over. As she screamed, he lifted Garit once more. He turned back and saw the forms of the soldiers in the distance, and then he took a deep breath and turned to the cliff. "Rylar, be merciful," he said. He lowered his head and kissed his friend on the brow, and he jumped.

XIII
What Dwells Within

Tristan hauled Garit to dry ground, quite certain his friend was gone. Then a groan of misery came from Garit's lips, and Tristan winced as he realized that tugging on the tunic had shifted the head of the arrow still lodged in his chest.

The river had carried them far, and Tristan was astounded at how fast the waters flowed. He didn't know how, but he'd found the strength to keep himself and Garit up, both fully clothed, and he'd seen Ella ahead swimming to the eastern bank.

Tristan had tried to follow her, but she'd come to shore well before he had. He'd hoped she spotted him and would be trying to reach him. He had no way of knowing — he had no way of knowing anything at all.

The river roared behind him as he worked to drag Garit further away from the edge of the cold water. His friend needed warmth, but he dared not think about a fire until he was certain the pursuers had been thwarted.

Vincent and the soldiers would have known they'd jumped, and they might have even watched them do it. Still, it would be a while before they were able to catch up and find a place to ford, unless they'd leapt in after them. That seemed highly unlikely, but Tristan scanned the water and the banks to make sure he observed no unfamiliar faces floating downstream or running alongside them.

Tristan found himself looking to see how much blood was coming from Garit's wounds. None was visible, but that might be for several reasons. Perhaps it was too dark for him to see, or maybe the cold water had pulled his skin tight against the arrow and was preventing further loss.

Most likely, though, was that he had little blood left to lose. He thought back to the wound he'd dealt Garit during the tournament and how long his friend took to revive from that. This would be worse if he lived.

"You can't die," he said aloud, and a moment later he became aware of approaching footsteps. He turned, but the figure was no enemy. "Ella!" he gasped out.

"Is he alive?" she asked, running up and pushing him aside. Once more she checked for Garit's pulse. "We have to warm him up and seal the wound."

"I know," said Tristan, standing and looking around. "I've no idea where we are."

Ella pointed. "I passed some sort of rocky formation on my way here. Great boulders and dry earth."

Tristan glanced back at the far bank. It was lower, and the pursuers — if there were any — would be over there until they found a way to cross. He grunted in approval. "Boulders? We may be able to use them to shield a fire from eyes on the other side of the river." She helped him lift Garit, and Tristan struggled to shuffle his feet. He had little energy left to spend, and he hoped they were done running for a bit. As Ella led the way, he realized she was limping. "Are you hurt?"

"Twisted ankle," she said. "Don't worry, oaf. You didn't hurt me by pushing me in. Though we'd not be in this mess if you'd stuck to the plan and not acted." She turned to him, an expression of weariness on her face. "You're a right pain in the arse." Guilt rippled through him, and he remained silent for the moment.

They moved uphill, and though Tristan couldn't see well, he clearly felt when the earth beneath his feet yielded to stone. Immense silhouettes of the boulders stood around them. "Do you think this will do?" Ella asked.

"This will be perfect," said Tristan. One boulder

loomed above them at an angle, creating a natural shelter below. Better yet, this put them facing away from the river. Tristan lay Garit down as gently as possible. "I'm going to look for wood," he said. "Have you your flint?"

Ella shook her head, but then reached in Garit's small pouch which still hung from his belt and found that he had his. "This will have to do, and I'll need you to help me pull the arrowhead from the wound soon," Ella told Tristan. He nodded and examined her face. Even in the near-pitch black which surrounded them, he sensed that something else bothered her by the way she held herself. "I can barely sense the White," she said. "It's there, but I don't know if it'll be enough, and I don't have any supplies with me."

"We'll figure something out," he said. After that, Ella stooped beside Garit, and Tristan went out for wood. There was plenty to be found on the ground, but the proximity to the river meant that a great deal of mist had drifted up this way, and the wood was not as dry as he would have wished. Still, this was all he could easily and quickly find.

Ella struggled to get a fire going, and as she worked, their haven filled with thick smoke. Once started, the blaze was a pitiful thing, and Tristan kept having to leave to find small bits to serve as kindling to keep it going. The night was half over before the flames were stable, and Tristan arranged other large pieces of wood nearby in hopes that they would dry out. "Are we ready to pull the arrow out now?"

Ella nodded. "Heat your blade. If I can't seal the wounds on my own, I'll need you to help." Tristan nodded and placed the end of his stolen sword in the flames.

The fire was hot, but the blade took a long time before it began to glow. Tristan thought about the sword which Ella's father had given him, and he winced to recall that he'd lost it. "Are you ready?" Ella asked. He nodded.

She ripped her cloak and wrapped the torn cloth around the arrowhead so Tristan could grasp it without shredding his hand. He knelt, and when Ella nodded, he pulled. The effect was terrible — the arrow did not budge, and as Tristan pulled, he heaved Garit up as well. Garit stirred and screamed in agony. Thankfully, he passed out after only a few seconds, but the event caused Tristan and Ella to wait before trying again.

For the next attempt, Tristan straddled Garit's stomach while Ella held his shoulders down. Tristan pulled, and he would have sworn he was also ripping out every piece of bone and meat which surrounded the arrow.

Again, Garit woke, but Ella stuffed yet more cloth from her cloak in his mouth. Tristan could hardly stand to hear his friend's cries, muffled though they were. Ella tried to reassure Garit that they were helping him, but the words were not getting through.

At last, the arrow dislodged, and Tristan was shocked to discover nothing more than blood clinging to it. The shaft was larger than the arrows he was used to carrying, and the head was broad and heavy. "Must have been embedded in bone," he said.

He tossed the dart away as Garit passed out once more, and Ella started using her skills. With the light from the fire, Tristan saw that she was trying to heal the wound from the inside out. The hole began to disappear, but great rivulets of sweat were running down Ella's face as she strained.

"Tristan, the sword," she said, and she collapsed to the ground. He grabbed the weapon and pressed the scorching blade to Garit's flesh. Tristan frowned, knowing Ella was in no shape to hold Garit still, but thankfully, Garit did not wake.

For a brief moment, Tristan wondered if the sword was not as hot as it appeared, but the sound it made as the blade touched Garit's skin and the smell of burnt flesh was far more confirmation than he wanted. He set his sword down and rolled Garit over onto his stomach, ripped his tunic open, and pressed the blade to the wound on his back. Again, Garit did not stir.

He rolled his friend over once more and tossed the sword aside. Garit's face relaxed now, and the faintest sound of breathing came from him. Ella stirred and pushed herself over to them and took Garit from Tristan's arms. "Let him rest," she whispered. "Pull him closer to the fire." She paused a moment and added, "Not too close, though—we don't need him sweating out."

Tristan did as she asked, but his anger was building. The sounds of his friend's cries of pain had woken a fury in him. He was upset that Ella was unable to do more for him, but he understood she had no control over that.

"I think I'm going to be sick," Ella said, clutching her stomach as she spoke. "We need to eat something. He needs water, and we all need sleep."

Tristan nodded. "Can I use your bow?"

"I suppose. It is yours, after all," she said as she handed it over. "I can't believe it survived the fall—I can't believe *any* of us survived the fall." She handed over her quiver as well. Tristan examined the bowstring and noted to himself just how badly it was frayed.

Ella was right. They were surrounded by the dark, but he'd find something—he had to. He patted at Garit's boots and took his friend's knife, slid it into his own boot, and began to walk away. He nodded to Ella as he passed, but she did not react. She was still kneeling over Garit when he took his leave.

As he walked, his anger only grew. He was tired and wished nothing more than to rest a while to regain some strength. Instead, he began looking for prey which he'd probably not find in a forest he was not the least bit familiar with. While he aimlessly searched, his brother-in-arms lay hurt—possibly dying—and Ella worked against nearly all hope to save Garit from his probable fate.

As he came to trees with smaller trunks and low branches, he reached up and searched among their leaves, hoping to find something edible. Dead leaves were all he found, many of them falling as he touched them. Winter was almost here, and he'd been so tired, he'd not stopped to consider that. No fruit would be in season, and he wondered if he should gather fallen acorns in hopes of sustaining himself and Ella. He had no idea what they would give Garit, save for water.

His legs crumbled beneath him, and he scooted back to a tree. He listened to insects chirp and flitter about, and somewhere in the distance a night bird sang a high tune. On any other night, this would have all been pleasing. On this night, however, he thought of how horrid it was that the world was this serene as everything in his life fell apart.

Something snapped. Tristan did not move at first, believing a dead branch or some such had fallen. A moment later, he became aware of a soft rhythm — footfalls. Something was walking. He tensed, knowing his pursuers had finally found a place downriver to cross. In this dark, he may be safe if he remained still.

As the steps approached, he discerned the strides of two foes. They came closer, and any hope he had diminished. He nocked an arrow and drew back, only for the string to snap. He gritted his teeth and stared hard at the brush ahead. His ears told him that any moment now, the enemies would emerge. The leaves moved as he eased Garit's knife from his boot.

A boar appeared, and what he'd supposed to be two men was four legs. The creature's coat was as black as the night, but Tristan distinguished enough of the silhouette to know the animal was massive.

A tiny part in the back of his mind was relieved, but the greater part centered on a rage he could not contain. Here was prey he could not hunt; food for him and his allies, but he was not capable of bringing the beast down bare-handed.

Tristan stared, trying to devise a way to kill it. He had Garit's knife, but he'd have to be within range of the beast's tusks to strike. He might throw the blade, but if the creature didn't go down—or worse, if he missed altogether—he'd be at the mercy of a charge more likely than not. His hand trembled as he gripped the knife, and the edges of his vision dimmed. Anger flooded into him, and he had no outlet.

He stabbed the blade into the ground and let out a cry of fury. This beast should have been his prey. The boar huffed, startled by his shout. It lowered its head and squared its body with him. A charge was coming, but Tristan was unafraid. His anger intensified, his rage beyond control now.

The boar took only a single step before stopping in its tracks. It shook its head and let out a deep rumble. A moment later, Tristan realized it was the beginning of a growl, but it soon devolved into a pitiful squeal as Tristan's own scream became louder.

If the beast would not dare to come after him, then he would go to it. He rose, and as he stepped forward, the boar turned sideways to him. Even in the night, Tristan saw the white of the creature's eyes. Fear—was the animal afraid of his yells? Surely not, but Tristan kept shouting, his head beginning to feel light.

In an instant, everything changed. Tristan became aware of the boar in a way which made no sense. He could almost feel the animal, though several feet separated them. There was a sensation, as if the creature's skin was under his fingers, and Tristan felt like he could reach into that skin and grasp the boar's beating heart.

Still yelling—his rage absolutely engulfing his entire being—he tried to do just that. He reached out his hand and slid his fingers around the heart of the boar which now existed in his mind's eye. The squeals of the animal intensified to an ear-splitting level.

Tristan had heard enough—enough of the boar, enough of himself. He reached in with his other hand, and with both he clenched and ripped the heart from its proper place. In response, the boar—which was still standing several feet away—dropped in place, its legs giving only the briefest of twitches. A gargling exhale replaced the squeals, and then the animal's presence vanished from Tristan's mind.

Tristan glared at his hands as though he expected to find blood on them, but he found nothing. He stumbled forward and collapsed on his knees beside the dead boar. After several minutes, the wave of dizziness had passed. All the blood had rushed to his head in his anger as all the air had fled out of him. None of this made any sense, and he couldn't think straight.

Crawling back, he retrieved his knife out of the dirt and began to cut into the animal. He reached inside, his hands practiced at the motion, and his fingers closed around the boar's heart. The organ was not connected to any of the blood pathways like it should have been, and his brow furrowed as he considered how this had happened.

The realization struck him that this had not been his anger. This had been his hatred made manifest—Tristan had used the Grey to kill the boar. He turned from the animal and retched, what little substance was in him coming out violently.

He regarded his kill with disgust and prayed he was wrong, but the proof lay before him. Not wanting to use what he now considered to be tainted meat, he rose to leave, but Garit was dying, and the meat was fresh. How to get the sustenance into his friend, he couldn't say, but he wouldn't let the meal stay here. He opened the beast up, emptied its entrails and conducted a hasty field dressing, and slung the boar over his shoulders.

As he began his walk back, he stumbled many times, exhaustion and mental fatigue both striving to bring him down. He did not wish to consider the implications of all this—that within him was the very thing which had killed his family—but how could he not?

He tripped over a branch and struggled back to his feet. He began to drag the boar now, his clothes clinging to his frame from a combination of the river, his own sweat, and the blood of the animal. He wondered if he'd be able to make it back at all. Perhaps he should find Ella and have her return with him to finish dragging back the beast.

"Ella!" he said aloud to himself. What would she make of this? How would she tell her he'd killed the boar? Almost without thinking, he drew his knife again and stabbed the creature behind the shoulder, the same place he would've placed an arrow if he'd wanted to shoot his game in the heart. The string had snapped as he readied a second shot—that would be the tale.

He was too tired to give this any more consideration. He stood and took a deep breath and noted a hint of smoke on the air. In the distance, he made out a soft orange glow. He was close. He sat still for a couple of minutes, and then he slung the beast over his shoulders once more and made his way forward for the last stretch.

He was well inside the light of the fire before Ella became aware of him. She was kneeling over Garit, her hands on his bare skin and her head bowed when she detected Tristan's approach. She came to her feet in alarm, but as Tristan dropped the boar and hit his knees in exhaustion, she recognized him and came rushing to his side.

"How's Garit?" he asked with what little breath he had left, but Ella did not answer him. She searched him over in what little light she had. "I'm fine," he assured her. "The blood is the boar's. I'm not hurt, only tired."

Her eyes shifted over to the boar, and she crawled over and looked down. She glanced back to Tristan with raised eyebrows. "He's fresh?"

"Aye, I killed him." He opened his eyes and saw the

look on her face. "An arrow in the heart." He offered no more, and Ella squatted over the boar but said nothing. She crawled over to Tristan, took his knife, and came back to begin preparing the kill. He turned his eyes to his friend. "Garit?"

"He's fine," she said, focused on her work. "There was a sudden surge of White a short while ago—not much, but enough. The wounds on the surface may have been closed, but there is still damage beneath. I was able to mend some, but I still have much more to do. For now, we must focus on getting food and water into him."

'A sudden surge of White.' At those words, Tristan's stomach turned—the tales of the Balance were true. When the Grey was expended, it gave power to the White, and likewise the White fed the Grey. "I bought this with death," Tristan muttered. "Life with death, and death with life." Ella turned and glanced at him curiously, but his eyes were already rolling back in his head. Sleep seized him in an instant, and he slipped into dreams and nightmares.

XIV
Back to the Pit

The sun was high overhead by the time Tristan managed to open his eyes. He didn't recall when he'd fallen asleep, but he'd been out for a long time. He was still weak as he began to move, and his thoughts seemed mired in fog.

He'd expected to find himself lying on the hard rock he'd collapsed on, but he was on soft earth not too far from the site where they'd made their fire the night before. The ground, so close to the river, was slightly damp, but he'd probably been better off here than on the stone. Garit, though, would have been left by the flames.

Tristan rose and stretched his weary muscles, aches greeting him as he did so. His eyes finally focused, and he found Ella sitting by the fire with her knees pulled up close. Garit was beside her, laid out on his back. His shirt, which had been removed the night before, was now bundled under his head as a makeshift pillow. Tristan smiled to see how well Ella had done with making them both as comfortable as possible.

"How is he?" Tristan asked as he approached. Ella started at his voice, and he realized she'd fallen asleep while sitting up. "Apologies," he said. "I didn't mean to frighten you."

She shook her head, a weary smile on her face. "No, it's fine. I just nodded off. The night was long." She looked from Tristan to Garit. "He lives. I was able to get some water down his throat last night, but he'll need more. For now, he's still fighting."

Tristan grunted and glanced over to the boar he'd brought back the night before, which Ella had butchered as he slept. He scowled as he recalled the events but said nothing. "Have you eaten anything?" he asked. She shook her head, and he moved over to some of the cuts of meat she'd set aside.

The night had been cold, but not enough to freeze, and the meat had not been moved far from the fire. Tristan came over with a few pieces, skewered them on some of the smaller branches which had not been burnt, and began to turn them over the flame.

Ella moved over to him, shivering. He held a branch with one hand, and with the other he motioned for her to come closer. "This'll warm you up. Both of us, for that matter."

"Your clothes are wet," she said as she moved up beside him.

"Aye," he said. "Someone tucked me in on wet dirt for the night."

"Oh," she said, her voice small before she perked up a small bit. "Well, someone pushed me off a cliff into a river." He laughed, and she smiled and laid her head on his shoulder. "You're not hurt?"

"No," he said. He pulled the meat away from the flame and offered the branch to her. "Let that cool a bit. I'm sorry, but this is the best I can do with what we have." He took up another one which he'd already prepared and began roasting his own breakfast. "I'm fine. Tired, but nothing more."

Ella straightened up and touched her food, testing how warm it was before taking a bite, and she placed it back over the fire. "Needs to go a little longer," she said. He nodded, and they both sat in silence as they continued to cook. The sounds of the river were amplified by the rocks which surrounded them, offering peace after the chaos of the previous night.

Ella pulled her branch back, and after the meat had

cooled, she dug in with an appetite which surprised Tristan. The night had been rough on her. "Have you slept much at all?" he asked.

She shrugged. "A wee bit," she said, her mouth half full. "I was able to nap here and there. I should've stayed awake to keep watch, but I couldn't do it. I couldn't even stir you to move somewhere more comfortable, and I tried nearly everything aside from kicking you."

"I deserve to be kicked," Tristan said.

"Aye, you do," Ella answered. "It should've been all three of us planning a rescue of Bartram, or an attack on Jules, or whatever else was needed. But no, we had to save your bloody arse with no neat way to go about it, and now this is the result!"

They sat in silence, Ella biting her tongue and trying not to guilt Tristan more than she already had, and Tristan wishing he knew the right words to say. Nothing came at first, but then he realized there was only one thing to be done. "I'm sorry," he said. "What I did was reckless, and I put everyone in an impossible position. I was a fool, and I hope my actions won't cost my friend his life."

Ella sat still a few more moments. After a time, she reached out and put her hand on top of Tristan's, and when he peered at her, she had tears in her eyes. "I'll not say it's alright," she began, "but we will manage, and we'll move forward."

Tristan nodded and stared down the path which led back to the river. "Vincent and his crew must've moved on. If they'd been looking for us, I doubt we'd have survived the night."

"Perhaps they believe we died in the fall," Ella offered.

"Perhaps." Tristan prayed she was right. The plunge to the river had seemed far in the night, and he hoped the men pursuing them would be content with the belief that they'd likely drowned. "We're lucky to be alive, but we aren't out of trouble yet. Garit's in a bad way, and we have no food, no supplies, no horses, no—" He stopped himself and exchanged glances with Ella. "The horses! Maybe they're still at camp?"

Ella nodded enthusiastically. "Might be. I fed them well yesterday, and they shouldn't want for anything desperately. They may be antsy, though, and we did make sure they were able to free themselves if threatened." She turned to face Garit. "I think we can move him safely, so long as we go slow. His wounds are closed. I had enough to finish that bit. He's fortunate."

Tristan held his tongue. He understood where the energy had come from. Perhaps the only good that would come of this was that the magic had helped with healing his friend. The Grey was inside him—had it always been there? A thousand questions began to form at once. "Tristan?" Ella startled him out of his trance.

"Sorry," he said. "I don't think moving too fast will be a problem. I'm tired, and he's not exactly light, and we're not sure of the way. If anything, I worry we won't move fast enough."

"So, what do we do?"

Tristan took a bite of his chop and considered their next move. "I'll scout ahead, see if I can find a way to cross the river. That's the first real obstacle. If we can reach the other side, we'll figure out the next part. One step at a time." Ella nodded, and they finished their meals without saying another word.

After they were done, they tidied up what little supplies they had. "I'm sorry I tossed you off the cliff," Tristan said. Ella turned to give him a playful glare but stopped as she perceived the sincerity on his face. "I realize I'm an arse, but it was the only way to save you— to save all of us."

"I know," she said, coming over to him and putting a hand on his arm. "I was never truly offended. I understand why you did it." He nodded and glanced aside. "Tristan?"

He stopped what he was doing and met her eyes. "I just want you to understand. I pushed because I care about you." Any hint of a smile faded from her face. He continued. "I'm more than aware that you'd rather I show my affections for you in other ways than tossing you off a cliff—and truth be told, so would I, but I don't have that luxury right now. I just wanted to assure you that I did it because I care for you—because I don't want to think of life without you."

"Your affections for me..." she began. Tristan opened his mouth, but she put a finger on his lips. "Let's leave it at that for now, shall we? We have other things which require our attention," she said, glancing over in Garit's direction. "Later, perhaps we can revisit this conversation. For now, I suppose I'll have to tolerate an occasional toss into the river if that is going to be the best way you can think of to tell me how you feel."

Tristan smiled, his first legitimate hint of happiness since before they'd set out for Emjaria. A few minutes later, he left the camp, moving downstream and hoping against hope that he'd find an easy way across the river.

He began by heading south, and before long he came across the place where he'd brought the boar down on the previous night. He tried not to stare, but his eyes were drawn to it. Flies were gathered on the entrails, but the sight which drew his attention was a small patch of dried blood which had trickled out of the beast's mouth.

He marched past and ventured closer to the river. He scanned over the brush and trees and found no sign of fire or smoke on either bank. He hoped this meant the others had not made camp during the night. Regardless, necessity drove him to cross.

He continued downstream and came to a bend. His heart leapt when he discovered a natural rock-bridge arching over the river. The water was no more than two hundred yards across here, and it appeared as though the flow had carved a path through one massive chunk of stone over many years.

The arch was thick, and Tristan dared to cross. The way was wet, but the coarse nature of the stone meant that it was not terribly slippery, save in a few spots which had been smoothed by years of wind and water. He crossed all the way over to make sure of the stoutness and returned to the camp.

Ella was waiting for him with an anxious expression. He'd expected as much. She was no warrior, and she'd been left to guard an injured man. That, and her archery counted for nothing after the loss of the bow. "Any luck?" she asked him.

He nodded with a smile. "Aye. A rock bridge, not a quarter of a league downstream." Her spirits lifted at the good report, and she began clearing out the space which they'd used the previous evening.

He did his best to sweep away any evidence of their fire. With Ella's help, he managed to get Garit onto his back, leaning forward so that Garit's chest was pressed against him as he carried one leg under each arm. Ella bound Garit's hands in front of him to keep them in place, and his arms hung limply over Tristan's shoulders.

Garit was not a small man, and Tristan would be needing frequent breaks. Ella was strong, but not strong enough to help bear this burden. She used a bit of cloth to carry the rest of the boar meat—or at least as much as she could manage—and with what little supplies they had, they set off.

They moved slow, and Tristan had to be more careful now than earlier. Walking with an injured man on his back affected his balance, gait, and reflexes greatly. Ella said nothing as she tried to pick their path ahead, going in the direction Tristan indicated, and trying to ensure that any loose rocks or branches were moved aside so Tristan had less to worry about.

They were coming near the place where the boar had been killed, and Tristan was about to guide them around when Ella caught the scent of the offal. "What is that?" she asked. She pushed through the brush, and Tristan was unable to stop her. He came up behind her a few seconds later, cursing himself for not burying the entrails. "I still can't believe you found prey so quickly."

"Luck," said Tristan, biting off the word and offering no more. Ella stared at the blood and organs on the ground, and he urged her onward. "Veer off to the right up ahead. The land near the river is smoother here." She shook her head at the gore and smell and moved on, much to Tristan's relief.

The rest of the trek that day was uneventful. Crossing the bridge proved to be the most dangerous part, as falling would have led to disaster. Taking his time, Tristan managed the task with little difficulty. Once on the other side, he and Ella were happy to discover the underbrush was not very thick and was altogether absent in many places.

They had leapt from a cliff overlooking the water from high above on the previous night. Now, having crossed at a place where the land and the river were level, they had to find a way to higher elevation. He feared they would come to an impassable bluff, but they soon discovered the terrain began to climb in a slight but obvious manner.

The incline made for arduous walking, and many breaks were needed, but as the afternoon passed, they came out on the same path they'd been pursued down on the previous night. The blood on the leaves was dried and brown, and Tristan was appalled at how much he observed. Had he been tracking an animal which left such a trail, he'd have had no doubts the beast had perished.

Garit still breathed in his ear, and Tristan was thankful for the reassurance. They arrived at the place where Garit had been shot and were shocked to find his bow and quiver still on the ground. Ella collected them, placing the arrows on her hip and testing the strength of the string.

At last, as the sun touched the western horizon, they reached the ruins of Emjaria once more. Looking about, it was clear the party had left in a state of disarray. They had no way of knowing what had happened after the events in the underground chamber, but the people had departed in a hurry.

Many belongings were abandoned, and Tristan wondered if they'd all been forced to leave in a hurry. One of the discarded items was a cot which had been overturned beside one of the crumbling buildings. That was where he lay Garit, cutting a stretch of cloth from a nearby tent to serve as a makeshift blanket.

He slumped down beside Garit and breathed heavy. Every muscle in his body was aching. "We have to find food and water."

"Aye," said Ella. "You stay here with him. I'll go and fetch the horses."

Tristan shook his head. "It's too dangerous. You should—"

"Stay seated." Her tone was sharp. He focused his attention on her, confused. "Tell me, are you afraid of these ruins?" Tristan examined the crumbling stone around him. Glancing back at her, he shook his head, and she raised one eyebrow. "No? Well, I am. And I'll not be left alone here."

"But why are you afraid—"

"I'll tell you later. For now, we need food and water and supplies. Besides, if I find the horses, they'll likely respond better to me. Should soldiers find me alone, it'll be no different than if they found me alone here with Garit. You are tired and sore and need to rest, so relax a bit while you can. I shall be as swift as possible."

She gave him no room to argue, but as she turned to leave, Tristan spoke up. "Should I be scared?" She stopped briefly, glancing over her shoulder at him. He went on. "Am I in danger by remaining here?"

She shook her head. "I'm not certain. When you asked me before, I was almost sure our teachings were little more than superstition, but now..." Tristan thought about the ritual which had nearly been performed in front of him the night before, but he still wasn't sure what Jules had hoped to accomplish. Seeing a look of confusion on his face, Ella's expression became one of calm. "Don't fret. I shall explain later. You need not concern yourself for now. If there had been a danger, I believe it has passed." Without another word, she turned and made off into the forest, Garit's bow slung over her shoulder. The sun had set, and the sky was fading into night.

He tried to make himself comfortable, but the pangs of hunger were stronger than his desire and need for sleep. Trying to convince himself to stay still and rest was useless. Tristan glanced over to the pack with the boar meat from the previous night.

He resigned himself to starting a fire. As he did so, a murmur from Garit reached his ears. He crossed over to his friend and found his eyes fluttering open. "Garit?" he asked softly.

Garit let out a weak moan, and his breath caught as his face twisted in pain. "Easy, my friend," Tristan whispered. "Your wounds are closed, but you should try to stay still and calm. You're going to be better very soon."

The words were not likely true, but Garit gave the tiniest of nods, made an effort to catch his breath, and then let it out steadily. "I'm preparing some meat. Ella has gone to find water. If you can stay awake, I'll have something for you as quick as I can."

As he spoke, Garit's eyes began to close again. "But, if you can sleep, then sleep. Don't fight it. The food will keep until you are ready." Another lie. The boar would ruin soon, and Tristan would have to hunt again.

Tristan moved about, watching his surroundings as keenly as possible. The light was failing, and he was beyond exhausted. With every action he took, he noticed the soreness which came of carrying Garit for so long.

The small set of ruins about them paled in comparison to the larger ones which lay beyond the reach of the last light of day, and Tristan wondered what secrets the underground chamber truly held. What did the place mean for the Order of the White? What did it mean for Jules?

He kept looking in the direction Ella had gone. With each minute, the way became less visible. He strained his eyes as the night deepened, seeking any sign of her, but she did not reappear. He tried to tell himself she had not been gone long enough to reach the horses, gather them— or at least their supplies—and return. He turned his attention to fire and food to distract himself. It was of little use.

In the end, he chose to wait to eat. He wasn't sure if the boar smelled wrong or if he was being paranoid, but he decided not to take the risk until he was certain that Ella wouldn't return with food. While it was true that he hunted in his free time, his knowledge of food preservation and preparation was limited. Still hungry, he crawled over to check on Garit. He'd fallen asleep once more, and Tristan did not wish to stir him.

He sat and studied the stars overhead. The fire blinded him to his surroundings and would serve as a beacon to any enemies. Many times, he told himself to put it out, but Ella was no scout or soldier. This fire served as a beacon for her as well, and this was the thought which won out as he continued to feed bits of wood to the flames. Time crept by, Garit slept on, and Tristan fought to keep his eyes open.

The sound of a horse whickering brought him to his feet. He realized in an instant that he'd been asleep, and his vision was not clear at all as he stumbled and tried to find his balance. He wasn't sure where his sword was, or even where *he* was for one confused moment.

"Calm yourself, Tristan," came Ella's soothing voice.

"It's me." He sat back down and rubbed the sleep from his eyes. Ella led the horses into the circle of light around the fire. He spotted their saddlebags, and relief rushed through him.

"I didn't mean to fall asleep," he said.

"You're exhausted," she responded. She settled the horses and moved toward him. "The events of the last few days are enough to rob anyone of strength. You've eaten?" He shook his head. "Here." She offered him a chunk of bread and a few strips of jerky. "I made a small meal from our rations in the supplies. I know we should save everything we can, but I didn't feel like I was going to make it back here before collapsing from hunger."

Tristan smiled and shrugged. "Let that be the least of your concerns. Starving yourself would have been even more unwise." She sat next to him. The night air was cold, and she shivered. "The fire will warm you quick enough. Even so..." He held his arm out. She moved close to him, and he wrapped her tightly about the shoulders.

For a time, they sat in silence. The fire crackled, and occasionally Tristan would lean forward to place another piece of wood. After a while, he let the flames burn lower. He and Ella rose at one point to move Garit closer to the warmth of the coals. Ella touched his neck and face and said she believed he had no fever. In the movement, Garit did not so much as twitch. Tristan told Ella he'd woken for a few moments earlier, and she said that was a good sign. "Sleep is the best healer, but the fact that he stirs means he is healing. At least, his body believes he is."

He had very little knowledge of the healing arts, natural or magical, so he simply nodded to her words as he watched Garit's seemingly serene expression. "I'm glad he's at peace for the moment."

She squirmed a bit as she surveyed their surroundings. "At least one of us is." The darkness had closed in around them, and Tristan recognized little beyond a few shapes of ruins in the shadows. Still, Ella peered into the gloom as if she perceived everything, and she wore an expression to show that she cared for none of it. "This place scares me. I don't believe I'll rest well until we are away from here."

"What about the ruins bothers you so?" Tristan asked. He had placed his arm around her again after they'd moved Garit, and as he asked the question, he rubbed her back reassuringly. "This place was destroyed centuries ago. What real evil does it hold, beyond a mere name?"

A shiver ran through her body. "You ask so easily, but I'm not certain I can give you an easy answer. The things which happened here—even before the Grey Empire built up the accursed city—are known to few. The knowledge is safely guarded in my order. You saw a hint, but I doubt you believed it was anything of note."

Tristan stared at the embers as he held her tight against him. "I'm not a good student of history, or even religion. I know nothing of what was here before the Grey Empire built the city. I know that while the rest of us hold Emjar to be the Cursed Helper of Rylar, the people of Felixandria held him in high regard and offered him worship."

"Aye," Ella said. "Felixandria came and conquered the people of Grauberg and Elinton. It was too much to rule them from afar, so they established a new capital between the two nations." She cut her words off and was quiet for a long time. Tristan thought she'd fallen asleep, and she startled him when she continued. "They made a discovery in this forest which changed everything for them. They built the city up around what they found."

Tristan nodded, his cheek resting on top of her head, and she stopped speaking again. When she did not resume after several minutes, he sighed. "Ella, I won't ask you to tell me anything you aren't comfortable sharing." She shifted beneath his arm, pulled back, and looked him in the eyes. He gave her his usual smirk. "But if you're going to start a story and end on a note like that, I'm going to push you off a cliff again."

She gave him half of a smile before rising and moving over to Garit. She checked him again for fever and nodded to herself. "His breathing is good, and he's warm but not feverish." She stood looking down at him before she turned her head toward the city. "Bank the fire," she said without facing him. "There's no wind, and we'll not be gone long. He'll be fine."

"Where are we going?" Tristan asked.

"Into the underground chamber."

The moon was more than half-full, but that was enough light for the two as they made their way through the ruins. They went cautiously, checking to make sure no one had stayed behind in anticipation of their return. They found no sign of anyone being present, but the marks of their passage were evident. Discarded packs, cloaks, and even food littered the ground. Nothing appeared orderly, but rather seemed to have been thrown aside in anger. Ella led and Tristan followed closely, hoping she'd figured out how to work the entrance to the pit. "What do you wish to find?"

She slowed her pace for a few steps and came to a halt. She turned and faced Tristan. In that moment, he took in her true beauty. Her features were half-lit in the moonlight, her bronze skin glowing softly. Her dark eyes reflected the light as if they were stars themselves. He had to catch his breath, and his resolve to push forward almost faded away. It was replaced with something else — something he wanted but refused to acknowledge. He shook the thought free, but not easily.

"Where did we come from?" Ella asked suddenly.

Tristan felt a sinking feeling in his stomach. "You're not lost, are you?" He turned to point where they'd come from, but she reached out and took his hand and kept him facing her.

"No, not that. I mean, us—people. How did we come into existence?"

Tristan made a face. "Well, if I recall the scriptures, we were created by Gui."

She nodded and began moving forward again. On they walked, and Tristan marveled at how much of the city he'd not taken in earlier. The moonlight reflected back from the cold stone, and as Tristan looked around, he saw how widespread it was.

The city had been much larger than he'd realized, and it wasn't crafted by simple stone. Much was marble, and in many places, smooth bits appeared to be fallen pieces of the heavens as they shone with the starlight.

He was snapped out of his thoughts when Ella spoke again. "Gui was the eldest of the Helpers. He was tasked by Rylar to give life to the races of the world. We are one, but there are others. You've listened to the strange tales which come to us from the Dytans, of people who are more animal than man, who reside in the lands far, far to the west. If they speak true, they trade with them, and some of the goods they trade with us come from those people."

Tristan scoffed. "They say that to try to earn more gold for their wares—make them appear more exotic."

"I'm not so sure," she said. "I believe them. I believe there are many races in our world, and we just haven't had dealings with them."

"Perhaps," Tristan uttered doubtfully. "But what has this to do with us? With this city?"

Ella stopped. "We're here," she said. In the distance, they noted the two posts which marked the entrance to the chamber. To the side was what remained of an old stone hut, and Ella steered them in that direction. "What do you recall of Emjar and his battle with Gui?"

Tristan thought back to what he had been taught as a child. "Emjar was the Helper charged with creating and keeping law and order." Ella nodded to him, and he thought more. As a soldier—and an orphaned one at that—religion and philosophy had not been a big part of his teachings. His close friendship with Garit had paid off in that he was afforded a chance to learn more than most commoners, but he was a poor student.

It had been a long time since he'd discussed the teachings of Rylar beyond generalities. He went on with what he recalled. "Emjar was jealous of Gui. He wanted to create living beings, as well. The other Helpers had created life in the forms of birds, beast, and fish." They entered the hut, and Ella walked over to a stone slab which was about waist high and began running her hand along the underside of it. "What are you doing, Ella?"

"The old city was destroyed, but its secrets remained hidden. We've long had rumors of the underground chamber, but none who escaped the devastation knew how to find it. The other night, while you were blending in with the crowd, Garit and I followed some guards at a distance. They entered here, and they gathered around this slab. I believe the switch to the chamber is—here!" She pressed, and the grinding of stone informed them of their success. The hole in the ground opened, and Ella took up a torch from a sconce in the hut.

A shiver ran up Tristan's spine as Ella fell into silence on their approach. No more words were spoken, and soon they were inside the chamber. He turned to Ella, and her silhouette motioned him forward.

Slowly, he advanced, and he soon found himself going down the flight of stairs. The air became still as he descended, but the temperature was the same as the night had been outside. In front went Ella's careful steps. She reached back with a hand to halt them, and he heard her striking flint. The torch blazed bright, and the area around them illuminated with a golden glow.

After they walked about a quarter of the way down, they began to note shapes in the distance. Tristan surmised that they were the stones which had been brought in for whatever ceremony Jules had wished to attempt. The closer they got, though, the more troubling the scene became. "What's that?" Ella asked, her voice quavering.

Blood stained the stones, but the two bodies were what frightened her. Nigel and Bartram lay motionless, throats slit. Lifeless eyes stared past Tristan and Ella, and she turned and buried her face in his chest. He reached up and clutched the torch, pressing it away before she burned both of them. "Quiet, now," he whispered into her ear. She trembled against him, and perhaps he shivered as well. Whatever the ceremony had been, Jules had gone ahead with it after the chaos of the pursuit. "What was the point? What are the Children he thought he would—Ella!"

She tore herself from his grasp and raced down the stairs. Tristan ran after, more careful of the steps he couldn't find now that the torch had gone with her. When he reached the bottom, he was standing at the mouth of the structure, which was far larger than he'd realized. He'd thought them to be catacombs, and now he was all but certain of it.

Ella had gone inside, and he went in after her. All about him were raised platforms. The torchlight was not far away, and Tristan was able to make out Ella's form. As he approached, she turned to him. "They didn't succeed," she said, her voice full of relief.

"What do you mean? Who are they?"

Ella turned back and held her torch up. All around them lay tombs—dozens of them, perhaps hundred.

"Emjar turned from the law he had sworn to keep, and he created a race which would honor him," Ella said. "He shaped them, but he did not have the power to give them life. So, they were buried deep, in a grave no one should have ever found."

Tristan's eyes widened. "Are you saying the Felixandrians truly believe this to be—"

"The Children of Emjar, aye. And one day, they *will*

wake up to serve his will."

XV
Resumption

The next morning found Tristan and Ella exhausted. They had returned late, and neither had slept well. Both had taken turns to keep watch, though they had no need of it. Jules and his followers were gone, and they were more than certain of that now.

Ella had been quiet since seeing the catacombs, and Tristan had chosen not to press her for information. He now understood her uneasiness a bit more. Not only was Emjar the Cursed Helper, but he was also—according to the teachings of Rylar—the father of the Grey. This place was the ultimate opposition to her order.

He had known that already, but he'd put no more stock in the city than its name. Now that he understood its contents—or at least what those contents were *claimed* to be—he better understood her desire to quit the place.

Garit had stirred after their return, and the night had grown quite cool by the time they made it back. They'd debated a fire, and they decided warming him was worth the risk. Morning came, and Ella was troubled to find that he'd managed to reopen his wound while squirming in the night, and his skin was hot to the touch. "I fear this is truly a fever now."

"Is there anything I can do to help?" Tristan asked. She shook her head, never taking her eyes off Garit, and Tristan grunted in frustration. "Can you sense the White here?"

"No," she replied. "I'm not sure if the problem is the cursed ruins or what, but no, I can't sense it." Tristan turned from her and closed his eyes, but he didn't know how to 'sense' the Grey.

What he did feel was an overwhelming need to go out into the forest and kill something; what he couldn't decide was whether this was because he was being influenced by the magic, or if this was his desire to go out and use the Grey to restore some of Ella's ability to use the White. Or, perhaps, he just needed an outlet for his anger.

"Are you alright?" she asked, snapping him out of his thoughts.

"Aye," he said. He turned back to her and walked over to peer down into Garit's face. He was pale, his features sunken. "Can we move him? Would you have a better chance somewhere else?"

Again, Ella shook her head. "I don't think so. Sure, sometimes the air teems with the magic in one place, but in another it may be fainter—but you'd have to travel a long distance for the kind of change you're suggesting, probably several days. I can't even find a trace here." She observed Garit again, her face anxious. "He doesn't have that time. Not like this. If I can't mend him—at least to close his wound and rid him of this fever—he won't last much longer, Tristan."

Garit made a face, and Tristan wondered if he'd understood her, or if it was merely a coincidence. In any case, the true meaning of her words hurt in a way he couldn't begin to explain. He thought to himself and decided that speaking the words aloud would push his resolve into action. "He's dying," he said.

Ella met his eyes. She appeared wounded, as though not saying the words would have made the reality any less. As much as he may detest the Grey, using it now would help his friend. Even if Ella was certain the Balance was a myth, he was certain it was true. Now, he was going to prove it to himself. "I'm going hunting," he said in a flat tone.

"What?"

"I'm no use here," he said. "We need food, and so will he if he ever wakes up. I'll not sit here and wait for him to die. I'm going to go and try to be helpful somehow." Ella was watching him now, her lips pursed. "I have to do something," he pleaded. "And I'll also keep an eye out for any herbs which may help draw out the infection. I don't have much knowledge about healing, but I was taught a little as a soldier."

She nodded. "I've some small store with me, though most of our medicinal stores were in my saddlebags on Rose..." Her voice trailed off. Tristan wanted to say something to her, but he was not sure what good his words would do. The anger which was building inside may be quelled if he took the time now to be sentimental.

He decided not to let that happen. Commander Walter had told him the Grey was crafted by hatred. So, without another word, he picked up Garit's bow and arrows and turned to leave. As he walked away, Ella called after him. "Don't be too late getting back," she said. He stopped but did not turn back to her. "Please," she added. "I don't want to be alone here." He grunted and vanished into the forest.

The chill of the morning began to ease as he made his way deeper. He decided to go east, which was the same direction they had fled in when they had been pursued by Vincent. At the very least, this way would eventually lead to the river, so he would know where he was. Still, he tried not to follow the exact same path they had followed two nights earlier, as it had been thick and difficult to navigate. Thankfully, he didn't have a grown man thrown over his back this time.

The trees here were varied, but still bore nothing which would serve as food. No birds sang, either gone for the season or avoiding the cursed ruins. In the distance, Tristan noted the rushing of the river, but the sound was faint. If anything moved in the vicinity, he should be able to detect it.

He crept along, looking at the ground more than anything else. His eyes scanned for tracks, broken branches, or any other sign that game may have come through. To his dismay, the only prints and signs of passage he found belonged to him and his companions, or else to the soldiers who had pursued them.

His empty stomach rumbled, and his hunger mingled with his lack of sleep, concern for his friend, the uncomfortable environment, and self-loathing about what was inside of him. The feelings were too much, and a storm churned in his mind.

Soon, he discovered the corpse of a soldier not far from the path. Tristan realized they had seen no dead men during their return to Emjaria, but Ella had dropped a few of them. Perhaps some had been carried back by their comrades, or perhaps they had crawled into the undergrowth, not sure of where they were going, but trying to survive.

In the stories, soldiers always seemed to die the moment they were struck. The truth was grimmer. The man Tristan was looking at had left a lengthy blood trail. He had pulled himself a fair way down the path and into this undergrowth. Death had not found him quickly, nor had it been a peaceful passing.

The man's face was twisted in agony. Flies buzzed around him, and the reek of decay was heavy on him. Tristan stared down and studied his remains. He took the man's arrows. His bow and sword were nowhere to be seen, likely picked up by one of the other soldiers. With no more loot to be found, Tristan slipped deeper into the forest.

Soon, he scented another corpse, and moments later he discovered the start of another dragging trail. This soldier had started shedding his armor as he went, likely in an effort to reach the wound easier.

After a few minutes, he found the body, and he was met with a gruesome scene. The man's belly had been torn open, and something had feasted on him. A sound up ahead reached his ears, and he readied his bow. Whatever had done this was no carrion bird.

He began to creep back, but he'd not gone ten steps before the first snarl sounded. He told himself he had imagined it, but then came a second one. He glanced down and spotted a print in the dirt, overlooked when he was following the blood trail—a wolf. The paw was exceptionally large. Hunger gripped him, but he had no desire to hunt wolves, or to be hunted by a pack. That was when he realized the wind was blowing from behind him.

A wolf snuffed the air, and then another took up the scent—at least two of the beasts. A moment later, he noted that while these two were sniffing, something was still eating noisily a little way off to the side. A third wolf, likely with a portion which had been ripped from the body.

After a moment, the sound of chewing from that direction stopped, and he listened as the third beast stirred to its feet. A rumbling growl came toward him from straight ahead, but he could not see anything yet. He squatted, drawing back his arrow. If he waited until they were upon him, he'd be too late.

He only had one chance to shoot—perhaps the others would flee if he shot true. He listened and caught the soft padding of paws heading in his direction. They were stalking. Beyond the underbrush in front of him, one of the lower branches moved. He loosed his arrow and was rewarded by a sharp yelp. The wolf retreated, but the others did not follow their wounded fellow. One emerged, and he had no time to draw another arrow.

He dropped the bow and was drawing out Garit's knife from his boot when the wolf lunged at him. He got it up just in time, and the jaws of the beast snapped down where the blade met the handle.

It did not seem to realize it had missed its mark, and Tristan wasted no time. He drew out his sword and stabbed into the creature's underside. The beast growled through clenched teeth but did not let go of the blade in its mouth, even as its blood and entrails begin to spill from its belly.

As he tried to pull the blade free, he realized that the wolf had one of his fingers as well. It was the forefinger of his left hand, and before he could give the matter any consideration, the beast shook its head violently. The dagger was ripped from Tristan's grasp, and his finger came away as well.

He stared down at his left hand for only a moment before the pain hit him. A wave of dizziness crashed into him and brought him to his knees. At that moment, the third wolf appeared. His muzzle was thick with blood, and his forelegs were coated as well from whatever chunk of meat it had been dining on.

A fresh pulse of blood burst from the severed knuckle, and Tristan spun back to the two wolves before him. The wolf which had maimed him was sinking down, his own fatal wound getting the better of him.

To his left, the new challenger began to hunch down, his muscles tensing as he prepared to pounce. Tristan paid him little mind as he held up his left hand with its missing digit, grabbed the wolf by the throat, and slammed the creature to the ground as soon as it launched. He gripped hard, choking the beast, all the while keeping his eyes on the one which had taken his finger.

He stretched out his right hand. It was like the boar— he was able to reach into the wolf without touching him. In his mind's eye, he reached down its throat. The creature tried to bite him, but Tristan's phantom limb could take no harm. He was determined to rip the animal's heart out of his chest, but the wolf succumbed, choking on an arm which was not there.

Not content, he faced the foe in his left grip. It was only now that he realized the creature was several feet away, and he choked this one with the Grey as well. The beast lay on his back, thrashing with all four legs at a foe who was strangling him and not touching him.

He did not bother with going through the mouth. With his right hand, he reached in and grabbed its heart. He pulled so forcefully that the chest split open as the heart came sprawling out on the grass. The wolf ceased moving immediately as blood poured from the gaping wound.

Tristan panted heavily as he stared at the gore before him, and he scanned the grass for his finger. The pain in his hand began to radiate as his focus drifted more toward the seeking of his lost digit and away from his anger. He found it, bloody and mangled, and clutched it tight with the remaining fingers of his left hand.

In a short time, the pain brought him to his knees once more. He gritted his teeth and clenched his eyes shut, holding his injured hand around the wrist. He lifted his left arm to his mouth and bit into the sleeve, chewing a tiny hole and ripping the fabric off.

It was clumsy work, but he managed to tie the strip somewhat tight around his left wrist. This helped to stem the flow of blood, but the throbbing intensified until his hand was hammering harder than his heart.

He pushed himself up and began to make his way back. He didn't stop to consider bringing any of the meat back with him. "What would wolf taste like?" he thought, and then he laughed. "I just used the Grey to kill wolves, lost a finger, and I'm thinking about how they'd go with a meal."

He realized he was talking aloud to himself, and continued to do so, hoping his musings would serve as a distraction. "Why me? Of all the people who could have been cursed with this, why me?"

He closed his right hand into a fist and consciously tried not to move his injured hand more than necessary. "The very affliction which killed my family, and I have it!" Sweat trickled down his forehead as the blood continued to drip from his wound. He lifted his left hand and resolved to hold it high.

His consciousness danced between his past and the present. Images of one of the wolves flashed through his mind. He stared hard at the pain he was inflicting, then a sword pierced through the beast's flesh, passing through the crack in the floorboards and slicing his face.

He reached up to clutch the wound, but the only blood he found was coming from his stump of a finger. Growling, he hurried back to camp. He did not try to be sneaky on the return and chose to follow the road.

Before long, the scent of fire and breakfast reached him, but his stomach was in knots. As his friends came into view, Tristan glimpsed Ella standing over Garit before the edges of his vision began to darken. "Ella!" he called out.

The word had no sooner passed his lips than he crumpled to the ground in a heap. A wave of misery washed over him as his left hand crashed into the earth, and the severed finger slipped from his grip as he succumbed to blackness.

Someone held him, rocking him as he cried. She wiped away drying blood as he tried to bring his sobs under control. Beside them, a little girl sat down and took his hand in hers. She didn't smile, but instead gave an expression which said nothing more than, "I'm here."

She reached out to his right hand, tracing over his fingers, especially his forefinger. Then she laid that hand back on his lap and reached over and took his left hand in hers.

This hand was missing a finger. Panic was setting in when little Ella placed a hand on his forehead and shushed him. He lay still as she let her fingers glide over his hand.

"Oh, Tristan," she said. The words were those of a woman, though, not this girl who sat beside him. In the next moment, she was the woman he now knew. "It comes so easy with you," Ella continued. She spoke as though he wasn't there. "If only you could understand how easy this is—and how damned frustrating."

Something cold came into contact with his stumped knuckle, and she wrapped her fingers around it and closed her eyes. "With anyone else, I'd have to say the words, but not with you. Never with you."

Tristan's eyes fluttered open, and he sat up. There was Ella, his left hand clasped in both of hers, and there was his finger—not severed and bleeding and dead, but attached and alive. He balled his hand into a fist and flexed and splayed his fingers wide. He wiggled them and reached with his right hand to touch the finger which should not be there. He gaped at Ella, astonished at what she had done—then threw up and passed out once more.

It was a while later before he woke again. He had been moved closer to the flames, and the sun was well on its way to setting. Something was cooking, and he lifted his head to see Ella tending meat. Two skinned rabbits, partially butchered, lay some distance away from them. The day was cold, the fire warm, and the scent made his mouth water. Tristan found himself thinking that rabbit would be much nicer than wolf, and he laughed aloud at the thought.

"This should be ready soon," Ella said without turning to him. "Took me a bit to find something."

He sat up and surveyed the area, and he found Garit sleeping beside him. He had fresh bandages, and the wrappings weren't as thick as they had been before. "Ella?" Tristan asked as she turned to him. "He's improved?"

"Aye," she said, and the tone in her voice was pleasant. "It was sudden. A bout of energy erupted and swirled in the air. I was able to reach for the White and close most of his wound. I would have mended it completely, I think, but then a certain fingerless sod came lumbering back into camp."

Looking down at his hand, Tristan flexed his fingers again, remembering everything which had happened. "Almost like I never lost it," he said under his breath. "I never knew you could do such a thing."

"It can be done, but it's supposed to be rather difficult."

He regarded her closely. "Supposed to be?"

She nodded, prodding the meat to see how well it had cooked. "I've read about the skill, but never actually seen it. This has probably only happened a couple dozen times in the last few centuries, since we started keeping written records and such—if that many."

"But you've been trained to do this anyway?"

She shook her head. "I've read about it, but I've never been taught how. It just came natural, though."

Tristan grunted to himself. "Well, you were saying it comes easy." He glanced at her, and she had gone stone still. The expression on her face was one of embarrassment. "What's wrong?"

"When did I say that?" she said, her voice little more than a whisper.

Tristan shrugged. "I thought I was dreaming. I was the little boy in the stream, and your mother was cradling me. You were there, holding my hand. Only when you started talking, the voice was yours. Your voice now, I mean—a grown up voice. You said it came easy with me. It's all a bit hazy, and I can't be sure what was dream and what was real." He stopped and realized her terror had only deepened. "What's wrong, Ella?"

"Did you hear anything else?" she asked. Her voice was still quiet, but now hurried as well. He stared at her blankly, wondering what she was so afraid of. "Tristan, answer me!"

The crack of her voice shocked him. "Something about not having to say the words. I didn't understand what you were talking about—I'm *still* not sure what you were talking about." He turned his body and fixed her with a direct stare. "Ella, what words?"

She opened her mouth but only stammered something unintelligible.

"You two are really loud, considering we're probably still in danger for our lives." Ella jumped to her feet, and Tristan turned back fast. Garit's eyes were open, and he was patting about his wound with his hands. "Well, I'm clearly not dead." Tristan began to chuckle, but it caught in his throat as a sob as he dropped to his knees by his friend. He reached out and clutched at Garit's hands, taking them firmly in his own. "Hey, Tristan."

"Hey," was the only response which came to his mind. He sat and let tears silently roll down his cheeks but didn't try to say another word. Ella stood on the other side of the small cot and inspected the bandaging. "No new bleeding. I think our only concern now is getting food and water in you."

Garit turned his head to her. "Whatever you're cooking smells good."

"It's rabbit."

Garit smiled. "Well, that's something I've not had in a while. It sounds great."

Ella started to walk away, but Garit took one hand from Tristan and held it out towards her. She stooped and placed her palm on his, and he gently squeezed. "Thank you," he said. "You saved me."

Ella smiled at him, and Garit closed his eyes again to rest. Once he was asleep, the smile on Ella's face diminished. Her eyes flickered to Tristan, and she turned away as she realized he was watching her. "I'll finish preparing dinner," she said.

The meal was not bad, aside from being bland because of their lack of seasoning. The night passed in relative peace, and they spent several more days there, letting Garit recover his strength. They searched the ruins for anything which would aid them.

They took what food they could find—a few loaves of bread and some jerky, chiefly—and replenished their depleted provisions. What excited Tristan the most, though, was when he came upon the sword which Ella's father had gifted him. It had been taken from him when he was captured but must have been forgotten when Jules' group had departed. He bowed his head and offered a prayer to Rylar, thanking him for this small blessing.

His blade in hand and his friend mending, Tristan was ready to finish what they'd started. They'd had their brush with death—now, all thought was centered once more on their goal. Stocked and rested, the trio prepared to depart for Elinton and Jules.

XVI
Homecoming

It took me a while to recover enough strength to begin the journey again, but we finally managed to move on. Still, this has lasted far longer than we would have liked. Most of the trip ended up being on foot after all, and I've slowed our progress more than Tristan or Ella will ever admit, but at last, we are nearly there.

Elinton will be within sight no later than tomorrow. After that, it's only a matter of sneaking in without being detected, slipping into the royal palace, and killing a dictator who is surrounded by mages who wield a power we can't see but will still violently rip us apart. Sounds simple enough.

Why did I allow myself to get pulled into this again? If I make it through this alive, I'm punching Tristan in the face.

Elinton loomed in the distance, a stunning city atop a hill, encircled by golden fields. The sight was a stark contrast to what they'd grown up in. Grauberg was a grey fortress situated among grey mountains, but Elinton was a ray of sunlight on a mound of green, and the blue sea beyond was the backdrop which perfectly framed the scenery.

Even now, with winter threatening, the city was dazzling to behold. If Grauberg had been built for war, then Elinton had been crafted for beauty—even the invasion of Jules and his followers from Felixandria had not taken that away. Tristan had long expected to find ruins and destruction, but the vision was more radiant now than when he had beheld it as a child.

A deep valley lay between the three and their goal. The hill which Elinton crested was one of several, with smaller towns and villages standing atop the others. The fertile valleys between were home to farmlands and pastures. Many dotted the landscape: wide fields for livestock and empty tracts which had their crops harvested in the late autumn.

Still, Tristan noted many patches which appeared to be barren. Some were overgrown with tall grass and weeds, and even from this distance, the barns or homes were clearly abandoned. One of these would likely be his former home, unless other tenants had moved in after his family's demise.

"I have never seen such a sight," said Garit, still marveling at the view. "Is everything truly made of gold?"

The others laughed. "No," said Tristan. "The king's palace was gold-plated, almost entirely. Aside from that, many of the buildings have small portions which are thinly gilded. The city appears golden only when the light hits at the right angle. Wait until the sun has set, and you'll see that it's much plainer than you suspect."

"Still," breathed Garit, his tone almost solemn, "it is a beauty."

"Aye," Ella agreed. "It is, indeed."

The three were still on the road near the edge of Camtar Forest, and the sun was low when Tristan held up his hand. "Let's halt here."

"What? So close?" said Garit, aghast. "Surely one of the homesteads will take us in for the night."

"We aren't sure what we're riding into," Tristan replied. "The sun will be down soon, and I'd rather have a bit more information before we waltz into the unknown and ask for a room."

Garit raised his arms and let them drop in a dramatic fashion. "But I want to sleep in a bed!"

"Me too," said Ella, all her enthusiasm gone with the thought of sleeping in the forest again. She heaved a deep breath and resigned herself to their fate. "It's only one more night. Tomorrow, we'll make our way into the city — I hope."

Tristan grunted and turned his horse off the path. Ella rode double with him on Traveler, and Garit had the bulk of their supplies. They'd not been fast in proceeding from the ruins of Emjaria; the horses were too heavily burdened to be ridden hard. Therefore, they'd split their time between walking and riding.

For every ride, they shifted much of the cargo to Garit's mount so Traveler could carry two, and while they had gotten quick about it, this was still time consuming. The trip which had originally been planned to take about a week had stretched on considerably longer, but the end was in sight.

"I'll get a fire going," Garit announced as Ella and Tristan began to unpack their bedrolls.

"No." Tristan dropped some of the gear and rolled his shoulders. "No fire, not this close to the farmlands." Garit let out another dramatic sigh, which drew playful glares from the others. Tristan peeked at the last of their food stores. "We have enough for tonight. We'll not be hungry."

"Nor will we be satisfied," grumbled Garit, but he did not argue the point.

Ella made her way around, settling things and trying to make their small camp as comfortable as possible. Once the sun was down, she led the horses out to the edge of the forest and across the main road where there was grass to be had. She figured the mounts were likely tired of their bland diet, but this was all they had available to them.

When she came back, Tristan and Garit were chewing on some dry meat. "I'll be happy when we are done with this," she said. "Since we left the ruins, I swear the only things we've discussed are sleeping, eating, and the sores on Garit's arse."

"I don't complain about those much," said Garit, struggling to tear off a piece of tough meat.

"Yes, you do," Tristan and Ella said in unison. They faced each other and laughed as Garit glared at them with a mocked annoyance. "You're right, though," Tristan began. "I'm ready for this to be over, as well."

Garit sat up a little and leaned forward. "Are you, though?" he asked. Tristan turned to him, and Garit met his gaze with a solemn face. "You've come this far. It's one thing to anticipate being done, but are you ready to go through with it?"

"You mean, am I prepared to kill Jules?" The bluntness of Tristan's question seemed to bring the entire forest to attention. The wind quieted as the words hung. Ella looked from one to the other, unsure of what to say in the silence.

"Don't take my questions the wrong way," Garit said. "I'm not doubting your resolve. I understand what you lost. I may not feel it personally, but I understand. But—" He stopped and made a face, trying to find a way to put his feelings into words. He stared between his knees and moved a small clump of grass with his foot. "I'm not sure that I could do it, is all. Not even to that bastard, Vincent. Because of him, I had an arrow in my back. The bloody thing came out of my chest, and I'd be dead if not for Ella's magic. But even knowing that, I'm not certain I'd be able to kill him in his bed."

Tristan glanced down at his hands in the fading light. Soon, the grey sky would yield to black night. "Are you saying I'm acting dishonorably?"

Garit shrugged. "I don't think that's what I mean. I'm no philosopher, but I'm not one to say it's wrong to kill a murdering psychopath while he sleeps. It just seems simpler to think of it in the heat of a fight. In a battle, you don't have a choice. It's kill or be killed, but this—this is so deliberate. It weighs heavy on a man's mind is all I'm saying."

"I've heard that all my life," Tristan said. "I've listened to the stories from the older soldiers—the ones where they took a life. They say they still see the eyes of their enemies." Ella scooted closer to him and placed a hand on his arm. "But I've met others who don't appear to be bothered at all, and I don't mean the ones who come into the low hall and lose themselves in a tankard of ale. Some of the men did what had to be done, and they don't seem to miss a wink of sleep."

"Aye, but how many of those men assassinated someone? They killed other soldiers, and they killed them in battles."

Tristan stood abruptly. "I won't challenge him to a fair fight if that's what you think I should do. My only concern is killing him, and I don't care how I have to do it!"

"I don't think that's what he means, Tristan," Ella said. She came to her feet and moved closer to Tristan, wrapping her arms around one of his. "We just want to make sure you've thought this through. We want to be certain you have considered how this might affect you."

Tristan looked from one friend to the other. Ella let his arm go as he stood. He paced about, then turned so that he could see them both clearly in the twilight. The silence stretched out, almost uncomfortably long. "I'm ready."

Garit and Ella glanced at one another and back to Tristan. They nodded. Garit opened his mouth to speak, but Ella shushed him and turned to the road. "Horses."

"I don't—" Tristan began, but he cut his own words off as he caught the faint sound of hooves. They'd made their camp far enough to be off the road, but not so far as to totally lose sight of it. A few minutes later, they saw two dark shapes come into view.

Ella moved to the horses, but they seemed unconcerned. Tristan made his way toward the road. Behind him, Garit was moving as well, but very silently. The shapes became clearer as they came closer.

They were obviously guards, riding at a casual trot on two dark-colored horses. "Standard patrol," Tristan whispered to Garit as they stopped two dozen yards or so from the edge of the road. The men drew nearer, and Tristan and Garit held their breath. The soldiers were soon right in front of them, and just as quickly, they had passed, their hooves growing fainter and fainter.

"Probably a good thing we decided to camp instead of riding on, eh?" said Garit. Tristan nudged him in the ribs, and Garit grinned. "They'll likely come back this way again in a bit. Want to stay put until they've returned?" Before Tristan was able to think of an answer, a horse snorted in the forest behind them. "That was one of ours," Garit said, and a sinking sensation spread in their gut. They remained as still as possible where they were, hoping the patrol hadn't overheard.

A few moments was all it took to dispel this hope as one of the soldiers came riding back at a near gallop. He reined his beast in and sat still, listening. "I heard your horse!" he called out. "Come out, in the name of the Regent of Elinton!" Tristan and Garit did not budge, and they hardly dared to breathe. The man scanned the edge of the tree line, but he appeared to have no true idea where they were. "I said come out, coward!"

A few moments later, they heard the second rider approaching. He was coming back at nearly the same pace they'd seen him at before. "Yell some more," he said as he reached his comrade. "Yelling always works. Thieves in the woods always reveal themselves the moment you start yelling. Go ahead. Call out again."

"Oh, stow it," the first soldier said. "Someone's nearby."

"I didn't hear anything."

"Well, I did, alright!"

The second soldier sat for about half a minute before he started riding back toward Elinton. "Come on," he said. "Let's go."

"But I heard—"

"—a horse. Do you hear one now?"

"Well, no, but—"

"Do you plan on dismounting and combing this entire patch of forest in the dark?" The first soldier said nothing. "If someone is out here, you've no idea where they are. But because you chose to gallop back and proclaim yourself so boldly, you can believe he bloody well knows where you are! Whose throat is most like to be slit if you go into that forest, eh? Yours or his?" Without another word, he resumed his ride toward the city.

"Shite," said the first, and he snatched his reins harshly and kicked his horse to a trot. After a few minutes, both of the men were out of earshot again.

Garit and Tristan let their breath out. "That was too bloody close," said Tristan.

"I almost soiled myself," said Garit. He reached down and patted the seat of his pants. "Aye, I'm good to go." Tristan couldn't help but grin. Even after his near-death experience, Garit had been quick to regain his humor. "Let's go check on Ella, eh?"

Ella was close to tears when they returned to her. "He came galloping back, and he started calling out. I thought he'd seen you!" Her eyes were wild with anxiety. "I thought I'd killed you!" Garit stood in silence while Tristan pulled her to him and held her tight. "I'm tired of being left with the horses, not knowing what's happening!"

"I know," said Tristan. She was pounding his chest with her fist as she ranted, and he didn't stop her. "This will all be over soon."

"It better be over soon!" she all but yelled. "If we are pursued on the way back, the two of you can tend the bloody horses!"

The rest of the night passed quietly. They went to bed once their nerves had settled. Early the next morning, they all stirred at about the same time. They ate hard cheese and harder bread for breakfast as the sky began to brighten through the thick trees. No leaves remained on the branches. "So," said Garit, chewing determinedly on a chunk from his loaf, "what's the plan now? Do we go in on the road?"

"I believe that would be the least suspicious way to go," said Ella. "Won't someone be alarmed if three strangers cross their farmland from the forest?"

Tristan sat and finished his breakfast, his brow knitted in thought. "Does anyone enter on this road? Do some of the villagers still trade with Elinton, or do they all shun it? We have no way of knowing.

He reflected on the events of the previous night. "The road may be under watch, anyway. If that soldier was adamant when he returned last night, any guards might be suspicious of travelers coming in early this morning."

"Well, what should we do?" Garit asked.

"Some of the farms on the far edges may be deserted," Tristan said. "A few of them appeared to be abandoned yesterday, at least from a distance." He remained silent for a minute, and then rose to his feet. He began to tidy up his belongings as he spoke. "The farm my family lived on bordered on the forest. That's how I was able to escape all those years ago. I think we should check it out. If no one else has moved in, it might be our best shot."

The sight was what Tristan had expected, and yet his heart broke all the same. The farmhouse and lands appeared dilapidated. That was good for their current needs, but it hurt to see his childhood home reduced to little more than rotted wood and overgrown fields.

The grass was tall as they made their way out of the

forest. Wild bits of corn or grain or cotton grew all about. No doubt, seeds scattered from nearby farmsteads had taken root over the years from time to time.

He barely remembered his days of working out here, helping to pull up weeds and "odd crops" with his sisters. The girls used to scare him with stories, but they were also his playmates and his coworkers. Now they were gone, and the weeds and the odd crops had come to stay.

He had a sudden impulse to stoop down and rip up the cotton and the corn and whatever else he might come across, but he fought the urge down. His temper had gotten him into trouble many times, and guards may be stationed anywhere, not to mention nosey neighbors. The last thing they needed was to be discovered because of one of his tantrums now that they'd come this far.

They didn't move fast, but they weren't exactly creeping along either. Before long, they had passed through the field and emerged by the front of Tristan's old home. He hesitated, unsure of what he was feeling. Anger? Sadness? Yes, but also the small memories he held onto—memories of smiles and hugs, and dinner at the table in the corner.

He was startled by Ella's hand on his shoulder. "Do you want to go in?" she asked. He stared at the entrance. The door had rotted off the hinges and was lying flat. Beside the doorway, someone had painted the words "Grey Cursed" on the wall. "I'll go with you if you want to go in."

"I don't want to," he said. "But I need to." He reached up with one hand and patted hers, and then he moved forward.

As Tristan walked away, Garit came up to Ella. "Is this a good idea?"

She shrugged. "I'm not sure, but he needs this. This is everything he lost, Garit."

Tristan walked forward into the house, and his friends remained behind. He worried that he would find bits of cloth and bone, but there was no trace of his family. He hoped that meant someone had come along and given them a burial—perhaps the same person who made the warning on the wall outside. "Grey Cursed." That's what had happened inside this house—and what was happening inside him.

Garit and Ella stood silent in the doorway as Tristan's memories threatened to overtake him. His home had not been big—one large room which served as kitchen and common area, and one thin, long room on the end which allowed his parents privacy to sleep.

Tristan and his sisters had slept on cots in the common room. The cots remained, rotted and torn to pieces. Birds had clearly picked at the stuffing in the thin mattresses over the years, and the blankets were completely gone.

His blanket had been blue. Miriel had a green one, and Vanora had insisted hers be "all the colors of the rainbow." When his mother had stitched them together, he remembered how excited Vanora had been for hers. Now that he thought back, he recalled only blue, green, and red patches, but Vanora's quilt had been the envy of not just her twin sister and baby brother, but of their friends as well. Life had been so simple, for a blanket to bring so much joy and jealousy.

His eyes wandered over the floor to a place where the boards had been ripped up—his hiding place. The surrounding planks were marked with mud-colored stains, and to the side was another similar area. Old blood, long dried and soaked into the wood—his parents' blood.

He tried to look away, but instead he found himself transfixed by the sight. He sensed Ella standing in the doorway, warring with letting him have his way or running forward to turn him from it. She did not move, and though he stood in the ruins of his lost childhood, he was thankful for the restraint of his friends.

He began to walk away from the spot, but his eyes

lingered. After a few steps, his gaze swept the room and fell on the corner farthest from the door. This was where his sisters had died. When he had been pulled from his place under the floor, he'd had one brief glimpse of their bodies.

Like his parents, they were gone now, but one of their dolls remained. The dress which had once been blue was now a faded grey—almost white—and had mostly crumbled away. The doll no longer had her straw hair, and the material she was crafted from had nearly decayed.

Tristan knelt to retrieve it. Had this been Miriel's or Vanora's, he wondered. The girls had always been able to tell. The dolls were more alike to one another than his sisters had been, but they had always known which was which.

The dreams had always been vivid, and yet Tristan found that standing in the home, seeing the bloodstains, and holding the doll brought everything to life in a way he'd not believed was possible. The memory was clear. In this home, he'd lost his mother, father, and sisters. It had not been two random mages trained in the Grey, but Jules himself, and his bastard spawn.

Tristan tasted the bile in his mouth as he thought of how he'd sat in a room in the palace with the regent after being escorted by Vincent. Jules recognized who he was, he was sure. When he'd seen the scar and asked, he'd known.

Tristan wondered if this had been the first home assaulted. Is that why Jules was able to remember him? Perhaps his family had been the first people Jules and Vincent had ever killed with their cursed power.

The same power which now dwelled within. Tristan thought about his last memory of his mother's face, blood running from her eyes, nose, and mouth. The Grey had done that to her, and now, he planned to turn that same magic on Jules.

Tristan held the doll tight as he stood and faced Ella

and Garit. "That's enough," he said, and he was shocked at how hoarse he sounded. He realized he had tears flowing down his face but made no effort to wipe them away. Shaking with fury, he walked toward the doorway, and his friends parted to let him pass.

Once outside, he moved toward Garit's horse. He reached into one of the saddlebags and removed a small bit of cloth and gently wrapped the doll, and he hung it from his belt. Garit and Ella observed in silence. After a few moments, Tristan wiped the tears from his face and turned toward them, taking a deep breath and willing himself to calmness. He opened his mouth but found he couldn't speak yet.

"We understand, Tristan," Ella said softly. "We understand."

The corner of his lips gave the slightest of twitches, the faintest hint of a smile. "Sometimes you don't have to say the words, right?" She regarded him with a serious expression, and he thought of what she'd said during the healing of his hand. She may not have ever explained herself, and he wasn't sure of the exact meaning, but he felt pretty sure about which words had not needed to be said.

Still, this was not the time. He turned and faced Elinton, high up on the hill. "We still have to find a way into the city, and the more I think on it, the less I'm sure we'll be able to sneak the horses in at all."

"I think I might have an idea," said Garit, though his tone made it clear that he was less than sure of whatever he was thinking.

"Oh?" asked Ella. "Do elaborate."

Garit moved forward, his eyes gazing past his friends. Tristan's home lay between the forest and the hill on which Elinton stood, but it also had a view across the flat valley to the sea. Garit pointed, and Tristan and Ella saw something white in the distance on the water. "Sails," said Garit.

Tristan shaded his eyes. "A ship?" he asked. "How does that help us?"

Garit clapped him on the shoulder. "Tristan, my friend, you've much to learn. Let me show you."

XVII
Final Preparations

Garit led the way through the open country between Tristan's farmlands and the docks. He hoped that so long as they stayed on the outside of the farms, anyone working in the active fields might take them as farmers on their way to the city for trading. Of course, they weren't wearing the garb of farmers, but it wouldn't matter if they were able to reach their destination.

"Why won't it matter?" asked Ella, annoyed that Garit was not talking to them.

"Soon, my dear Ella," he replied. "All in good time."

Ella glanced at Tristan, who was wearing his smirk. "Helpers, help me," she muttered, "but I want to kick both of you."

The sails had not seemed large in the distance when they first spotted them, but they had not realized how far away they truly were. At first, they assumed the ship must be anchored offshore, but they were coming to see that the vessel was closer and much larger than they'd believed.

The ship was actually resting at the docks, and Garit had them marching hard. "We've got to reach them before everyone has disembarked," he said but offered no more.

They passed many properties along the way, many of them still producing crops. They had only passed a few which were overgrown like Tristan's had been. One of the other homes had the words "Grey Cursed" carved on the door, and one structure had been burnt at some point.

They reached the last of these farms, and on the other side stood the docks. Beside them was a small building that those coming and going would have to pass through, and a few people were on their way out as Garit led his friends closer. "Perfect," he said as he came to a stop.

"What's perfect?" Ella asked, her patience at its limit. "Enough with the blind march. What's your plan, Garit?"

"They are," Garit said, pointing at the people disembarking from the ship. Most were dressed in simple garb, though some had finer clothes of a much different fashion than anything these three had ever seen. The noble men wore pants which were tied off below the knee with high stockings and shoes buckled to their feet.

Their jackets had long sleeves which flowed open wide at the wrists and had bits of lace stitched inside. They didn't even cover the full backs of the men, ending abruptly above the waist, and the front edges were lined with golden or silver buttons which did not meet, nor were they intended to do so.

The women wore dresses which clung to their upper body in a way which was meant to show off their figures, with trimming which accented their curves, and lowcut necklines which revealed the tops of their breasts. "They're going to be cold soon," Garit said, forgetting that he was explaining his plan.

"Garit," Tristan said, masking his own annoyance which was, truthfully, as great as Ella's.

"Oh! Sorry," Garit apologized. "We'll follow along at a respectable distance. The passengers will think us farmers coming into town for the day. The guards at the gate will think us passengers with the rest of them. No one will ask questions and we'll be able to sneak ourselves and the horses in without issue."

Ella stopped short, her horse stopping with her. Tristan and Garit halted as well, with Tristan looking back and forth between the two. Ella's face was one of complete exasperation. "That's the plan? Sneak in with a bunch of strangers and *hope* no one bothers to ask questions?" She worked hard to keep her voice quiet, but her frustration was clear.

Garit shrugged. "I realize this isn't the best plan, but we needed an opportunity, and an opportunity is present. We may not have a better chance, nor do we have a better plan. I'm open to suggestions, but the window of opportunity to sneak into the city is closing quick."

Ella gave no response to this, and Tristan considered Garit's words. "This way will have us coming in from the docks, and they'll only be expecting the passengers from the ship, I'd imagine. As opposed to the eastern gate, where we would almost certainly be questioned. We might try sneaking in, but if a guard does find us entering in from any way other than a gate, we'll be put to the test for sure."

"But where are these people even from?" Ella asked, and Tristan and Garit answered in unison: "Felixandria." Her eyes widened. The answer was so obvious that she now felt silly for asking. No one from Grauberg was going to come by ship, and no lands were known of to the east—which left only Felixandria to the north. "Immigrants who wish to live here under the rule of Jules, rather than there with his father," she said. "Very well. I suppose we have no choice."

"I can't think of any other," said Tristan. "Just stay calm and keep your head down. But if we are doing this, we have to move now. I'd prefer to be in the middle of the pack than at the back."

With that, they all ventured toward the crowd. A couple of people noted them, but when the three gave no cause for alarm, the newcomers dismissed them—just as Garit had hoped.

Elinton was every bit as immense as Grauberg, and likely covered a larger area. Unlike Grauberg, it existed on a single level and was more spread out as a result. The city was not walled like a fortress, but regular patrols were stationed all about.

In various locations were guards who were assigned

a particular place, and Tristan noted others rotating from post to post, discouraging any who might try to sneak in between the regularly stationed sentries. Sneaking in would have been futile. The hill leading up to the city was covered in grass. No trees grew on the slopes, and with nothing to hide behind, intruders would have been seen long before they had a chance to take anyone by surprise.

The closer they got to the city, the more convinced Tristan became that this had been the best plan. They came ever nearer, and sounds began to reach his ears from within Elinton—the everyday milling about of city life, trading & bartering, hammers on the anvils of smiths, and swords somewhere in a practice yard.

He next began catching the different smells—fresh bread and smoked beef, sweat and body odor and horse dung. They all mixed in a familiar way, and yet still were distinct from Grauberg's.

Faint memories formed in Tristan's mind, of times he had come to town to trade with his father. It had likely happened often, but those images were all but gone now. As they neared the guards at the gate, he recalled a time when none had been posted here, and he had ridden on his father's shoulders as they entered.

"Helpers, help us," he heard Ella mutter under her breath. His eyes scanned about, but no one else was standing near enough to hear her prayer. In fact, he had not realized how close she had moved to him. He held his right arm out, and she looped her left hand through. He flexed his forearm and her hand squeezed back in response.

Garit was ahead of them, and he walked straight but not stiff, as though walking into the city of Elinton with a group of immigrants from Felixandria was something he did on a routine basis. Tristan and Ella did their best to match his confident stride. Moments later, a sense of elation washed over them—they had passed through the gates without so much as a glance from the guards.

"Well, that was easy," Garit said once they were several yards into the main byway. "Now, what do you think we should—"

"New arrivals, your attention please," roared a voice. Garit was stunned to silence by how loud it was, and those who had entered and were still flowing into the city turned to find a man standing on top of a podium. He was calling out through a grand horn which amplified his voice above the clamor.

"Those of you with horses, I would direct you to the stable located to the right of the gate you just walked through. Please tend to your animals and make any necessary arrangements with the stable's staff.

"Those of you who are nobles, please proceed straight down this street and directly to the regent's palace. Upon your arrival, you will be given a welcome worthy of your status. The men before you are members of the personal guard of Prince Jules, Heir to Felixandria and Regent of Elinton. They shall escort you." Tristan noted several armed men garbed in dark grey cloaks. Each carried spear and shield and wore a blank expression.

The crier went on. "Those of you who have trades—or those who come with employment secured in advance—please meet with the representatives of the city's various guildhalls to your left. There are also others not associated with the halls who are otherwise well acquainted with the many businesses of the city. Surely, someone can help you to your appropriate place.

"And lastly, to those of you who come with hope and little else: I warn you, you will receive no handouts here." The man's voice had a sudden harshness which took Tristan by surprise, and Ella's hand tensed on his forearm. He wasn't sure whether she was alarmed at the change in tone, or if she intended it as a reassurance to him.

The man went on. "We do not suffer vagrancy within the lands of Elinton. You will find a way to make yourself useful to our society, or you will be removed from it. If you should need help in this regard, you may proceed down this street to the Department of Appointments. When you arrive, you will be evaluated and assigned a means of contribution.

"Now, I believe my directions have been quite clear. You have been informed as to where you must report. I urge you, bear in mind all instruction you have received, both on the ship before disembarking and here in the city proper. Any who do not adhere will be dealt with accordingly.

"If you have any questions, you may approach me at this time. I trust that shall be precious few of you." With that, the man stepped out from behind the horn and descended a small stairway to the city streets. None approached him.

Garit turned to Tristan and Ella with raised eyebrows. "Charming fellow, to be sure," he said, and the uneasiness among them was broken as he smiled. "I suppose we should see to the horses if we wish to avoid questions."

The stables were kept up at the expense of the regency, and the three learned that only those who housed their mounts full-time were charged. They had no difficulty in bringing their horses in, and Garit's plan proceeded without any issues.

Tristan stood by as Ella and Garit tended to the horses. Garit grabbed his saddlebags and threw them over his shoulders as Tristan took his bags from Traveler. He glanced at Ella, and for a moment her eyes misted over, and he knew she was thinking of Rose.

He didn't like to think about the fate of the poor mare, so he patted Ella on the back, and she gave him a slight smile. They were given papers to reclaim their horses at the end of the day, and they left the stables as though everything were business as usual.

"So," Ella began, "what now?"

Tristan scratched his chin. "I feel that we had best

walk over to—what did they call the place? The Department of...?"

"The Department of Appointments," said Garit, smiling and happy to show that he was paying attention. "I think you're right. We can't afford to appear suspicious now. We'll go along with the flow and gather what information we can."

Ella sighed. "I hate making things up as we go."

"I know," said Tristan. "As do I, but gathering information is necessary. We have to start somewhere."

Ella and Garit gave one another a knowing expression. "That worked out so well last time," Garit said. He rubbed the spot where the arrow had pierced him, and Tristan had the decency to drop his eyes. Garit nudged him on the shoulder. "Just keep your head this time, and don't act blindly. I might not be so lucky next time."

Tristan nodded, and they turned and made their way down the street. They soon realized the office they sought was not near, and the saddlebags became a burden long before they reached their destination. Ella took some of the load from both Tristan and Garit, but no amount was enough to keep all three from being miserable before long.

"I wish that wonderful fellow with the big horn had told us what to do with these," Garit said through gritted teeth. "Remind me to apologize to my horse."

The bags were not loaded too much. In fact, they had very little weight compared to what they had started out with, but they were all exhausted from poor travel, poorer food, and terrible sleep. However, knowledge of how the packs *should* feel did nothing to alleviate the burden of the three friends in that moment.

At last, about halfway between the gate and the royal palace in the distance, they found the office. Three others were leaving as they walked in, letting their burdens fall to the floor in a clatter.

The sound brought a man out from a doorway in the

back. He was short, but stocky. "Took your precious time finding the office. I thought we were through with your lot for the day." He moved behind a desk in the center of the room, took a seat, and began looking through a stack of papers.

"We had horses to tend to," Tristan said, the tone in his voice declaring clearly that he did not like this man's attitude.

"And I've business to attend, so let's be quick about this. What are your skills?" All three of them exchanged glances, unsure of what to say. The man raised his eyes from his papers. "Well? What did you do in the motherland?" Again, none were sure of what to say. This was going poorly, and Tristan knew it. The man regarded them closely now. "Fine, if that's no good, let me ask a question which should be simple enough: how's the weather?"

Tristan turned to the doorway behind him. The door was framed between two windows which extended the length of the wall from floor to ceiling. Sunlight poured in, and the sky was visible above the buildings across the street from the office in which he now stood. "Sunny, as you can see—and I've got a decent sword arm, if that's of any use. I thought I might serve as a guard or a soldier."

The man stared at him. His eyes danced suspiciously between Tristan, Ella, and Garit—something was amiss here, but Tristan could not sense what that was. "A strong arm is not enough to be a soldier here," said the man, his voice full of contempt.

"I have more than a strong arm," Tristan said, the words coming out before he realized what he was doing. He only knew he had to find a way forward.

The man pushed back from the desk and stood. "Oh? And what do you have, exactly?" He was walking past them now, as though he were about to walk out the front door.

"The Grey," Tristan said. He had turned to follow the

man with his eyes and noted the looks Garit and Ella were giving him.

The answer stopped the man from leaving. He turned back and glared at Tristan with an odd expression. "Roundabout way of answering the question. You nearly gave me a start, coming in and behaving like that."

The tone in the man's demeanor had flipped. Tristan had no clue what he had said to alarm the man in the first place, nor what he had said to put him at ease. Still, it appeared he had accidentally done something right. The man moved back behind the desk and resumed his seat. "Now, tell me—what do you really have to offer?"

Tristan stared at him, confused. "The Grey," he repeated, hoping the answer would work as well a second time. The man leaned in close to him. "Is that a problem?" Tristan asked, keeping his voice calm and trying not to provoke the man to anger and alarm again.

The man scoffed. "Son, the Grey isn't something you can just say you have. Magic isn't a skill you can learn, but—"

"I have it," Tristan cut in. "I've killed a boar and wolves with it. I ripped their hearts out without ever laying a hand on them." Tristan didn't like saying these things out loud. Behind him, Garit and Ella remained silent, and Tristan made no movement to face them. The thought of looking in their eyes and seeing if they accepted this as truth angered him as much—if not more—as giving these memories voice. His anger was building inside, but he focused his attention on the man before him.

The man's demeanor changed again as he leaned forward and peered into Tristan's eyes. "Oh," he said, his deep voice surprisingly soft now. "I see." He cleared his throat and sat back. "Calm down, lad. I'll not prod you any farther."

He tapped his fingers on the desk. "The three of you go together, eh?" They nodded. "Well, they'll be welcoming the nobles tonight, and tomorrow will be a day of feasting and revelry. The ones who you'll need to report to are attending the regent at the moment. It'll be a couple of days before you can meet with them. I'll have to get tickets for each of you."

The clerk opened a drawer in his desk and pulled out three short slips of paper, then he scribbled a note on each. "Show these if anyone gives you trouble. Present yourselves back here in three days, and we'll sort you out."

He hastily wrote out notes on three more slips. "The barracks won't take you until you've been through the proper channels. Which means for now, you're homeless, and we don't have that here. So, take these to the inn. They can put you up until we resolve this. Direct the innkeeper to this office if there are any problems."

Tristan, Garit, and Ella took the papers, picked up their bags, and turned to leave when the man yelled out after them. "'Always Grey,'" he said in his deep voice. "Don't forget again—I almost pissed myself. Someone else may be quicker to raise an alarm than I was." Tristan nodded without being sure what he was acknowledging, and the three departed.

The inn was an impressive building, one that was far more occupied than Tristan would have thought, considering there couldn't be much in the way of people travelling to Elinton. He stopped to reconsider that idea—perhaps people came and went from Felixandria more than he imagined. Or perhaps there were villagers in Camtar Forest who still had business dealings here, as well.

Felixandria was said to be a land of hard earth and stone, with little in the way of farming and hunting. The people there had come to Camtar centuries ago to benefit from its farmlands and wildlife. When they'd been forced back to their home, Tristan imagined they'd been reduced to a rather small nation. Perhaps they had, but it seemed with Elinton open to them again, many were ready to return.

"What should we do now?" Garit asked. He stood over the saddlebags, which had unceremoniously been dumped in the corner as Tristan and Ella sat at the edges of their beds. "Go out and gather information?"

Tristan gave an uneasy nod. "That would be for the best, but one slip and we're done." He still wasn't sure exactly what had transpired in the appointment office, but it had been narrowly avoided. He was painfully aware of that, and he did not wish to repeat the experience. "I suppose we could stay in until nightfall and venture out then, but we'd be going blind."

"What if they have a curfew?" Ella asked. Tristan and Garit appeared startled, neither having considered this. "The city most likely has a curfew if Jules rules as a tyrant as we've always believed. Instead of passing in the night as strangers, we might be arrested if we're seen."

"He may not rule as a tyrant, though," said Tristan. "We've always believed him to be evil. He's strict, for certain, but when we were at the ruins in Emjaria, one of the soldiers there was Elinian. He was from here, not Felixandria, and he sounded proud to be a member of the guard. I overheard a family speaking in much the same way in the Chamber of the Children. What if the people here have embraced him? What if they don't want him overthrown?" Tristan didn't speak of the fact that the soldier, Nigel, had been the one sacrificed—the entire ordeal still sickened him.

Garit raised an eyebrow in the direction of his friend. "Having second thoughts?"

Tristan shook his head, but then gave half a shrug. "It's not that. Regardless of how people perceive him, he is evil. He murdered families—including mine—in cold blood. His men killed Ella's grandparents." She flinched at the sudden onslaught of the memory, but he pushed forward. "How many others? We can count how many Elinian orphans and refugees reached Grauberg, but what of the people who didn't—those who died here, in their own homes for the crime of being in Jules' way? Or those who died of their injuries on the road or in the forest while in flight for their lives? They died because Jules decided he wanted to take their home. I want my home back."

Ella reached out and patted his hand, but the gesture was weak. Tristan wondered what she was thinking, but he did not wish to put her on the spot in front of Garit. After a few moments, she spoke anyway. "We are planning to do the same to him as he did to us," she said. "That's what keeps going around in my head. Garit tried to voice his thoughts last night, and that's when I started thinking.

"I don't believe I've quite understood why this bothers me until now, but that's why—because we are coming to do the same thing he did." She faced Tristan with the slightest hint of tears in her eyes. "Does that make us the same as him?"

Tristan was stricken. As much as he'd thought of Garit's comments since last night, he had not thought of them in that particular light. "I—I don't—" he stammered out. "No! No, it's not the same thing!"

"Are you sure, or do you just *choose* to believe so?" Ella asked, a slight chill in her tone. "You've almost always acted on emotion, Tristan. You surprise me sometimes with logic and common sense, but then you do something stupid like almost kill Garit in the melee of a tournament or botch our plans like at Emjaria!"

Tristan reddened and turned his head to Garit, who was slowly nodding. "She does have a point," he said. "We need to be certain that we aren't becoming monsters by doing this, Tristan. I love you. You're my best friend, but we can't make this decision like boys who've had their toys taken away."

"I didn't have my toys taken away," Tristan said, his

uneasiness fading into something else. "I had my sisters taken away! And my father and my mother—my home! I lost everything that day, not my toys!" He had gotten to his feet at some point, and his fists were clenched at his side. In front of him, Garit and Ella both appeared to be suddenly fatigued. He unclenched, let his hands rest at his side, and took a deep breath.

"I'm sorry, Tristan," said Garit, shaking his head. "That's not what I meant. I'm sorry."

"I know," Tristan mumbled. He glanced at Ella, who regarded him with a curious expression. He sighed and tried again. "I know that's not what you meant," he clarified to Garit, his eyes shifting from him to Ella. "It isn't just what he's done, though. To say that makes it sound like I'm looking solely for revenge. I could try to be noble and say I'm seeking justice, but it wouldn't be entirely true. I do believe it, but vengeance is wrapped up in it, as well. Real justice can't be about vengeance. I realize that, but I'm not doing this for vengeance or justice. I'm not here only because of what he's done—I'm here because of what he will do."

He pointed out one of the windows in the room. The inn was three stories tall and had a clear view over much of the city. The window Tristan motioned to looked out over the road they'd traveled to come here. "Elinton is not the only home I've ever known. Grauberg took me in, gave me food and training. I met you there, Garit—and you on the way, Ella. I've grown close to your families. I barely remember Elinton. I am more familiar with the lower level of Grauberg than I ever was with the markets here.

"Grauberg is my home, and Jules is going there next. You know it, just as well as I do. My family is dead, but your father still lives, Garit, and your parents, Ella. All the friends and comrades we've made—Jules means to kill them and take what they have. Why should we let him? If I can stop what happened to me from happening to someone else—if it is at all in my power to do—I will."

Silence followed, and Garit sat looking down at the floor. Ella still stared at Tristan, but her eyes held him more warmly now. "Those are not the words of a selfish boy," she said. "I needed to be sure, Tristan. I think I would have come with you regardless, but I'm glad to hear you speak like this." He smirked at her and started to open his mouth, but she cut him off. "You're doing so well—don't ruin it."

Garit laughed, and the tension in the room was gone. "Well, that's that," he said, putting his hands on the mattress and pushing himself to his feet. "I suppose we'd best go out and try to gather a bit of information then, eh?"

Tristan nodded. "Probably, but before we go..." His words trailed off, and he moved over to the bag which held the bulk of his own property. He stooped down and began rummaging, removing items to reach for something in the bottom. When he turned back to them, Garit's breath caught. "I thought you might want this back."

Tristan held out the head of the spear Garit had broken on the day he'd been called a traitor. A short bit of the shaft was still attached. "I picked it up. I didn't want you to regret leaving it behind for the rest of your life."

"I *have* regretted it," said Garit. "I still feel sick about what happened, but..." His breath caught again, and Tristan sensed a sob was fighting to break out, as well. Garit took a moment to collect himself. "Thank you, Tristan. And you're right—we can't let what happened here happen in Grauberg." He tucked the shaft of the spear into his belt, then moved his cloak to conceal it. "I will have this in hand when we strike at Jules."

Tristan nodded. He turned to Ella, who was fidgeting with her fingers. "Garit," she said, her voice unusually shy. "I'm still not sure what happened in Grauberg. I mean, with the soldiers coming after us and everything. I'm not sure if you've thought I blamed you. I just..."

Now it was her turn to catch her breath. "I want you to know I'm not mad at you—not even a little. Whatever happened was a terrible misunderstanding, and I don't blame you for it. I know you and what you would and wouldn't do, and misleading your superiors and friends—well, it's not in your character."

Garit bowed his head to her, and she almost jumped at him to wrap her arms around him. "Careful of the spear," he said, his tone light. "Thank you, Ella. And for your peace of mind, no, I never felt like you hated me or believed me a liar."

"Alright," said Tristan, his slight smile now a broad grin. "That's enough sentiment. We have to go if we're to have any daylight left."

The three left the inn and found themselves looking over a fairly quiet street. They proceeded to the markets, where most of the indoor shops were still open, but many of the outdoor vendors had started taking down their wares. The sun had an hour or so before it would set, but these merchants appeared to be preparing to close shop for the day. In Grauberg, the vendors remained in place until the last of the light was gone. Tristan wondered if Ella's theory was correct about a possible curfew.

"There's a smith," said Garit, pointing to a building up the street. "Want to pay him a visit? We can at least sound somewhat knowledgeable about weapons and such while we pry for information."

"And there's an herbal shop," said Ella, indicating a structure across from them. "Divide and conquer?"

Tristan nodded. "Sounds like a great idea, but be careful. Change the topic or leave If you feel like you're losing your grasp on the conversation at all." Ella nodded, and she turned and walked across the street as he and Garit made their way to the smithy.

The shop was hot when they walked in. The forges were in the back, and though the work was done for the day, the heat lingered. A man with strong arms and a broad chest met their eyes when they came in. "Help you?" he asked.

"We've come to view what you have on offer," Tristan said conversationally.

"You new here?" the smith asked.

"Aye," said Garit. "Arrived today. We've been told we're to be guards, but they can't get us started with them for a couple of days."

The smith crossed his arms over his barrel-sized chest. "Got papers from the appointment office?" he asked.

Tristan reached and realized he had set them down with his saddle bags. He faced Garit, but he, too, was empty-handed. "Think I left them at the inn," Tristan said, keeping his voice calm. "Will you be open a bit longer? I can run and retrieve them if —"

"What's the weather today?" the man asked without a moment's hesitation. Tristan recognized it now, not as a question aimed at slow-witted new arrivals — this was a countersign.

"Why does —" Garit began, but before Tristan was able to shut him up, they heard someone shouting down the street.

"Intruder!" came the call. "Imposter at the healer's shop!" Others were taking up the cry. Garit and Tristan exchanged a glance. They looked back at the smith. He was taking a deep breath, and as he raised his hands to cup his mouth for his own shout, Tristan blurted out, "Grey! It's Grey! It's always Grey!"

The smith pulled his hands down and gave them a look of relief. "Bleeding hell, I thought I had imposters in my shop, too. Now, out of my way." He had reached up and grabbed a mace from the wall with one hand, while pushing Tristan and Garit out with the other. "Ella!" Tristan and Garit hissed to one another, and they followed the man out of the store.

Outside, the street which had been so quiet was now

drawing a decent crowd. "They said it was a woman," one person shouted, and then another cried out, "She broke a window and went out the back." Even with that knowledge, the mob seemed content to stand out front and to relay every bit of information which reached them.

Tristan expected to hear a lot of false information begin to crop up, but he was amazed at how accurate the reports spreading were. They relayed Ella's height and hair color and described her stature and even her tone of voice.

"She was wearing purple!" one voice called out. This one was wrong, and he realized the shout had come from Garit. "She had a sword on her hip!" Tristan shouted. Like wildfire, the word spread.

Tristan and Garit were on borrowed time. After a glance and a nod, they shifted through the crowd and toward an alley in the back. Ella had not been found yet, but if they made themselves obvious, perhaps she would find them.

They called out their false information to people coming toward them. "A well-muscled woman, armed with a sword and wearing purple," they told several, raising their voices louder as they went. "Headed for the western gate!" Garit shouted, and Tristan hoped he wasn't accidentally correct. Some went on toward the mob, but many were diverted to the false route.

"Where is she?" Tristan asked after no one else was around.

"Not headed for the western gate," came a voice from a shadow behind them. They turned to find Ella emerging from behind a crate. "Nor am I garbed in purple or carrying a sword, but I do like to consider myself in decent shape." She gave her friends a smirk which brought one to Tristan's face as well. "Come," she said. "I've a plan of my own, this time."

"Oh?" said Garit, "Making things up as we go, are we?"

Ella turned and smiled. "Opportunity, my dear Garit."

"And what is this idea?" Tristan asked. Ella made her way deeper into the city as the others followed.

"The city is distracted," replied Ella. "Soon, every guard will be looking for us, or at least me, and we are going to use the opportunity to sneak into the royal palace."

XVIII
The Royal Palace

Ella frowned as they walked through the city. "'Always Grey,'" she said. "Bloody hell, I missed that one entirely." She had been smiling moments before, but then Tristan had revealed where things had gone wrong. "I was only in there for a moment, and then the shopkeeper was asking me about the weather. I thought to myself, 'Is everyone here a sky-watching pain in the arse?'

"I told her if she wanted to see the sky, she needed to open her eyes and go outside. She gave such a start that I thought I'd offended her. Figured she was blind or something. Next thing I know, she's screaming that I'm an intruder and an imposter and a few other choice words. I ran through her back office and broke a very nice window to get out."

"I missed it as well," said Garit. "The smith asked us, and I was about to say something snarky. Must've been something the new arrivals were told about before they got off the ship. Tristan caught it, but we were about to be in the exact same situation."

Tristan smirked. "I'm just good. Keep your eyes on me, and you'll learn a thing or two." Ella and Garit both punched him, and he let out a groan. At least they were able to find merriment in the proceedings. All around them, the city was coming back to life. It had been on the verge of sleep, but now shouts rang out in the distance.

Every time Tristan, Garit, and Ella met someone new, they gave out different details. Soon, word of a dozen intruders was running rampant. No one asked them for the countersign, but merely took the information and relayed it.

"The first mob was pretty disciplined," Tristan said. "Jules has done well in that, at least. His people understand what to ask and how to spread information."

Ella nodded in approval. "You were clever to spread lies."

"No," said Tristan, pointing to Garit, "He was the one who started that."

Garit smiled as they proceeded deeper into the city. They weren't running, but their pace was quick, and they were drawing nearer to the palace in which Jules resided. Only a hundred yards stood between them and its gates.

To their surprise, those gates opened, and a group of soldiers emerged and headed toward them. The three moved to the edge of the street—out of the way of the men, but not in such a way as to appear suspicious. The patrol drew closer.

In the distance, a bell sounded the alarm. Moments later, other bells had joined in. The city bustled with activity again, like a beehive knocked from a tree. "Stay calm," Garit said under his breath, as much to himself as to his friends.

The soldiers continued straight down the street, but at the very last moment, the man leading them held up a fist. Without a second of hesitation, every man stopped. The soldier turned to them. "You three!" he shouted in a commanding tone. Tristan, Garit, and Ella went to him— there was no other choice. "What do you know?"

Tristan and Garit both shrugged, as if to say they weren't sure, but Ella spoke up. "We've caught a series of conflicting reports," she said, her tone frustrated. "We've been told a man, then a woman. Some say tall, some say short. The one thing I'm positive of, though, is that whatever happened all started at the stables! I believe they were stealing a horse and trying to leave town." Tristan guarded his expression, but inwardly he was impressed and amused with Ella's cunning.

The soldier nodded and fixed his eyes on her. "And the weather?"

"Always Grey," all three said.

"You," the commander called to one of the men behind him. "Return to the palace. Gather more men and set out for the stables." He faced forward and grunted. "This will be a long night," he said with a hint of a growl in his voice. "Forward!" he called, and the company began moving again, save for the one soldier returning for reinforcements.

"Follow him," Tristan said, and they did, jogging along at a respectable distance. Luck favored them. The soldier did not return to the front gate, but rather began to trail around the wall which surrounded the royal grounds until he came to a small door. The three friends ducked into the shadows just before the man glanced their way.

He knocked on the door, and someone on the other side said something. The soldier replied, but both of their voices were too quiet for Tristan or his friends to hear. The door opened and the man disappeared inside.

"What did he say?" Garit and Ella asked together. Tristan shrugged, reached for his belt, and cursed. "What's wrong?" asked Garit.

"Left my weapons at the inn. No dagger or anything," Tristan said, then he began muttering to himself about his own stupidity. "How about you two?"

Ella shook her head. "I'm in the same predicament as you."

"I have my spear," Garit said, pulling his cloak back. "Slightly shortened, mind you." He laughed nervously, and Tristan knew his friend did not wish to use it.

"It'll have to do," Tristan said. "Let me have it. We're probably going to need to, well—do something about this guard."

Garit nodded and handed it over. "I didn't think we were going to make it through this without some blood being shed, but I do hope it's minimal. What do you have in mind?"

"Trust me," Tristan said, deciding to take a note from Garit and Ella and lead his friends blindly for a minute. He crept toward which the door the messenger had passed through. He knocked lightly. "Let me in," he whispered through the wood. "They'll kill me. They have our men trapped in the square. Let me in!"

"What's the secret word?" a voice called out from the other side, full of uncertainty.

"Keep your damned voice down, you bloody sack of filth!" Tristan hissed. "You'll bring them down on us. Let me in or I'll shove this spear up your arse as soon as I get my hands on you!"

Nothing happened. The door stayed closed, and Tristan thought his gamble was a loss. A moment later, though, the door opened without warning. A head peered out, and as soon as the man inside laid eyes on them, Tristan leaned forward and slit his throat with the spearhead. The man reached for his neck, but he'd lost consciousness before his hands even touched the blood.

He fell face first through the doorway. Tristan and Garit each grabbed an arm and dragged him into the shadows they'd been hiding in moments before. "Let's go," Tristan said, taking a dagger from the man's belt and handing the weapon to Ella. She stared down at the dead man for a moment longer, and then the three were inside the walls of Jules' home. As they passed through the doorway, Tristan picked up the spear which the man had dropped.

The palace was surrounded by courtyards, but the one here on this side was not as immense as the one they would have met by going through the front gate. The sun had almost disappeared, and in the distance, men formed up to assist with the hunt for the city's intruders. No one stood between them and their goal. "Fortune favors us," Garit said.

"I don't believe in fortune," said Ella. "But today, I'm willing to make an exception." They covered the open ground and soon found themselves against the palace itself. It had many floors, all full of windows. "There!" Ella blurted. Tristan and Garit moved their heads and spied what she was looking at—a ladder leaned against the wall and a bucket of dirty water. "Window washer?"

"Who cares," Tristan said. "Let's move before we're seen out here." He grabbed the rungs, spear in hand, and began to pull himself up. Behind him, Garit and Ella stayed on the ground to keep an eye out for soldiers.

He climbed all the way to the top, but the windows on either side of him were secured from within. He descended a few rungs to the next level and pressed against a window to his left, but the pane wouldn't give. He tried the window on his right and found it to be unlocked. He pushed it open and carefully climbed through.

A quick glance revealed no guards, and he leaned out and motioned for the others to follow. In the next few minutes, he hauled Garit and Ella through as well. Inside, all was mostly dark. A few candles had been lit, and several doors lined the wall. "Let's figure out where we are," Tristan said.

The others nodded in agreement, and they hastily moved to one of the doors. Tristan pushed his ear to the wood as Ella and Garit kept a watch down either end of the hallway. No steps approached, and Tristan detected nothing on the other side of the door.

He pushed the door open to discover a bedchamber. The room was elaborately furnished, but a staleness in the air spoke of disuse. Still, Tristan let out a small laugh of relief.

"What's so funny?" Garit asked quietly.

Tristan pulled the door closed. "We're in the residential wing."

Garit looked confused, but Ella realized what he was

saying. "Jules' room is somewhere near, then?"

"Aye!" Tristan's excitement was evident, and he had to work to keep his voice quiet. "Let's check the others." They moved to the end of the hall and began making their way down. Most of the doors were locked, and the few which were open revealed rooms which were more or less the same as the first. After checking every door on the hall, they came around a corner with an identical corridor. Again, they worked their way down. At the end, they'd found nothing of note, but they had come to a stairwell. "Up?" Tristan asked.

"I'd think so," said Garit. "I doubt they would have people sleeping above the regent himself."

"Unless he doesn't sleep in this wing," Ella added.

Tristan gave her a teasing glare. "Don't doom our luck now," he said in a playful whisper. She smiled at him in the flickering candlelight, and they were about to make their way up the stairs when they noted footsteps above.

They moved beneath the stairway and hid in the shadows, but if someone looked straight at them, they'd be seen. The steps grew louder on the floor above, and then they began to descend the stairs. Tristan gripped his spear, but Ella reached out and touched him. He peered at her and recognized the plea in her eyes. "Only if I have to," he said, and she nodded in reluctant gratitude.

The lone guard came to their floor, but he passed by them as he made his way down the hall. He walked with the attitude of a man who did this patrol often, checking a couple of the rooms casually, walking into none of them, and seemingly unconcerned. He was complacent, and Tristan was thankful for that. "Let's go," he said after the guard's footsteps had faded.

They moved up the stairs which the guard had just descended. The floor above was better lit, but there were no doors in this first corridor. They made their way down and took the corner and found themselves standing in a carpeted hall.

Small statues stood on pedestals at regular intervals between windows on their right. On their left were doors, though not so many as had been on the floor they'd come in on. "Larger rooms," Tristan surmised. "This is it—the hall of the royal chambers."

"Stay sharp," Garit said. Ella nodded, though one glance at her face revealed how tense she was. Tristan thought to himself once more that she had no training for anything remotely close to this. He and Garit were soldiers, trained for dangerous situations since childhood. She had none of that, but here she was, standing with them anyway.

He didn't deserve her friendship, and that made him value it even more. He only hoped she understood how much he treasured it, though in truth he'd rather show her. He shook his head—this was not the time for those thoughts. Garit tapped him on the shoulder. "You alright?"

"Aye," he said and began to move forward. Five doorways lined the wall. The first two were simply crafted, one panel each, and both were locked. The third was a grand set of double doors. He reached up and twisted one of the knobs, expecting to find them locked tight. The knob turned in his grip, and he paused for a moment. He sensed this was Jules' room—every instinct in his body screamed that it had to be. This is why he'd come. Would Jules be inside, sleeping? Would they have to conceal themselves until he came in? There was only one way to find out.

He pushed the door open and crept in, and Garit and Ella followed swiftly. It quickly became clear that Jules was not there, and Tristan closed the door behind them.

The room was dimly lit. Dark drapes hung on the wall over the windows, as well as over the canopy bed. The chamber was huge but scarcely decorated. Tristan was certain it had been richly furnished when Elinton still had a king, but Jules had stripped it nearly bare—"the old ways," as he had called his style of living when Tristan met with him in Grauberg.

In the center stood a small, square wooden table, surrounded by four simple chairs, and a wash basin rested on top of a chest of drawers. Tristan was shocked to consider how much Jules' room was like his own, and the thought unsettled him. Garit and Ella were looking around, finding little to inspect. The drapes would be the only place to hide if Jules returned, or possibly under the bed.

Tristan moved closer to examine the bed in the center of the room. He was about to kneel to search under it, but something nestled between the two pillows caught his attention. He shook his head and rubbed his eyes, certain that they were playing tricks on him—they weren't.

Between the pillows on which Jules slept was a doll like the one which was tied in cloth and hanging from his belt. Her dress had not rotted away, and she was much better maintained than the one he'd found in their home, but there was no mistaking it. This doll had belonged to one of his sisters.

Footsteps sounded behind him. Ella or Garit, he wasn't sure. His vision misted over as tears filled his eyes. "Why does he have my sister's doll on his bed?" he asked aloud.

"Tristan," the voice was Ella's—soothing, but he did not wish to be soothed.

"Why," he growled, "is this here?"

"This is a trap," Garit said with certainty. "He's expecting us. Somehow, he knows who you are."

Tristan knew it was true—he'd already figured out that Jules had to know. He'd discerned as much in Grauberg. Had the prince been tracking them through the city? None of this made sense. "He has this in his bed. What—" His mind turned over all types of scenarios and schemes. At best, Jules anticipated his coming and had planted this to provoke him. At worst—"What kind of monster is this?" His voice was shaking.

"Tristan," Ella began again, placing a hand on his shoulder.

The door behind them cracked open, admitting the light from the hall. All three turned and froze. Jules stood in the doorway. He took two steps into the room before he noticed them.

The prince was wearing a robe and he carried a small cup. He was barefoot, and his thin frame appeared skeletal beneath the open robe. An odd expression was in his eyes, but Tristan wasn't sure what it was.

Jules began to inch back toward the door. "No," Tristan said, and he was shocked at the venom in his own voice. "You're not getting away from here tonight." He let the doll drop from his hands as he charged forth, and Jules turned and bolted, dropping his cup as he fled.

"No!" Ella shrieked, and Garit yelled something as well. Tristan didn't know what, and he did not stop to find out. Jules ran out in the same direction they'd come from and headed for the stairwell at the end of the next corridor.

Tristan was amazed at how fast Jules was moving. He was keeping pace but not gaining ground. As they passed the locked doors, now on Tristan's right, something clicked, and one opened.

A soldier came out, but Tristan drove his spear into the man's throat. More troops were in the room. Tristan ripped free and ran on. Behind him, pounding footsteps filled the corridor. He stopped long enough to turn and see Garit and Ella fleeing as well. The guards were behind them, but very close. Garit was right; it was a trap, but that didn't matter—not with the monster within reach.

Tristan turned and charged ahead. Jules was nearly to the stairwell when Tristan took the corner. He ran hard to catch up. "Tristan!" Ella yelled, but he did not turn back. Had they been caught? There were too many soldiers to fight if he stopped, and he had to go after Jules.

He finally reached the stairwell and looked down, but Jules was out of sight. Tristan began to go down, using the wall and rail to descend in giant leaps. His lungs were on fire—weeks of poor travel had destroyed his conditioning. He sucked in a deep breath and kept going. Jules couldn't escape. Not after they'd come this far for him.

Above him, someone else was coming. "Tristan!" came a shout from Garit. Ella echoed him, and a wave of relief hit Tristan. They'd not been caught yet, but was there an escape for any of them?

Useless to consider. Jules was here, and nothing else mattered—Jules, who murdered his family and had his sister's doll in his bed. "The filth!" Tristan uttered aloud, a wasted breath when he couldn't afford it, but that was of no consequence. He was determined to catch and kill his foe.

He reached the bottom of the stairs, glanced to his left, and found nothing. To his right, he witnessed Jules stumbling down a corridor. The prince spun back to face Tristan, then turned and picked up his pace. The edges of his robes flapped up as he disappeared through an immense set of double doors.

Tristan took a deep breath and pressed forward, his steps echoing loudly down the passage. He reached the doors and found them closed tight. He rammed them with his shoulder, and they gave way a little, but no more. He stepped back and kicked, and they flew open.

He raced forward and found himself surrounded by a dozen spears. Just beyond them stood Jules, breathing hard but not winded, his mouth quirked in a twisted smile. Before Tristan had time to think, someone hit him in the back of his knees, then in the back of his head.

He thought he had been blindfolded but soon realized he was dazed. His vision was hazy, and he observed only silhouettes moving about the room. He closed his eyes and fought the urge to vomit.

He was on the ground with someone kneeling on him. He couldn't breathe, and his hands were being tied behind his back. In the hall behind him, he heard Ella's screaming. He began to shout, but a boot to the ribs silenced him.

"Bring the prisoners forth," Jules commanded, his voice calm but stern. A guard hauled Tristan up by his bound hands, and he thought his shoulders would rip out of their sockets. He was brought forward and shoved back to his knees.

Shouts and curses rang out as Ella and Garit were brought in and deposited on the floor beside him. He opened his eyes again, and most things were clear enough now.

They were in the throne room. Torches were lit in sconces on the wall, as well as numerous lamps overhead. The mere thought of looking up seemed painful to Tristan's aching eyes. Jules came to stand before them. Vincent joined him, and a couple of hooded servants in grey stood with them.

Jules let his robe fall off. His figure was thin, but he was far from frail, as Tristan had first supposed in the ruins of Emjaria. He'd never known that a man could be so skinny, and yet so fit. Jules wore simple leather pants, no more. His black hair hung free around his shoulders, balding on top. "Welcome home," he said with perhaps a hint of amusement in his voice.

Tristan turned his head to his right, and Ella was kneeling beside him. Blood dripped from her forehead, and the left side of her face was swollen. To her right, Garit, too, was kneeling, and his face was a blood-soaked mess. He breathed hard from his mouth, and at least one of his teeth had been knocked out.

Both Ella and Garit had their hands bound behind their backs as well, and the weariness in Tristan faded as his anger began to rise. "I'll kill you," he said, trying to inject as much rage as possible into the words, but the threat sounded feeble.

"No," said Jules dismissively. "No, you will not be killing anyone tonight." Tristan glared at him. He struggled hard to focus his hatred on the prince, and his exhaustion was working hard to claim him. He tried to will himself into wakefulness and anger.

His head throbbed, and he winced from the pain. Still, he stared at Jules and tried to imagine reaching into him. He made a choice—he would kill him with the Grey here and now. He strained at his bonds behind his back, and a primal roar erupted from his lips.

On the dais before him, Jules tilted his head in curiosity. He laughed, and the very sound broke Tristan's spirit. It would have brought him to his knees if he'd not already been there. "Tristan, my boy, are you trying to use the Grey *on me*?"

Tristan let his head drop. After a moment, he became aware of the looks Garit and Ella were giving him—confusion from Garit, and confirmation from Ella. Was it also condemnation? When had she begun to suspect? "I'm sorry. I should have told you."

Jules and Vincent both laughed, but the soldiers and servants remained still and silent. Jules descended from the dais and stood over him. "Tristan, there is so much you don't know."

"I know you killed my family!" Tristan spat out. "I know you killed other families when you stole my home."

"Stole?" Jules asked, his tone amused. "Tristan, I stole nothing. I took back. This land once belonged to Felixandria. This was a part of our glorious empire—the Grey Empire. Then your people betrayed us.

"How many were killed when Felixandria was betrayed by Elinton? How many have died in the centuries since we've returned to our barren land of rock and misery? I am royalty, and I grew up not knowing if I was going to eat each day!"

The hint of amusement was gone, and now an

indescribable venom crept into his voice. "If it was that way for me, imagine what life is like for our smallfolk! And my father has done nothing but sit on his throne and wear a crown. I will not sit and wait to die of starvation while you and your ilk go to bed with full stomachs every night and tell stories of how evil my people are!"

Tristan had no reply. His hatred was stifled. It was not truly gone, but he could not find it in him to think clearly about all the reasons he had to hate this man. Not now — not after he'd just listened to all the reasons this man had to hate him. He was chilled, and he realized with certainty that he was not going to survive this night. "Don't kill my friends," he said, his voice small.

"Begging for your life?" Vincent asked.

"No." He tasted bile as he fought to control his temper. "Not for mine, but for theirs, I will. This was my idea. Let them live. Kill me."

"Tristan," Jules said, his voice having regained its collected tone, "I won't kill you. You are raw and untrained, but I sense what lurks inside you. I will not allow such potential to be wasted."

Tristan scoffed and spit without thinking. "You expect me to join you? Even now?"

"Even now. You have yet to have your eyes opened, but that will come in time. I shall teach you how to think as one befitting your power. Your father was taken from you — in his place, I will instruct you how to be a man."

"You're the bastard who took him!" Tristan said, almost choking on his own words. Vincent moved forward and slapped him with a gauntleted hand.

Jules chuckled. "You come here with nothing, Tristan. No power. The only thing you bring is the rage of a boy. A lesson is needed, I think." He stepped in front of Tristan and placed a hand on his head, then ran his finger down the scar on his face. "My son's sword did this to you."

Tristan's eyes blazed as he glared helplessly, and Jules spoke on. "You hate me. Did you know that's what they say the Grey is? Hate given form?" He placed his fingers under Tristan's chin and raised his face up. Overhead, the lights were piercing. "I don't hate you, Tristan."

As he let go of Tristan's chin, Jules moved over to Ella. "Ah, the mage of the White from the tournament. You performed splendidly that day, my dear. We have so few in Felixandria who are able to touch the White. It simply is not prevalent in our bloodlines, I'm afraid. Your kind stayed behind when the Grey was banished."

"Don't touch her!" Tristan attempted to yell.

"Have no fear," Jules said. "The Balance necessitates the existence of the White. If we kill their mages, then eventually we will be cutting off our own power." He gave Ella an appraising look. "I'll not kill you—we need you, and I believe you can serve other purposes." The change in tone left little doubt as to what was implied, and the leer from Vincent confirmed it.

Ella did not move. She trembled where she knelt, but no more. Tristan strained against his bonds, but something jabbed him hard in his spine. He glanced over his shoulder briefly. So many soldiers—dozens of them. There was no escape from this room. He turned back, and Jules now stood in front of Garit.

"Master Garit Tyon, yes?" Garit did not respond. "My men thought you had died after your failed ambush at Emjaria. It seems our White mage is more powerful than I anticipated." He regarded Ella with an expression of something almost approaching admiration.

His eyes darted back to Garit. "And what's this?" He reached down and pulled the bit of spear from Garit's belt. "Ah, the family heirloom, dating back generations to a time when our people were at war. This will make a fine trophy." He turned and motioned. One of the hooded servants stepped forward, and Jules handed her the weapon. "I will keep it well. It has been used against my people, but I will honor it. This is the spear of a warrior."

He walked a slow circle around Garit. "I want to see the scar." Two soldiers moved forward and ripped Garit's tunic open. He'd received several cuts—and a stab wound in his side—while fleeing the men and chasing after Tristan and Jules.

"Let him go," Tristan said.

"Quiet, now," Jules said as if speaking to a child. He knelt and studied the slight scar on Garit's chest. "You did your work well, Ella." Jules stood, and now he raised his voice to address all in the hall. "Before me kneels Garit of House Tyon of Grauberg. He has trespassed into our city, come into my home, and attempted to kill a member of the royal family of Felixandria."

He faced Tristan. "It is time for you to learn your first lesson. You've managed to make it this far with your crimes forgiven. That ends now—you must be taught that your actions have consequences."

Jules moved his hand out and pointed his finger at Garit's chest, letting it come to rest at the spot where the arrow had wounded him. "Garit, son of Gerald, your people hunted mine. You drove us to a barren land and condemned us to feed on rock and stone. You have traded in lies for years, and your family has reaped the rewards of nobility for your role in reducing my noble people to all but ash.

"You tried to kill my son. You have killed my soldiers, and tonight, you tried to kill me. You are filth, not worthy of having your name remembered, and I hate you."

A roar unlike anything Tristan had ever heard erupted from Garit. Ella screamed and pleaded, but the sound was drowned out by the cries pouring from Garit.

He dropped to his side and rolled to his back. His spine arched, bending in any way it could to try and allow him to catch a breath, but Garit was unable to quit yelling. Tears flowed with his blood down his face as he thrashed about. At last, his scream gave out, but his face remained contorted as he convulsed on the floor.

"You can't do this!" Ella screamed. "Stop! This will lead to war!" Even now, she tried to use logic with Jules. She had the clarity to know that an emotional appeal would do nothing. "He's the son of a noble. This will mean war!"

Jules did not face her as he spoke. "Your threats are empty," he said with a tone of pure contempt. "War is already coming. Still, I suppose this might serve as my official declaration." He spread his fingers, and for one brief moment, Garit found his way up to his feet. Whether it was intentional or an act of desperation, Tristan could not say.

A moment later, he collapsed to the ground again. This time, he lay motionless. Beside him, Ella shrieked. She closed her eyes and mumbled under her breath. "Stop her," Jules said, and two guards stepped up behind her. One hooked his forearm around her neck and applied pressure until she passed out, and the men removed her from the room.

Tristan was still on his knees, too stunned to move. Vincent stepped forward and kicked Garit, but there was no response. Tristan stared hard, unable to tell if his friend lived or not. He watched Garit's chest, searching for any sign of an intake of breath. Then two men stepped forward and hauled Garit away. "Is he dead?" Tristan asked, but no one answered. "Is he dead?!" His voice was a piercing plea, and the only response was Vincent's laugh.

"You bastard," Tristan said. Then he roared, "You bastard!" He surged to his feet, but Vincent smashed his unprotected face with a fist. Tristan's feet came out from under him as he went sprawling to the ground. He landed on his bound arms, and at least one of his shoulders slipped out of place with the impact.

He rolled to find the remnants of the doll, which had been folded in the cloth on his belt, now lying on the floor—the doll which had once been a twin to the doll that now lay on Jules' bed—the bed of the man who had just killed his best friend.

One of the hooded servants stepped forward. Tristan flinched as a hand reached down for him, but instead of grabbing him, the servant's fingers closed around the doll. She stood and pulled back her hood. The other servant moved forward, pulling her hood back as well, and Tristan noted how much they resembled one another.

The one with the doll in her hand stared down at him. "This one was mine," she said. Tristan's eyes widened as someone hauled him up. An arm slipped beneath his chin, and he lost consciousness before he was able to speak their names.

To be continued..

Special Thanks

I would like to thank the following:

-My family, for pushing me forward. I love you.
-My friends, for always believing in me. You're amazing.
-My beta readers, for your invaluable input. 'Thank you' is not enough.
-Yirafiel (twitter @yirafiel), my amazing cover artist. For giving a vision to my words. It's wonderful.
-The Writing Cartel, for cheering me on and shenanigans. This never would have happened without you.
-Cryst (past, present, & future), my online family. Bloodkin or not, you are my people.

Thank you.

About The Author

Living in the Southeastern United States, Edward Patrick and his family and their collection of fur babies enjoy country living. He enjoys reading and writing fantasy, and he is also a gamer.

edwardpatrickwrites.com
Twitter: @edpatrickwrites
Instagram: edwardpatrickwrites

From the Author:
I hope you have enjoyed reading this as much as I enjoyed writing it. I look forward to many more stories to come. This adventure is just beginning, and I hope you'll stick around for the ride (and tell your friends about it)!

And please excuse my social media. This is a new adventure for me, and I'm learning. If it's scarce now, know that I will remedy that moving forth! I look forward to hearing from you!

Made in the USA
Columbia, SC
28 March 2022

58237946R00188